July 7th

a novel

July 7th

a novel

Jill McCorkle

Algonquin Books of Chapel Hill
Chapel Hill, North Carolina   1984

The lines from Loudon Wainwright's "Talking Big Apple - '75" are used by permission of Snowden Music, Inc. © 1975, Snowden Music, Inc.

Library of Congress Cataloging in Publication Data
McCorkle, Jill, 1958– July 7th.
   I. Title. II. Title: July seventh. PS3563.C3444J8
1984   813'.54   84-16766   ISBN 0-912697-12-1

ALGONQUIN BOOKS
Post Office Box 2225
Chapel Hill, N.C. 27515-2225
ISBN 0-912697-12-1

SECOND PRINTING

For my parents,
Melba Collins McCorkle
and
John W. McCorkle, Jr.,
with love

July 7th

a novel

1

If you like action come to N.Y.C.
they got murder and rape and robbery,
they got all kinds of violence can happen to you,
they got broken glass and dog doo-doo,
a Saturday night special every night of the week.

Now this kid with the shaved head has been saying the words to this song for the past 450 miles, over and over, ever since the trucker picked him up just outside of the Holland Tunnel. He just keeps mocking Loudon Wainwright III who in that song mocks Bob Dylan who never mocked anybody that the boy can think of. That's what he's going to do; he's going to not mock anybody; he's going to write words that nobody has ever heard before; he's going to create worlds that are worlds better than this piece of crap and he's going to be somebody. Just as soon as he gets somewhere, he's going to be somebody. But for the time being, he's gonna ride, just gonna sip bourbon and ride, might ride right on down to Florida, put orange juice in the bourbon, write down all of these thoughts that lately seem to stick in his mind, thoughts like life sucks, might sing Jimmy Buffet songs; Jimmy

Buffet doesn't mock anybody, saw Jimmy Buffet one time, football stadium full of college students, cold beer, barefooted, Saturday afternoon. "Changes in latitudes, changes in attitudes, nothing remains quite the same."

"Can it, kid." The trucker has spoken. The boy had forgotten that the trucker was there, forgotten that it's this big hairy truck drivin man that makes the wheels turn, makes the rubber burn. "Can't you talk?"

The kid nods, takes a sip from his bottle. He finished off a pint around D.C., put the empty bottle in his canvas duffle bag that he has between his feet and pulled out another one. His eyes are glazed, one hand on the bottle, the other on the top of the bag. The trucker keeps thinking that this guy will pass out soon and he can put him out by the roadside somewhere. He nudges his foot under his seat to make sure that his metal box is still there, bought himself a gun during the strike, bought it mostly for weirdo hitchers in case they got smart like that bruiser a few weeks ago that was wanting to bugger. He broke that queer's jaw and threw him out somewhere around Richmond. You just never can tell. This kid looks harmless enough, looks young, stinks like a polecat, drunk as a skunk, says "excuse me" after every hiccup, has on brand new looking Nikes, but you never know.

"How far you going?" the trucker asks. He's asked this question for the past ten hours and has yet to get an answer.

"Don't know."

"Why'd you leave New York?"

"They got murder and rape and robbery . . ."

"Yeah, yeah, broken glass and dog doo-doo. You said all that already." The kid just shrugs and takes another swallow. "You ain't from New York, ain't got a New York voice."

"Everybody sounds the same these days."

"So where you from?" Usually the trucker doesn't give a damn, but there's something about this one, something that's made him curious.

"The world will be homogenized but never pasteurized."

"I said where bouts you from?"

"I want to go somewhere, somewhere different, Howard Johnsons look the same, blue and orange, and McDonalds with yellow arches. It's all the same." His voice is slurred and now the damn kid looks like he might cry. The trucker is sorry now that he ever got him to start talking.

"I'm from North Carolina, nothing special, Howard Johnsons, Texaco station, high school; people date and get married and have children that learn how to walk and talk; everybody does things like that; everybody might have herpes one day."

"We're in North Carolina. Where you from?"

"A town." The boy shrugs and rolls that shaved head to one side. "They got bars in New York that never close, got bars where people take off their clothes."

"Got 'em everywhere, boy. Wanna stop so you can get yourself home?"

"Got 'em everywhere, damn right. Homogenized but not pasteurized." The boy stares up ahead. He's tired of talking to this man; he liked it better when he forgot that this man was here; this man just doesn't understand, doesn't know that he has all of these things to think about, things to decide, things to create, things like the way that all those letters on that glowing green sign run together to spell nothing.

"Think I'll pull off and stretch," the trucker says. "Might grab a cup of coffee."

"Might grab a cup of coffee."

"You sure could use one," the trucker says and pulls in at an all-night convenience store right by the service road. This kid is really getting on his nerves now, the shaved head, his drunken mumblings. "Hey, you, aren't you getting out?"

"Nah, been in these places before."

"Come on, get out." The trucker nudges him and the kid shakes his head back and forth. "Come on."

"Got my bag."

"Well hell, bring it with you." The trucker walks around and opens the other door, stands there waiting until he slides down, the bag clanging against the floorboard. "What you got in there anyway?"

"Typewriter." He sways for a minute and his knees start to buckle. The trucker starts to grab him but he throws up his hands. "Sam Swett walks alone," he says and weaves behind the trucker, pulling his bag behind him. Sam Swett, most likely to succeed; he only missed getting that by a few votes, almost most likely to succeed. The bells on that door ring so loud that it jars his whole skull, and the light makes his eyes burn, makes

4

him feel dizzy. The trucker is talking to the fat man sitting behind the counter, so he walks over and looks at what's on the shelves. Chef Boy Ardee; you can go anywhere in the country and buy Chef Boy Ardee, and the candy bars, rows and rows of candy bars: Three Musketeers in red, white and blue the patriotic appeal, Zero in that cool blue, M&Ms. He remembers eating M&Ms: he would sit down and open the pack, segregate before eating; there were blacks, light skin blacks, Indians, Chinese and Martians; there were no white M&Ms; there was no race with orange skin; orange ones were the white people, no other choice, but then came the big decision, which race do you devour first? And he got older but there were still M&Ms, same wrapper, only difference that the Indians had become extinct, stripped from society, made children hyperactive. He would segregate them, figure the population percentages, integrate them back within the bag and pull them out one at a time, try to guess which race was melting in his hand before he popped it into his mouth. Then he was in college and his mother would send a shoebox wrapped in brown paper, filled with cookies, a check, athletic socks and M&Ms. He would open one corner of the bag and pour the contents into his mouth, homogenized. What do kids do now? There are no colors for Puerto Ricans, Cubans, India Indians, Iranians. It would be so difficult to be a child, so difficult to segregate and discern the differences, just say they're all M&Ms, they're all people. It's all junk food: Fritos, Ruffles, Cheetos, Doritos, Doritos Light, Sour Cream and Onion, Sour Cream and Chives, Nacho;

it's enough to drive you fucking crazy; there are too many choices. "You have so many choices, Sammy," his father had said, pride in his eyes, the keys to a new car in his pocket. "Used to people just had to get out and find something to do, didn't have much choice." It's enough to drive you fucking crazy.

"Can I help you find something, son?" It is the voice of the man behind the stool.

"I can't decide." He shakes his head and walks back around to the counter, the top of the duffle bag clenched in his hand, the empty bottle clanging against the typewriter, his only pair of clean underwear covering the keys. "We gotta leave, going somewhere," he mumbles and looks around. "Where is that man?"

"Were you with him?" The man looks surprised, the loose sallow skin of his cheeks glowing under the fluorescent light with a greenish tint. Give this man a green M&M. "He left about ten minutes ago."

"Where am I?"

"Marshboro, North Carolina." The man does not take his eyes off of him. Marshboro, N.C. He is only about two and a half hours from home, two and a half hours from central air, clean sheets. "Do you want some coffee? Anything?"

"May vomit." He feels his stomach churn, tightness in his throat, the man's face slowly covered in little black specks. "Bathroom."

"Sorry, it's private. You'll have to leave." The man has shifted a little now, his hand near the phone. Who does that man think he is? Some kind of derelict? He was almost most likely. He turns and goes out the door, the bells clanging over his head. He makes his way to the corner of the store and squats there in the darkness, cold sweat running through the prickles on his head, dropping like dew onto the green surgical shirt.

Charles Husky breathes a sigh of relief when the door closes and the kid disappears into the darkness. He's used to getting the late night weirdos, but it doesn't happen that often. Usually it's a slow night which is why he doesn't mind working the late shift. He's been working here ever since the textile plant started laying people off last December. His first night of work was Christmas Eve, Merry Christmas, and Maggie and his daughter Barbara had come down there and sat with him for about an hour. Still, it's almost peaceful here now, on this vinyl stool, the canned goods to his right, the Slurpee machine behind him softly gurgling like a baby nursing, like his little baby Barbara had done and Lordy, that's been a long time. Barbara is thirty with a gurgling baby of her own, way off in Montana, coming home for Christmas every other year. But still, Charles likes to think about all of those things and he has plenty of time to do it during these late hours when most people are asleep, when it seems, the whole town is asleep. He found out a long time ago that things just ain't like they are on T.V. where someone comes tapping on the door wanting a jar of Miracle Whip. It just doesn't happen that way and if this town wasn't right here on I-95 where truckers and travelers are passing through all night long, there wouldn't even be any reason to stay open this shift, and then maybe he could get on in the daytime, and at this time of morning he'd be spooned up with Maggie, his arms wrapped around her plumpness in a warm bed. Whenever he thinks of Maggie, he thinks "warm" and it always sounds so good to him, as good as the first time he ever wrapped his arms around a much thinner Maggie, even though right this minute he has his oscillator fan fixed so that it won't oscillate and will blow right on him. It is ninety degrees, only dropped six degrees since afternoon. Maggie's tomato plants growing along the back fence ain't ever gonna make it through this and she works with those plants, digging and replanting, fertilizing and watering, and all because he likes fresh tomatoes with his eggs when he gets home at seven.

Not many people even stop; oh maybe every now and then they do but it's only for a thirty cent cup of coffee like that trucker. Charles Husky doesn't blame them. Why would they stop for a cellophaned sandwich that you stick in a toaster when they can ride on down the road and find an all-night diner? No, the only regular during this shift is Harold Weeks, been coming in every single night since he left home a couple of months ago. Right now, Harold Weeks is in that back room, either guzzling coffee or stretched out on that cot sleeping it off. Harold never should have left Juanita over that one mistake she made; he was lucky that she ever married him in the first place, him being thirteen years older and all, and Juanita's a real looker, too, got her own business, gave

8

Harold two fine children and what does he do but up and leave her the first time she makes a mistake. Somebody needs to tell Harold a thing or two, tell him about forgiving and forgetting, but Charles Husky isn't the man to do it. Charles just ain't the kind to get all tied up in somebody's business. Besides, Charles likes having Harold around late at night, not to talk to, of course, but just so he's not alone. Ain't no way that you can talk to Harold Weeks when he's had too much to drink. He has a filthy-sounding mouth when he's sober.

This real nice song called "Tight Fittin Jeans" is playing on the radio when two headlights appear almost out of nowhere and a big Chrysler New Yorker screeches to a stop. Boy, Conway Twitty can sing, all right, there's a tiger in these tight fittin jeans. Charles reaches down and begins wiping off the counter where he and Harold had had one of those cellophaned sandwiches with tomato slices just a little while ago. These two young boys get out of that car and start walking up. Charles never has gotten used to seeing young high school kids driving around in big fine cars. The bells ring and this skinny one with sun bleached hair comes in first, followed by a larger one with a bad case of acne. Little Barbara never had a car to drive around in except Maggie's old Rambler but she never had face or teeth problems, saved them a fortune he's sure.

"Hi boys," Charles says and smiles. "What can I do for you?"

"Keep your shirt on, man, we'll see," the skinny one

says and goes over to the drink cooler. That kid's eyes look funny, red and glassy, ought to be at home and in bed. His Mama is probably worried sick right now. The larger one just stands near the door, his hands deep in the pockets of his Levis, and stares down at the paperback book collection there in front of the counter. That's such an embarrassment to Charles. He hated that Christmas Eve when Maggie and Barbara came in and saw all those books. Harold Weeks calls them "beaver books." Harold sometimes reads one while he's sobering up. The skinny one has his head in the cooler now and is fumbling around.

"Hey, Ronnie," he yells to the larger boy who is now flipping through one of the books. "They ain't got shit here, all the beer's hot."

"Son, it's after one. I can't sell you any beer anyway." Charles looks up. He had been distracted by this other song he really likes, "Swinging." The boy whirls around and glares at him. "I'm sorry as I can be but that's the law, thought you were going after a soda."

"A soda? Do I look like I want a soda?"

"I'm sorry." Charles says and watches that kid pace back and forth. Kid probably isn't even old enough to buy beer, about seventeen, probably. Her Mama was in the kitchen cuttin chicken up to fry, her Daddy was in the back yard winding up the garden hose and I'm out on the front porch feeling love down to my toes and we were swanging, justa swanging.

"Yeah, well what are you gonna do about it, old man?"

"Hey man." The big one tosses down the book and

steps closer to the door. "Just buy the rolling papers and let's leave."

"Hell no!" The skinny one goes back to the cooler, gets a Michelob and opens it, the most expensive kind they sell and that kid just gets one and opens it. Charles reaches for the phone. He doesn't want any trouble, especially with a child who ain't got sense enough to go on home. "Hey, I'm just teasing, old man, I'll pay you for this one." He steps closer, picks up a loaf of bread, wanders down another aisle and gets a box of Saran Wrap. This kid is worse than that other one that was in here. "Pack of Marlboros, and some rolling papers."

Charles gets the papers and the cigarettes and rings it all up. He doesn't even ring up the beer, just stretches his hand out for the money. He watches the boys walk out and just stand there in front of the store. An old one, I beg your pardon, I never promised you a rose garden. That fool kid stands right out there and dumps that whole loaf of bread on the sidewalk. There's got to be a little rain sometime. He comes back in, stretching the bag, twisting it around, and the big one follows him, his eyes still on those "beaver books." The next thing Charles knows, that big one has jumped over the counter and is holding both of his hands behind his back, even before Charles could ask why that kid had dumped out the bread, and that big one had seemed like a nice boy. He is being robbed. His hands are being wrapped and knotted up in that plastic bread bag. This kid is strong as hell, too. "Harold," he says, but he can't seem to speak loud enough. The skinny one turns up the radio. Better look before you leap and don't be sorry, love shouldn't be so melancholy. "Harold. Come on kids, cut it out. I'll give you some beer."

"Shut the hell up," the skinny one says and crams all the napkins that are beside the coffee maker into Charles' mouth. He picks up the Saran Wrap and starts wrapping it around Charles' face, round and round, pulling it tightly. He can't talk; his vision is blurred, the creases in the plastic buckling around his eyes. He can barely hear the radio, barely hear the big one. "Hey, don't do that, come on, just get the cash and whatever you want and let's get the hell out." These kids probably have big allowances. Why the hell are they doing this?

"Ah, he can get loose. That plastic will pull right apart." The big one pushes Charles to the floor, that cool tile floor, sandwich crumbs, God, he can't breathe. Where's Harold? He barely hears the cash register open, barely hears something about trying nigger wine, barely hears the gurgling of the Slurpee machine. He is gasping, face down, the specks on the tile floor jumping and leaping toward his face. He doesn't have the strength to move his wrists. How many nights has he stared at these specks of color in the tiles? He would trace the specks into patterns and shapes just like Maggie always did with clouds. There's a rabbit pattern beneath the stool, a sea gull in front of the Slurpee machine. Now he sees black spots mingling with the specks, the plastic creases over his eyes. The gurgling is getting further and further away. He thinks of Maggie, spooning with Maggie in that warm bed, he thinks swinging, justa swinging, the gurgling gurgle of the Slurpee machine, gurgle, the sea gull in the tile, that damp cool sea gull, gurgle, just like little Barbara all those years ago, gurgle, swinging, gurgle, justa swinging. And here's one you'll all remember, Buck Owens up there in the Big Apple when he did Carnegie Hall, I got a hungrin for your love and I'm waiting at your welfare line. A cellophaned sandwich ruffles under the breeze of the fan; the receipt that was just rung up is caught and held for a second like a leaf in the wind and then settles as easily as a feather to that cool tile floor.

At the far end of Main Street there is a boarding house, a two-story brick structure with old time windows framed in lumber, a porch that wraps around the front and sides and supports the various creeping vines which over the years have reached all the way up and neatly entwined the two upstairs windows as though it had been planned that way. Once when this was a central location in town it was a very fashionable tourist home, and in the summers the gray-planked flooring of the porch creaked under rocking chairs, feet gently pushing an old glider, a swing. Now it is at the edge of town, separated from the bottoms only by a broken-up and overgrown railroad track. What little brick is left unexposed by the creeping vines is dark with age, and it seems at a glance that it could all crumble down with the slightest tremor, yet the brick is very strong, its texture intact, only the appearance has changed.

Now a yellow light illuminates the porch where there is an old chipped-up kitchen chair propped against the wall, cigarette butts along the cement steps, an empty Coke bottle propped between the spindles of the railing. Moths hover around the light, beat themselves against the bare bulb without venturing into the dark recesses where the vines fall like curtains. There is a small pair of jeans hung on the ledge of the upstairs window on the left. They belong to M.L. McNair, who is six years old and lives in this room with his grandmother, Fannie McNair. Earlier in the day she had washed out his jeans as she always does and hung them there to dry. Now she has forgotten them. Now she can be seen in the dim light of her window like the pupil of a large tired eye, as she sits in her overstuffed chair, a reading lamp behind her casting a glow that clings to the sweat on her dark forehead where her knotty hair is pulled tightly back and bobby pinned in a straight line. The radio is turned down low, just low enough that she can still hear it but so low that it doesn't wake M.L., who is curled up on his side of the low double bed in the corner. Fannie McNair spends all of her evenings this way, just sitting and listening to the gospel music that plays after midnight, even though she could fall asleep at any given moment. It is her time to "think and pray," as she always tells M.L. when he stirs over there in the darkness and calls out her name. This is what she is doing now, thinking of her husband Jake, wondering where he might be, if he's still alive, if he's living with some other fool woman, if he's sprawled out dead as a doornail in the alley of some big city street. It'd serve him right, God knows it would, but no, Jake deserves as much hope as any other body. And it wasn't always bad, not always.

There was that rainy Thanksgiving when just the two of them were together and he surprised her with a radio that he bought at Sears, the very one that she's listening to now, and they had stayed in bed near about all day listening to the radio and the rain and hadn't even eaten their hen and stuffing until nine-thirty that night. There was something special about that day, special because she has always been certain that that was the very day her daughter took root inside of her. It was just like Elizabeth in the Bible, because she was thirty-five years old and had just about given up on having children other than those that she was paid to keep. God, it was a happy time when that second month had passed without a trace of bleeding. Then her stomach got to where it was pushing out and she had to go to work with her skirt unfastened. It was a miracle, truly it was, and she had more energy than she could ever remember having, wasn't sick a day, and kept right on working and going about her life. She was sitting right there on the front pew of Piney Swamp Baptist Church on a day that was just about as hot as yesterday was, when her water broke. There was so much commotion and jubilation in that building that she just stood up and clapped and yelled with the best of them and made her way out of the church without anybody even noticing what had happened. She caught a ride with a farmhand who went back inside the church to find the doctor, and off they went to hers and Jake's house which stood just on the other side of the tracks where there is now a warehouse. It wasn't much of a house, but that day it seemed like it was, especially when she opened her eyes and heard that cry. "His name is John," she had said, releasing the grip she had held on the edges of the mattress, "and he's a Baptist."

"You'll have to wait for the next one," the doctor said and held up that wrinkled little baby.

"Elizabeth, then."

Jake didn't have much to do with Elizabeth, looked at her, pulled out a bottle of liquor and then disappeared for about three days. All those years he had blamed himself for them not having children, and had spent years worrying about Fannie finding a man who could give her what she wanted. Now that Elizabeth had come, he had somehow come to think that it was all Fannie's fault, and she though he must have spent a lot of time thinking about all the seeds he could have planted elsewhere. Fannie knows it probably was her with the problem, it probably was some sort of miracle that she should even have had a baby. But Jake had spent all those years believing what most people always have believed, that black women are just like watermelon vines and once one gets ripe, there's another right behind it. She reckoned Jake was for the first time proud of his manhood, and took it out on her that he had doubted himself all those years. Before Elizabeth was even a year old, Fannie was already having to unfasten the tops of her skirts. It didn't seem like such a miracle that time, because Jake was gone before she even got to wearing big loose frocks with no waist to them. She named that child Thomas because it was all that doubt and resentment that had brought him to her.

She tells herself that there were some blessings to come out of it all, that she has forgiven Jake for leaving the way that he did, forgiven Elizabeth for going to New York and leaving M.L. with her to raise from the time he was a year old. She tells herself that her children deserve better if they can find it, though she's proud of her life, proud of the fact that she is sixty-five years old and gets up and goes to work every day, cooking and cleaning for the Fosters who live in one of the big houses out in what she still calls Piney Swamp even though it has been given a fancy name that she never can remember. One day M.L. will have himself a fine house with a long table set with matching dishes and silverware. M.L. might just be a doctor and that would be fine, but for Fannie McNair, the most important thing is that M.L. grows up to be decent and proud, hard working and loving, not fighting to prove he's something that he ain't like Thomas, who lives somewhere right in this town but hardly ever comes by. M.L. ain't gonna sit and watch his mailbox for the government to send some kind of check.

She goes over now and leans down close to M.L. where his face is buried down in the stomach of an old stuffed monkey that he calls F.M. after her, and she can feel the warmth of his breath against her cheek. This is a ritual that she performed with her own children and did with M.L. before he was even left there with her, and now, with the reassurance of his measured sleep, she goes back to her chair for a few more minutes of thinking. Her gnarled fingers work in and out while she hems the dress that Mrs. Foster is going to wear to a party tomorrow night that is being given for a couple about to be married. It's a pretty dress, green and silky, cool to Fannie's fingers as she slides the material around. The dress smells like Mrs. Foster, clean and a little spicy like those crumpled-up dried flowers that Mrs. Foster has in little bowls in the bathroom. It smells like the Fosters' house and it makes Fannie feel for a minute that Mrs. Helena Foster is right there in the room with her, though of course she's not; Mrs. Foster has never been inside of this room or right out front on the street, or if she has Fannie doesn't know it. Mr. Foster picks her up in the mornings and brings her back home, or if he is out of town, Mrs. Foster gives her taxi money the day before. That's the way it is, Fannie tells herself, though there have been times when she would have liked for Mrs. Foster to come up here and see her home, see the quilts and afghans that Fannie has made, because Mrs. Foster is real interested in homemade things like quilts, rugs, bread and jelly, though as far as Fannie knows Mrs. Foster has never made a thing in her life, probably not even a bed.

It makes Fannie smile just to think of how that whole house would fall apart if she wasn't there to keep things right. But she likes Mrs. Foster. Sometimes she just likes to look at her because it's so hard to believe that a woman getting close to forty with two children could look that way, that frosted blonde hair that she pulls up in a loose bun, those long nails always glazed in clear polish, those bright plaid pedal pushers that she wears around the house or to the grocery store. It is something, the way that Mrs. Foster looks like she's always about to go somewhere even when she isn't. She wears earrings every day of the week.

Fannie breaks off the thread and carefully hangs the dress back on its hanger and carries it into the bathroom to hang it on the shower rod so that nothing will happen to it. She pulls out the skirt and lets it rock back and forth like a ghost dancing there. She does like to think and wonder about the Fosters, to think of how Mrs. Foster's voice changes a little when she has company, how she doesn't spend much time with Fannie when other people are there. Mr. Foster is real quiet most of the time and Fannie never has been able to decide if he's mad or if he's just a soured person. He isn't even smiling in that wedding photograph that Mrs. Foster has on her dresser.

Fannie goes back to her chair and now that that dress is out of the room it's a little easier to forget about the Fosters. She will be back with them soon enough, back with Billy Foster locked up in his room all day long, asleep till noon and before she can get in there to make his bed, he's already back on it, just sitting on top of rumpled covers and playing his record player full blast. He reminds Fannie of a scrawny little chick who goes around acting like a bantam rooster till somebody crosses him and he goes crying to his Mama. M.L. ain't that way. M.L. don't act a bit bigger than what he is and he isn't a crybaby, never has been. But that Billy Foster is something. Fannie can't quite figure it out. How did such a cute little boy grow up like that, except that he's spoiled rotten. He has all these posters on his walls, of people with their faces all painted up like some kind of freak show. "Kiss," it says below these awful faces. Fannie McNair wouldn't touch one with a ten foot pole, let alone kiss one. Fannie supposes that he comes by this sort of taste for pictures naturally, though. Just the other day, Mrs. Foster called Fannie away from her cooking to come into the living room and see the new picture. "It's a Primitive," Mrs. Foster said. "We got it at an auction. Isn't it wonderful?" Fannie nodded like she was agreeing, but she thought that it was more than primitive; she thought it was downright scary with that head too big for that child's body like some kind of poor dwarf. Mrs. Foster talks about all these things like she knows something about them, but Lord knows, she don't know too much. She doesn't know a thing about the history of Marshboro; she didn't even know that her house is just a hop and a skip from where Piney Swamp Baptist Church used to be, and even though the Fosters are members of a church in town, Fannie has not once heard them discuss a service and has never heard a hymn sung in that house, until she herself began singing while she works.

Sometimes it makes Fannie feel proud that she works in such a fine house with all that silver to polish, like she owned it all or something since she's the one to care for it. But other times, she feels guilty for thinking that way, for forgetting herself and wishing that M.L. had his own bathroom with a little towel with his name on it like Parker Foster, who is only twelve years old and has everything that most grown-up women don't even have. Sometimes it goes on and on until that pride turns a little to doubt and resentment and she can't help but remember being a young woman and going to the movies, having to sit in the balcony where it said "colored," using a bathroom that said "colored," and it makes her feel a fever deep in her body, the same fever, she is certain, that Thomas McNair has felt every day of his life.

There is a soft rapping at the door and Fannie realizes that she's been thinking about the Fosters again, thinking about all those old sad things that have happened in her life. She tiptoes across the old hardwood floor, her stocking snagging on a small splinter. "Who's there?" she whispers, though she's certain it's Corky Revels from across the hall.

"It's me, Fannie," comes the voice so she takes off the chain and opens the door. Corky is standing there in a blue cotton gown that reaches her thin calves; she has one foot curled around the other. "I saw your light beneath the door. I didn't wake you, did I?"

"No, honey, you know I sit up late as I can stand it." Fannie motions for Corky to come in and then closes and locks the door. Corky goes over and sits on the footstool in front of Fannie's chair. "I just couldn't get to sleep," she whispers, her large pale eyes magnified by the dark circles below them, her light hair slipping from the ponytail on top of her head and falling around her face. She waits for Fannie to settle back into her chair. "I guess I just wanted to talk for a minute."

"You've got to get some sleep." Fannie leans forward so that she can talk without waking M.L. "Don't you work in the morning?"

"I go in at seven." She seems to relax a little, stretching her feet out towards Fannie's chair.

"It's well after one, now," Fannie whispers. "Can I fix you something to eat?" She is hoping that Corky will say yes because she's as thin as a rail, but she just shakes her head and the tears well up in those large sad eyes.

"No thank you," she whispers and then she just stares out the window. Fannie doesn't mind Corky coming over in the late hours; she does it often and Fannie never knows exactly what to do except to sit there. Corky told her one time that that's what she needed, to be with somebody.

"Are you frightened?" Fannie whispers. "Cause you can get right over there and sleep with M.L., you know you can." Corky blinks those long lashes and the tears roll down her cheeks while she shakes her head. "Are you all right?"

"Yeah, yeah, really I am," she says and pulls the neck of her gown up to wipe her cheeks. "I know, Fannie, tell me about the house where you work."

"Well, what part of it?" Fannie has been over that house with a fine tooth comb with Corky. Corky could probably make her way around the Fosters' house blind-folded and she has never even set foot there.

"Tell me about that bedroom suit that they have that is as old as George Washington." Fannie is not sure if that's right or not. Mrs. Foster had told her that it was just like

that she has fallen in love with and married, moved to that little yellow wooden house over on Maple Avenue which is in a good section, though not like where Fannie McNair works. In her dream, she has lots of children; some of them have pale blonde hair and gray eyes and the others match the faceless father of the dreams. When she's in that house on Maple Avenue, she furnishes it with all kinds of things that she's either heard about from Fannie or seen herself, like the big braided rug that Granner Weeks has in her house with the heathered blues and grays, or like the big brass coat rack that Rose Tyner, Granner's granddaughter, has by her front door. In the dream she wears a pink silky dress and in the background there is slow dancing music, candles burning, a blue satin bedspread turned down just right.

Now she is curled up on her bed, right in front of the window, the sheet pushed down below her feet. The window is open but the white ruffled curtains just hang in limp folds all around the ledge where there is a large doll made of corn husks, its hair made from silks bleached as light as Corky's. There is a shelf above her bed with smaller dolls just like the big one, another used as a centerpiece on a table set for two with one red candle stuck in a wine bottle. Her breath rises and falls in sleep; her cotton gown clings to her back, the droplets of sweat forming at the nape of her neck. Something in the stillness causes her to jerk, pull her knees closer, shake her head quickly, softly, her lips parted in a silent cry, and then just as easily it goes and her breath falls into rhythm with the chirping of the crickets and tree frogs that fill the darkness beyond the yellow glow of the porch light, and the darkness spreads until it reaches the slight glow of the streetlight at the corner.

Granner Weeks has tossed and turned ever since she went to bed at nine-thirty, she is so excited. Now it is July 7th; it is her birthday and at seven A.M., give or take a few minutes if her Mama's memory was correct, she will be eighty-three years old. She just wishes that she could get a little rest so that she won't be slam wore out when her party starts mid-afternoon. It's two o'clock now, so she only has about twelve to thirteen hours to wait. She has already gotten up once for warm milk, once for a cup of hot water so that her body will perform first thing when she gets up so that she won't have that full uncomfortable feeling. Now she is eating a bowl of Product 19 because she has found that that seems to help the system as well. She knows she needs to get a good night's sleep, but every year it's this way. It's more exciting than being a child and listening for Santa's deer and sleigh bells. More exciting than even thinking you hear that fat man creeping out of your fireplace, like she did as a child once and she didn't even have any kind of big Christmas like most children nowadays. She was lucky if the fat man left her some fruit and nuts and maybe some shoes and socks, and it was still exciting. Lord knows, if she had ever had a Christmas like her great-granddaughter, Petie Rose Tyner, with all those talking and wetting dolls, she would have tossed and turned all year long waiting. But now she's old; she's just about eighty-three and times have changed since she was a girl. People buy nice presents, or at least they got the money to. The actual niceness comes down to whether or not they got any taste about them. It's gonna be a nice birthday this year, with lots of nice presents, Granner can feel it in her feeble bones.

Imagine, Granner Weeks, formerly Irene Turner of Flatbridge, turning eighty-three years old! She can't stand it. It really is just like waiting for Santa Claus to come! She has baked a big coconut cake just like she does every year, and has already pulled out a big box of fireworks and her flags that she hangs out every year on her birthday. She has a North Carolina flag that she hangs in the kitchen, the American flag of 1776 that was a gift to her in the Bicentennial year that she drapes over the dining room buffet, her American flag (the modern one that includes Alaska and Hawaii) that she hangs in the entrance hall, and of course the Christian flag that she waves out of her bedroom window, but the real treasure is the great big Confederate flag that her granddaddy passed down to her. She can just see him, just hear his voice! He was sitting out on his front porch swing, with one leg of his pants just sort of hanging limp and swaying back and forth. "They took away my leg, yes sirree, but they can't take away this flag. Wave it proud, girl. Do it right!" Granner Weeks does do it right. She always has done it right, and every July 7th she hangs that flag out on the front porch and lets it wave all day long. It makes her weep every time.

Her custom of flag-waving started way back, back when her husband Buck was still alive, back when little

Kate was just a tot and had never laid her eyes on Ernie Stubbs. Back when her son, Harold Weeks, was still a nice child. She had thought it was silly to have two holidays right there together; it just made things too hard on her, having two big parties in one week. She had said to Buck, finally, after years of being pooped out on her birthday, "Let's combine the holidays, Buck. Let's celebrate this country's birth with my own birth."

"All right by me," Buck had said, because he was a very agreeable person, unlike his son Harold Weeks. "You won't mind gettin your presents three days early?"

"I ain't thinking of changing my day," she had said. "I was thinking it would be easier to change the country's day, so that I'll have three extra days to plan."

"All right by me," he had said and it has been that way ever since. It's a big celebration, with the flags waving, red white and blue Uncle Sam hats, and balloons. You name it. All the family comes and Granner always likes to pause for a few minutes to think over the guest list to see if there are any additions or subtractions. Lord, that was a sad July 7th when she had to cross Buck out; every year it's sad when she has to cross Buck out. Let's see, she thinks, and pushes away her half-eaten bowl of Product 19. She is too nervous to eat. There's her daughter Kate, and Kate's husband, Ernie Stubbs, who has made quite a name for himself around here as a real estate salesman, especially since he was raised over there on Injun Street, which as far as Granner can remember has always been a rough, cheap part of town. Ernie has done so well that he built them a fine house out in the country, a house with two and a half bathrooms and four bedrooms, even though there's just the two of them now. What's more, he can afford to run his air-conditioner all summer long. Of course that doesn't mean much to Granner, because she's cool natured now that her blood has slowed, but still that's a sign of somebody with money to burn. It bothered Granner a little when she heard that they were building themselves a house in the country, because used to people with money moved to town, just like she and Buck had done.

Her yard right here on Main Street is a far sight bigger than Kate's and prettier, too. Ernie chopped down all of their trees to make room for that big house. Still, he's done all right by them, built that big brick patio off of that house just so he'd have some place to put up those Tiki torches when they have a party.

"I don't see you too much now that you've moved to the country," Granner said one day.

"Not country, mother," Kate had said. "It's called Cape Fear Trace." Granner just calls it "out there" because an old woman can't be expected to remember everything. That Kate always did take it in her head that she was a notch or two better than everyone else; pitched a pure fit when she wasn't asked to be a debutante up in Raleigh. Granner explained time and time again that Buck hadn't come from such fine lines, though he was the best looking man in all the county. But no, all Kate wanted was to be in high cotton, and how did she get there but to marry somebody off of Injun Street! Even if he has done well, he still came off of Injun Street and all that money don't change that, don't change the fact that his Mama died poor as a churchmouse. Granner is happy that Kate is happy and got just what she wanted, because for the longest time she had had her doubts, due to Kate not being the best looking thing. "She's a real plain Jane," Buck said one time when Kate entered herself in a beauty pageant and nobody had the nerve to tell her that she didn't stand one bit of a chance, and it hurt Granner's heart to hear that about her very own child, although she knew that it was the dead truth. Buck Weeks, rest his soul, wasn't the smartest man around, but he always told the dead truth.

Kate's daughter Rose looks just like her Mama except she got Ernie Stubbs' squared-off chin. Granner always has thought that Rose would look all right if she had been a man, but she wasn't, so there ain't any need to even think of it. Rose is sweet, though, the salt of the earth, and not a bit uppity. Of course she can't afford to be uppity, because everybody in town knows that she did get herself in trouble some four years ago with Pete Tyner because that's exactly how old Petie Rose is, but there's no need for that to ever be discussed, not EVER. Pete is simple and kind, a wiry little thing, white as a sheet, works like a dog for Ernie in that land business, and he married Rose just as soon as everything came to a head. There's no reason for Petie Rose to know the truth or that new baby that they're expecting any day now. That's six, counting the baby on the way.

Then there's Granner's son, Harold Weeks, who is handsome as can be with that dark curly hair and tanned skin but rotten to the core. Granner likes Juanita even though she has recently shamed the family name, because Juanita will tell you the truth, lay it on the line. "They got their noses in their asses," Juanita said one day about Ernie and Kate, and it made Granner laugh till she cried, even though ordinarily she doesn't make fun of family. And cute children, that little Patricia and Harold, Jr. Harold couldn't have done any better. He was thirty-seven before he even got married. Granner doesn't know if she can count on Juanita, Patricia and Harold, Jr., being there or not, with things being the way that they are. And that's not fair, wait all year for something and then they let some little marriage problem ruin the whole thing.

Granner thinks it's something the way that things work out; she and Buck both had good looks and enough money to keep them up in a nice way; Kate and Ernie got all the money and no looks, and Harold and Nita got good looks and not near as much money. What puzzles Granner the most is how money can make ugly people think they got something over on everybody else, when the truth is that you can't go out and buy yourself a new face or a new body like the one Juanita has got herself by going to that Nautilus center.

Then there's Granner's great-niece, Corky Revels, who took up with Granner when she first came to town. Corky is a strange-looking little girl, pale and thin with that almost white hair, creeping around like a kitten and then right out of the blue throwing a temper tantrum like you've never seen. Corky has good reason, Granner reckons, and she makes eleven if Juanita shows and the new baby is born; she wants a boy that they can name Robert Lee Tyner and call Buck for short.

Granner takes a bite of soggy Product 19 and goes over to her kitchen window. Her yard is all lit up; people can probably see her house from blocks away. Those floodlights that Harold hooked up for her was the best investment that she ever made. Nobody would come creeping around a house so well lit. God, she hopes that Kate has gotten her one of those whirlpool foot relaxers like she's been hinting about ever since she saw one in the new Sears catalogue. After all, she's almost eighty-three and everybody knows what that means. Well, she may not live to see eighty-four. Lord, if anybody can afford one of those machines it's Kate and Ernie. There will be twelve people at the big party counting herself and the baby on the way, unless of course that Iranian man that has been calling her on the phone should happen to come.

Nobody believes that this man is calling, just because they aren't there when it happens. Kate says, "Now, mother," and Harold laughs his fool head off and says that man must be blind and crazy, and Rose's eyes get all misty and she comes over and rubs Granner's back and pats her like she's some blubbering fool. Now why would anybody in their right mind make up a suitor from Iran? If she was going to make up one, it sure wouldn't be some greasy-looking foreigner who helped to keep all those Americans locked up a few years ago. My God, Granner hates foreigners; she hates they were ever let into this country, and she told that Mr. Abdul that, the last time that he called her on the phone, which was just yesterday. She said, "Mr. Abdul, I want nothing to do with your kind. I'd date a Negro first."

Harold Weeks can go on back to the trailer park now because he isn't seeing two of everything any more, must've dozed off, which lets him know that he might have had about one drink too many. Anybody that can fall asleep right in the middle of a beaver book more than likely had one drink too many. He gets up from where he had been sitting and leaning against a stack of drink crates. He feels like he has been hit by a transfer truck, like he plowed a damn cotton field with his mouth. His head is pounding, and worse than all of that, he's got to drive out to that trailer park where he's renting a place. He thinks about all those nights that he'd get home and find Juanita acting like she was asleep until he got the covers pulled up over him good and then she'd start, screaming in his ear that he drinks too much, and then when she had done that she'd snuggle up beside him and say that she wanted to do it, and she'd keep right on until he said okay, and then she'd say that he had to rinse off first because he smelled like a field hand. It was like a goddamn broken record, the way that she did that. Juanita could probably write one of those beaver books herself, and she's just forty. Harold wished off and on that she'd go ahead and go through the change of life and maybe she'd slow down a little bit. It got to where he just couldn't go on, and now what's he doing but getting drunk and reading beaver books. God, if he had just gotten up to rinse off and do it more often, then he wouldn't be going to some old trailer park, wouldn't be riding by the YMCA pool hoping to catch a glimpse of Patricia or Harold, Jr., or even Juanita in that pretty aqua suit she bought on sale just before he left home. God only knows who's seen inside of that suit since he's been away. Sometimes when he's still a little drunk he thinks that he ought to go on home, tell Juanita that he loves her more than anything and that he'll forgive her if she'll forgive him, but then he thinks better of it all. He thinks that she ought to come beggin after what she did. After all, a man's got pride; he isn't some old pussy that can be taken advantage of; he's a man's man who just happened to have a little difficulty getting up to get it up from time to time, and she should have known that when she married him. It's her own damn fault.

He stretches, scratches the hair on his chest where he's got his shirt unbuttoned, and walks into the store. Those lights are so bright that it makes his head hurt all over again. He gets a Goody powder off the shelf, then goes over and gets a Coke out of the cooler. His Mama always told him that Goody's were cheap nigra medicine, that that's how they used to get a buzz, by taking a Goody's with a Coca Cola. Of course, his Mama also thinks a foreigner is wanting to take her out for pizza. He pours the powder into his mouth and takes a big swallow of Coke. "Hey Charlie," he yells without turning around. "Ring me up, better get on, got an early day tomorrow." He chugs the rest of the Coke and rubs his head. "You'd tell me if you'd heard anything about Nita, wouldn't you? I mean if she's going around this town putting out,

I gotta right to know it." He turns around and starts strolling up to the front. "Ain't gonna bother me. I could have just about anybody I want myself, you know? Hey Charlie?" The radio is louder than Charles usually has it and he isn't answering, probably knows something that he ain't wanting to tell. He looks up and down all the aisles then leans up against the counter. Charles is face down on the floor, looks like some kind of plastic on his head. "Charles?" Nothing. He reaches down and shakes Charles' shoulder but he doesn't move, lifts the hand, the hand resting there under the Slurpee machine and it is cold, slaps against the floor when Harold lets go. "My God, Charlie." Now his legs are like rubber, numb and heavy like in a dream. He turns Charles over and starts peeling the plastic away from his face. "Charles?" Nothing. He's got to call the police, there beside the phone, the emergency number in Charles' handwriting. He lifts the phone and squats down on the other side of the counter so that he won't have to look at Charles Husky. He cradles the phone under his chin and uses his other hand to hold his finger still so that he can dial. It seems like it rings forever, but there, there's a voice. "Help," Harold whispers. "the Quick Pik off of 95." The man on the other end yells for him to speak up, but Harold can only whisper again, only this time he says please, only this time he is crying and his hands and shoulders are shaking so badly that the phone slips and clatters to the floor. Harold crouches forward, his hands over his face, his forehead on the floor. He opens one eye and glances to the side where there is an opening at the end of the counter, and he sees Charles Husky's hand resting calmly on that tile floor, there in front of the Slurpee machine. Goddamn, he never would have seen this if Juanita hadn't done what she did.

Ernie Stubbs built himself a new office not long ago. He used to rent out space in one of the old buildings downtown, but once he knew he was really going to make it, he built the new office over near the new shopping center which is near the new highrise retirement home that he built and the new apartment complex. He built the office about the same time that he was building his house, and he got a lot of good deals by doing this, buy more of the same thing, same brick, same roofing. Ernie Stubbs knows how to squeeze every drop of good out of a penny, which is how he has made it this far. Even the slump in real estate hasn't hurt him one bit. Kate already owned the property where he built the retirement home and the apartment complex, a nice big piece of land that her Daddy left her, and so with just a few investors, Ernie Stubbs has been able to parlay that land into quite a sum. He figures people are always going to get old and children will always pay out more than they'd like to so that they won't have to have their parents live with them. Hell, it's a lot like putting somebody away for good— buy the best casket so you don't feel guilty, same with putting an old person in a home. It's a real nice home, too, everything an old person could want; fire alarms so they don't burn themselves up, bars close to the toilet so they won't fall off, wide doorways so they can wheel around, low counters so they can eat right there in their chairs. He's been trying to talk his mother-in-law into moving over there, even told her that he'd put her in the deluxe model which has a microwave built right in and a Jacuzzi hooked up to the tub.

"I'll lie down and die before I move from my home," she always says, and Ernie doesn't pressure her, though it would be for her own good, though that lot of hers right there on Main Street would bring in quite a lot of money, good place for a doctor's office, straight shot to the hospital. Of course, that would mean getting the old house back from his daughter, but they ought to be out some place like Oakwood Village where there are lots of young couples and children for Petie Rose to play with anyway. Ah, but he can wait. After all, he waited years to have what he's got right now, years and years of hard work, which is why he's working late right now, why he works late lots of nights. He's a long way from Injun Street, but he can't ever get too far away, and the way to get further and further away is to make more money. There was no reason that he should ever be reminded of it again. There's no reason to be reminded now. The circle that he runs with now is mostly comprised of people who came to Marshboro long after he made it off of Injun Street, doctors, businessmen and such that don't even know that Injun Street exists. It's only people like his mother-in-law and brother-in-law and even Kate sometimes who will bring something up about his background. Over the years, Kate has learned not to do that, but not Harold Weeks.

Ernie is fifty now, fifty years old and just finally coming in to what he has always deserved: a fine new Williamsburg home in the best neighborhood in town, two cars, his maroon BMW and Kate's blue Audi, the colors matching perfectly with the Williamsburg tones of his house, a pool where little Petie Rose can come and play, instead of having to go to that cheap YMCA like Harold and Juanita Weeks' children, and most importantly a circle of friends who can recognize his class, a circle of friends who enjoy a cocktail party, getting all dressed up and sipping the finest wines and liquors, sometimes getting a little wild, but maintaining some semblance of dignity, unlike someone like Harold Weeks who merely belts down shots and gets stumbling drunk and says things that are crude and unacceptable. Hell, he's got everything going for him and a fifty-year-old man ought to have even more, make hay while the sun shines, make up for lost years before he gets old and decrepit and starts imagining things, like his mother-in-law who on this very day will turn eighty-three years old. How in the hell has she lingered this long?

Tick tick tick. He watches the second hand going around the brand new oak encased schoolhouse clock that Kate picked out for his office. Two o'clock. He's been watching clocks for way too long, counting hours, days, years, decades that would separate him from Injun Street. He would sit in school, watching the big old Seth Thomas clocks, thinking that things would be better at three when the school bell rang. He's always waited for something better to happen and it always has, by dammit, and he's made it happen, he's made it all happen, by himself, and he'll keep right on doing it.

Now he watches little Janie Morris out there typing away, typing up the new land proposal that he has drawn up for a new business area downtown. She volunteered to work late; of course, she is getting overtime and to a secretary, that's a lot of money, Ernie supposes. She'll probably go out and buy herself another cute little outfit, new shoes, things like that. He can sympathize, indeed, with somebody less fortunate working their buns off for a washing machine or a color T.V. He's been there, years ago he was there. Yes, she's going to work out just fine, only been here a week and already those files are neat as a pin, can type like hell, too. A young single girl trying to make good, and she acts like she's real interested in business, too, says she wants to get her real estate license. Now, there's a girl with sense, getting in the right place at the right time, putting herself in the position where she would meet all of the upper-middle-class housewives who have decided to work. Ernie took on one of the young doctor's wives just the other day. Yes, he sees a lot of potential in Janie Morris, and that name fits her, Janie, fits her petite little self and those little fingers rapidly typing up a deal that could be worth thousands and thousands. It's a shame that his daughter Rose never showed such promise; all Rose ever wanted to do was teach art. Imagine, teaching art—no future in that. Ernie supposes that Rose figured that she didn't have to worry, since her Daddy was making it so big and had agreed to take her husband into the business, and God only knows what

Pete would be doing otherwise, probably still working as assistant branch manager over at Federal Trust. And Corky Revels; there isn't a prayer for her, working at that coffee shop, not even trying to go off to school, and she even came from a fairly decent background, at least until a few years ago.

The second hand is ticking in rhythm with Janie's fingers, in rhythm with the way that she swings her leg back and forth, just her toes keeping that little spectator pump from clattering onto that solid heart pine floor. His eyes follow her leg with every tick, the foot swinging back and forth, the little pump holding onto those toes, connected to that slender ankle, the little muscular calf, sturdy hips, slim waist, that low cut silky blouse. Tick tick. This girl's got the right potential all right, little heavy on the makeup, could brush up on her English, groom herself on the right topics so that she could make some comment on world affairs, Dow Jones, music, literature, wines, all of the cocktail topics. Kate has done it though she makes an occasional faux pas, but he bets this girl will be perfect someday. He's seeing the raw workings, the lump of coal that can be squeezed and pressed into a perfect diamond, a woman like Dr. Miller's little wife, Nancy. God, what a dish.

He can just see Janie Morris throw back that curly head and shudder when he told her all about what he hopes to do in the future when he gets all the rest of that land along I-95. "You're some businessman," she had said, and had taken a sip of coffee, a tiny little delicate sip, her pinky even lifted. He hears those words over and over, sees the admiration in her eyes, hears it in her voice, sees that little foot swinging with every tick tick tick. He doesn't quite know what is coming over him, this surge of power, this tightening in his groin.

"Wow, that's some complicated stuff." Janie slumps in and leans against the doorway, stretches her back from side to side, like Kate's cat Booty, who has just had her ninth litter of kittens by some old prowling tom. Booty is a full-blooded Persian, papers, two hundred dollars worth of cat, and every time she's been knocked up by some stray tomcat. "Sorry it took me so long but I like to be real careful." She stretches again and she does look like Booty, a purring kitten, like Nancy Miller.

"I'm real pleased with your work, Janie," he says, now aware of her perfume; nice brand, too, he's smelled it before at a cocktail party. "You know I'm certain that there's a place for you in this business."

"Wow, do you really think so?" She steps closer, got to get her to stop saying "wow." He can't get his mind off of Booty, that night that one of those toms sat outside of his bedroom window, making the call. Kate had slept through it, but he hadn't. He had heard every screeching Mmmmrrrreeeeooooowwww! To cats that is passion in its rare and true form, and at the time what did Booty care that her old tom didn't come from good lines? Maybe she saw potential in him; maybe she felt such a strong attraction that it didn't matter at all.

"I really think so," he says and leans forward, his hands folded on his desk. "Hope I haven't kept you from anything tonight."

"No, no plans and I can really use the money."

"Or anybody? A pretty smart young girl like you has got to have somebody."

"Well, there is one person, but you know, no strings."

"Play the field, huh?" Ernie sits back in his chair and props up his feet. "Have a seat, unless of course you're in a rush." He motions to the chair in front of his desk.

"Actually, I'm wide awake. Once I sit up this late, I sort of get my second wind." She smiles and those little dimples seem to sparkle on that young lineless face.

"Yes, you will be my protégée." He places his fingertips together and works them in and out, bending his knuckles.

"What is that?" She looks embarrassed that she would have to ask.

"It's a French word." He leans closer now, sweat gathering suddenly where his thick salt and pepper hair is parted and styled. "It means that I will take you into my care and help to further your career in the real estate business."

"Really, you mean it?" Now she has jumped up and run around the desk, standing there in her stocking feet like a helpless little child. "Oh, Mr. Stubbs, nobody has ever been as nice to me as you have this past week." She leans down and kisses him on the cheek and just the brush of her lips, the trace of Dentyne on her breath, brings the tightening back and before he even knows what he is doing, he grabs hold of those little hands and kisses them, nibbles the thumb, got to get her to change that nail color, something more subdued, sophisticated.

"Mr. Stubbs." She backs up, those hazel eyes widening. "I hardly know you."

"But you want to, don't you?" Ernie stands up and it is like he has no control, it is like the ticking has exploded into a surge of power, the power that he has been deprived of all of those years that he was working his way from Injun Street. "I mean look at this office, my business, you want that. Don't you think about how you want this?"

"It's crossed my mind, yes, but you're married." Now Janie Morris looks frightened and he didn't want to frighten her. It's his strength and power, too much for her to grasp.

"I'm sorry, sorry," he says and steps closer to her again. "I just lost control. You are so perfect, so attractive."

"But we just met the first of this week. I haven't even gotten my first paycheck." Now her voice has softened.

"You're right. I don't know what happened to me. I'm under so much pressure. Can you imagine how much pressure is involved in a big business? Can you?" He goes back to his chair and puts his head in his hands.

"Oh yes, I'm sure there is." She is creeping closer, like a cat, he can see those stocking feet from where he is peeking through his hands. He's got to slow down, got to take things slowly; he hasn't come all the way from Injun Street to blow it all on one woman. How do all of those men do it? How do they so easily have a little fling, something to tell the boys on a deep sea fishing trip when Ted Miller takes out his big boat. Even Ted Miller has stories to tell about women and brief flings, and he's got that beautiful wife at home, never suspecting a thing; or what about old Dave Foster and all of his escapades on his business trips when he's got Helena, one helluva Helena is what all the men say. Hell, Ernie Stubbs can handle it. It's like old Dave Foster said one day on the golf course, "It doesn't mean you don't love your wife, just means you want to spice up your appetite a little bit; even a hotdog tastes good if you've eaten steak for every single night for the past seven years." Damn right, and as far as Kate is concerned, Ernie figures he's had meatloaf for twenty-nine years. Now Janie Morris' little hands are on his shoulders. He could reach his arms around the chair, grab her, flip her over onto his lap and take her with force. No, he's got to go slowly, make it all happen slowly. "I'm sorry if I made you angry, Mr. Stubbs." He lets her talk, makes no response. Now her fingers are working in and out of his neck, massaging the muscles and it feels so good. "Can I still be your whatever?"

"Protégée?" he murmurs.

"Yes, protégée." He shrugs, her fingers still working over his shoulders. Tick tick tick—something is going to happen and those little paws on his neck feel so good. It's just like when he was a child over on Injun Street and had to work all those summers cropping tobacco. He rode every day on the truck with this black girl, a young black girl, with round firm breasts showing through her thin cotton blouses. He sat right in front of her and she was so intrigued by that straight silky hair that she just had to touch it, had to plait it, and those times he had thought about asking her to stop because it felt so good to him, but it felt too good to make her; he was like putty and even imagined throwing her down on the bed of that truck and climbing on top of that warm brown skin; of course he never did, he never would have even kissed a black girl. "You're gonna get cooties," his Mama said one day when he came home and she saw that plait in his hair, and he remembered those words, but once those black nimble fingers worked their way up and down his head, he was helpless. That girl could have plaited his whole head and he wouldn't have stopped her. MMMrrreeeeeooooowwwww!

"Can I, Mr. Stubbs, still be your protégée? I'm a hard worker!"

"We'll see," he whispers, making the words linger in what he supposes is a suave sexy voice.

"Really, I'll work hard. I know I can do it." She's weakening, every tick, weakening, just about to do anything. God, when is that deep sea fishing trip planned? Two weeks? He will have to check his calendar, but not now, no, not right this second, tick of a second.

The bells above the door ring and it makes Harold lurch forward. He turns around just in time to see this kid with a shaved head stagger in, a duffle bag clenched in his hand. It's him; it's the person returning to the scene. Harold's face is white now, and the pounding in his head is getting worse by the second. The kid keeps walking, his head cocked to one side like a confused dog while he looks at Harold. "Don't come any closer!" Harold jumps up and holds his hands out in front of him.

The kid stops, cocks his head to the other side, then rolls his head forward and all around. He stands there staring at Harold, opening his mouth like he's going to say something and then closing it back, shaking his head from side to side. "Want some water."

"The police are on their way," Harold whispers. "They'll be here any second."

"Huh?" Sam Swett is confused now. He reaches into his bag and pulls out the empty bottle that has been slapping against his typewriter. "Can put water in this or throw it away." He stands for a minute staring at the bottle, and then leans over the counter to toss it in the trashcan. "Two points," he mumbles and then is silent. "Goddamn." He puts his hands up over his face, rubs his eyes but he can't wipe away what he just saw, that fat man, blue in the face. He peeps through his fingers and feels his stomach starting to churn again. "They got murder and rape and robbery, murder." He turns away, his fingers spaced in front of his eyes and there's that big hairy man. He picks up his bag and starts walking backwards to the door, can't take his eyes off that man. "Didn't see it," he says. "No, no, didn't see."

"Hey, you don't think I did this?" Harold moves toward the boy. "This man was my friend. I wouldn't kill him."

"No, no, you wouldn't kill him." Sam Swett shakes his head and keeps backing up.

"Who the hell are you anyway? Where'd you come from?"

"I was in a truck."

"That don't answer my question." Now Harold is mad. Charles Husky is dead and here's this strange-looking kid that's all drugged up.

"Asked him to use the bathroom, had to vomit, sent me outside to vomit." He is leaning against the glass door.

"And that's why you did it?" Harold yanks the bag out of his hand and steps back, puts his hand down in the bag without taking his eyes off of this freak. He gets his hand down there and pulls out a pair of underwear.

"That's my clean pair," the boy mumbles, and Harold throws them down and steps on them, a big black footprint right on the crotch.

"What the hell?" Harold glances down for just a second. "A typewriter and a couple of bottles of booze?"

"I drink bourbon, drink straight bourbon."

"Hell, I can read, got you some Jim Beam, damn, got you some Wild Turkey. What'd you do, bump off a booze store, too?"

"Bought it."

"Like hell. You grabbed what you could. If you had had the time or money, would have bought yourself a fifth of something and saved some money."

"Couldn't decide."

"Shit, tell it to the cops. You move one step and I'll kill you."

"They got bars where a fella can pick a fight, and if you want you can spend the night behind bars."

"You ain't gonna pick a fight with me!" Harold grabs him up by the collar of that nasty green shirt and shakes him.

"No, no, not gonna pick a fight."

"So why the hell did you do that?" Harold presses that boy's head up against the door. "Couldn't decide what booze to buy but you decide to kill a man." He wraps his hand around the boy's neck and pulls him over to the counter, pushes him down on his knees right there beside Charles, the Saran Wrap still bunched around Charles' neck.

"I didn't." Sam Swett closes his eyes and turns away, feels like he's going to choke. He went outside, vomited a couple of times, took a little nap; things are clearing up. The trucker left him and he was looking at M&Ms and then he felt sick and then he left and then he came back and saw this big man with the dirty fingernails squatted over here with the dead man. It is hard to focus his eyes with his head turned this way, with this man shaking him so hard that he can almost hear his brain sloshing up against his skull. "Drink bourbon, not that shit." He points to the countertop where there is a bottle of wine, doesn't drink wine, spilled wine all over his prom date. She called him a jerk and got put on restriction. "I thought you were a nice boy," that girl's Mama said; girl didn't say she drank all but what was on her dress.

Harold stops shaking and glances over at the half-empty bottle of T.J. Swann Easy Nights. Charles Husky didn't drink at all, never touched a drop. Somebody's been drinking that nasty nigger wine. Harold lets go of the boy's neck and can't help but look at Charles again. That boy crawls off to the other side of the counter with his head turned away and Harold follows, yanks him up on his feet. "Breathe, boy," Harold says and braces himself for what is to come.

"On you?" The boy cocks his head to the side and looks like he's going to be sick.

"Breathe, I say!" Harold's nostrils flare and he waits. One thing he knows is the smell of various alcoholic beverages. He knows that cheap wine would stay on a person's breath even if they had had something else on top of it. Damn, sour vomit and bourbon. He loosens his grip on the boy's shirt, flexes his fingers, his Mason ring catching Sam Swett's attention. Sam Swett has to blink several times before he is certain that that is what the man is wearing. He remembers getting to be a Mason; he remembers his Daddy wanting him to become one. "Almost every President of this country has been a Mason and it's something to be proud of, something that should be passed down from father to son." Sam Swett thinks it's a pile of shit; he doesn't want to belong to any club, doesn't want to be homogenized. He reaches down and gives this man the secret handshake. At first that man pulls away like he's crazy, God, if he could remember the password. There are too many words in his head, a dead man, think, think, there; he whispers the word and that man's eyes get big and he lets go of him.

Harold steps back. How in the hell did somebody like

this get to be a Mason? It's hard as hell to be a Mason, probably wouldn't have made it himself if his Daddy hadn't been such a damn good one. "Where are you from?"

"Born in South Cross."

"Nice area." Harold shakes his head, glances out the door. Where in the hell are the police? It's been well over ten minutes since he placed the call. "Mind if I get a drink from you?"

"No."

"Lemme try that Wild Turkey." Harold stares at the boy now, that shaved head and filthy shirt. "You don't look like a Mason. You're drunk and filthy dirty."

"You don't look like a Mason. You're drunk and your hands are dirty."

"Give me the shake and word again." Harold sticks out his hand. "You might've just gotten lucky." Nope, he does it right again, both things, and a Mason sure as hell wouldn't kill anybody; they don't allow riffraff in the Masons. They don't allow riffraff over in South Cross on all them golf courses, either.

"My Dad's a Shriner." Sam Swett picks up his underwear, gets the bottle out of his bag, takes a swallow and passes it to the man who takes an even bigger swallow and then half smiles at him. This man is impressed that his Daddy acts like an idiot, riding around on a Moped with that shitty hat on his head, trying to get people to go to a fish fry.

"Good stuff," the man says and takes another swallow, passes the bottle back. "You know, boy," he says. "Me and you are here in this store with my friend dead over there behind the counter.

"Dead man."

"The police may think that's a little odd." Harold takes the bottle back. "We got to tell them where we were when it all took place."

"I was sick, still feel sick." Sam Swett squats down and puts his head between his knees. He spins when he closes his eyes; he sees that dead man when he closes his eyes, got to stare at the bag, got to go somewhere.

"I was passed out in the backroom." Harold takes another big swallow. "Hey, boy, you got to get up, can't pass out with the cops coming." They've waited fifteen minutes; Harold hopes that the police will wait just a couple of more. "I got it, now you get up and go along with everything I say, just nod your head with everything."

"Nod my head with everything you say." Sam Swett nods, feels the slosh, wants to put his face on the floor but that big man pulls him up, pushes him against a shelf, tells him to stay. There are blue lights flashing around the store, through the glass, doors slam, bells ring. Now there are two cops, agree with everything he says, nod to everything he says, if you want you can spend the night behind bars, hell no, scared of that, never been to jail, nod to everything he says.

"Harold, should've known that was you on the phone at this late hour," one of the officers says. His name tag says Bobbin; the Mason's name is Harold; cop looks like a bird with that sharp nose and large Adam's apple like a turkey, when the red red robin comes bob bob bobbing along.

"Where the hell have you been?" Harold screams. "Look!" He points his hand over the counter without looking. "Charles Husky is dead!" Bobbin walks around and looks while the other cop is talking on his radio.

"Damn," Bobbin says. "Wish I'd known, could've been here sooner, had a domestic over on Injun Street, had to take all the cars over there cause you never know what might happen on Injun Street."

"My brother-in-law was raised over on Injun Street." Harold can't help but throw that in whenever he gets the chance.

"Ernie Stubbs?" Bobbin stands up and shakes his head. "Never'd guess that, him being high society and all." He nods his head toward Sam Swett. "Who the hell's that?"

Harold nods his head like he realizes that he's forgotten to introduce this boy. He doesn't know his name. "Introduce yourself, son."

"Sam Swett."

"He's from over in South Cross. His old man is a Shriner."

"Hmmm, he don't look like his old man would be a Shriner."

"No, no he doesn't, let me tell you what I saw." Harold is talking fast now. "You see this bottle here, Bobbin?" Bobbin nods. "Well, this is evidence. We ain't touched that bottle cause we knew that it was the evidence."

Harold is pacing again. "Now, I ask you Bobbin, who drinks T.J. Swann Easy Nights wine?"

"Niggers." Bobbin nods his head. "Never known anybody else to touch it. Tried it myself one time just to see what kind of kick they get from it, you know, so I'd know what to expect when I meet up with one in a alley who's chocked to the gills."

"Okay, well, I had just pulled up and was standing out there to smoke a cigarette because Charles Husky hated smoking, hated smoking and drinking, and I saw this nigger man come out of the store and drive off. Bout the time I was coming in, a trucker let this boy out right off the ramp over there and he came strolling up. We came in together and found Charles just like he is now cept he was face down. I knew I shouldn't have touched him but I was thinking maybe it wasn't too late, maybe I could give him some artificial breath."

"What did this nigger look like?" Bobbin whips a pad and pen out of his pocket.

"Now you know they all look alike," Harold says and thinks a minute. "But I can tell you what he was wearing. He had on one of those big loose bright-colored foreign shirts."

"Dashiki," Sam Swett says without thinking. Is Harold telling the truth? He doesn't remember any of that. He only remembers going around the corner and vomiting. Isn't right to call black people niggers, not right at all, a violation of civil rights; people are just people. He doesn't remember any of this, just those M&Ms, how they are homogenized once they escape from their society within the bag.

"What about the car?"

"Big one, an old one, hell, I don't know what kind it was, didn't think I'd need to know what kind it was."

"Hey, call the ambulance, tell 'em it's gonna be D.O.A." Bobbin says and gets a very serious look on his face. He always gets a serious look when he uses abbreviations. "Guess you boys can get on," he says. "You look worn out, Harold, and it looks like you need to take a bath." He looks at Sam Swett and shakes his head.

"Come on, Sam, I'll give you a lift," Harold says and he looks at Charles Husky one last time. It's a damn shame is what it is, a damn shame. He feels sorry for whoever it is that has to tell Maggie. "Where you want to go?" he asks when they get in his truck which is parked on a side street that runs in back of the store.

"Somewhere," Sam Swett says and pulls out a bottle. He passes it to Harold, but Harold shakes his head.

"Don't drink and drive except to come here to the store," Harold says. "Don't reckon I'll be doing that any more, hate that son of a bitch that's here in the daytime."

"Hate that son of a bitch."

"Son, you ain't sobered yourself at all. You need to sleep it off."

"Need to sleep it off."

"How bout going to a motel? I would take you home with me but I ain't got much room in the trailer."

"How bout a motel?"

"Now you're talking. Got any money?"

"Visa, few bills, Exxon card."

"Here's Howard Johnson's right up here."

"Can't stay in Ho Jo's, oh no."

Damn this boy's crazy, drunk and crazy as hell. "I'll take you to the Marshboro Hotel," Harold says and heads toward Main Street.

"Marshboro Hotel."

"Ain't bad, little run down, hell of a lot cheaper than the ones on the highway." Harold keeps driving while Sam Swett slumps forward a little. Oh no, he shakes his shoulder. "Hey, don't you puke in my truck, son, just got it vacuumed."

"Don't puke, dead man."

"Just hold on and I'll have you there soon, right across the street from the bus station, too, in case you're wanting to catch one in the morning."

"Catch one in the morning."

"That's right, that's it, hold on, now." Harold is getting close to his Mama's house, can spot it from three blocks away with all those damn floodlights, looks like a prison yard. He pulls up in front of the Marshboro Hotel and stops. "You want some help getting in?"

"Nah." Sam Swett shakes his head and Harold is relieved. He knows several of the people that work in there and he'd hate for them to see him with the likes of this, even if that boy's Daddy is a Shriner. He waits while the boy gets out of the truck and staggers up to the big glass door. Vacancy, there's always a vacancy at the Marshboro Hotel. Harold watches until the big door swings shut and then it hits him, Charles Husky is dead, dead, and he saw him, and he lied to Bobbin to protect that odd-looking boy, to protect himself. He waits a minute before pulling away because his hands are shaking again, his head pounding. He sits and stares over at that yellow glow around the corner, the only part of that rundown old boarding house that you can see at this time of the morning.

He's sober now, completely sober, but it's a strange feeling, a scary numb feeling, as if his body is doing everything without him having any say-so. A light comes on in an upstairs window of the hotel and he sees the curtains open, then the shaved head pausing there. God, he wants to get away, to forget about everything. Without even thinking, he drives right down Main Street and turns on Maple; he's just about to pull in the driveway when he realizes that he's driven home and right there in front of him is his old bedroom window, where right this minute Juanita is probably stretched out with some fool thought running through her head or some damn fool man beside her, and at the moment it doesn't even make Harold mad. He's too tired, too fuzzy feeling to get mad, so he just parks across the street where it is dark and watches the house, that house that he built himself. God, why didn't he just rinse off a little more often?

"Loping through La La Land with Juanita Suggs Weeks," Juanita whispers to herself and sprawls her leg over on Harold Weeks' side of the bed. That's a game that she made up way back when she was still in electrologist school and couldn't get to sleep for thinking about shocking and tweezing people. Now that Harold has left, it seems like she can't sleep at all, and even though it was this very game that got her into trouble, she can't stop playing it. The first time that she ever played this game she was just counting sheep and those sheep were jumping and jumping and pretty soon there was just one sheep going around and around in a circle, and she realized that what she was seeing was that bill-board on I-95 that tells you to take a siesta at South of the Border, which reminded her of her very first date with Harold Weeks who she had just met at a little country bar out in the county, when they went to South Carolina to play putt putt in Pedro's country and drink those sunrise drinks that Juanita is still so fond of, but before she could even think through all of that she was wondering about those worms that Harold Weeks had told her lived down in tequila bottles, and that made her think of that garden snake that she had seen out in her Mama's yard, which reminded her of those big snakes that'll choke you to death like one that she had seen on Wild Kingdom when they were over in Africa. So she had to go back to South of the Border, back to those wild colors and bright lights, and that made her think of carnivals and candied apples and don't sit under the apple tree with anyone else but me, Adam's apple, Harold Weeks' Adam's apple, Adam and Eve sitting around in the buff knowing one another just like she and Harold had done in Pedro's motel, and so on until she was dead asleep, thought out. Through the years she kept playing this game on those nights that Harold was out at the lodge getting soused and those nights that he refused to get up and rinse off. It had gotten to the place where it seemed like she was playing it every night and sometimes even in the daytime, except for on the Sabbath when Harold would stay around home and finally do all kinds of personal things with her.

It had gotten to where all of her days and nights were near about the same—get up and go to Hair Today Gone Tomorrow where she is the owner and fully trained electrologist, perform her time-consuming, tedious professional skill, then come home and wait around for Harold, who very rarely showed up in time for dinner. Then by the time that Harold, Jr. (who looks just like big Harold except for the fact that he's a little jug-eared) was sound asleep with his little plastic E.T. doll watching over him from the night stand, and Patricia was asleep with her transistor radio blaring away beneath her pillow, she was pooped out, too pooped to sleep actually, and she'd say "loping through la la land with Juanita Suggs Weeks." Harold always said "Juanita sucks weeds" and it tickled the children to death. Patricia's name is pronounced Patree-sia because Juanita wanted her to have a Mexican-sounding name like her own, knowing that when they had a Harold, Jr., that they'd call him Harold, Jr., not to mention the fact that Patricia was conceived during a siesta night over at Pedro's when they didn't really siesta, and also because all that Juanita wanted the whole time that she was carrying Patricia around were sour cream and bean burritos from Ace Macho's Nachos, which is a real dive just up from Injun Street but the best burrito-making place in town. Patricia has had a hell of a time in school with that name.

Juanita thinks now that this game is more than a pastime; it is like being born again, a religious experience, being on drugs, a conscience-raising like she has read about in *Cosmopolitan*. She can drift back and see so many good things that have come out of these thinking times, and just good times in general like in that song that she loves so, "do you remember the times of your life?" Once business got real slow because all the women with moustache shadow that could afford her services were too embarrassed to go to Juanita, and would go out of town instead for fear that someone would recognize them. She'd come home crying, that's how bad it was, and Harold would lean her back on that crushed velvet spread that's right now bunched around her feet, get right in her face and say, "Baby, you run into this much shit and there's bound to be a pony close by," and then they'd make love right then and there on top of that spread. Then he'd take the kids to McDonald's so she could get herself feeling better and she'd just lay there and watch the sun set, those pink clouds floating by the window, and pretty soon she'd be in la la land where there was a virus going around that caused women to sprout hair on their chins, knuckles and chests. Those were good times, but there were some bad times as well, and once it all gets started Juanita just can't get it to stop even if she bunches that pillow all around her head like she's doing now. It got to where Harold didn't push her back on that spread any more, even though occasionally she still had a bad day and her thoughts would get to where Harold would fall down and get run over by one of those big tractors, and be laying there between rows of corn with half his head cut off. It seemed that the harder she tried not to think bad things the faster they would come, just like being a child and thinking of a word that you knew was bad and it would just repeat itself in your head, just like a song will do if you especially hate the way that song sounds. As a child she once thought, fuck fuck fuck, knowing that it was bad and it wouldn't shut off, said it to beat the band. Her mouth would be saying yes or no and her head would say fuck, just like that. The more Harold got to where he didn't want to make love, the worse those thoughts seemed to get. She even confided once to Judy Carver who was an old high school friend and whose inner thigh hair she was thinning out for free, and she got real shocked-looking and lay there chewing her nail, partly to keep from wincing when the root was shocked, but mostly because she was shocked, clearly she was, and Juanita was shocked because she thought that everybody had had those thoughts from time to time pass through their heads. Finally, when she had finished her work and was dabbing Judy's stripped follicles with witch hazel, Judy took her nail out of her mouth and said, "Juanita, I think that you need to see somebody about that. You need to see somebody that knows about mental things." It was bad enough that it was all happening, but to think that her best friend thought that she was mentally out of whack just made it worse. It was like being a child and going somewhere in the car and she'd have to pee so bad she thought she'd bust, and her Mama would say, "Don't think about it. We'll stop when we see a clean place." Every time her Mama said "don't think about it," she'd have to think twice as hard and it would sound something like gotta pee, gotta pee, gotta pee. She'd see somebody creep up and push Harold into one of those big pieces of machinery and he'd get all mangled up or else he'd be buried in a grain bin and rattlesnakes would bite the fire out of him. She'd cry and cry while laying there on the bed but it kept right on playing. There was a funeral and she wore tight black jeans and a fringed western shirt and boots and Ace Macho was carrying the casket all by himself. It was just after that episode that she thought that maybe Judy Carver was right, and she started to ride over to South Carolina and find that psychologist who is married to a former client of hers (she had long black hairs sprouting on her toes) but then she changed her mind and went to the preacher instead, thinking that the problem might be deep in her gut instead of her head. He didn't know Juanita that well because of what she had done for years on the Sabbath Day, even though in recent months Harold had cut her off and spent his Sundays fishing with Charles Husky. The preacher was nice; and said he knew her sister-in-law Kate Stubbs real well and that Kate was such a fine person, and Juanita didn't even correct him. He said that people can't control what they dream, that it wasn't her fault and that God knew it and had already forgiven her. It made her feel somewhat better, even though she didn't tell him that she wasn't really asleep when these thoughts came to her but in la la land, which is a lot like that place that Catholics say is between heaven and hell. She was feeling much better, especially when Harold found out that she had had to talk to a preacher and decided that he would take a rinse so they could do it. She was doing fine, almost asleep beside Harold who was already snoring, when suddenly she saw that preacher all dressed up like a rock and roll star, moving his hips all around like Elvis and right in the middle of Jailhouse Rock when he had called her up on the stage to sing harmony, Harold stood up to clap, fell down a flight of stairs and broke his neck. She tried her best to think pretty words but there came the bad ones, scrotum, scrotum, scrotum, and she couldn't make them stop, prostrate, prostrate, prostrate, and then gesticulation. Those words always have sounded so nasty to her; make her think of Ralph Waldo Emerson Britt who used to work at the Winn Dixie and would stand up in that little manager's box with his little red bow tie. She'd think prostrate and then she'd see him nuzzle up to her ear and he'd whisper, "scrotum prostrate." It just never ends, even now it's getting away from her and she sees Ralph Britt whispering those words, and she sees what Ralph Britt really did to her and how Harold stormed out of the house and moved to the trailer park without even letting her explain that she thought that she was dreaming it all up when it happened. She tries to think of something a little lighter, like Ernie Stubbs (who is full of shit) saying that he had heard about a man who played the same game and had written seven books about it. She never should have told Ernie about her game, but that was before he got to the big house and wasn't quite as uppity, aside from the fact that they had all had too much to drink after Granner went to bed. Ernie Stubbs pinched Juanita's titty one time and said he knew what kind she was, even though he didn't know what kind she was. She should have told Harold about that but she didn't. Juanita could write a book. On nights like this when it's so damn hot and she can't get to sleep even though she worked out with heavy weights at Nautilus, and even though she's trying to keep la la on track but can't, she ought to write a book. She ought to get up and just write down the real story of what happened and why it happened and how she knows that if Harold Weeks was here right now and had rinsed off and said that he'd come back to her for good and had said all that about the shit and the pony, well, then she could sleep. She gets up and untwists that velvet spread where it has slid to the floor, shakes it out and puts it over the chair. She can see those bright green numbers of the digital clock radio that she gave Harold for his birthday, 2:30, and she is wide awake. The clock is set to alarm at 5:30, just like Harold always set it, and she hasn't changed it so that it will be just right when he comes home. She hears an engine crank and feels her way around the end of the bed over to the window. She pops her head through the curtains in time to see two rear lights getting smaller and smaller on Maple Street. If she didn't know better, she'd swear that they were the taillights of a Chevrolet truck just like Harold's.

Sam Swett is still sitting in front of the window at the Marshboro Hotel, a Kleenex that he found in the drawer rolled into his typewriter; he's got to record what has happened to him before he passes out. It is getting harder and harder to remember what has happened. Why is he here, in this room, cracked green walls, an air-conditioner that sputters and shakes, putting forth as much air as a two-year-old blowing out a candle? There is a chrome straight chair with a plastic orange seat, like in a school cafeteria; he remembers a school cafeteria, remembers having to buy his lunch, slimy plate on a slimy tray, while other kids had little brown bags and thermos jugs with good stuff from home. One day somebody said that there was rat hair in the pizza stroganoff and he had run run run to that rundown bathroom, got sick, went home. Got sick, ought to go on home. Got to remember why he's here. There's this lumpy bed, bicentennial bedspread, stars and stripes forever with a big bald eagle resting its head where his ought to be and he hates that fucking bird with its fucking bald head but what's a man to do when he can't decide, when there's murder and rape and robbery everywhere. That's why he left New York, car got stolen, most of it got stolen, left him the backseat and two doors, a dashboard; got robbed, stereo, T.V., liquor, cash, got scared, shouldn't get scared, people watch on the subway, get you; all of them look alike, shaved his head so he'd look different, so people would be scared, got rid of everything so people wouldn't want it; yes, he tossed all of his clothes from the fire escape except these, just these that he has on, and people came like ants after a piece of bread, nine minutes is all it took, in nine minutes it was all gone, but they couldn't get enough, came back for more, just like everybody, had to have more, couldn't be satisfied, and he was afraid of becoming just like them, thinking like them, not sleeping like them, sick and starving. He is a modern hunger artist, witnessing the death of society, of America, the world. There is a story in all of that, but it will not come to him because he can't keep his head held up, like a ton of bricks. He rubs his hands around and around his head, feels the stubble, sees the vacancy vacancy vacancy neon sign, red and green blinks like a short-circuited Christmas tree. He can see himself between blinks, his hands on his head, looks like someone washing a coconut, vacancy, looking for the monkey face, vacancy, to drain the milk all of that sweet rich milk, vacancy, split the skull to get that rich white meat, vacancy, eat it up. He can't remember the last time that he ate. But that makes him different from these ants crawling around, formication, eating and sleeping defecating and fornicating, eventually dying. He can be above all of that; eat just enough to keep him alive, detach himself from the gluttonous world, remain an individual even though everything else is becoming the same, then he will be able to tell it, in his own words.

"I saw a dead man." It takes a long time to type that, because he has to hold onto his head as well, but he does and then leans forward and stares at the words. Never in his life has he seen a dead man that was not all fixed up and in a casket, not even in New York. But you can't escape it, can't escape unless you shut yourself away from everything. He tries to remember more but all he can see is that man with napkins stuffed in his mouth. He could be anywhere and that fucking bald bird propped up over there like it's something, a symbol of some sort. That bird means nothing, a symbol of nothing, and this realization, the man with the napkins in his mouth, makes his stomach churn, heave upwards into his chest, but there is nothing left to come out; all traces of human weakness have dried up and he is cleansed, sick as hell but cleansed, crying like a baby. He rubs his head furiously, tries to remember more, types a row of zeroes, big fat zeroes, zero, zero, zero, Zorro, he remembers a black caped man named Zorro; he remembers a beach towel around his neck and he mounts a broom or is it a rake. He mounts something and rides away, far far away from South Cross. Zorro! Zero! He remembers a candy bar, creamy white caramel. He bobs his head rapidly with these memories and he can hear that sweet rich milk sloshing around. The memories are as close as his prickly scalp, as far away as another planet, but there is slosh, he hears a slosh, milk behind his very own monkey face. He has never been this drunk in his life, never had such thoughts flowing into his head from such tangents, brilliant thoughts. He failed as a great writer because he could not live in New York, but he will drink like a great writer; everyone knows that they are alcoholics, homosexuals, suicidal, schizophrenic! He could be all of those things, maybe, maybe. He has never tried any of those things. Now, the idea. He will write about the country as it will be when fully homogenized and people will all look just alike, a colony of clones with plastic bug eyes who all live inside of Howard Johnson's, all committing murder and rape and robbery until there is only one left, the cream rising to the top, showing that homogenization cannot continue and then the world will end and start all over and the narrator will have been a young, middle class person like himself who had the sense to lock himself away and observe the process.

Call me Zorro. Some years ago—never mind how long precisely—having little or no money in my bag, and nothing particular to interest me on earth, I thought I would fly and hide a bit and see the slimy parts of the world. This is my substitute for pistol and ball.

There, he has started, going through the Kleenex but he can read the words, words so true and so real that they almost sound familiar. All great works should sound familiar even though they have never been said before. He must do it again, again and again, until it is just perfect—

Once upon a time and a very bad time it was there was a fucking bald eagle coming down along the road and this fucking bald eagle that was coming down along the road met a nicens little human named baby Zorro. Baby Zorro had his own song that he liked to sing. It went: If you want action the world you'll see, they got rape and murder and robbery, got all kinds of things can happen to you, got broken glass and dog doo-doo.

There, but again it is as if he remembers all of that. It's got to be original, painful, truthful, so difficult that nobody else will ever understand it. After all, isn't that the mark of excellence? Something so difficult, so far beyond the human mind that only the author understands it? That's what will make him different. Yes, yes, the sweat trickles through the coconut stubbles; it makes him cry, all of it makes him cry, a little Sammy playing Zorro all by himself, eating school food all by himself, living in New York all by himself, being anywhere all by himself, afraid to go home all by himself, afraid someone will put napkins in his mouth and leave him to die all by himself. He pulls the Kleenex from the typewriter and wipes his face, the ink smudging on his cheeks and around his eyes. It will never work; he cannot stay awake, can't drink another drop, can't kill himself all by himself, and sure as hell can't be gay. What's a man to do except to climb on that lumpy cover, rough but cool, face on top of the eagle, pitiful bald bird close to extinction, like society, his Toyota. He is a failure, a drunk, tired loser, his eye staring right into the eye of that eagle, that pitiful fucking bald-headed bird that reminds him of that pitiful fat bald-headed man, napkins in his mouth, dead.

Ernie Stubbs feels cheap, used; powerful and manly, but cheap and used. He has done it, after all these years he has been unfaithful, and it is more difficult than he would have ever thought, mainly because he thoroughly enjoyed himself, because he could lose everything if Kate ever found out. He is as sordid as Juanita Weeks, no, not quite. Juanita Weeks is an example of lower class animalism and he has merely fooled around, had a little fling as the boys say. It is confusing because the actual thought of being unfaithful never entered his mind when Rose was a little girl, when his hours were filled with work and reaching a goal. It was only after the goal had been reached, only after plans were made for the new house that he had begun to think, that he even made a move on Juanita one time. She never told Harold; obviously she never did, besides if she did, all he'd have to say is that it was the other way around, especially now that Juanita has shown her true colors. Adultery, it seems like a lower class and upper class thing to do, and how can that be, that the same thing that goes on over on Injun Street could be going on in Cape Fear Trace as well? No, but it's not the same thing. A poor man does it because he's ruthless and crude, doesn't know any better, a dog after a bitch in heat. But men like Ernie Stubbs are different; they aren't attaching any strings, a little friendly recreation simply because there is too much power bottled up inside of a successful man to limit his limits.

The ticking reminds him; he is aware that the comfort of those nimble fingers has worn off, reminded that his mother is going to be furious that a black child was playing with his hair, reminded that he might have to get one of his doctor friends to give him a shot or something to ward off any diseases. He is aware that he is standing in his office, in a pair of baby blue boxers that Kate picked out for him. Kate picks out all of his clothes. He is aware that underneath his Polo oxford cloth shirt, there on the floor, wearing nothing but chipped up putridly pink nail polish, is Janie Morris. Her head is rolled to one side and there's a little piece of Dentyne hanging out of one side of her mouth. Her blue shiny eye shadow is smeared up to her brows. They always say that they don't look near as good afterwards as they do before; it's funny, a man's joke to be told on the boat or golf course. And she had acted like she wanted no part of such. All he had to do was dangle the carrot, protégée, ha! That's all it took, that cheap little tramp, and she was ready willing and ever so able. She's cheap, as cheap as Juanita.

"Hi, tiger," Janie whispers and sucks that Dentyne back into her mouth. "I really like this overtime."

"Overtime? For the whole time?" Ernie throws back his shoulders with his superiority, sucks in that white fleshy roll around his middle.

"Why sure, I mean your wife's been doing the payroll for you, hasn't she?" Janie Morris tosses his nice starched Polo onto a chair and stands up, turns around in front of him with her arms raised like some kind of deformed ballerina. "Wow, I've never been a protégée before. You know I help Tommy out sometimes when he's making pots, but that's about it."

"Who's Tommy?" Ernie quickly puts on his shirt and buttons it, wrinkled, what's he going to tell Kate?

"Just a friend, a close friend really, but don't let that

bother you a bit." She creeps over and rubs her hand through his hair. "Hairspray, I've never known a man who wears hairspray." She wipes her hand on her bare thigh. "Hey, but don't you worry about Tommy. You know, we play it loose. I mean Tommy wouldn't get upset at all over you." She bends over and pulls up her underwear, nylon bikinis that say "sock it to me." God, nobody has said "sock it to me" in years, and they're raggedy and frayed on the elastic, must be a hundred years old. Kate doesn't have an ass like that but at least she wears clean-looking underwear.

"Why wouldn't he care about me?" Ernie stuffs his shirt into his pants and zips up his fly.

"Well, you know, you're sort of old."

"You didn't think I was that old a little while ago. I mean what young man could have ever accomplished all that I have unless it was handed to him on a silver platter?"

"Oh, for sure, for sure." She puts back on those little spectator pumps and pulls on her skirt and blouse. "What time should I come in tomorrow, I mean today, wow it's after 2:00. I really am going to have the cash come Friday, huh?"

"Take it off."

"Oh, now you know I would, but I just got all dressed and really need to go." She smiles great big with her head thrown back and he can see fillings, silver fillings in her back molars. "Don't you ever get tired?"

"No, no, the day, take the day off."

"Oh, I couldn't let you work alone."

"I've got somewhere to go tomorrow, family thing. Just come in Friday."

"Oh great!" Her feet click clack over to where he is standing and she kisses him on the mouth. "Maybe we'll work overtime Friday?"

"We'll see." Now, he cannot bear to look at her, and to think that just a little while ago he was feeling so passionate, a surge of strength that made him feel like there was nothing but that very tick tick of a second. He had wanted so badly to fulfill his appetite, a change of diet, a bite of lobster, only to find out that he has wasted himself on perch. Now she'll hold it over his head, blackmail him for sex and money. He never would have made it where he is if Kate hadn't been willing to claw and scratch her way to the top, to have big dinner parties with the most prestigious people, to buy him all of the latest clothes, to give him all of that land.

"See ya," she says, and her feet click click over that heart pine floor, the door closing behind her. Ernie sits in his desk chair and runs his hands through his hair. Maybe it wasn't worth it. He feels as much shame right now as he ever did over on Injun Street, and it's not his fault; it wasn't his fault that he was born and raised on Injun Street, and this is not his fault.

Juanita Weeks has walked all around her house four or five times, done situps and the waist twister and still her mind is thinking on and on. That very well could have been Harold Weeks, though she doubts it; "I am washing my hands of you," he had said that last day when she came running in from the Winn Dixie to find him packing a bag.

"I can explain," she said and grabbed his arm, but he pushed her down on that crushed velvet spread and left her there without touching her. "You're not leaving, are you?"

"Does a wild bear shit in the woods?" Those were his last words and that was so like him to answer a question with a question, and he had turned and left, just like Rhett Butler, and she had sunk down on the door stoop because they don't have a staircase, and her thoughts had wandered off to all the various reasons that Harold Weeks had for leaving her, even though Harold didn't know about most of those things. There was that time when she was eight months pregnant with Patricia and she had this awful craving for sour cream and bean burritos. Harold wasn't home so she drove down there all by herself. Ace Macho was there alone, sweeping the floor under those dim lights that they use so that people will know they are closing. Ace was goodlooking at the time with his big hairy arms and thick moustache, and she always has just loved to see people who could wear body hair and have it look good on them, though heaven knows she is thankful for those whose body hair is not attractive on them or she wouldn't have anything at all. She knocked on that door and bent down so that Ace could see her under the Closed sign. Sure enough he did and he let her in. She remembers exactly what she had on, too. She had on terry cloth slippers and one of

Harold's big work shirts and some of those stretchy pants that have the little stirrups so they won't ride up. "What can I do for you?" Ace Macho asked after giving her the one two.

"I want two sour cream and bean burritos." She watched him shake his head and glance back at the empty counter. "Anything hot," she said, "spicy hot, a taco, nachos, enchilada." She was feeling desperate, and there Patricia was kicking up a storm. She always has thought that Patricia may have had a touch of that womb perception and knew that something was going on.

"Ain't no law that says I can't whip up something." He went over to the freezer. He pulled out all sorts of good things and started heating up that big oven. Once he turned and grinned and it was a pretty smile.

"Does this suit you?" Ace asked and set before her two bean and sour cream burritos, a little basket of nachos, and a chicken taco. He got himself a beer and sat there staring while she ate all of that, sour cream and hot sauce running down her wrists. He said, "Motherhood agrees with you," and she just nodded because her mouth was crammed full of burrito. She ate every bite. "How much?" she asked right when she swallowed that last nacho.

"It's a favor," he said and came around to pull out her chair for her. He got real close and he was wearing this heavy musky smelling cologne that she can catch a whiff of right now when she thinks of it. She told him that her husband could afford for her to have a Mexican meal, and even if he couldn't she could, because she was a professional woman herself. The next thing that she knew, he had rubbed his hand over little Patricia and kissed her hard on the mouth like in a movie, grinned great big and pushed her away. "Now, we're even," he said and kept on grinning. She left feeling funny and then cried, and cried once she got home that such a thing had happened. Even now it makes her want to cry, just to think of what Harold would have done to her if he had known. It makes her cry more to think of Ralph Waldo Emerson Britt, him as ugly as he is, and that's why Harold left her, and it never would have happened if she had known that she was really awake and really in the Winn Dixie instead of on her bed in la la land. Even now she thinks that it's possible that really she is out somewhere doing some of these thoughts instead of being here in the bed. She slaps her cheeks, turns on the light over the bed. She's here all right; Harold's side of the bed still empty, the clock still set for five-thirty and she hasn't had one wink of sleep. Besides, she's got to figure out whether or not she's going to take the kids over to Granner Weeks' party. Harold might slap her down or something.

Bob Bobbin is still out cruising in his squad car even though his shift is up. It's relaxing, after a hectic night, especially like this one, his first big murder scene and all he has to go on is a bottle of T.J. Swann Easy Nights and Harold Weeks' description of a nigger, which ain't much to go on considering they all look alike to Officer Bobbin. He rides past the old boarding house and slows down. It looks like Corky is sitting in her window, but he knows it's probably that big old doll that she puts up there sometimes. He starts to blow the horn to let her know that he's watching out for her, that she's safe as can be with Bob Bobbin on the scene, but the last time that he did that she got furious, said he woke her up and her neighbors. Her neighbors are black and he's told her before that she ain't got no business living someplace with niggers. She just got mad all over again, when all he wants to do is watch out for her.

He turns up Main Street and everything is dark except for the streetlights and, of course, Granner Weeks' yard. That old woman is forever calling the station to report something that ain't even there. "You better quit crying wolf," Officer Bobbin told her one day when she had reported that a man was up on her roof trying to get in a window. "You better do your job, ugly, and if you do you'll not have to worry with me," is what she said, and right there in front of her family, called him ugly, which really isn't true, especially now that he grew his moustache and sideburns to fill out his face a little. Ernie and Kate Stubbs were standing there to hear her talk that way to him, and how about that, Ernie grew up on Injun Street. He never would have guessed it, ain't even going to ride down Injun Street now that he's off duty, because something is always going on down there.

The hospital is all lit and he rides on by and out into the country, past the new highrise for oldies, past the new apartment complex where he has just moved, and it's nice, perfect for a bachelor like himself, and it will even be okay for a young newly married couple. He turns in the big gate that leads into Cape Fear Trace and circles around. All these big houses are always well lit, and with good reason. If somebody was wanting to pull a robbery, this is the place to come, not some Quik Pik where the sign even says that there's only twenty-five dollars in the register after ten. Twenty-five bucks and a bottle of T.J. Swann, that's what Charles Husky was worth, and it's a shame, a damn shame, but that's the law business, the work of the men in blue. Everything looks fine out here so he swings back on the main road and heads toward his apartment. He has the one bedroom model, "perfect for a single person" is what the brochure said, and it's true, got a little bar, and Bob was even able to pick out his own carpet and wallpaper, red shag and that black and red sort of velvety paper. Mrs. Stubbs had called and asked several times, "Are you sure this is what you want? What if you move and nobody else wants this combination?"

He assured her that he would live there a good long time. He knew what she was thinking, a little bold, maybe too masculine, but he's the daring kind anyway. A woman would walk in and see that decor and know right away what kind of man Bob Bobbin is, a daring bachelor, and when he gets his new furniture, that suit of Spanish Mediterranean with the matador lamps, and one of those bearskins to go in front of the portable fireplace, he's going to ask Corky Revels over for dinner. Corky's the kind of woman that needs to be spoiled with all the good things, and God knows she deserves it. Sometimes she looks so lost and frail that Bob thinks he could crush her ribs if he pulled her up to his strong chest. She plays hard to get, but Bob Bobbin has never yet to meet a woman that didn't play hard to get with him. That's how he knows that women find him attractive; women only play hard to get with those men that they want the most.

The case of Charles Husky is still the most important thing on his mind right now, not much to go on, send the bottle of T.J. Swann to the M.P.D. lab room, get fingerprints, maybe get them off that bread bag, those napkins that they had to pull out of Charles' mouth. Got to unwind, a little champagne before bed. He goes to the refrigerator and gets himself a little bottle of Champale out of the sixpack, best way in the world to buy champagne if you frequently sip from time to time like Bob Bobbin, because it doesn't go flat. He pours some into his glass that he just got at Burger King, swirls it around, holds it to the light, takes a sip; you must always sip. This is what he'll serve when Corky comes, might buy a can of smoked oysters, or some of those snails, maybe some anchovies. He takes another sip, tosses his cap over on the bar, loosens his tie, pulls off his shoes and socks, unbuttons his shirt, unzips his fly, steps out of his uniform. Now, he's comfortable. He spreads a kitchen towel on the floor so he won't get his briefs dirty and sits there, leaning against the refrigerator.

He stares over at the wall where he's got his outstanding service plaque and the newspaper article framed beside it that tells all about how he saved that old niggerman's life. He remembers everything about that night, was reminded of it all when he got to the Quik Pik. He was down around the bottoms when that 911 came through, got the address, old shack on the other side of the tracks. The door was locked so he busted a window and crawled through, found that old man stretched out on the floor with the telephone receiver beside him. Old man was breathing by the time the rescue squad got there and carried him off. "You saved his life," those guys had said, and that old man opened one eye and was trying to say something but they carried him away.

"Kissed a nigger," one of the guys at the P.D. had said and laughed. "Did you slip the tongue?"

"Shut the hell up," he had said, "I couldn't let him die."

"You could've, and the way you're always talking about niggers, I'd think you would've."

"It's different" Bob had said, decided that he wouldn't pin that newspaper clipping up on the bulletin board, spelled his name wrong anyway.

"That was something what you did, Bob," Corky had said.

"It was nothing."

"You saved a life!" she had said and smiled; she had actually smiled, and that coffee shop had been full of people looking over there.

"A nigger's," he had said, and made several of the men in there laugh. Corky hasn't smiled at him since, that he can remember; she's not even smiling in that little snapshot that he's got of her stuck in the corner of his bedroom mirror. It's her senior class picture and she didn't even want to give him that; he had to bug the hell out of her. Hell, he wasn't going to have all those guys riding his ass like that. He was glad when the whole thing died down and was forgotten, though he still gets cards from that old man from time to time, can't make out a word of that scrawl, saves them though, thinking that some time maybe he'll have the time to sit down and figure out what that old nigger was saying. Everybody's just about forgotten it by now, even Corky, but sometimes he can't help but think about it, to remember how he pumped that man's chest and breathed life back into him. Old Charles Husky wasn't so lucky and that's what's on his mind now, that and getting to sleep so that he can get down to the Coffee Shop first thing before his shift starts. Sometimes he thinks he ought to stop going down there, that maybe Corky would wonder where he was if he didn't show, that maybe she'd wonder about him, but he never can do it, never can ride by without stopping just to see her, to see the flush in her cheeks when he says, "Coffee, no c&s, ASAP."

2

Frances Miller pulls out of her drive in Cape Fear Trace at exactly seven o'clock, right on schedule. She passes the little sign on the main road, "Marshboro city limits—Population 10,000—Awarded the Governor's Community of Excellence—Speed Limit 35 mph." Lordy, what a dipshit town, tacky, just tacky something awful. She can't believe that a successful doctor like her father would live here. Nobody drives 35. Frances is in a big hurry to get to Myrtle Beach because she knows it's going to be a perfect day. She looks at herself in the mirror and she really does look so good today! Her frosting job turned out to be a terrific idea. Now her hair is a beautiful ash blonde and has so much body that it curls and falls around her face and shoulders with a sort of Farrah Fawcett look. A lot of people have said that she looks like Farrah but she can't decide. she thinks that she sort of looks like Olivia Newton John and this is why she has a little twisted headband up on her forehead. Carl loves Olivia; he loves that song "physical" and he is bound to notice the similarities now that her hair is blondish. Frances is certain that Carl is the one for her, and her parents agree; he was a Phi Delt; his father is a big-time tobacco man; grew up in Greensboro on the finest golf course. In just an hour and a half, Frances will be lounging on the beach in front of the big Ramada Inn where Carl works as bar manager, a temporary fun little thing for him to do before entering his father's business, of course. She will be lounging there in her new bikini with the G-string effect that she has on right now under her terry cloth coverup, sipping a daiquiri, planning the wedding. After all, she's twenty-two years old!

There is a stoplight up ahead so she shifts down in her brand new Datsun 280-ZX; she loves this car with a passion, almost as much as she loves Carl. It makes her feel powerful when she shifts down and back up. She likes to hear the engine rev a little. She's got it all! A Datsun, good looks, knockout figure, blondish hair, a K–3 degree that she has no intentions of ever using, and best of all Carl.

Frances locks her doors. Her Daddy always has told her to lock her doors if she had to ride down around Main Street. It does look bad around here, run down and all, and she wishes that there was another way to get to the highway except to come through all of this. She is getting the spooks; she has never ridden around the bottoms all by herself, and when she gets to the end of this rotten street that's exactly where she'll be. She speeds up and pushes in her Olivia Newton John greatest hits tape. "Let's get physical, physical." She shifts into fourth. There probably aren't even any cops around this part of town.

"I want to get animal, animal." Cruising down Main Street at fifty mph.

"Happy birthday dear Granner, Happy birthday to you!" Granner sings like a bird and goes over to stand by the window. Yessirree! It's a beautiful day, hot and plenty of sunshine, and it's the day of her birth. It's exciting, maybe not for everybody, but for a woman who is possibly entering her last year it's exciting. Granner ties her warm flannel robe around her tightly, and pulls up her crew socks that she likes to wear around the house, so that she won't get chilled when she goes out to get the paper. She has saved the *Marshboro Gazette* edition of July 7th for the past twenty years because the editor always remembers to put a little something about her. It'll say something like "Happy Birthday, Mrs. Irene Weeks."

Kate and Ernie would have a pure fit if they saw her walking around in these socks, because last birthday they gave her some of those big fluffy shoes in an all-right lavender color. They have never been out of the box. They make her feel like she is walking around with dust mops on her feet, and an old woman shouldn't feel like she's doing housework ALL the time. She gives good presents. She gave Kate one of those vegetable pulverizers that makes carrot juice and all sorts of good things, and she gave Ernie Stubbs four pairs of argyle socks and a paperweight that's shaped like a bowling ball. He said, "My, how nice, I haven't bowled in years." And then Kate had to put in her two cents, said, "Bowling is such a blue collar sport." Granner can tell when somebody's giving her the dig, even if it's her own family member. She said, "Well, he's got on a blue shirt, better hop to it," and they both just laughed like she didn't know any better. She hopes they don't try to get her back. She wants one of those whirlpool foot relaxers more than anything in the world. The thermometer on the front porch is already up to 96 degrees. Isn't that nice? Granner won't be chilled all day long.

"Hi, Petie Rose!" Granner yells. Without a doubt she is the cutest child with those red pigtails, come out cute as a bug, which sometimes makes Granner think that it was someone other than Pete Tyner who got Rose in trouble. Granner was so glad when Pete and Rose moved into the old house that she and Buck gave Kate and Ernie in the first place. Seeing a child out playing is what an old woman needs to keep her living from day to day. "What you doing, Petie Rose?"

"Looking for Tom!" Petie yells back in that gruff little voice.

"He's probably out prowling. You know what special day this is, Petie Rose?"

"Nope!" Petie Rose is crawling behind the azalea bushes.

"It's Granner's birthday!" Granner picks up her paper and stops right there in the yard to open it up.

"Tom! Tom! Tom!" Petie Rose screams and stomps her little feet. My, that child's got a temper, a fiery temper, and Granner likes that so much. Of course, it's a blessing that the new baby is on the way. Another year and Petie Rose wouldn't stand for a new baby.

"You'll find him, sweetie Petie."

"TOM!" Petie Rose's face is now as red as her hair.

"Petie, calm down. He'll come home." Rose is out on the porch now with her stomach swoll up like a blimp. "Happy birthday, Granner!"

"Thank you, Rosie." Glory be! Can't an old woman have no peace to read her very own birthday greeting? Granner likes to save things like letters and important pieces of news for when everything is quiet and she can direct her full attention. "See you later! Hold onto that baby, now. Don't work and move around till it drops out before you're ready."

"I wish it would drop out," Rose says, and from this distance across the yard Granner can even see the twisted look on that squared-off face. No doubt about it, Petie Rose don't look like either of them. Granner can't hardly wait. She closes the door and spreads that paper right there on the floor and starts looking over every speck. Ain't on the front page, and you'd think that by now it would be front page news. Not everybody is alive and well for so long. Granner keeps flipping those pages and finally has to go get her glasses before she sees it. It's in the smallest print that it's ever been in, and it ain't on the society page, either. It says "Irene Weeks turns eighty-three today," and that's it, no happy birthday or kiss my foot, and it's right above an ad for The Salvage Bin which is a junk shop over near Ernie Stubbs' old neck of the woods on Injun Street. It says, "We take old, used, worn-out things that get in your way."

Well, the nerve of it! She bets Ernie Stubbs put them up to this so that she'll think about going over to that highrise, or else because she gave him that bowling ball that he probably has in a drawer somewhere. It crosses her mind to call the police in on this but then she decides to handle it herself. She'll just call Mr. Stubbs up is what she'll do, and let him have it. It ain't decent to toy with an old woman and especially one that's already so upset about that Iranian. "I wish to God he'd have a stroke or something and then he'd see who's old, then he'd see who needs to live in that highrise with commode bars and such!" Granner is on her way to the phone to say those very words to his face through the phone when she hears this awful screech and Petie Rose screams. It sends a chill through Granner's scalp. "Oh God, I didn't mean that wish. I take it all back. Don't take it out on Petie."

Granner runs out her front door about as fast as any woman with a slight touch of arthritis can do and catches her chest with a sigh of relief when she sees Petie Rose standing by the roadside, still screaming, but alive.

"Get up!" Petie Rose screams. "TOM!" She stomps those feet but Tom doesn't move at all. Petie Rose keeps screaming even when her mother and Granner come and pull her away from the street.

"I'm so sorry! So sorry!" That blonde-headed woman with the string around her head squats down and tries to get Petie Rose to look her in the face. Petie Rose doesn't want to look her in the face. Petie Rose wants Tom to get up.

"You fix Tom!" Petie Rose screams. "You make Tom get up!"

"Sweet Pete," Granner says and hugs Petie Rose close. "Poor old Tom is hurt too bad to get up. Tom's dead."

"Tom's dead?" Petie Rose screams. "You killed Tom!" Petie Rose pulls her pigtails so hard that it hurts her head. She pulls them until her Mama makes her stop pulling.

"I'm so sorry," that lady says. "I'll do anything to make it up to you."

"You couldn't help it," Rose says. "Old Tom wandered all the time. It was bound to happen sooner or later."

"How fast were you driving?" Granner asks. "You know it's twenty here on Main Street. Always has been twenty, due to there's lots of old people around here and some children like this one. That could have been Petie Rose here that you killed."

"Granner, please," Rose says, and nods down to Petie Rose who is crying up a storm, her nose dripping like a faucet on her pretty little top.

"I hate you! I hate you!" Petie Rose screams and starts to run away. Petie Rose is going to go inside and turn the T.V. set up as loud as it will go. That's what she's going to do, all right, and what's more, she's gonna take her crayons and scribble all over the living room wall. She's gonna scribble and scribble and throw her Legos all over the house just as soon as Granner will let go of her.

Frances Miller watches that little girl twist away and

run up to the house, crying and carrying on, and who can blame her? Her pet that she loves is dead.

"I'm so sorry," she says. "Can I get her a new kitten? My father is Dr. Ted Miller."

"I don't care if St. Peter's your Daddy, it ain't gonna resurrect Tom there." That old woman steps closer to Frances. "I reckon you might have been going too fast." The old woman goes out into the street, picks the cat up by the skin of his neck and slings him into the yard. "Gotta do something with him, Rose," the old woman says. "It will just kill little Petie to see him again."

"Here, here, put him in my car and I'll take him. It's the least I can do!" Frances can't believe what she's saying, but the old woman takes her up on it and picks the cat back up and carries him over to the car.

"My, my, a young person like you driving a sports car!" The old woman says, and sways back and forth with the cat. Frances can't stand to look at that cat. She opens the hatchback and watches that woman plop that cat right down on that pretty new ice-gray upholstery. "It's a killing machine all right, a fast little car like this. Hope you wear a seat belt."

"Granner please!" the pregnant woman says, and the old woman turns on her.

"Granner please! You say that like I don't know a thing I'm saying, like I'm old as dirt and need to be put away. That's all your Daddy can think of is to have me put away just like something old, used up, and in the way. All of you act like Mr. Abdul ain't really so, act like

I should have just sat back and done nothing that day that that man was crawling around trying to get in my windows."

"Oh my," Frances says and covers her mouth.

"Oh my, is right." The old woman stops and stares at her again, those beady little blue eyes suddenly widening. "Did you say your Daddy is Dr. Miller?"

"Yes, yes," Frances nods.

"That's who I took my Buck to when he had a little chest pain and next thing I knew your Daddy come out and told me that Buck was dead, D-E-A-D, dead, as dead as Tom."

"Granner, granddaddy had a heart attack, nobody could have helped him."

"Heart attack, foot. He had a touch of the gas, told me so himself. He's the one that drove the car, too, and I sat right there in the passenger side and told him where to go. A little gas don't kill." The woman eyes Frances again. "Cept when it's inside of a machine like that, then gas'll kill."

"Why were you getting Grandaddy to the doctor then?" The woman grabs the old woman's arm and speaks slowly to her like to a child.

"I was going to see if they'd give him an enema."

"Oh Granner."

"Believe what you want. I know that little bit of gas isn't what killed Buck. The gas ain't responsible for me being a lonely old widow."

"Am I responsible? I mean, can you forgive me for

killing the cat?" Frances opens her door and stands there with her head pressed against that hot ice-gray metal. Her Kleenex is all soggy and she has to use her Olivia Newton John headband because her nose is still running. Her mascara is running.

"I thought you were gone!" That old woman says and stomps off to the house next door.

"It's okay," the pregnant woman says, but keeps watching after that old lady. "You couldn't help what happened. Petie Rose will understand what happened. You go on now. You were nice to even stop." The woman waddles up her own driveway, stopping to pick up her paper, and Frances gets in her car. She is driving ten mph, watching the road through watery eyes almost as if she expects a cat to jump out any minute. "I've never killed anything," she sobs. "Here I was riding along above the speed limit thinking of myself and now that little girl and her old Granny will hate me forever! Forever they will remember the blonde that looks like Farrah Fawcett that was driving the Datsun 280-ZX, that ice-gray Datsun that ran over her kitten! That little girl will grow up and go to pajama parties and when they all start telling sad stories, that child will speak up and tell about that awful streak-haired woman in a skimpy coverup driving a gray killing machine that ran her cat down and killed him." It makes Frances cry that much more; it takes away the joy that she was feeling just a little while ago. Frances sees this filthy-looking guy with a shaved head squatted down in front of the Coffee Shop at lower Main Street and she wants to speed up so that she can hurry by, but she can't speed up. At this speed, it will take her until noon to get to Myrtle Beach.

Corky Revels pours herself another cup of coffee and goes to wait on Harold Weeks, who has just come into the Coffee Shop and is sitting there talking to Bob Bobbin. She wishes that just one morning she could come into work without Bob Bobbin standing around out front waiting for her. Bob Bobbin doesn't even notice that she can't stand him, doesn't even notice that strange-looking boy that's strolled up and is sitting right outside the shop. "Can I get ya'll something?"

"Coffee," Harold says. "Gotta go over to Woolco's and get something for Mama's birthday. Reckon I'll pick up some little something and stick Harold, Jr., and Patricia's name on it, cause I know Juanita ain't going to do it."

"You don't know," Corky says, because she likes Juanita. Just about everybody likes Juanita.

"Ah, her head's too full of other thoughts." Harold looks up and his eyes are all red and puffy. Corky would think that Harold had been crying, but that's impossible. Must've pulled a bad drunk, like he's done regularly since he left home.

"What happened between you two, Harold, not being nosey of course, happened to wonder just last night when I was sipping a little champagne." Bob looks directly at Corky when he says this and she turns away. She gets so damn sick and tired of hearing about his champagne and his apartment.

"What have you heard?" Harold pours some of his

coffee in his saucer and then drinks it from there.

"Heard something about Juanita and Ralph Britt," Bob says and it makes Harold clench his teeth. "Is that true?"

"Does a fat dog fart?" Harold pours some more coffee into the saucer and spills it all over the counter.

"You don't have to be crude right here in front of Corky. All you had to say was yes or no."

"Cause it ain't your business. Your business is police work."

"Anything else?" Corky asks Bob and starts figuring up his bill so that he'll leave. He never even leaves her a tip.

"Got any English muffins and marmalade?"

"Why do you ask that every single morning when you know good and damn well that we don't?" She rips off his bill and hands it to him.

"Just teasing, Corky," he says and then looks at Harold. "Private joke."

Corky comes close to saying that he's the joke, but she knows that the sooner she completely ignores him, the sooner that he will leave.

"Got a full day down at the P.D. Gotta find the man that murdered Charles Husky."

"What?" Corky puts down the pot and sits on the low table behind the counter. "Mr. Husky was murdered?" Corky can't keep her eyes from getting all watery. Mr. Husky was without a doubt one of the sweetest men that she'd ever met. He and his wife were regular lunch customers.

"Yeah, time of death approximately 1:00 A.M. Wouldn't have anything to go on if it weren't for Harold here."

"You were there?" Now Corky really is amazed. To think that Harold Weeks, of all people, is the one that was there.

"Saw the man leaving." Harold shakes his head back and forth. He practically has himself believing that he really did see that black man in the dashiki. "Then I went in and found Charles." Harold puts his head down on the counter and Corky wishes that he wouldn't do that. It doesn't look nice to have dirty hair on a countertop where people are expected to eat, but in this case she forgives Harold.

"That's horrible," Corky says, and pours some more coffee into Harold's cup.

"Yep, suffocated him with Saran Wrap," Bob Bobbin says, "gagged him with paper napkins, got the weapons right there in the Quik Pik. Husky's eyeballs were close to popping out of his skull when we got there, blue-looking."

"Just shut up!" Corky screams. "I don't want to hear all of that, and you ought to be out there looking for the murderer anyway." Corky notices now that that strange boy is squatted down in the doorway with his hands up to his shaved head. "Bob," Corky whispers, "Don't look right yet but there's a strange-looking person outside, might be the man." Bob whirls around, draws his gun and then starts laughing. "He ain't black, Corky, and he ain't wearing one of those bright foreign shirts." Bob sits back down and blows into his coffee, and he looks like a turkey with that big Adam's apple bobbing back and forth and coffee getting all over that puny moustache.

"Well, I didn't know!" Corky slams down her cup. "How was I to know? That's a stranger out there and he looks strange, strange enough to have killed somebody."

"Ah, Harold knows that kid, knows his Daddy is a Shriner."

"Didn't say I knew him. Said he got out of that truck after Charles was already killed and we went in together to find him."

"You gave him a ride home."

"I took him to the hotel, said he'd probably catch a bus this morning, probably waiting around now to catch one." Harold turns and glances at that kid. Yep, it's him all right, not cleaned up a bit. "But he is a Mason, knew all the secrets."

"I've thought I may be a Mason," Bobbin says, and looks at Corky again like she might be impressed.

"You don't just say you want to be a Mason, ain't like getting in the Jaycees."

"I've thought about the Jaycees, too." Corky doesn't even look his way at this one. Bob turns and looks out the door again. "I swear though, even if he is a Mason, he's filthy dirty, and with that shaved head looks like he might be a cult member, like those that go around with that Chinese preacher, you know?"

"Maybe he's been in the service." Harold doesn't even look again, though now Bob Bobbin is staring.

"Bad image for the Masons. Don't that upset you?"

"Does a dog use a rubber?" Harold is getting fed up with Bob Bobbin, especially today when he feels so damn bad for so damn many different reasons. "Masons takes all kinds from Presidents to farmers like myself, greatest place in the world to be."

"I think Cape Fear Trace would be a great place to be."

"Stop staring at me!" Corky screams at Bob, and starts wiping off the counter, now that Harold has his head raised back up.

"I wasn't staring at you."

Corky just ignores him and keeps looking out from time to time at that boy. He sure doesn't look like a Mason, looks a little kooky. Kooky. That's what Granner Weeks used to call Corky. Granner Weeks always has said that Corky needed to find herself a man that is as Kooky in a nice way as she is. But that boy looks bad with that shaved head and all. Corky goes back behind the counter when he starts to stand up, his whole body swaying and he keeps holding onto his head. The bells jingle when he pushes in and both Harold and Bob Bobbin turn around and wave at him.

"What's new, stranger?" Bob Bobbin asks. "Thought you would have left town. Wasn't a pretty sight you saw last night."

The boy looks like he wants to say something, but then he goes and sits at the table by the window. He slumps over and lays that shaved head right on the table! What on earth is going on today? Corky is going to have to take Lysol to every counter in the place.

"Bet it was drugs," Harold says. "I bet that murderer is

on drugs. I mean, he'd have to be wouldn't he? To do what he done?"

"Some people are just plain mean as dogs," Bob Bobbin says.

Corky gets up her nerve and walks over to the table with a coffee cup and the coffee pot. "Can I get you some coffee, sir?" That boy doesn't even look up, just rolls that shaved head back and forth. "Hey, you," She shakes his shoulder in spite of the fact that she really hates to touch his clothing. He lifts his head and squeezes his eyes tight several times before he opens them and looks at her. "How bout some breakfast?" He turns his head to one side like a confused dog and keeps staring at her. His eyes are hollowed out, looking like somebody who hadn't slept for weeks.

"What time is it?" he asks, and it sounds like his whole mouth is full of cotton balls. "I smell food."

"It's after seven o'clock and you ought to be smelling food. This is a restaurant. What can I get you?"

He keeps staring at her, and Corky can't help but notice that he's got real pretty eyes, great big and brown, if he'd just get rid of those awful bags under them. "Hey, are you okay?" She shakes that nasty shoulder again.

"What day is this?" he asks and now he's staring at her eyes as hard as he can, turns his head from side to side, staring at her eyes.

"It's July 7th, Thursday, July 7th."

"Just Thursday?" He puts his head back on the table, but this time with it rolled to one side. He is still staring at Corky's eyes, then her mouth; it's like he can only see one thing at a time.

"Hey, are you sick?" Corky sits down across from him and whispers. "You know, have you maybe just been let out of somewhere or something?"

"New York City."

"You were locked up?"

"Sort of." He looks up and he really does have pretty eyes; they look a little like Dr. Zhivago's eyes. "Sort of locked up, still not free."

"Are people looking for you?"

"Huh?"

"The people who locked you up." Corky notices that Bob is watching her, so she pours a cup of coffee and pushes it in front of this Kooky person. He lifts the cup to his mouth and starts drinking, and that's hot coffee. Corky always serves piping hot coffee. "Good," he says. "This is good."

"You need some food is what you need." Though she doesn't want to, Corky touches his face and lifts his head so that he has to look at her. "Probably made you sick to see what you saw last night, didn't it?"

"I was sick last night. Cool," he says and rubs her hand over his head.

"It ain't cool; it's bad is what it is."

"So cool," he says again and rubs her hand through his prickly hair and back around his eyes. He's sweating like a pig.

"I believe you're still sick. Honest to God." She takes

her hand away and wipes it on her apron. "I'm getting you some breakfast. Just don't move. Stay right there."

"May be in shock," Harold says. "Too, I never seen anybody as drunk as that boy was last night. May still be drunk or bad hung over."

"I still think he must be in one of those cults as well as the Masons," Bob Bobbin says. "Did he ask you to give up your stuff, Corky?"

"I beg your pardon! That's a bad thing to say, Bob Bobbin, just cause I won't go out with you." Corky goes and starts mixing up pancake batter.

"No, Dizzy Dame, I mean things like your home and car and clothes and money, you know, to follow that Chinese." Bob laughs great big. "Course you ain't got a bit of anything, do you?"

"I got what I need and no, he didn't ask none of those things. He's feeling sick is what he's doing, and who wouldn't if they had seen what he saw?" Corky pours the batter into neat little circles on the griddle and fixes some sausage patties while she waits for that batter to bubble. She looks back over to make sure that he's still there. He's filthy, all right, but he's got the prettiest, saddest eyes that she's ever seen, and it makes her think of things that usually hurt her to the core, but somehow, now it doesn't hurt as bad.

"I saw it, too, and you ain't going out of your way to help me get over the shock." Bob stands up and pulls his cap down low. "Harold saw it, too."

"But you're trained in it, Bob, that's what you said." For some reason, she is feeling better, feeling better enough even to be a little nicer to Bob, especially now that he's getting ready to go. That boy is staring at her; it seems like he's watching her every move.

"You're right," Bob says and takes his hat back off. "Maybe I'll just have a couple of those hotcakes myself to get my energy up."

"Well, I ain't got time for this," Harold says and stands. He leaves a dollar on the counter and walks to the door. "Hey Sam!" He turns and yells and that boy looks over. "Maybe we'll meet at a convention of some sort some time." The boy just nods and rolls his head back toward Corky. It's a damn shame that that boy's feeling so bad. Some people just can't hold their booze, Harold reckons. He steps outside and already it is hot as pure fire. He thinks for a minute that he ought to get in his truck and drive right over to Maple Street, tell Juanita all the things that he's thought of to say, tell her she ain't fit to raise his children, give her a slap or two and tell her to go live in that damn trailer park, but he doesn't have the time or energy, not when he's got to go see Maggie Husky, and especially not when he's got to spend the afternoon at his mother's.

Harold gets in his truck and decides that he'll head on over to Maggie's before all the church women arrive to cry and carry on reading old sad poems and singing those sad songs like "The Old Rugged Cross." His Mama had enough balls to tell those women to cut it out when his Daddy died but Maggie Husky ain't that kind of woman. She's sweet and kind and Harold can't even stand the thought of facing her. There ain't a car there but Maggie's old Rambler, and he's relieved that he can speak to her by himself and then leave. He walks slowly up the walk where Maggie's got some great big pretty pepper plants. He figures instead of flowers, he'll just tell Maggie that when his melons are ripe that he'll bring her all the honeydew, cantelope and watermelon that she can eat. He rings the bell, takes off his John Deere cap and steps back.

"Why Harold Weeks!" She has on her bathrobe, curlers in her hair. She opens the door and steps back. "Come on in."

Harold steps in sideways so he doesn't brush against her and just stands with his hands behind his back, a couple of feet from the door. This is a nice house, neat as a pin. Juanita could have taken some lessons from Maggie Husky way back. There's a plate on the kitchen table with fresh tomatoes, a big bowl of scrambled eggs, some bacon strips. "I'm sorry, Maggie, didn't want to interrupt breakfast for you."

"Oh, I've eaten already. Have a seat, Harold." Her hands immediately go up to her curlers. "I'm afraid you caught me looking a sight. Charles ought to be here any time now. That new man has been coming in late to relieve him all week long."

Harold sinks into the big overstuffed chair and rubs his hand over his face. "Maggie, I . . ."

"Oh, I'm so rude, how about some breakfast?"

"No, thank you, I'm not hungry, I don't . . ."

"If you're in a hurry I'll just tell Charles you stopped by."

"Hasn't anybody been here to see you?" Harold gets up and paces over to the fireplace. On the mantle is a picture of Charles and Maggie, with Charles holding up a great big bass.

"Well no," Maggie says and then her voice softens and Harold can hear her creeping across the room. "Harold, nothing's wrong is it?" Her eyes are wide, and now as Harold watches, the color drains from her face. "Harold?" Her voice is trembling and her hand is on his arm. "Something's wrong. I can feel it."

"Maggie, I'm sorry, I don't know how to tell you but—" Harold cannot look at her face any more. He turns away and rests his head on the mantle, and he can see his reflection in the glass of the picture. He can't keep himself from crying and he puts his fist up to his mouth and presses it against his teeth.

"Was there an accident?" Now Maggie is crying and squeezing his arm. "Please."

"He's dead, Maggie." Harold wraps his arms around her and he can feel the wetness on her cheeks soaking into his shirt and against his chest. He can't say anything else and just stands there rocking her back and forth like she might be some large stuffed doll. It seems like he has been standing there forever when the doorbell rings and he pulls Maggie away, gets her to sit down, and he goes to open it himself. Harold sees the Chief of Police's car parked behind his truck before he even notices the man.

"She already knows," Harold says and wipes his face. "Where the hell you been all this time?"

"Sorry," the chief says. "That goddamn Bobbin didn't tell me till just now." He steps inside. "I'm sorry, Mrs. Husky."

Harold goes over and squats by her chair, holds her hands. "Let me know if I can do anything, Maggie. I'll do anything I can." He squeezes her hands but she doesn't look up. "He was a fine man, the damned nicest man a person could know." Maggie just nods and pats his hands. He can't stand it any more, can't stand to see that breakfast sitting over there for Charles to come and eat it when Charles ain't ever gonna eat breakfast again.

"Somebody ought to string you up by your ass," Harold says to the chief. "I could break your fucking neck." Harold is ready to knock his face in, but he hears Maggie sob and turns to see her hunched over in that chair with her hands over her face. "Stupid son of a bitch." He runs out to his truck, cranks it up, scratches off.

Fannie and M.L. go out on the front porch of the boarding house to wait for Mr. Foster. Mr. Foster is always there right at eight o'clock and Fannie is always out on the porch so that he won't have to wait. Mr. Foster gives M.L. a ride either to the YMCA where this nice young lifeguard agreed to watch him or over to the playground at the recreation department. It's the nicest thing in the summer that M.L. can go to these places or go to Bible School when it's in session, and Fannie doesn't have to worry about him all day long. That boy can swim like a fish, and it makes Fannie so proud the times that she has taken a taxi over to the YMCA to watch him. None of her children ever learned to swim that she knows of, and she never did herself. The only pool to swim in before the YMCA was that country club pool where she had never been, and Sherman River. she used to go down to the river and sit there under a shade tree while Jake splashed around, but that current was too strong and there were snakes, too, big old moccasins. Lord knows how many people drowned there in Sherman River.

"I'm gonna jump off the diving board today, Fannie," M.L. says, and goes and sits in that old kitchen chair that is propped against the porch wall.

"Don't you get too fancy," she says. "You make sure somebody's always watching after you."

"Jesus watches after me." He hops out of that chair and walks up and down the porch, stopping to put his foot in each opening between the spindles. "That woman at Bible School says that Jesus watches everybody all the time."

"That's the truth, too, M.L. But, that means Jesus is so busy he might not could pull a little boy outa the water fast enough." She sits down on the concrete steps and fans herself with a little notepad that she keeps in her purse. "Gonna be hot today. You got your lunch, baby?" M.L. waves the brown bag and then puts it back down right beside his towel. Fannie knows deep down that she probably loves that child too much. It might not be right to love one as much as she loves him. She watches him going around and putting that little foot in all those holes. He's got on a nice little swimsuit, bright red and blue, that she found at J.C. Penney's with a little terry cloth shirt that matches. "You remember not to be out there swimming right after you eat that lunch. Might cramp up."

"Okay." M.L. walks over and sits right beside her, moves an old cigarette butt around with his toe.

"I thought I told you to put on your shoes, mister."

"I got 'em." He grins at her and she can't tell if he's fooling her or not. It's gotten to the place that that child is wanting to pull all kinds of tricks on her, come home one day with a little rubber spider that some boy had give him and had it perched up on Fannie's radio.

"Well, where have you got 'em? Upstairs in the closet?"

He just grins again and presses his face into her arm. "They're under my towel, Fannie, fooled you."

"You let me see," she says and pushes him away. "Go get your stuff so we're right ready to go. Mr. Foster is a busy man and ain't got time to fool with us."

"Right here." He holds out a pair of sneakers in one hand, his towel and lunch bunched up under his other arm.

"Well, you weren't really fooling old Fannie."

"You ain't old." He puts his things down beside her and starts dancing around. It tickles Fannie to death to see him dance like that and he knows it. He'll do it to her every chance he gets, especially if they're out in public, had those people down at the Piggly Wiggly in stitches one day and he was singing a song right along with it. He told Fannie it was a Michael Jackson song and she didn't know where on earth he had listened to such. He sure didn't hear it at home, so it must've been either at the playground, the YMCA or maybe even from Corky Revels, because Corky is forever playing music when she's at home and M.L. loves to visit her because she always is giving him cookies or bubble gum. "You dance," he says and does a little turn and it makes the tears come to her eyes.

"You're a sight, you are. I wish I could snap your picture and send it to your Mama." Fannie doesn't really mean that. Sometimes she feels like she has to mention his Mama, though, so he won't forget that he's got one. Every now and then Elizabeth sends a letter, and every single birthday M.L. gets a little something, and on Christmas, but still, Elizabeth don't know what she's missing.

"When am I gonna see my Mama?" He stares at Fannie with those brown eyes wide open. They go through this every now and then. Every now and then he starts getting curious, and more and more now that he's older and sees other children with one or both of their parents.

"Would you like to?"

M.L. just shrugs. "I bet she don't look like that picture no more."

"Any more."

"Bet she don't look like that picture any more."

"She might. Your Mama's a pretty woman and that's why you're so handsome."

"And what about my Daddy?" They have been through all of this before, too, and Fannie always answers him even though she does hate to lie.

"He was as handsome as you'd ever see." Fannie is relieved to see that big Chrysler round the corner because she hates to lie to M.L. She hates it mostly because she knows that one day she's gonna have to tell him the truth, that she don't know who his Daddy was and doubts if Elizabeth herself knows.

"Hey Mr. Foster!" M.L. scrambles into that big backseat as soon as the car stops.

"Good morning, Fannie," Mr. Foster says and Fannie gets in and closes the door. Even this car is cold as the inside of a refrigerator. Some mornings M.L.'s lips get to quivering before they even let him out.

"Morning, Mr. Foster." Fannie doesn't much like to talk to him because he always acts so aggravated.,

"I want to go to the YMCA today," M.L. says and leans up against the front seat. "Can we play music?"

"Now, M.L., he might not want that radio blaring this early."

"It's fine," he says and turns it on. The news is on and Mr. Foster doesn't even try to find music, knowing full well that's what M.L. was wanting. The three of them ride along without saying a word, now that good morning is out of the way. M.L. leans up and kisses Fannie's cheek when they stop, and he hops out and stands there waving just like a little man, and then Fannie catches a glimpse of him running up to a group of children.

"Nice sunny day, isn't it?" Fannie asks and puts her notepad back into her purse. She sure doesn't need to be fanning in this air conditioning.

"Hot."

"Yeah, sure is hot." Fannie doesn't really like to talk to him anyway. She just likes to ride and look out at all the pretty green lawns and flower beds, the vegetable gardens. It gives her a good feeling to be in a car and riding, makes her feel like she's really going somewhere when she knows all along what's waiting for her, beds to make, breakfast dishes to wash, and probably a basket full of ironing. They pull through that big gate that says the name of this area and then down the curve and up that long driveway.

"Mrs. Foster may still be asleep. I know the children are."

"Okay." Fannie opens the door and gets out.

"Tell Mrs. Foster that I may be later than usual today. You may have to get a taxi today."

"Okay." Fannie slams the door and doesn't even try to say good-bye, because that's something Mr. Foster won't do. He'll say good morning first thing, but he ain't about to say good-bye or anything else. He's a soured person, and Fannie thinks it's a shame when Mrs. Helena Foster acts so friendly much of the time. The sun feels good during that short walk between the car and the front door, but then it's cold all over again. Fannie gets her sweater from where she keeps it in that front closet and goes into the kitchen to make some coffee. One thing she does before she starts working is sit down and have herself a cup of coffee. She sits right there in the kitchen and stares out that big picture window at the pretty shrubbery and that fine bricked patio with the pool. She has thought so often how nice it would be if she could bring

M.L. with her and let him swim out there. He could probably teach that little Parker Foster a thing or two about swimming, cause she can't even do the back float and stay there, not like M.L. showed her that day. And that Billy Foster, she has yet to even see him get in that pool with his skinny self.

This is the prettiest kitchen that Fannie has ever seen, with that nice stove that don't have real burners but has them drawn onto that flat top so all Fannie has to do is wipe over it with a rag, and those big copper pots and pans hanging from the ceiling, a pantry full of good food, and all kinds of little spice things that smell so good, makes the whole house smell like a florist; cool and spicy, that's the way it is, and spic and span once Fannie gets done. She likes to get her cleaning done bright and early so she can watch the story that she likes that comes on T.V. at one. If she misses it, though, Corky Revels can tell her exactly what happened and so could Mrs. Foster, but Fannie hates to ask her.

"Good morning, Fannie." Mrs. Foster comes into the kitchen and she is still in this slinky pink gown and robe. She pours herself a cup of coffee and sits in the chair right across from Fannie. It's okay when Fannie sits here by herself but it makes her feel funny with Mrs. Foster or Mr. Foster sitting with her, makes her feel lazy. "I didn't mean to sleep so late," she says and takes a sip of coffee. "I'm glad Dave picked you up on time. We have got so much to do for the party." Mrs. Foster always says that every time there's some sort of party to be had, and there never is that much work to it, fix a little food, iron the tablecloths, set flowers in water, do the regular cleaning. Fannie could have it all done right by herself and still get to watch the story, but for some reason Mrs. Foster don't feel like she's going to have a party unless she rushes around all day long, stepping back and staring at flowers or plates and such. Fannie probably won't get to see the story today and that bothers her a little, because she looks forward so to seeing that crazy Opal Gardner and Phoebe Tyler Wallingford. Those white women are the biggest sights that Fannie McNair has ever seen and they tickle her to death. She better get up and start doing something before Mrs. Foster thinks of something for her to do.

Fannie opens up the dishwasher and there it is, crammed full of dirty stuff, and when she left here yesterday around three there wasn't a thing dirty to be found. She fills up the sink with hot suds and starts washing some of the dishes herself, turns on the dishwasher for those other ones. She told that good-for-nothing Jake once, way back, that she'd love to have herself a dishwasher cause she had just seen one for the first time.

"Got me a dishwasher," he had said, and pulled on her tit. It used to bother her so the way that he'd do that. "One that makes money at it, too. Ain't no machine that can go out and earn money or I'd have married one of them."

"Go on with your lousy self," she had said and kicked her feet where she was sitting there by Sherman River. She remembers exactly what she was wearing, too, some stretch black shorts and a loose white blouse that had a little lace around the collar, and her stomach was starting to push out a speck with Thomas. Elizabeth was wrapped up in a cool piece of sheet and laying under the shade tree. Fannie remembers it so well, the wisteria hanging out of those big trees and smelling so good, the hot white sand and cold brown water. She remembers watching Jake wade out in that river to where he was chest deep and he'd walk around out there, couldn't swim a lick, and she remembers wishing right then and there that she wasn't going to have no baby, that she didn't even want the one that she had, and she wished that Jake would go under and never come back up.

"What are you thinking about so hard this morning?" Mrs. Foster is standing there filling up her cup. She has time to sit and drink more than one.

"Oh, thinking about old Sherman River."

"Where's that?"

Fannie throws back her head and laughs now. Mrs. Foster can be as funny as that Phoebe on All My Children sometimes. "It runs right back here behind Piney Swamp."

"There's a river back there?" Mrs. Foster is truly shocked. Imagine living right here and not even knowing.

"Yeah there's a river, bout a mile or so down. That's where I used to go to swim or rather to get wet. Ice cold water and those old snakes would be curled up in trees looking like limbs." Fannie watches the look on Mrs. Foster's face and knows that she can't stop with that. "Those old snakes would be swinging in the breeze and looking around just waiting for a boat to pass so they could hop a ride."

"Oh my, Fannie, why on earth did you go down there in the first place?"

"It was cool down there, I reckon. Most everybody I knew went down there. Good fishing from time to time."

"Wasn't there a swimming pool?" Fannie can't even believe Mrs. Foster sometimes. Imagine that.

"There was the country club, I reckon," Fannie says, and grins great big and shakes her head back and forth. It makes Mrs. Foster turn red as a beet. "Honey, we were lucky to have a river around here. When I was a girl and went a ways out to see my cousin, there wasn't a thing to do in the summertime but sit under the pump and have somebody pump that water on your head and down around you. We took turns just a pumping that water."

"Well, I certainly didn't know that there was a river with snakes right near here."

"Yes, ma'am, and big snakes, heads as big around as my fist and long as from your foot to mine." Fannie scrapes some chicken bones into the trash.

"Do you think there are still snakes around here?"

"It's swampland, all right. I told you that this area was called Piney Swamp and that's why, not a thing but pine trees and swamp, couldn't hardly even have a churchyard when I was going to the Piney Swamp Baptist cause every grave that was dug filled up with water. Our preacher said those bodies would wash right on down to the river."

"Oh Fannie, you're teasing, aren't you?"

"No, ma'am, got to where we all would sing 'Shall We Gather at the River' come a funeral time."

"What happened to those graves?" Mrs. Foster has sat back down now and is staring out into the yard, like she might be listening to Fannie or like she might have her mind on something else.

"I reckon they either washed out or they're right out here under some of these houses." Fannie turns off the water and begins drying the dishes that she washed.

"That can't be," Mrs. Foster says and turns from the window.

"Well, I knew several people that were buried out there and I never heard of 'em being dug back up."

"Oh dear, don't you dare ever tell Parker that. It would scare her to death." It looks like Mrs. Foster is near about scared to death by now. Fannie doesn't know why that meanness gets into her like that sometimes, to make her want to have that woman believing such a story. That little cemetery is still right where it always was, as far as Fannie knows, right down near the river, but the graves really did all fill up with water, that part was true. Fannie is fixing to tell her about the time they dragged the river and found ten dead men all fish eaten and bloated but there's a knock on the back door.

"I'll get it, Fannie. You go on with what you're doing because we've got to get started on the party in just a few minutes." Mrs. Foster opens the back door, and who's there but that Mrs. Stubbs from next door. Fannie can't stand that woman, her old fat face and that bleached yellow hair like she might be a teen. Fannie knows that

Mrs. Stubbs has got to be at least fifty, and bleaches out her hair and wears those same kind of long shorts like Mrs. Foster's like she might be as young as Mrs. Foster, and clearly she ain't. It amazes her sometimes, the friends that Mrs. Foster has, several of 'em old as a coon. Now Corky pays visits but that's different, because they don't act like they're two children in the same grade at school. Fannie likes to think that she is sort of a mama to Corky or a great-aunt, she don't pry into Corky's person or ask questions when Corky has a man in except to ask if she had herself a nice time, that's it, but now that Mrs. Stubbs is going on and on like she might have just been asked to the prom. Course, it is right pitiful the way that those other women make fun of Mrs. Stubbs behind her back. Even Mrs. Foster does it sometimes, laughs and says how she just pushes and tries too hard to make friends. Though Mrs. Stubbs gets on her nerves, Fannie figures it's better to try too hard than not try at all, like Thomas McNair.

"Oh Helena," Mrs. Stubbs screeches, and even Fannie knows that it's not Hell-eena like she says but Helena. She would correct her if she was Helena Foster, just as she has always corrected people that say Mac Nair instead of McNair. "I brought the ladies golf tournament tickets, thought you could sell a few."

"Oh sure, I'll be glad to. Come on in, Kate." Mrs. Foster opens the door and here she comes, long britches and all, and those pants big enough for Fannie and M.L. to camp out in. "I've been lazy this morning, would you like a cup of coffee?"

"I sure would." Mrs. Stubbs sits down at the table and

her eyes are taking in every square inch of this room. "I left Ernie still in bed. I declare he's working so hard these days."

"I know the feeling." Mrs. Foster carries that cup of coffee to the table, and now it is like Fannie ain't even there. She starts wiping the counters real slow like, because sometimes listening to these women is better than the stories on an average day. "Dave has had to be away on business twice this week and he's always late. Of course, he says he does it so that I can have the life that I deserve."

"Same with Ernie, but my goodness, Hell-eena, how much more could we ever want?"

"Oh yeah," Fannie says, and they both look at her like she might be that big green man that M.L. likes to see on the T.V. reruns. "Mr. Foster said to tell you that he might be late, that I might have to take me a taxi cab home."

"Oh dammit." Mrs. Foster only says that when she's really aggravated, so Fannie can overlook it even though she herself doesn't use strong words. "He couldn't have forgotten about the party, after all the planning that I've been doing the past few days! I mean he was standing right there when I called the jewelry store and ordered that place setting of china."

"That's what he said." Fannie picks up the coffee pot. "Want some more before I rinse this up?"

"I would, uh, I'm sorry, your name has slipped my mind." Mrs. Stubbs holds up her cup.

"Oh I'm sorry," Mrs. Foster says. "I thought sure you two had met. Fannie, this is Mrs. Stubbs."

"Fannie, of course, I had completely forgotten."

"I had forgotten yours, too." Fannie pours her some coffee and is so tempted to spill some right on those loud-colored pants. People are forever saying how black folks like the bright colors; well, those people ought to step out here in Piney Swamp for a peek or two.

"I better call Dave right away." Mrs. Foster reaches for the phone. "Excuse me a minute, Kate. Fannie, why don't you go ahead and press that shirt I have hanging for Mr. Foster, and maybe touch up that gray suit."

"Lordy, I plumb forgot your dress."

"Oh dammit!" Fannie has never seen Mrs. Foster look so ill at her. "Dave Foster, please, this is his wife and it is very important!"

"I'll have the taxi carry me and bring me right back, I reckon."

"No, I need you to help serve tonight and you'll have to be here by six, so you can bring it then." Now, she is talking away to Mr. Foster, and that soft voice ain't so soft any more. Mrs. Foster hadn't even mentioned Fannie serving until now; she doesn't know if she can or not. Now Mrs. Foster is smiling, and Mrs. Stubbs raises her hands over her head and claps like they might be watching Ali or something, nodding like some big fight may have been won. "Bye bye, honey, I know you're busy." There's that sweet angel's voice again, and Mrs. Foster hangs up.

"Mrs. Foster," Fannie says and steps up a little. For some reason it makes her so nervous to have to speak up to somebody that she really deep down likes. "I didn't know nothing about tonight and you know I've got M.L. to think of."

"Well, Fannie, you know that I always need you when we have a party."

"I bet the girl that comes for me might can do it," Mrs. Stubbs says, and eyes Fannie like she might just be the help, instead of the person that keeps this house going.

"I'd feel better if it was Fannie," Mrs. Foster says and gets real sweet again. "Maybe M.L. could come with you. I'll pay you double your usual."

"Oh, it ain't the money." Fannie keeps wiping the counter so that she'll have something to do. She could use the extra because M.L. is going to be going off to first grade come the end of August, and he'll need all sorts of new clothes and booksacks and such. "I bet maybe Corky Revels will watch him, and if she can't I'll just bring him and he can sit right here in the kitchen and help like he does at home."

"Oh, thank you!" Mrs. Foster squeals and clutches the neck of her thin robe like Fannie might have just pulled her out of Sherman River. "I'll tell you what. You can go home earlier than usual if we get it all done, and then I'll send Billy over to pick you up at six and I promise that he'll take you home just as soon as the meal is served." Mrs. Foster touches Fannie's arm. "And I meant that about the money, too."

"Thank you very much," Fannie says and goes on about her business. She likes to show her pride as good as anybody, but she knows when it's best to stop as well. If she sets up the ironing board where she usually does, she can disappear all over again and listen to these women, the way that one will every now and then slip up and say "ya'll" or "ain't" and then catch it and go back to that little accent that they all use.

"Are we going to be out by the pool tonight?" Mrs. Stubbs asks, and before Mrs. Foster can even answer she keeps on going. "Ernie and I have been toying with the idea of a barbecue except of course we'd have filet mignons, except it's so warm these days."

"This will be inside, and if some of the younger ones want to go by the pool after dinner, they can."

"Oh, that's a splendid notion. I suppose we could do the same thing, maybe get somebody to come and grill for us and then just eat inside where it's cool." Mrs. Stubbs talks faster than any white person that Fannie has ever heard, talks faster than a Yankee even, but still keeps it real Southern-sounding by putting little uhs and ahs at the ends of her words. "I really am looking forward to it. It's so much fun to mingle with the younger couples."

"That's why I decided to have something for the bride and groom instead of just a tea for the bride."

"Well, I don't even know the bride or her family." Mrs. Stubbs pushes her coffee cup to the center of the table. She has no thoughts of carrying it over to the sink and rinsing it like an able-bodied human. Fannie thinks it's because she ain't able-bodied, and it makes her just laugh while she goes around that collar with the hot steam iron, and that steam feels good, too, spraying up around her hands, because it's colder than usual in this house to-day, always is when there's going to be a party. "I don't blame you since you are giving the party because of the groom and his family. I mean from what I hear this girl's daddy is a small farmer out in the county somewhere."

"That's what I've heard but she's a pretty girl, or at least her picture in the paper was."

"You can't go by the paper in this town. Rose's picture turned out just awful, all dark and ugly, and you know how Rose looks."

"Lovely."

"Well, the Raleigh paper did a much better job. I wonder if this girl will have hers in the Raleigh paper?" Fannie spits on the iron so it'll hiss, just because she wants to interrupt Mrs. Stubbs' gossip talk. It doesn't work. "You remember Rose's wedding, don't you?"

"Oh yes, lovely." Now Mrs. Foster looks like she's wandering right out of that window again, and who can blame her?

"You've got a long time before a wedding, Hell-eena."

"I hope so! Parker is only twelve. Billy is seventeen but he doesn't seem the least bit interested in girls. Goes out with the boys every night."

"That 'going out with the boys' gets younger and younger, doesn't it?" Mrs. Stubbs shakes her head. "Can I help you do anything before I go?"

"I believe that Fannie and I can get it all done, probably. I'll be worn out and sweating but we can manage." Mrs. Foster stands at the same time as Mrs. Stubbs and stretches. "I haven't even showered and dressed. Look at me."

"We all get lazy every now and then." Mrs. Stubbs goes to the door. "I've got to go get Ernie up and then go and get a birthday present for my mother. Every year she has this little get-together for all of her family. You know she's so feeble."

"How quaint," Mrs. Foster says. "I'll see you tonight."

"Yes, and don't you worry one bit, Hell-eena, it will be simply marvelous as always, I'm certain."

"I hope you're right, and I'll take care of these tickets." Mrs. Foster stands out there on the brick patio with that door standing wide open, letting all of that paid-for air slip away, dollars just floating away. "Now Fannie," Mrs. Foster says when she finally closes that door, "everything must be perfectly spotless and I've got to call the florist and the grocer, and I am having a caterer bring in the hors d'oeuvres, the gift will be delivered. Oh my, I don't know if it'll ever get done."

"You go right on and relax yourself in a tub bath. I'll take care of all the cleaning." Fannie waves her hand and is glad when Mrs. Foster disappears down the hall. This is when she really likes her work, when she feels like she is all alone in this house and can walk around on those soft carpet rugs, smell those dried flowers and think of how it's gonna be someday when M.L. is all grown up. If Thomas wasn't so full of hate and worthlessness she wouldn't have to count on little M.L. for every hope she has; after all, M.L. ain't but a baby, and sometimes Fannie even gets to wondering if she will even see him all grown up and on his own. Lord only knows what would become of that child if she were to up and die.

Sam Swett is on his third stack of pancakes, and they are so good. He can't remember when anything was so good, can't even remember when was the last time he ate. All he remembers is getting a ride with that trucker, CB blaring, remembers stopping and getting out, remembers seeing that man that was just in here and the one who's sitting at the counter, but then it all goes blank. Now, his stomach is so full it feels like it might explode, but he can't stop until he's had that last bite, that last sip of orange juice, milk, coffee. He has gorged himself, succumbed to the weaknesses of human nature, but who gives a damn? He's got to keep up his strength, got to decide where he'll go, got to find out where the hell he is. The girl said that it is July 7th and he is certain that he left New York on July 6th. He remembers picking up a newspaper and it was only yesterday, only yesterday about this time that he put his typewriter in his bag, went to the liquor store, started looking for a ride. Only yesterday, and it seems like forever.

"Can I get you something else?" the girl asks and brings him a cup of coffee.

"No, no, I think I'm full. I might could eat some more but I think I'm full."

"You were starving," she says and picks up his plate. She has the tiniest fingers that he has ever seen and he likes to see her joints move, fingers around the rim of that plate. "Bet you feel lots better." She sits down across from him. "So exactly where in New York were you locked up?"

"Huh?"

"You know, I asked you if you had just been let out of somewhere and you said something about New York." She looks over at that man at the counter and lowers her voice. "Did they have you in one of those shirts that wrap around you?"

"A straitjacket?" Now, he's getting scared. What if he's done something that he can't remember doing? "Why do you ask that?"

"Are you teasing with me?" She wets her finger in the circle and draws a "C." "I mean you said that you were locked up and you know I'm not making fun. I know a real nice person who's been in one of those shirts before."

"I never have that I can remember."

"You said that you still weren't quite free, though," she whispers "free" and those beautiful gray eyes flash, a blink, a wink. It is coming back to him, being free; it is his whole purpose to distinguish himself from the horrors of the world, to detach himself from the weaknesses of human nature, to decide how in the hell he will spend his life.

"I remember, now."

"Well good! For a minute there I thought that I was the crazy one, I mean feeling crazy, you know, because after what you saw I think you have every right to feel that way." She has leaned forward again to whisper the word "crazy." This beautiful-eyed little urchin thinks that he is crazy, and she even knows why he might be.

"I wasn't physically locked up like you're thinking," he says and watches her tilt her head to one side, that pale hair falling over one shoulder. "I've been locked within myself, you know, trying to find lots of answers to a lot of things, struggling to understand society, human nature, to figure out why things are the way that they are instead of the way that we would like to believe they are. I want to define human nature." Ah, it is all coming back to him. "I want to understand why people settle for things as they are, why they don't try to change things or themselves, but settle for what's been done before."

"I don't get you," she says and shakes her head. "I don't get that about everybody settling, and I don't see what it is you plan to do."

"I'm going to observe life." He's on a roll now, things have not come this quickly in a long time. "I'm going to stand on the outskirts so that I can see what's happening without being trapped into being a part of it."

"Like sitting back and watching T.V."

"Something like that I think." Now she's confusing him. She looks a little confused herself.

"Corky!" That bird man at the counter yells. Is this her name? Corky? "Get me a little more coffee and make it strong, ASAP."

"I'll be right back," she says and Sam hopes so. He has so many things that he wants to ask her.

The man at the counter whispers something to Corky

and then looks over at him. She shakes her head and sticks her tongue out at bird cop. She has a beautiful tongue connected there at the back of that little mouth, the full pouty lips, moving so slowly inside that cavern edged with pearly white teeth, shaping the slow words of a perfect Southern accent. His mother sounds that way and he used to, a while ago; it seems that sometime or another he had made a conscious effort to change his voice so that he wouldn't sound like everyone else in the South. But the trucker had recognized that he did not have a New York accent. God, he has no accent. He is the example of what everyone will soon sound like. Such a shame for that girl's voice to change. He would like to lock her away and protect her as a relic of passing time.

"You reckon he's really a Mason?" the cop asks and she shrugs, her shoulders lifting the neck of her blue uniform like he imagines it would do if she were to breathe deeply. How does the cop know that? Now, that cop gets up and walks over to the table. "Hey, can you prove that you're a Mason?"

"To another one," he says and watches Corky walking back over. Her feet don't even make a sound.

"Well give it to me then, Buddy." The cop steps even closer and squats down beside the table.

"Don't tell him a thing. He's not one himself." Now Corky is standing by the table, too, a pot of hot coffee right over the cop's head.

"Shut up, Corky, this is police work."

"Don't believe him; he's trying to get your secrets so maybe they'll let him in." She gives a mean look to the cop. "If you were doing police work, you'd be out look-ing for that murderer." Murderer, they got murder and rape and robbery. He remembers giving the secret word and shake. It was to the man that was in here a little while ago. Then this man came in and that other man did all the talking, something about a black person. He is remembering.

"Are you sure that you didn't see anything going on at the Quik Pik?"

"Huh?"

"Leave him alone, Bob, Harold told you what hap-pened." She puts the pot on a dishtowel and sits back down. "Go on and finish your coffee so you really can go to work."

"You need something else?" she asks, and he loves the way that her tongue pushes up against her teeth when she says things.

He shakes his head. It's finally starting to feel better. "Did he say a murderer?"

"Yeah, you know what you saw last night." Before she even finishes the picture comes to him fuzzily and then clear, so clear, down to the napkins in the mouth, that bluish color around the lips and nose.

"Oh God." He puts his face in his hands and shakes his head. "You see what I mean? It's happening every-where, the same thing."

"Hey, I know you're upset." She reaches over and rubs his hand. "Where bouts you from?" Her voice lightens and she tugs on his hand, lets go.

"South Cross," he says without lifting his head from the table.

"Wow, I've heard of that. I've heard it's sort of swanky."

"Some parts." He cannot help himself, human weakness; he has to look at her, to reach across the table and touch her hand the way that she had touched his. She glances over at that cop and he's staring right at them. She acts nervous, pulls her hand away, puts more coffee in his cup. She stares without blinking one tiny blink. "Has anybody ever told you that you look a little like Dr. Zhivago?"

"No." He shakes his head, that shaved head that he shaved so that he would never look like anybody. But for some reason, he doesn't mind, doesn't mind being compared to Omar Sharif. "It's your eyes, so brown and sad looking."

"Your eyes are not like any that I've ever seen." He hadn't meant to say that. He is losing control. He hadn't planned to reach over and brush away that sprig of hair right near her eye but he does it. "You're different. I've seen a lot of people but no one that seemed as different as you." He leans forward. "I saw that dead man and I didn't want to see it but it was like a symbol of what happens. That man could have been anybody or nobody, it didn't matter. What mattered was that human nature had struck out again."

"But he was somebody. Charles Husky was somebody and it's not like he could have been just anybody to his wife and daughter or to me, or anyone with any feeling.

I can't believe you'd say that it doesn't matter." He has made those eyes fill up and overflow onto her face; made her take a deep breath and lift the neck of her dress. He has made her feel something. Now she has her face in her hands, her shoulders shaking. "I think it's awful. It's not human nature, either; it's crazy is what it is! It's wrong!" The bird cop has swung off of his stool and is loping this way.

"What did you say to her, boy?" The man grabs Sam by the collar. "Mason or not I don't care, nobody gets Corky all upset and gets away with it." The man shakes him and he feels like his head might fall off. "You saw the dead man, big deal, do you know whose job it is to go out and find his murderer? Mine, that's whose!"

"So why don't you do it, instead of butting into private conversations?" She wipes her face. "It wasn't his fault I got upset. I know what he was saying, kind of."

Sam is thinking that he'd like to show her his driver's license so that she could see him with hair; suddenly for the first time, he is self-conscious about his hair and clothes.

The cop tries to hug her, but she pushes away and starts picking up Sam's dirty glasses. "He ain't going to mess with you any more. He looks like the kind that would take advantage of a little girl like you, looks like the kind that probably knows a lot about niggers." He puts his thumbs under his holster belt and laughs, his head bobbling all around. "Maybe I could use him on the case after all. Have him sniff down that nigger."

"Shut up, Bob! Just shut up!" She spins around and throws a cup to the floor. "I'm sick of hearing what you've got to say and sick of you acting like I'm some property of yours to watch out for, and sick of your ugly talk!"

"What ugly talk?"

"Try N-i-g-g-e-r, try that!" She kicks the pieces of the broken cup into a little pile. Sam watches her gray eyes harden, watches her kick her feet.

"Oh, I forgot. I forgot that you moved out of Granner Weeks' house when you got yourself that high school diploma! I forgot that you moved into that rat's nest of a boarding house where you got niggers for neighbors!"

"It's none of your business!"

"Just watching out for you, Corky, a dizzy little girl like you. You got no business living with trash, nobody to care for you when you could settle down with a nice smart man that would look after you." The cop, this bird Bob, perches back on his stool and laughs.

"I reckon you mean yourself? Well, let me tell you something, Bob Bobbin, I wouldn't touch you with a ten foot pole, and that's why you're always picking at me. Cause I never have and I never will touch you!"

"You been with worse, Corky Revels. Matter of fact, you been with about everybody I know. I reckon you're saving me for marriage."

"Go to hell!" She screams until her fair little face is all red. Sam Swett thinks that he ought to do something, to say something, but no, he's going to watch it all. Bob

Bobbin is walking away now. He turns at the door, his hands on his hips, his hat pulled low on his forehead. "Whore!" he says.

"Whorehopper that can't find nobody to hop!" Corky swings around and walks to the door, her dishtowel all twisted up and ready to pop like Sam used to do as a child at the swimming pool, and what made him suddenly remember that? "Cause you're uglier than a mud fence full of worms and stupid to boot!" She tries to swat his face but he runs out the door, laughing still though his face is beet red, gets into his car and drives off. Corky stands there a minute breathing hard, and Sam is enjoying that breathing sound, those little gasps for air.

"I reckon you heard all of that," she says but doesn't look over.

"Nah, wasn't really paying attention."

"Being nice don't work on me. I'm too smart for that. People may not think so, but I am." She turns and her eyes are wide open now, taking him in, his eyes, his head. Now, he is really embarrassed; he is trying to remember exactly what the picture on his license looks like. She is still staring when she sits back down. "I know you heard all of those terrible things. Go on, admit it!"

"Yeah, I did, but first I want to tell you that I'm real sorry that I upset you. You know, even though I didn't know that man, even though it happens all the time, it still made me sort of sick." It really did make him sick, even though he was already sick. Now he just wants to make her smile again, to feel that cool hand over his face again. "I don't know why I said all of that."

"It's all right," she says and bites her lip, that perfect little pouting lip. "I sort of got what you were saying, you know, so much bad happens, to where you just don't want to go on feeling." She sighs and sits back. "It's okay." She looks out the window and he sees her profile like white on black, like those that everyone made in kindergarten, but add the color, the freckles on that tilted nose, the dark lashes framing that pale gray eye.

"You seem like a smart girl to me," he says and then continues, afraid that doesn't sound quite right. "You know, not dizzy and kooky like that guy said."

Finally she laughs. "You're about the first person that's ever said that to me. Everybody else seems to think I'm crazy just because I like to be by myself sometimes, or because I haven't gone off to school, or because I don't run my mouth all the time."

"They're wrong." He cannot help but reach across the table and touch her arm again.

"I know that. I just never knew anybody else who thought the same."

"So, now you have; Corky's your name, right?"

"Yep, I knew you must've listened." She moves her arm away from him and crosses both arms over her stomach. "What's your name?"

"Sam, Sam Swett." It sounds so funny to hear his name out loud.

"Sam, I like that," she says and smiles. "And you're nice. You're a little different from most people around here, but you seem nice." She is staring, staring like she can see straight through him, and when he inches up on his seat she looks away. "So why is your hair all cut off, the service?"

"No." He shakes his head and tries to think of a good reason. "I can show you a picture with hair." He pulls out his wallet and hands her his license. "It isn't a very good picture but you can see what I look like with hair."

"I like you with hair." She hands back the license. "Will it come back, or is it gone for good?"

"I just shaved it myself. I don't know why, you know, it was sort of a dumb thing to do." He rubs his hands over the prickles and shakes his head from side to side.

"I got a brother that's ten years older than me and he used to have long long hair, down to here." She draws a line with her finger around her elbow. "Then he got it all shaved off."

"Why did he do it?"

"Service." She looks away again. "He still keeps his real short."

"I never had real long hair, you know, all that was sort of over with when I came through. I'm twenty-one now."

"Same here. I'm eighteen."

It gets quiet for a few minutes and he doesn't want that to happen, he doesn't want her to stop talking and for it all to end. "What did that guy mean when he said that you went with everybody in town?"

"Now, you see, you heard every single word and not a bit of truth." She bends down and picks up a paper napkin from the floor. "Why do you even ask?"

"Just wondering, you know, figured you must have a

boyfriend or maybe that he used to be your boyfriend or something." Sam Swett hates that term "boyfriend" but he doesn't know what else to say.

"No I don't, and I've never run around with people like Bob Bobbin said." Now the flush is in her cheeks, a pale pink on white like a china doll.

"Never?" For some reason, a reason that he is uncertain of, he is determined to push this subject. It is as if he wants to feel jealous and envious, and that's ridiculous, considering he hardly knows this girl, considering that those emotions, any emotions, are what lead to destruction.

"Look, I don't even know you." She pulls away right when the bells ring and a young couple come up to the counter and sit on the bar stools. She goes over quickly and gets two water glasses. "Coffee break, right?" she asks and the two nod. "Two cinnamon rolls and two coffees, right?" Again they nod and she disappears into the back. He can't let her get away this easily. When she reappears and serves the people, she walks back over. "You might should leave, you know?"

"Can I see you later?" He reaches for her hand again but she moves away and holds her pad and pencil right up against her chest. "Please." He knows that he is begging, becoming a desperate animal and he can't help it. He is past the objective point and he is objective enough to realize this, objective enough that he knows he doesn't care.

"I get off at one," she says and steps a little closer.

"Now we can sit here and eat lunch or something but then I've got somewhere to go at three."

"A date?"

"No, a birthday party." She shakes her head and for some reason starts laughing again. "You think maybe you could get yourself a shower before lunch?"

"Yes. Yes, I'll take a shower, be here at one."

"Okay, here's your check." She very carefully tears his check off and places it right beside his waiting open palm. He pulls out his wallet and keeps looking up at her while she shifts from foot to foot.

"Do you take Visa?" Now he remembers, he has no cash, just plastic money, gotta pay that hotel bill, too, get it for another night.

"Just forget it." She steps back so that he can get up and she walks a few steps in front of him to the door. "See you later," she whispers and he walks out, around to the window where she finally waves, again. He doesn't know what he's going to do until one. That's three and a half hours away.

3

Juanita Weeks is having to rush around like a chicken with its head cut off because she overslept. God knows she had every reason to oversleep after those thoughts keeping her up near about all night long. She bends over and brushes her hair forward and then shakes it back so that it falls around her shoulders in a bushy mass of frosted curls. She loves her curly perm; she loves to let hair that should be where it is go free. "That do suits you to a tee," Harold had told her, "kind of loose and free and sparkly." Of course that was before all that other happened. She pulls on a pair of aqua terry cloth shorts and a striped top that matches. After all, she can put on her white jacket when she gets down to the shop, and it's too durn hot to get all dressed up.

"Come on, kids," Juanita screams, and bundles up her swimsuit and towel so she can take a dip herself after work. She's already decided that she's going to close at noon, and she does that a lot in the summer so that she can spend time with the kids, but mostly because she herself likes to sunbathe and swim. Patricia comes slouching out in her new suit, a tiny bikini that don't do a thing for her since she's so flat-chested. Juanita tried to tell her, right there in Belk's, but Patricia would not hear of it, pitched a fit until Juanita bought that suit and now what does she do but slouch around to hide the fact that there's nothing in that top. "Stand up straight, honey, you don't want your spine to stick that way."

"Oh mother." That's just about all that Patricia says these days is "oh mother." Juanita has an idea that Patricia has heard all about what happened, or worse, some updated rumor, and Patricia ain't about to talk about it. Patricia flops down in a chair and starts messing with her necklace, or acting like she is. She is really peeking down her top to see if any growth has occurred overnight. Lord knows, she's just fifteen and Juanita keeps on telling her she's still got plenty of time, may just be a late bloomer, which she herself was not.

"Come on, Harold, Jr." she screams and here he comes, a cowlick sticking straight up on the top of his head just like his Daddy's used to do.

"It's Granner's birthday today," he says and levels his eyes at Juanita. He is the oldest eleven-year-old that she has ever met. The only thing childlike about him is that E.T. doll, and he hides that if a friend comes over. "We're going, aren't we?"

"You know we're not," Patricia says and stands up, pulls her coverup all the way around her and holds it that way. Lord knows, Patricia needs a perm or something to give that dirty blonde hair a little body, and more than likely she's gonna need a little inner thigh thinning if she keeps it in her mind to be a flag girl at the high school in those skimpy suits. It always has amazed Juanita that hair will be thin where it's supposed to be, and thick where it ain't. Thank the Lord that she can handle all the hair problems for free.

"She's not about to go where she might see Daddy." Patricia prances by and lets the screen door slam shut.

"Well, I think we ought to go." Harold, Jr., is still staring at her. "Granner will be awful mad if we don't."

"I think you children should go." Juanita goes out the door so that Patricia can hear what she's saying as well. "Slam that door good now Harold, Jr., so it'll lock." Juanita has to talk louder because Patricia is already at the car. "I think you two should go, never thought otherwise, else why would I have gone out after work yesterday and bought a nice present for you to carry over?"

"Oh mother." Patricia gets in and slams her door. "You know how Aunt Kate and Uncle Ernie treat us anyway. They'll say all kinds of things when you don't show up."

"Your Daddy is going to be there and they won't say a thing about it." Juanita pulls out her Foster Grants before cranking the car. "I know that pool's going to feel good today."

"I'm tired of the YMCA." Patricia slouches back in her seat. "And so is he." She nods toward Harold, Jr., but he doesn't say a word. Juanita can just look in that rearview mirror and tell by that frown on his face that he's thinking about his Daddy.

"Tired of it? How can you be tired of it on a day as hot

as this?" Juanita just doesn't understand Patricia these days. If Juanita says that something is white, she'll say it's black and so on.

"I'm sick of looking after him."

"Now don't you let me hear that again, you making Harold, Jr., feel bad for being underage. Next summer when he's twelve he can go by himself, and you'll be sixteen and will probably have a job to keep you busy."

"A job?" Patricia turns on her and that face is all flushed. "Oh mother, be serious." Juanita just ignores her, because it's simply not in that child's nature to carry on this way. She blames her mother for Harold's leaving home, can't see the kind of things Juanita was having to put up with beforehand. Juanita stops right in front of the YMCA.

"Have fun, kids." She smiles and tries to make up with Patricia. "I'll be here at noon and then when we leave, we'll go to Burger King, how about that?"

"Hey, can I get a Return of the Jedi glass?" Harold, Jr., finally smiles, bless his old acting heart.

"Sure you can, and Patricia can get herself one, too."

"Whoopee." Patricia slams the door and doesn't even wait for Harold, Jr. He runs on up yelling and waving to some boys close to his age, but Patricia doesn't wave to a soul, probably won't, either. Every day when Juanita picks them up, Patricia is sitting off by herself near that Coke machine, knowing full well that she shouldn't fill herself up on cola. Juanita pulls away, thinking that she ought to go on down to the shop, but then thinks better since she only has a little paper work to do, no appointments today. It seems that's getting to be a regular thing. She decides to go on to Nautilus and get her workout out of the way just in case she should happen to see Harold if she decides to go to the party. Lord God, she stops at the stoplight and it is like she has radar, the way that the first thing she sees is Harold Weeks coming out of Woolco. The whole time that they were together, she could go out and about all day long and never lay her eyes on him, and here all of a sudden she's seeing either Harold or his truck or a truck like his truck everywhere she goes. He looks so good even from this distance with those tan strong arms wrapped around a bag, that cap pulled down over that thick curly hair. The car behind her toots because the light is green so she moves on, deep down hoping that he sees her car; there aren't too many bright yellow Toyotas that she's seen around town.

Nautilus isn't too crowded on the weekday mornings, due to the fact that most people have jobs. That's why Juanita likes being her own boss. She can get right in and get a bike first thing. She gets on and Al Taylor is right beside her. She can hardly stand to look at Al Taylor because he's an old friend of Harold's, and more than likely reports to Harold every time that he sees Juanita in Nautilus, probably tells Harold that she flirts with the boys who work there which she doesn't. There's a big difference in flirting and being friendly and she has tried to explain that to Harold Weeks since she first met him, but he's too damn hardheaded to listen.

"How's it going, Juanita?" Al asks and grins at her. The bell on his bike rings and he struts over to the first machine. Just what she was hoping would not happen. She was hoping that Al would skip the leg machines and go on to his flabby arms and stomach like he sometimes does, but now she's got to go right behind him which means it could take forever the way that he's always stopping to flex his muscles and catch a glimpse of himself in that mirror that's down at the end of the room for the aerobics group.

"Just fine, Al, thank you."

"You're looking good, considering." He lies flat on his back and straps himself into the hip and back machine. "I'm sorry, but you know what I mean."

"I know all right." Juanita wishes that young instructor would come over and talk to her just so she could stop listening to Al, but that boy is over on the arm machine working with a new person, a little Chinese-looking woman. Juanita has never seen a Chinese in Marshboro before.

The nerve of that man anyway, saying those things to her, knowing that she ain't going to say anything back to him. Sometimes the thought has crossed her mind just to pick out a spot on the map, load herself and the children and her electrolysis equipment and move on, so she won't have to put up with all of this. Of course, that would be saying that she's ashamed of herself, which she is, but also saying that she can't take it, that she's a weak woman who can't take what she dished out. Too, Harold Weeks would never come back if she moved away, because he ain't about to leave all that farmland of his

Mama's that he works with so hard, especially when he knows that Ernie Stubbs is dying to get his hands on it. And that's another bone to pick; she ain't about to let Ernie and Kate be right about her. All these years, treating her like she wasn't fit for anything, and treating Harold and their children the same for that matter. Well, she'll show them all. She'll go to that party and just see who's a big person. Harold Weeks may cuss her out or slap her down, but she's willing to take that chance.

By the time that Juanita has used all of the machines, she is drenched with sweat and old Al is hanging around that water cooler like a big white whale.

"Going to get in the hot tub whirlpool, Juanita?"

"No, I'm in a rush today." There ain't no way that she'd get in that hot tub with Al Taylor. She doesn't even get herself a drink of water, because she knows how Al smells once he's worked out. She just gets her purse and leaves, heads on down to the shop.

The shop is in an out-of-the-way place, located in a small gray cinderblock building behind Belk's, so that clients can come and go without everybody in town knowing their hair business. Lord knows, it seems that people would give her the same respect, but it ain't tit for tat, never has been and never will be. What if Juanita was to go through her files and pull out all of those women from Cape Fear Trace who have had moustache shadow or chin hairs, and fanned that around? Kate Stubbs had the hairiest toes that Juanita had ever seen, was ashamed to even wear barefoot sandals until Juanita took care of her.

Of course that was way back when Kate was trying to be nice, even though it was a putdown kind of nice, but Lord, that has all changed.

Juanita is worn slam out from her workout, but it's that pleasant kind of tired, so she just stretches out on her table and stares up at those nice colorful posters she has of magnified follicles. She feels like she might could even take a little nap, and Lord knows she could use one. She closes her eyes and still she can see those follicles just like they're stamped on the inside of her eyelids; she sees those roots that have to be tweezed way down where they begin. It's a little sad to think of uprooting. She couldn't just uproot Patricia and Harold, Jr., even though it seems that that is what has happened. A wild hair should be uprooted though, growing where it ain't supposed to be, a wild hair, that's all it was, a thought, that's all. Ralph Waldo Emerson Britt never really said things like "prostrate" in her ear, not really, but it seemed so real, just like a wild hair can become to look like it belongs somewhere even when it doesn't. She just went to the Winn Dixie and the next thing that she knew, she was up at that little office at the front of the store where Ralph Britt was standing there in his bow tie and she said, "Pardon me, Ralph, but I can't find a single pork chop," which was true because she had already been and looked. Ralph Britt glanced at her out of the corner of his eye. Ralph Britt is not handsome and she had never thought so, nothing compared to Harold. Now, she wonders why Ralph even got into la la land in the first place, except maybe because he was ugly. He is a little man with stringy blonde hair that he brushes back and fluffs when it's clean, itty bitty eyes, sharp nose, and no trace of facial hair, unlike Harold who keeps a sort of Fred Flintstone shadow on his face even after he shaves because he's got such a thick beard. She loves that on Harold. She just knew that Ralph Britt was gonna say "scrotum" at any given second. He stepped down beside her and was so close to her that she could see a filling in his mouth. "I'll go and help you," he said, still staring with those itty bitty eyes, and that wasn't new, that staring. Ralph Britt had stared at her for years and maybe that's why she came to think of him in the first place. She walked back to the meat counter and Ralph nodded at this youngster standing there in his meat apron. That boy must have been just a speck older than Patricia and not the slightest facial hair. He was helping a woman who did have facial hair pick out a country ham.

"I'll check myself," Ralph Britt said in a real exasperated way and winked at her, at least she thought he winked at her. "Come on, you can just pick what you want," he said and she followed him, knowing that at any minute he'd say "gesticulation" and then she'd come to and be lying on hers and Harold's bed, watching those late afternoon pink clouds passing by. She went back into that room with Ralph and lo and behold, those were two-way mirrors out there. She always had wondered why they had mirrors over vegetables and meat, cause most people would not like to see what they look like during an average trip to the grocery. She said, "I never knew," and sort of shied away because she was standing right in front of that woman examining a country ham, though she now thinks that she must have known, considering it was in her own thoughts that she found out.

"It's fun to watch people," he said, and opened this other door where there were huge hunks of meat hanging. "I've watched you lots of times."

"Oh my," she said, thinking that now's about the time for the ear whispering. She followed him into that meat room and it was like she was really smelling it all, salty, hickory, meaty smells. It was barbaric, almost savage smelling, and she happened to think that if somebody could bottle that smell for a man's aftershave, they'd make a killing. She couldn't tell what were chops because everything was so big, huge hunks of meat swinging around on hooks like the ones Rocky beat on, and for a split second that reminded her of Harold because he loved that movie. She kept staring at Ralph Britt to see if she could tell what he was thinking and he was staring back. It was getting cold in that room. "I don't know which are chops," she said and walked over to where he was standing. Next thing, she and Ralph Britt were in a prostrate position on top of some crates and there was a big ham swinging overhead. She thought that ham ought to fall down, hit her in the head and wake her up, but it didn't. That's what she was thinking when she turned her head to one side and realized that she could see out the mirror right into the Winn Dixie from that position. That same boy was helping a woman she had seen once at a donkey softball game, and that was something the way that she should happen to think of that woman. It seemed like all kinds of people were passing through. Then there came Harold walking up to that meat counter, her canvas purse slung over his arm, and that was funny, because Harold never went to the grocery store; it was so funny the more she saw it, the more she knew that she was in a prostrate position right by herself on top of that velvet bedspread, which is why she didn't even try to get up. It got more and more real when Harold came through the door and was in that meat room. "Juanita? Juanita?" She could hear him clear as a bell. "You ain't gonna buy anything without this. Went right out and left your purse." She was doing fine with all that talk coming from Harold, until she realized that Ralph Waldo Emerson Britt was hearing it, too. It got more and more real, the most real when Harold socked Ralph Britt right off of those crates and onto that filthy sawdust floor. It seems her memory fails at this point because that's when it got so real that it liked to have killed her when she got out in that bright sunlight with Harold squeezing her arm, and she knew for sure that it was real. Harold got home before she did and he was already packing up. That's when he set off for the Tonawanda Indian Village Trailer Park out in the country, and that's when she sunk down onto that door stoop. Nothing's been right since.

Juanita sits up now and her heart is beating fast and her face is all flushed, just like it all might have just happened again. It makes her sick as a dog to think of Ralph Britt; it makes her miss Harold so bad that she aches deep inside. There's no way she'll get a lick of work done in this state. She'll go on over to the YMCA and try to relax. She'll go to Burger King just like she promised. She'll do anything under the sun to make it all up to those kids and to Harold if she ever sets her eyes on him again. She'll start by getting herself looking so good today that it'll make Harold ache to see her. She'll step out of her Toyota to let Harold, Jr., out of the back seat with Granner's present and Harold will get up from that rocker on the front porch and come down those steps slow motioned, his John Deere cap in his hand against that fine hairy chest. He'll walk right up to her, tears in those sweet bloodshot eyes, bury his face into her swirling hair and breathe into her neck real softlike. "I can't stand being away from you no more, Juanita. I forgive you that mistake. I understand how you got a little confused. I know that you never would have got a little confused in the mind if I had been the kind of husband I should have been, the kind of husband I'll be if you take me back." He'll look at her, those pleading eyes glistening with teardrops, those strong hands with the little ridge of hair on the back of them, trembling. "Can I come home, baby?"

"Does a fat baby poot?" she will ask.

The first thing that Ernie Stubbs sees when he opens his eyes is Kate standing there in the center of the room in those loud shorts. She is looking at herself in the mirror, turning from side to side to get the stomach profile, and the rear view which does not even compare with what Ernie saw at the office last night. This is the third time that he has awakened since he got home, took a scalding hot shower and crawled into bed where Kate was flat on her back, her breathing so raspy that it would occasionally turn into a heave, a snore, and each time that he has awakened he has momentarily forgotten what happened, pulled the covers over his head to avoid that initial confrontation with Kate.

"Oh no you don't." Kate walks over and plops down right beside him. "I know you had a late night but you've got to get up. We have to go to Mother's today, remember?"

"Oh, do we have to?" Ernie rolls over and Kate runs her finger along his side, grabs him around the hip and jostles him. She does have a gentle touch.

"It's the least that we can do. I don't want to go sit in that morbid hot house a bit more than you do. We can leave early and we do have the Fosters' party as a good excuse." Kate is up again and at the closet. "I can't decide what to wear tonight, because it's not going to be like a club party considering there will be young people there."

Ernie has closed his eyes again. He's got to think through every course of action, make sure that he never slips up. How the hell does everyone else do it so easily? Practice?

"Poor Ernie, so tired." Kate has pulled out a bright-colored sundress with big yellow circles that look like fried eggs. "Maybe my Malia?" She comes and stands, that bright dress right in front of him. "Goodness, I would think that you had gone out and built a building yourself. What time did you get in?"

"I don't know." Ernie rolls over on his back, stares at

his lovely stuccoed ceiling, the huge oak beams. "Must've been around one."

"Oh, it was after one I'm sure, because I happened to remember an idea that I had for our barbecue and got up to write it down." She goes to the window which looks right out on the pool. "What do you think about big fruit bowl floats on the water? Maybe even a floating bar, wouldn't that be novel?"

"Maybe it was after one. I don't watch the clock while I'm working."

"I know, dear. You'd forget about everything if I wasn't here to remind you." She smiles, those lines stretching out from her eyes. "You and Dave Foster."

"What?" Ernie gets up now, walks to the bathroom. Kate keeps talking the whole time that he's in there.

"You know, work, work, work. Helena and I decided that we've got everything anyone could ever want and that you two need to take a little play time." She is right outside the door; she would come in and talk while he peed if he hadn't told her before not to do that. A man must have his privacy. He stares at himself in the mirror, not a trace of guilt. She doesn't suspect a thing or she would have said something by now. He's home free.

"What were you saying, dear?" He comes out and goes over to his dresser, puts on a nice starched shirt. Nothing feels so good as a starched oxford cloth shirt.

"You've got to relax a little, Ernie." Kate is making the bed now. Nothing goes undone with Kate around. "What good are you to me if you have a heart attack or a stroke?"

"Good God, Kate, look at me. I'm not old; besides, I've seen days when I worked harder." Ernie gets a pair of pink golf slacks from his closet and puts them on. Everyone always does say that he is the best-dressed man on the course. "What time do we have to be at your mother's?"

"Around three, but we can be a little late." Kate is brushing her hair, tossing it from side to side for that natural look because it doesn't do that naturally and then she holds her hand over her eyes and sprays it that way. "You know Harold will be rudely early as usual if there's food to be had."

"Especially now that he's left Juanita."

"Don't remind me." Kate puts on her add-a-bead necklace for that youthful look that she likes. "I have been living in fear that one of our friends will have heard about Juanita in the Winn Dixie."

"We all have skeletons in the closet." Ernie walks out of the room and he can hear Kate scampering right behind him.

"That's true, as a matter of fact, I have heard that Ted Miller has been seeing someone. You know I've been wondering why Nancy has seemed so upset lately, and that must be it."

"Probably just a rumor." Ernie pours the last cup of coffee from the percolator and sits down, carefully, so as not to wrinkle his slacks.

"I don't think so. Seems that there's this little nurse who is chasing him around. I'll never understand women like that, women like Juanita."

"I can't believe that Ted would cheat on Nancy." Ernie is sweating a little around the neck, under the arms. He takes a sip of coffee and looks out at that cool blue pool of his, and it's concrete, too, not that plastic stuff like the Fosters have.

"Well, you know that if it was put right there in front of him he might would. Imagine a woman doing that to a man."

"Yeah, can't be true."

"I hope you're right, because we've got that big couples dinner slated for Labor Day Weekend and I don't know who we'd get to replace the Millers, I mean a table just doesn't look right with eighteen places instead of twenty. There's nobody else in this town who would fit in, and it would be a shame to try out someone who would possibly feel left out or you know, not good enough."

"Yeah." Ernie is watching that water, the sun hitting it, shimmering. He is home free, just that easy. Here he is, a man with everything. He can remember the first time he ever saw a pool. He was working construction when the Country Club was first built. The workmen were not allowed to get into the pool once it was completed. They were only allowed to stand back and see their accomplished work enjoyed by others. Ah, but never more. He had stood by that pool and told himself that one day he'd be there and he'd have more, a self-made man who is in with the best of them!

"I swear Ernie, Mother is worse than ever. Rose called and said that Mother got all upset this morning about something in the paper, said it was your fault."

"She blames everything on us." Ernie turns his attention back to Kate. "And here we are the ones offering the financial assistance for her to move where she can be cared for."

"Mother has never been real appreciative. Of course, look at my father, land rich and pocket poor, and didn't even care, didn't even try, knowing how much it meant to me to have nice clothes and go off to school."

"You had it far better than I did, Kate, at least you had electricity."

"Well, your mother was no problem like mine."

"She died." Even now it makes Ernie a little sad to think of his mother dying, to remember getting that phone call that she was dead, and he didn't mess around, either, wasn't about to put her out in that graveyard near the swamp where his Daddy was buried, bought her a fine corner lot right in the new cemetery in town. She was put away right, all right, everyone said so. Kate even went out and bought her a lovely silk dress, because none of his mother's clothes in that house were appropriate for the viewing. He was good to his mother. "Your mother is probably going to be around another fifty years."

"I'm going to have a talk with her again about the retirement home." Kate pulls out her cross-stitch and starts working, a lovely pineapple welcome sign. "Harold doesn't want her to move because he thinks that he's going to get that house and move in when she's dead."

"But we own the lot next door."

"Well, I know, but Harold just doesn't think, he never has. If he did, he would have tried to get himself cleaned up a little and found somebody other than Juanita Suggs." Kate's plump fingers work in and out, in and out, she works so hard on these cross-stitch designs that some days her fingers get tired and stiff, and framing, she used to do her own framing but it got to be too much for her. "Speaking of dying, Ern, Petie Rose was all upset when Rose called because that old tomcat was run over this morning."

"Oh my," Ernie opens the paper and shakes his head. "It's a shame that Booty's kittens aren't going to be pedigreed, or we could give her one of those."

"She needs a house cat, that's what I told Rose, or a little puppy like a schnauzer or shih tzu, but Rose says that she isn't going to have an animal in the house with that new baby."

"Don't blame her. Poor Petie Rose. She's got to learn that life isn't always easy."

"Serves that ugly old tomcat right for being out and prowling. I wish that all the old stray toms were dead."

Ernie looks up from his paper just as seriously as he can without giving any indication of his guilt. "That's not very nice, Kate. He was only doing what tomcats do."

"Prowling and screwing anything on four legs, like Booty!" With this Booty waddles over and rubs against Kate's chair, arches her back, those little paws not making a sound, so gentle. It just doesn't seem right that a tomcat would be punished for simply doing what he was put on earth to do, even a male pedigreed would do the same.

Bob Bobbin has been riding around Marshboro all morning and has yet to see anything unusual, any stranger that resembles Harold's description. He hasn't even seen that many people out and around, and he doesn't blame them; a person would be a fool to be out in this heat instead of finding themselves a nice cool spot in front of an air-conditioner. That man that killed Charles Husky is probably long gone by now, probably got right out there on 95 and is now halfway to either Miami or New York with that little bit of money in his pocket.

Ahead on the right is one of those roadside markets that set up every now and then, where they got all kinds of artwork like black velvet tapestries all painted up in glow-in-the-dark paint and lamps made out of a bust of Elvis Presley. Bob has always found it amazing, the similarity that those busts have to Elvis. It's quality art, all right, though he would never buy an Elvis for himself. He'd rather have one of Marilyn Monroe or one of those coiled up cobras. All kinds of people stop at these markets so he decides to pull off for a while and see if these people have seen anybody today or last night that fits the description.

He gets out of his car and stretches, puts on his sunglasses. Those lamps really are nice. If he can ever get Corky to give in, that's what he'll give her for her birthday or Christmas. Corky loves Elvis Presley music and even wired some flowers to Tennessee when he died.

"Interested in that lamp, officer?" this cute little curly-haired woman asks. "Give it to you at a good price." She sure is a business woman, out in this hot sun, and yet dressed to kill, right down to those little two-tone shoes with the dots all over them like so many professional women wear. Bob Bobbin saw a picture of a girl in *Hustler* one time who said she wanted to be a lawyer one day, and that's what kind of shoes she was wearing. It always has bothered Bob to see those women showing all they've got, even though he does like to look, can't help but wonder what their Mamas and Daddys must think.

"Not buying today, ma'am, though I really think that's a fine piece." He pushes his hat back on his head so that he can see better. This woman is real nice looking. She ain't Corky Revels, but she's getting close. "No, gotta ask you a question or two."

"We have a license."

"I'm sure you do, not that at all." Bob bends over to get a closer look at Elvis. "There was a murder right near here last night."

"Near here?"

"Right down there at the Quik Pik, got a description but it ain't much to go on." Bob picks up one of the lamps and holds it arm length in front of him.

"I haven't heard a thing about a murder," she says and then steps closer. "Only one man has stopped here all morning."

"Nigger?"

"No white, said he might come back and buy all five of those Elvis lamps. Was the murderer a black man?"

"Yep." Bob puts the lamp down and stands back up. "When was he coming back to buy those, today?"

"He didn't say."

"Do you live here?" Bob pulls out his handkerchief and wipes his forehead. He wishes that girl would at least ask him to step into that trailer parked in the shade.

"No." She waits a minute and then volunteers some information. "I live near here, though." Damn, he wants her address, not all this playing around like Corky does.

"Married?"

"No way!" She laughs again. "Now about that lamp." She picks it up. "It's even got Elvis' autograph right here on this scarf around his neck. Difficult ceramics."

"Never seen you around. You from this area?"

"No, I'm sort of new in town, but I really like it here, got myself a good job, a few friends."

"Oh, so you make these lamps, huh?" Bob is liking this girl more and more and he knows what it feels like to be new in town; he knows how hard it is to find a spot for yourself.

"Oh no, matter of fact I don't work here at all. I help out from time to time." She puts the lamp back down and brushes away some dust from Elvis' hair.

"Where do you work, miss? Oh, by the way, the name's Bobbin, Bob Bobbin."

"Like in the song," she says and then hums Red, Red Robin. "I'm sorry, you must get a lot of teasing about that."

"I don't mind a little teasing," which is true, he's used to teasing by now and it doesn't bother him when it's coming from a nice-looking woman.

"I'm Janie Morris and I'm a secretary over at Marshboro Land and Real Estate Company."

"Ernie Stubbs' outfit! Well, that's something. I rent one of those new apartments right near that office. It was Ernie's brother-in-law that saw that murderer and gave me the description." Bob steps closer to her. "So why you hang out around here? You know, who's here all the time?"

"Oh, I'll go get him," she says and walks over to that trailer. "Tommy, honey, there's somebody that wants to meet you." She goes into the trailer; she called that man honey. Well, that still doesn't make her unavailable, because she is single. Bob checks his watch, almost noon. He can go to lunch pretty soon, try to make up with Corky, might surprise her and come in with this one on his arm. Even if she does have a boyfriend, she was being mighty friendly. Good God, what's a cute woman like that doing in a trailer with a nigger?

"Tommy, this is Bob Bobbin. This is Tommy McNair."

"Janie tells me that you're interested in a lamp."

"I've never seen you around here before." Bob takes off his sunglasses and stares at this man, the bright loose shirt that he's wearing.

"Haven't been around in a while." He puts his arm around that little woman's waist. "I'm from here but you know, been traveling around."

"We met in Richmond," she says and grins at that man.

"Is that your car?" Bob asks and points to the red Granada parked beside the trailer. The man nods and steps closer to Bob. "What's with all the questions?" This guy is big, too, probably ought to box or play basketball instead of making ceramics.

"Do you drink any alcoholic beverages?"

"What? Man, I got work to do. Do you want that lamp, or don't you?"

"Answer the question," Bob says and rests his hand on his gun.

"Scotch, I like scotch, okay?"

"Where were you between midnight and one A.M.?"

"Hey, wait a minute, man, what's this all about?"

"Routine questions, got a description that you match."

"You mean that murderer? the description of that murderer?" Janie steps in front of that man. "Tommy wouldn't murder somebody!"

"Of course I didn't. Don't you accuse me of something."

"So answer the question. Where were you?"

"In bed and asleep."

"Right there in that trailer?"

"No, I don't live here. Live in a trailer park outside of the city limits."

"Got any proof that you were there and asleep?"

"What the hell? Yes, Janie must've seen me. She came in after I was asleep. I went to bed at ten."

"I thought you said you live near here," Bob says and looks at her now. He may as well forget this one.

"I do, but sometimes I stay with Tommy."

"Tell him, Janie, tell him that I was at home so he can get the hell on and I can get back to work."

"Tommy was asleep when I got there." She goes and picks that lamp up again. "Are you going to buy this, officer?"

"Maybe, business first." Bob takes the lamp from her and places it beside his foot. If he does buy one he ain't going to take her word for it; he'll check over every one of those lamps to make certain that he doesn't get one with a chip.

"You know everybody thought that Elvis was a black guy when he first came out." Tommy McNair shakes his head and laughs. "That white man could sing."

"Don't go changing the subject with some lie I don't want to hear." Bob turns back to Janie Morris. "What time did you get home, miss?" He waits and she looks at that man. "Don't look to him for an answer. Remember, I know your boss and whatever your story is, I'll check it out."

"Well, I was a little later than usual." She is looking at that man, shying away like he might hit her or something, and he probably does hit her from time to time. Bob bets they do all sorts of crazy things like he's read about before. "I got home after two."

"What in the hell were you doing until two?" That Tommy is mad now. He twists her arm and makes her face him. "Of all goddamn times. Where were you?"

"I was at work, honey, we had a lot to do. Don't be mad at me." She puts her arm around him but he pushes her away. "I made lots of extra money and I'm going to be up for a promotion soon."

"A promotion? What the hell did you do, or is it because of that young white face?"

"Tommy! Don't talk to me that way. Everything I do is for us, so you can go back to school. You know love is colorblind."

"Plain damn blind is all," Bob says and pulls out his handbook that he always keeps with him.

"I worked late for us, honey."

"Forget it," he says. "I know I was at home and asleep."

"Still got to take you in," Bob says, "get the witness in to look at you."

"But I didn't do anything!"

"It's procedure." Bob pulls out his wallet. "Now, how much for that lamp?"

"It's not for sale!"

"How much?" Bob looks at the woman this time, those eyes filling up with tears cause her man ain't being all sweet to her, cause there's a chance she's been living with a murderer. "I got every right to buy it. You're open to the public and I'm public."

"Thirty dollars," she says, and doesn't even look at him or at her boyfriend. Bob hands her the money and goes and picks up a lamp that neither one of them have touched that he's seen, and puts it in the trunk of the squad car. Not a bad price for it at all.

"Okay," he says and opens his book. "You have the right to remain silent . . ." but Tommy McNair isn't silent, raises hell to the point that Bob just about has to take him by force. He pushes him into the back seat and that woman is crying and carrying on all over his back window, saying how she's going to put everything away and get down there as fast as she can. That man raises hell all the way to the station, calls Bob crazy, ignorant, some words that Bob has never even heard before. It seems to Bob that an innocent man wouldn't carry on this way. They'll just keep the guy until Harold Weeks comes down to see him, can only keep him twenty-four hours, but Bob wants to make damn sure that all the guys see that he's run in this man. He wants them to see the guy and to hear him tell how he found this nigger that matches the description. Then they'll never call him nigger lover; then it'll all balance out and he can go back to saying Negro or black outside of the station, of course; then he could be proud of the way that he saved that old man's life. He could tell Corky that he never meant all those things that he said; he can tell her how weak and frightened and relieved he was when he lay back on that old man's bed and watched the rescue squad carry him off. Corky will smile at him again when she hears all of that, probably will rub his head, the way that she was rubbing that filthy boy's this morning. Hell, he could explain it all to Corky anyway, tell her never to tell that he sent a card to that old man, never to tell how good it all made him feel deep inside. And he bought that lamp for her for just thirty dollars. Good investment, and if this guy does turn out to be the murderer and winds up sitting on death row in Raleigh that lamp will probably jump in price. Matter of fact, he should have bought another one, one for Corky and one for his bedside table; then, if they got married, they'd have a matched set.

Rose Stubbs Tyner has finally gotten her deviled eggs and baked beans ready to go to Granner's party, and now she is checking to make sure that everything that she is supposed to have is in her Lamaze bag. It is very important to make sure that her bag is ready to go at all times. For Rose it is almost like being pregnant for the first time. With Petie Rose she had been so nervous and upset and having so much trouble that they had knocked her out and done a C-section. Not this time, though, not with Pete right there with her, not with the doctor who has told her repeatedly that he sees no signs of trouble. After all, Petie Rose had been backwards. If they hadn't done a C-section, Petie Rose would have come out feetfirst and Rose is certain that that would have killed her. But Rose isn't scared now. If Lady Di and Charles could do it and turn out with such a fine looking baby as little William, then she and Pete Tyner can, too.

She stands and stretches, her hands on the small of her back, her eyes focused on her stomach. Granner swears it's a boy, the way that she is all out front, and Granner wants a boy; Pete really wants a boy though he isn't saying; her Daddy wants a boy, thinking it will be named after him, when Rose has no intentions of ever naming a child Ernie; the only Ernies that she will have around are her Daddy, who doesn't have time to come around too often, and the one on Sesame Street that Petie Rose loves so much. Her mother wants a debutante, Petie Rose wants a kitten, and Rose just wants a baby; she just wants a baby that will hurry up, because the days are getting hotter and hotter and the only way she has of getting cool is to put on one of those sacky lightweight dresses and stand over the air-conditioning vent and let a current of air whip up her full body. It's a struggle these days even to get into the bathtub. She could go out and sit by her parents' pool because they have said it would be okay, but God knows what she would do if she was out there with just herself and Petie, and the baby started coming. Ooh, it's too hot. She stands over the vent, wishing that she could just take her dress off and stand there without a stitch. Oh boy, and now she's got to go to Granner's house, and Granner has never invested in central air; Granner only has one window unit that she doesn't even use because it chills her. Lord knows, it will probably be a hundred in that house by the time everybody gets there and Granner starts heating up food. These parties always get a little heated anyway, and not just because of the weather. That's why Pete doesn't like to go. Deep down, Pete has always liked Juanita and Harold, and then if he spends much time with either of them her parents get mad at him. They even get mad at her if she is nice to Juanita, or if Petie Rose plays with Harold, Jr.

"Rose!" Pete comes running in, his face white. Pete's face is always white. He gets a little sun and turns bright pink and then it goes right back to white, never gets a bit of tan. Rose is glad that Petie Rose got her complexion and hopes that this new child will, too. "Have you seen the living room wall?"

"No, what on earth is wrong?" Rose hangs her Lamaze bag back on the door.

"Look, just look." Pete pulls her by the arm. "We just got everything fixed up to have your parents and my parents over, and look." There is red and purple crayon all over the wall from one corner to another. There's a road, a house, a car, a cat, a dead cat, and then lots of scribbling in black.

Pete heads back down the hall to Petie's room and Rose catches up with him. "Honey, don't be too hard. She was already upset about the B-a-b-y and this morning Tom got run over."

"Granner was trying to tell me something when I was coming in, going on and on about the horrible thing, the worst thing on earth, and I figured she was talking about the Iranian she made up."

"Well, if you had heard it from her, she would have had it all stretched out of shape. It was a real sweet little girl and she was so upset about it." Rose sometimes loses all patience with Granner and her tall tales. Granner is the one that started going all over town voicing suspicions about Petie's red hair when hers is dirty blonde and Pete's is blonde. Granner said that that suspicion took people's minds off the fact that she and Pete had to get married, which makes no sense at all, especially when that isn't true.

"Tom got hit by a killing machine!" Petie throws her

Caspar book to the floor and stomps both feet. "A fat ugly woman killed Tom."

"Petie, don't be like Granner and make up stories." Rose walks over. "That was a pretty young woman and it was an accident."

"POOT!" Petie Rose screams and runs around in a circle. She learned that from Harold or one of his children, Rose is certain.

"Petie," Pete says, and makes her stop running. He picks her up and Petie calms down immediately. She does that for Pete every time, but does she do it for Rose? No, never! "I'm sorry about old Tom but you shouldn't have crayoned the wall. We've told you about that, haven't we?"

"Yes, Daddy," Petie sobs and her entire little face puckers up for a second. "I'm sorry," she wails.

"I know, baby," Pete says and rubs her head. Petie has pulled one of her pigtails until the rubber band is way down at the bottom and her hair is all knotted up in it. "And that was an ugly word that you just said."

"I'm sorry, Daddy!"

"Where did you hear that?" Rose goes over and stands near Pete when he asks this.

"Uncle Harold." Petie sniffs and squirms so that Pete will put her down. Lord, surely this new baby won't have a temper like Petie. Rose cannot even bear to think about it. Pete Tyner has no idea what goes on all day long.

"That wasn't nice of Uncle Harold," Pete says, and looks at Rose as if she has something to do with it. If it's not Granner it's Harold, and if it's not those two, Pete has had a bad day with Ernie, or Pete is tired of Kate's opinions on where they should live. She cannot take responsibility for her relatives when she already has so much on her, and Pete just doesn't understand, blames her for everything.

"But he said it," Petie says and gets her Farmer Says off the floor. She sets it on pig and pulls the string—oink-oink-oink! "He said a fat puppy poots."

"Okay, okay, Petie," Rose says and twists to one side. All of a sudden, she had a little pain. Now it's gone, and thank God, Pete hadn't noticed. He is so nervous and edgy these days. "You've told us where you heard it, now just don't use it any more." Now Rose is burning slam up. If she doesn't get over one of those vents, she will die.

"But Tom is dead!" Petie starts crying again.

"That reminds me, Rose, you know that old guy that worked at the Quik Pik?" Pete follows her to their room just across the hall.

"Fat one that used to eat all the time?"

"Yes, the one that always asked us about Harold." Pete whispers. "He was murdered last night. I heard that Harold saw the guy that did it."

"Where did you hear all of that?"

"Stopped for a pack of cigarettes there this morning."

"How awful." Rose stands over the vent and it feels so good. "Honey, you need to cut down on your smoking."

"I will when the baby comes," he says. "Think I'll take a shower before going to Granner's. Bet Harold will have some wild tale about the old man at the Quik Pik."

"Oh Jesus, you know he will." Rose flaps her dress around and feels a little queasy all of a sudden. "By the way, maybe you could go back to the store and get Petie a Slurpee when you get out." Rose has to yell now because Pete is in the bathroom. "She loves those things, and I'd sort of like one myself."

Sam Swett is faced with a difficult dilemma. He has showered and lathered his entire body, including his prickled head. He is clean, smells like soap, and his entire body is tingling while he stands naked in the middle of his hotel room, trying to decide what to do. He is clean, but his clothes are filthy, even his one pair of spare underwear has that big footprint on the crotch. He remembers now, remembers that big hairy Mason stepping on the crotch of his underwear. Somewhere way back, it seems that he learned that one should never put filthy clothes on a clean body, or was it the other way, that one should never put a filthy body into clean clothes, a filthy body onto clean sheets? He remembers; it is all of those things. For some reason, this concerns him. It concerns him mostly because he is afraid to break a rule, the law; he is afraid to be different, and he knows this because of the way that he gorged himself on pancakes, the way that this girl, this Corky has stayed on his mind. He is weakening, weak and helpless.

He has an idea, a real idea. He can wash his clothes out in the shower and hang them outside the window to dry. He can just walk around the room naked until they are dry enough to put back on, until one o'clock, which doesn't leave a great deal of time, and it does feel good this way, clean and naked like a newborn and just as helpless. He bundles up his clothes and takes them to the bathtub, rubs the bar of soap all over them and then holds them under the water and watches them suds up. He even washes his tennis shoes. For some reason he cannot keep himself from singing; for some reason he wants to sing "when the red, red, robin comes bob, bob, bobbin along." And he is aware of the quiet on the street below, aware of the fact that he is no longer in the city. He is in his home state, in a small town, in an old hotel. He still has not decided where he's going to go and what he's going to do, but somehow that doesn't seem to worry him as much as what he saw last night, a real body, somebody's husband, somebody's father, somebody that Corky liked, and the thought of her cool hand, her small tilted nose, makes even that seem less horrible and frightening. The thought of her, those full lips, makes him scrub harder. Wake up, wake up, you sleepy head . . .

Mrs. Foster is still running around like she's crazy even though Fannie has got everything under control. That house is spic and span and now all they're waiting for is the florist to come and set up the flowers. That long table is all set with one of those lacy cloths and Mrs. Foster's very best set of china. It's hard for Fannie to tell the difference between those three sets cause they all look like china, you can hold up every piece and see the light coming through. The best ain't even the prettiest, plain white. If Fannie had been asked to pick the best, she would have picked that set with the pretty light pink and blue border. Her Mama gave her a set way back that looked almost just like that, except hers was what they called crockery and you couldn't see through it. Her children and M.L. have just about done away with that set, except for the creamer and sugar bowl that Fannie keeps on the table. That's why Fannie herself wouldn't have nothing but crockery, so that she didn't have to tell her children to watch out, don't tap your fork, don't stack those plates, like Mrs. Foster has to do all the time. Come to find out, that pretty set is the cheapest of all three of those sets and you'd never know it.

That's one problem about being in a house like this, cause you can't tell what's valuable and what ain't, just like those vases that Mrs. Foster had her wash just a little bit earlier. "Be very careful, Fannie," Mrs. Foster had said. "I could never replace these vases." That makes Fannie nervous as a cat when Mrs. Foster does that to her, said those vases was Waterford crystal and cost a fortune. Fannie wouldn't have known if Mrs. Foster hadn't told her. They looked like any other old crystal, thump the edge and they ring like a handbell. Still, if you backed way off and looked at them, they looked like some you could find at the dime store. Lord knows what they did cost though, cause even pretty cut glass is high these days. Mrs. Foster had this real pretty cut-glass pitcher and tumbler set that Fannie thought was so pretty, she took it upon herself to put it in the china cabinet with the rest of that stuff. Everyday she'd put it there, and when she'd come back it would be boxed up and back under the sink. One day it wasn't there any more and Fannie got the point, she didn't have to be hit with a ton of bricks to see that Mrs. Foster didn't agree with her. Mrs. Foster didn't even ask her if she wanted that set, and she would have loved to get it; it probably went to some rummage sale or such. It aggravated the devil out of Fannie sometimes, and she is feeling aggravated when the phone rings.

"Foster residence," she says and stretches with the cord so that she can see the clock. Her story is going to be starting soon and she intends to watch it if Mrs. Foster can calm herself down.

"Mama, is that you?" Fannie goes over and sits down at the table. She hasn't heard Thomas' voice in months, not since he came to borrow some money from her to get himself set up in a trailer. He has yet to pay her back.

"Thomas? Is that you?" She doesn't like to admit it, but it is good to hear his voice. A woman just doesn't stop loving her children even if they have caused heartache and headaches. "Lord, I had just about forgot that I had a son named Thomas."

"Mama, you've got to help me." Fannie has to press the phone closer, cause there's lots of noise behind Thomas. Ain't that like him, though, act like the big black man, or worse, act like the big black man that wants to be white, belittles her and her work, and then calls like a spoiled white child for his Mama when he needs something. Fannie doesn't say a word, just waits to hear him through. "I'm in jail."

"Lord boy, what have you done?" He doesn't even correct her for calling him "boy," so she knows he's in trouble bad.

"That's the thing, Mama, I haven't done anything at all." Thomas is breathing heavy. "They got me down here because they say I fit the description of a man who killed a man."

"Did you?" It is like Fannie's heart has stuck right up in her throat.

"No! I don't know what's going on. This cop came by where I was working and the next thing, he was carting me off, just because I'm black, too. That's the only reason is because I'm black and I can't prove that I was at home and asleep last night." Fannie has heard similar stories from Thomas before, all that "just because I'm black."

"Son, they don't take somebody in for no reason. Now, you tell me what happened or I'll hang up on you." Fannie's voice gets louder and now Mrs. Foster is standing there in the kitchen. Mrs. Foster can't stand it when somebody calls Fannie on the telephone.

"I swear, Mama, that's all." She can hear Thomas sniffling a little, and she hasn't heard that in years. "They made me take off all my clothes and searched me and they've fingerprinted me, and now they're going to put me in a lineup."

"Thomas, I don't know what I can do." Fannie keeps watching the way that Mrs. Foster is picking up things and replacing them in a heavy-handed way. "I'm at work."

"Please, I thought there wasn't going to be any problem, and now I'm getting scared." Fannie has not heard this kind of talk coming out of Thomas' mouth since he was a small child and scared of the dark, just like M.L. is. "Mama, I know you've been mad at me but if you've ever loved me, you'll come get me, come tell them that I ain't a murderer." It's been years since Thomas said "ain't," too. He's worked so hard on his English. Fannie can't help but feel herself getting a little upset.

"I don't know what good I'll be, baby, but I'll come down there."

"Thank you, Mama, and I swear that things will be different when I get out of this, I swear it!" Fannie hangs up the phone while he's still there making all of his promises, prayers in the dark as she always says when somebody suddenly gets on their knees and begs. Don't matter even if he don't keep those promises; he is her son.

"What on earth was that all about?" Mrs. Foster has stopped her fiddling, now that Fannie is off the phone.

"My son's in jail and I gotta go down there."

"But, Fannie, what about my party?" Mrs. Foster comes and stands right by Fannie's chair. "I mean, I'm sorry that your son is in jail, but what can you do? I mean, why is he there?"

"Looks like a murderer." Fannie shakes her head from side to side.

"Murder?" Mrs. Foster backs away now and stares at Fannie. "Did he do it?"

"Says not, and I believe him." Fannie turns to the yellow pages for the number of the taxi service. "I'm sorry, Mrs. Foster, but he wants me there and I aim to go."

"I know, I know." Mrs. Foster is twisting her hands now. "I think I can probably get the rest done. But what about tonight? Will you be able to come back at six?"

"You plan on it, and if I see that I can't, I'll let you know in plenty of time to get somebody else." Fannie dials the taxi number and then waits. "Yes, I need a cab. I'm at the Fosters' house on," Fannie holds the receiver away and looks up at Mrs. Foster. "What street is this?"

"Primrose." Lord, she should have remembered that, being led down the primrose path.

"Primrose Street out here in that new neighborhood that used to be Piney Swamp." Mrs. Foster is shaking her head, mouthing that it's boulevard and not street, mouthing that name of this place, don't matter, that old taxi driver knows exactly what she's talking about. "As soon as you can get here, thank you."

"Fannie, I would offer to take you but you know, the florist is coming, and to tell you the truth, I don't even know where the jail is."

"Don't matter." Now Fannie looks up the number of the Coffee Shop to ask Corky if she can sit with M.L. a while tonight. That Corky is a sweet girl and Fannie doesn't even tell her what's going on, cause she knows it would worry her. Corky doesn't even ask where Fannie is going tonight, just says, "sure thing."

"Well, M.L. is taken care of," Fannie says, and goes to get her purse so that she can wait by the front door for the taxi. "Now I gotta take care of Thomas."

"Oh, that's so good that you found a sitter. I tell you Fannie, I'll pay the sitter for you, too." Mrs. Foster follows her into the living room, and Fannie looks out the glass storm door so that she won't have to look at that pitiful child hanging on the wall.

"No need for that. Corky don't charge me. We do favors back and forth for one another."

"Hey, Ma." Billy Foster comes into the room and slumps down on one of those fine pieces of furniture that is, in Fannie's opinion, made for looking and not sitting. "I need some money. Think I'll go to Burger King."

"Okay, Billy, just a second." Mrs. Foster suddenly looks upset. "Oh I knew that there was something that I forgot, Billy and Parker's rooms. Oh, I guess I can close their doors. No one will go upstairs anyway." Fannie doesn't make any comment. She ain't about to run up those stairs and make up behind those lazy children, when her own child is in trouble.

"Oh God, is tonight that party?" Billy slings his dirty blue-jeaned legs over that fine cherrywood arm that Fannie just dusted to a red shine.

"Yes, and I'm going to need your help, too. You'll need to pick Fannie up at six and take her back home after dinner."

"Oh great! There goes the whole night." He makes a face that Fannie feels needs to be slapped, but Mrs. Foster doesn't do it and Fannie doesn't offer to use the taxi service tonight, either. He gets up and slumps back toward the kitchen; she hears him open the refrigerator, pop a top. Fannie knows that every soda in that refrigerator is in a bottle and that Billy Foster has gone in there and gotten out one of his Daddy's beers, just like that. Mrs. Foster knows it, too.

"Dave lets him have one every now and then, you know he'll be eighteen soon." Mrs. Foster smiles at her, that same smile that she gives women like Mrs. Stubbs.

"I see," Fannie says, and thank the Lord, here comes her taxicab up that long drive. "I'll let you know if I can't make it, but until then you can count on my coming."

"Oh thank you, Fannie. I don't know what I'd do if you weren't here. I guess maybe I could serve myself." Mrs. Foster follows her onto the porch. "I've never done it that way, but I guess if it's an absolute emergency, I could manage."

"I feel certain I can make it," Fannie says and heads down the steps.

"I hope so," Mrs. Foster calls. "And I hope everything is okay, Fannie. I really do!" Mrs. Foster is already back inside the cool when Fannie gets in the taxi and slams the door. "Take me to the jailhouse," she says, and looks that driver square in the eye.

Bob Bobbin only has a few details to work out on the case before he goes to lunch. He's got to get Harold Weeks down to the station to get him to identify the man, but first he's got to go talk to Ernie Stubbs and make sure that Janie Morris is telling the truth. Of course, it seems logical that she would be, cause she could have protected her boyfriend and lied. It just doesn't make sense, and it's these kind of details that seal up a case. A man with no alibi is usually guilty as sin. Bob swings through those big gates of Cape Fear Trace and almost sideswipes one of those old taxicabs that is such an embarrassment. Bob has suggested that Marshboro get itself a transit service, buses and such, but the chief or nobody else pays much attention to what he says. That'll change after today. He pulls up in front of the Stubbs' house and gets out; nice house, too, got that old look to it even though it's brand new. Bob doesn't care for that look, but he can appreciate it. In his opinion, when he's got something brand new, he wants everybody to know that it's brand new. He wouldn't mind being called what people call "new money" or that other way to say it that's in a different language, wouldn't mind being known that way at all. Ernie Stubbs is new money or must be, if what Harold told him about Injun Street is true. That's something else that Bob is curious to prove, because if it's true, then he knows that he can do the same thing himself. Hell, he'd have a far shorter way to go, considering he's living in that complex right near here. He rings the bell and steps back with his cap in his hand.

"Yes?" Mrs. Stubbs is a lady you'd never forget. She's got that same husky sort of build as Harold, though there's no resemblance in their faces, Harold with that thick dark hair and tan, and her with that yellow hair and sort of white skin. "May I help you?"

"Is the husband home?" Bob steps right inside, figuring it's okay since she hasn't come outside and hasn't closed the door. It's nice in here, all right.

"Yes, he is, but may I ask what this is about?" She backs up and watches Bob the whole time. Bob thinks he'd like to have a pair of those shorts to put over his alarm clock so he wouldn't have so much trouble waking up.

"Police business, routine questioning."

"Ernie!" Mrs. Stubbs turns her head to one side to yell

while she keeps her eyes on Bob. "Honey, a police officer is here." She smiles but doesn't offer him a seat and he sure would like one, rest a minute. Mr. Stubbs comes through the hallway, his little half glasses on his nose, the newspaper in his hand. He's reading that fine print financial section, and Bob always has liked to see somebody that could read all of that.

"What can I do for you?" Mr. Stubbs asks.

"Well, first, do you remember me? Bob Bobbin, I advised you about the security of your new office and I also rented one of the new apartments."

"The red shag," Mrs. Stubbs says, suddenly remembering, and it makes Bob feel good to know that he had made a favorable impression on her. "I remember."

"Why yes, Bob." Mr. Stubbs sticks out his hand and Bob shakes it. "What's this all about, haven't been robbed, have I?"

"No sir, keep a tight watch on that building." Bob steps in a little closer, hoping that they'll offer that seat, but they don't. "I'm here about your secretary."

"Oh?" Ernie feels his knees getting weak. What if she's accused him of rape? That happens sometimes. He's heard of that happening before. Or what if she was found dead and he is the last link, another Chappaquiddick? God, maybe the Kennedys could afford that but he can't.

"Yes, there was a murder last night." Bobbin takes out his pad. "Surprised you haven't heard, since it was Harold Weeks who gave us an I.D. of the murderer."

"We don't deal with my brother often." Mrs. Stubbs leans against the doorway. She ain't about to offer one of those seats, or even offer him something cool to drink.

"Well, I can see that." Bob nods, gives Mrs. Stubbs that look of his that says that he knows exactly what she means. "A person just can't afford to be that close to Harold, you know, no offense intended."

"I don't see what this has to do with . . ." Ernie cannot complete his sentence before this Bob character starts up again.

"Charles Husky was the victim. Doubt if you know him, didn't lead much of an exciting life, not like most of us if you know what I mean?"

"I know," Ernie says and nods, so that this man will hurry up. What does Janie have to do with it all? He did know Charlie Husky, so did Kate. Charlie Husky grew up right near Ernie; he was in their class at school. It makes him cringe to remember. "That name doesn't ring a bell with me."

"Or me," Kate says, and looks at Ernie, knowing that they both know otherwise.

"Anyway, Harold got a description and I arrested a man that fit it." Bob pauses for a minute for them to congratulate him, but they don't. "Any way, it so happens that the murderer's girlfriend is your secretary."

"What?" Kate steps closer. She is taking in every bit of this, and Ernie doesn't want her to hear it, he's afraid for her to hear it, but if he asks her to leave the room she'll get suspicious. He can't let her get suspicious.

"So what do you want from me?" Ernie asks.

"I want to see if you can verify her story. You see this man ain't, excuse me, doesn't have a alibi and her story still didn't give him one. But still, I have to check it all out and need to ask a few questions."

"Okay." Ernie feels that he is maintaining a very cool, calm dignified appearance, even though he is feeling sick.

"What time did Miss Janie Morris, the woman in question, leave your office last night?"

"Night? I thought she got off at five!" Kate looks at Ernie, stares at him.

"I had her work later than usual, big land deal coming through."

"What time?" Bobbin has his pencil ready to write.

"I gave her a dinner break and then we worked straight through." He looks at Kate. "She must have left around midnight."

"Midnight!" Kate puts her hands on her hips. "You went all these years without a fulltime secretary, and all of a sudden she's working till midnight? What on earth did you do before you got one?"

"It took a long time to get the work out, that's what."

"Something's fishy," Bobbin says and shakes his head. Ernie would like to knock his head off. "Little lady told me that she didn't get home to this boyfriend until after two. For some reason, she's lying."

Ernie's head feels like it's spinning now. He's got to make his story go along with hers without getting Kate all upset and wise. If he doesn't go along with her story, Janie Morris will probably tell everything! "You know I'm awful about time," he says. "You can ask Kate. I work so hard that I never know what time I'm getting in."

"You got in well after one last night, though," Kate

says. "I told you that I was up at one to write down an idea and you weren't home. Did she work as late as you did, Ernie, or what?"

"She left right before I did, I swear, though it didn't seem that late. Of course, I lose myself in my work."

"Know what you mean." Bob Bobbin steps closer to Mrs. Stubbs. Her name is Kate. No reason why he can't call them Ernie and Kate. "So, Kate, if you verify that Ernie here was in closer to two than one, and he can verify that Miss Janie Morris, the woman in question, left just a speck of time before he did, then I reckon we can believe that little lady which means that without a trace of doubt that man has no alibi and more than likely is just the man that your brother saw leaving the Quik Pik which was the scene of Charles Husky's brutal murdering." Bob waits for their response. "Now, is that correct? You can verify that?"

"Yes, yes," Ernie says and both of them nod. Ernie steps forward, hoping that this man will leave. "Anything else?" he asks, an exasperated tone in his voice that Bobbin doesn't even notice.

"Yeah, how much do you know about your secretary?"

"What do you mean by that?" Ernie shakes his head. "I try not to know about my employees' lives outside of the office."

"Good policy, but I feel I gotta let you in, considering all of this will probably make the papers."

"Go on," Kate Stubbs says, and Bobbin almost hates to tell her, a lady doesn't need to hear such.

"You know I told you that it's her boyfriend that she

stays with sometimes that's accused of the murder."

"Yes." She didn't tell Ernie that she had a regular boyfriend. She didn't tell him that she sometimes lived with someone; play it loose, no strings, is what she had said.

"Well, what I didn't tell you is that her boyfriend is a niggerman, uh, Negro."

"Ernie, I thought you said you hired a nice girl!"

"She seemed nice enough," he stammers. "She can type and she seemed like a nice girl."

"I think you ought to fire her! Just look at what she did to you as well!" Kate steps closer to Ernie, those shorts like a bomb exploding.

"What? What?"

"All that overtime! She knew what she was doing. She's been there long enough to see how you lose yourself in your work! She was probably sitting on the phone with her black boyfriend or filing her nails and letting the dollars and cents add up!" Kate is through now, out of breath, wheezing a little.

"I didn't mean to cause a ruckus," Bobbin says and puts his pad back into his pocket. "Got all I needed. Told you what I felt was my duty, Ernie." He puts his hand on Ernie's shoulder. "Keep on using that timer on the lamp in your office. Best security around these days next to the force."

Ernie stands at the door and watches Bobbin disappear. He can feel Kate's anger.

"The nerve! Honestly, it's a shame that you can't find a

secretary who doesn't act just like a secretary, cheap little money-hungry nothing!"

"Kate, honey," he puts his hands on her shoulders. He is safe now. "You were a secretary once."

"That was different!" She shakes her head and not a hair moves. "I knew that I wasn't really like all the others!" Ernie knows those words well. He thinks them every time that he looks back at how he got where he is.

"But did everyone else know?"

"Why are you doing this to me, Ernie?" Kate pulls away. "Don't get all guilty-feeling if you fire this person. She deserves it!"

"Maybe so." This pacifies Kate enough that she goes back to her cross-stitch, says that she doesn't know why they allow people as stupid as that man who was just here to become a policeman. "God! What's it coming to?" she screams from the other room. "I mean what if your business is linked to this hideous scandal, and believe you me it will be if my nasty brother has anything to do with it.

"Yes, dear," he says. "Don't you worry your pretty little head about it. We're not associated with any of that." It's amazing how those two words "pretty" and "little" can appease Kate so quickly, two little words that in reality make no reference to her.

"You're right, honey. Why don't we have a cocktail before we go to Mother's?"

"Fine." He goes and mixes Kate a vodka martini just the way that she likes it and pours himself a straight shot of scotch. Kate sips hers and he goes over to his chair in the den and stares out at the swimming pool. He downs the shot and closes his eyes. It seems lately that Injun Street is not that far away, not with the mention of Charlie Husky, a man that he probably once identified himself with, not with the realization that he has gone through those same weak desires that he had as a child, to throw that brown-skinned girl down on the bed of that truck, to feel manly and powerful. And he had done it, not with a black girl, but with the closest thing, a white girl who sleeps with a black man. That's not exactly the kind of thing that anyone would tell on the golf course or on a drunken deep sea fishing trip. There's not a soul that he can tell, and he can't fire her, either. Sometimes, like right now, he thinks that it may have been easier if he had never even tried to get off of Injun Street, if he had been living right nearby when his Mama accidentally turned that pot of boiling grease on herself and bashed her head on the counter, if he had just been there to pick her up, to mop up the grease.

Corky keeps looking at the clock. Already, it is a little after one and Sandra Rhodes has come in to relieve her. She ought to just leave is what she ought to do, as if there isn't enough going on this day, with Mr. Husky's dying and Granner's party only a couple of hours away. But then again, she doesn't mind waiting a few extra minutes, just in case he does come back, though now she's thinking that he might have hopped a bus and be long gone from Marshboro. Lordy, it must be the weather that's got her feeling so funny. Lord knows, she's been out with boys cuter than this one, boys with hair on their heads, boys that come out smelling of Old Spice or Aqua Velva, boys in clean clothes. She goes over and sits at that table where she sat with him a little while ago. That Sandra, eyeing her that way, like she's got no right to sit in the coffee shop after work. Sandra just wants to fix herself up some big lunch and sit there and stuff her stuffed self. Sandra Rhodes would give her eyeteeth for a date with Bob Bobbin, and takes it out on Corky that he never asked her. Corky can't help Bob liking her; if she had her way, he wouldn't, that's for sure. Now Sandra is standing over there tapping that spatula up against the stove like she's about to jump right out of her uniform. Sandra is about as much fun as Columbus when the Indians shot him, or whatever that is that Harold Weeks is always saying. If he's not answering a question with a question, he's saying one of those that's-about-as-funny-as things. That's about as funny as a bubblegum machine on a lockjaw ward. That's about as funny as ExLax on a diarrhea ward. She is staring out that window, when all of a sudden she sees that shaved head rounding the corner. He is staring down at his feet and doesn't even see her, so she gets up and gets a stack of menus to sort through so it won't look like she's been sitting there waiting for him. She doesn't even turn around when the bells ring over the door and she hears the squeak-squeak of his shoes.

"Sorry I'm a little late," he says and shifts from one foot to the other. He smells clean like soap, and those prickles have a little fluff to them, not much, but a little. His clothes and shoes are soppy wet, though.

"I hadn't even noticed," she says and flips back through the menus. "Looks like you showered in your clothes."

"No, I showered first." He sits down across from her. "Then I showered off my clothes."

"Well, that makes loads of sense." She puts the menus down on the table and stares real hard at this Sam boy. "Don't you have any more clothes?"

"Nope, threw them all away before I left New York."

"Oh," she says, like that makes a whole lot of sense, because it very well may make a whole lot of sense. He could've had a good reason to do that and she doesn't want to look stupid. For some reason, she wants this boy to like her and to go right on thinking that she's smart and all, like he said earlier. Still, she can ask an intelligent question. "Did you get cooties or something?"

"No," he shakes his head. "Claustrophobia, paranoia."

"Oh." Corky feels a little nervous and she can tell that he is, too, the way that he keeps rubbing his hands through that stubble. "Feel better?"

"Yeah, yeah, check me." He picks up her hand and rubs it on his face, from his cool forehead down to his cheek. He's got a little bit of a beard, not much, soft brown hairs like goosedown on that smooth cheek. His head ain't downy, though, even with that little bit of fluff.

"It's hot outside," he says and keeps holding onto her hand.

"Yeah, it sure is." Corky can't ever remember feeling at such a loss for what to say to somebody. "You hungry?"

"Sort of." All he says is sort of. Now, what is she supposed to say to that? "Oh, I've got some money now. I found it." He reaches in his pocket and pulls out some damp bills all clumped together.

"Where'd you find it?"

"It was in my pants, all that time, right there in my pocket, and I didn't even remember putting it there." He gets this awfully confused look, sort of a helpless look like a kitten or a baby, and Corky gets that feeling that she wants to squeeze him as hard as she can, love and squeeze him so hard that it makes her grit her teeth, the way people always do when they hug a teeny little helpless creature, a kitten or a puppy. If Sandra wasn't standing over there taking it all in, Corky probably would've squeezed him that way.

"Seems like you don't remember a whole lot."

He shakes his head and stares directly into her left eye, then her right one. "I'm starting to remember things. I think I drank too much for too long, you know?"

"Bad habit to get into."

"But it's not, a habit I mean, I had never done that, haven't done anything, really."

"I know what you mean." Corky pulls her hand away so that Sandra won't have that to talk about, and he looks that funny way again, like she might've just scolded him or told him to go to hell. "You remember last night, though."

"Some of it, yeah. I was in this truck, you see, and I got sick."

"That must have been when that trucker let you out,

right there near Quik Pik." Corky lowers her voice and leans forward. "Harold, that man that you saw in here? Well, Harold said that you got out of that truck and that the two of you together went in and found Charles Husky dead."

"Oh." he shakes his head. "You see, I don't remember that. I remember being in the store and getting sick and then seeing that dead man."

"But you didn't see that black man leaving like Harold did?"

"No, no, I don't think so."

"Can't tie up this table, Corky, what's it going to be?" Sandra is standing there with her pad and pencil.

"I see how busy you are," Corky says and waves her arm back toward all of the empty tables. "Just bring us two specials." Sandra just stares at Sam, rolls her eyes and then lopes off to the kitchen.

"No, I don't remember any of that part, don't remember even seeing that Harold man until I got inside of the store. It seemed like I had been there before."

"Oh, I get those a lot where you feel like you've said or heard or done the exact same thing."

"Déjà vu."

"Huh?" God, if this boy starts talking crazy again or acting show-offy like Bob Bobbin, she's gonna give up on him right now.

"That's what you were talking about is called, but it wasn't that way with me, not really." He rubs his head again and then smiles at her, with straight white teeth.

"You must've been real drunk." Corky leans back in her seat. "Bet it sobered you up to see what you saw." She stares out the window and her face gets solemn, her eyes dull.

"Not so much as it made me realize that this is the world, violence and death. People talk about life and the real world and this is it." He stares at her like she's supposed to say something back. He's getting her a little confused.

"Granner Weeks always says that you're alive until you're dead." That is all she can think of to say, and she waits to see what he'll answer back. It takes him a while, so she shuffles through those menus again until Sandra snatches them out of her hand.

"Two specials," Sandra says and stares at Sam. He stares back without blinking. Then he stares down at his hot roast beef sandwich, bends over and smells it. Sandra rolls her eyes again and gives Corky one of those "you're stupid as hell" looks. What does Sandra know? Corky watches until Sandra is back behind the counter with her cup of coffee and romance magazine.

"You do have a life if you're alive," she says, and takes the pickles off of the top of her sandwich. "Tell me about yourself."

"Not much to tell," he says, with his lips pushed forward, his right cheek bulging with sandwich. He nods and holds up his hand to let her know that he will finish when he swallows. "Grew up in a small town, went to school, went to college, got out, went to New York to find out what it is I want to do with my life, left New York and still haven't figured out what to do. I mean there are so many bad things happening and people settling down to the same old things, you know?"

"Same here, I guess, cept I never went to college, never been to New York." Corky takes a deep breath. "But about that other part, well, I've known all that goes on for as long as I can remember. I know that I'm alive."

"But everything else is dying, falling apart." He leans forward and is almost in her face. "That's why I want to shut myself away from it all, you see, before I lose all of my desire for something better; I don't want to become like everybody else, like her." He glances over at Sandra, who has now opened a bag of potato chips and is sitting over there crunching.

"Nobody's like her, I'll guarantee," Corky says. "I work here with her every single day and I'm not like her."

"But you might get to be like her. You may fall in the hole with everyone else." He points to the floor like maybe it might open up, or like he sees a big hole there. This has gone about far enough. He may sound smart and maybe he did go to college, but what he's saying now is crazy. Imagine, her getting to be like Sandra. Sandra is divorced, and Corky hasn't even been married yet.

"Sounds to me like you're feeling scared and sorry for yourself for some reason." She pushes her plate to the center of the table and she hasn't even finished one half of the sandwich. "You're just scared of what you might see or what might happen. I bet nothing bad's never happened in your life!"

"Maybe that's how I can see it so much better, see it objectively, a process of elimination." He picks up part of her sandwich and starts eating it.

"That's a lie!" she says, and she doesn't even care that Sandra is staring over at them. "I'll tell you how I know it's a lie that what you're saying works." She props her elbows on the table and cups her face in her hands. "My Mama left home when I was fifteen, no warning, no nothing, she just up and left. All my Daddy did was sit around and say what you're saying about the end of it all and all that. He didn't care a bit about me or how I felt; he didn't care a bit about anything but lying around in his bed, drinking and crying and saying how his world had fallen down." She turns and looks out the window. "Wouldn't talk, wouldn't eat, just shut himself away from it all like you want to do, and do you know what happened? Do you?" She can feel the blood pumping to her face and she wants to stop, to forget all about it, but now she can't, now she has to say it all and be done with it. "He blew his head off, right in that bed, just like that!" She snaps her fingers and looks at him now, those gray eyes hard and glassy. "On a Sunday morning, do you hear? A Sunday morning in the dead of the summer!" She leans back and takes several deep breaths. It makes her mad all over again just to think about it.

"Maybe he did what he had to do. Maybe he wanted to take control of his life before somebody else did it for him." He doesn't even raise his voice.

"Ha! It was stupid and it was easy. He didn't have to strip off those bloody sheets. He didn't have to see himself lying there with half a head! He didn't have to do nothing about a service. He didn't have to be right by himself, like he left me." Now Corky is crying and she can't help it, she can't help but see it all again. "And now Mrs. Husky is left all by herself, and Mr. Husky couldn't help it. He never would've left her all alone on purpose, but still, she's alone and he wanted to live. You don't feel alive when you hear all of that? It doesn't make you thankful that you're not one of those numbers you been talking about?"

"I'm sorry." He pushes his plate to the center, reaches across the table, but she jerks away. "I didn't mean to upset you again. Really, I had no idea."

"That's what I been saying." She glares at him and her eyes are all red. "You haven't got any idea of what it's like, because if you did, then you wouldn't talk the way that you do. You think I'm just gonna fall apart because I knew people who have?"

"You misunderstand me, really. I don't know what I'm saying."

"No, you don't know what you're saying, because you don't understand. You might have gone to college but you don't understand a whole lot."

He shakes his head and she just shrugs, her brows wrinkling again like pale white circumflexes. The bells ring, and for the first time in her life Corky is glad to see Bob Bobbin. She'd be glad to see anybody that could put a stop to this crazy conversation.

Now Bob is standing close by with one of those tacky

Elvis lamps under his arm. Corky wishes that people would just let Elvis rest in peace, let her Daddy rest in peace, let everybody dead rest in peace.

"Hi there, Bob," Sandra says, and giggles. Sandra is far too old to giggle that way.

"Hi." Bob is watching Corky now, and it makes her so mad for him to watch her this way. Every time that they've had it out good and proper and she thinks that she's gotten rid of him, he comes back and looks at her this way. "Corky, can I talk to you a minute?"

"What for?" she asks, and now Sam Swett has sat up straight in his chair and is squeaking his wet tennis shoe back and forth on the floor. He is watching every move that Bob makes.

"In private," Bob says, and walks right around Sandra to the back room.

"Hey, you're not supposed to be back there, and neither is Corky after her shift is up." Sandra gets off her stool and stands there with her hands on her hips.

"Just this once, Sandy." Bob pinches her cheek like he might be some old movie star, and Sandra is desperate enough to fall for it.

"Just this once." Sandra smiles at him and then glares at Corky when she passes.

"What is it, Bob? Can't you see that I've got a lunch date?" Corky leans against the doorway, her hands in the pockets of her apron.

"With him?" Bob carefully places the lamp beside the sink and steps forward. "A lunch date?"

"That's what I said, now what did you have to say?" Now that he has moved closer, she stands up straight with her arms crossed over her stomach.

"I just wanted to say that I'm sorry about earlier." Bob shifts around and Corky knows what's coming before he even takes off his hat. "It's just that I care."

"And I don't." There, she told him. His ears are turning red and he stares down at his big black-handled gun fastened there on his belt. "Was there anything else?"

"No, not one damn thing." He glares back at her and watches her turn and swing out, hears her talking to that crazy boy. Bob goes back and picks up the lamp, cradles it in his arms. "I thought you might like this Sandy, real fine piece." He hands the lamp to her and keeps his eye on Corky, who is now holding hands with that boy.

"Why Bob, how thoughtful." Sandra takes the lamp and puts it up on the counter, steps back and looks at it. "How bout some lunch for you? It's on the house!" Sandra rushes over to get a plate and silverware.

"Raincheck, got some big business going on." He puts his hat back on and looks one last time at that lamp. Corky isn't even paying any attention, isn't even trying to hear what's going on between him and Sandra and he can't hear what's going on between Corky and that boy because they're both leaning up and talking real low. "Take care of yourself, Sandra, don't work too hard."

"Now, Bob, you know what they say about all work?" Sandra giggles again. "I've never been accused of not playing enough."

"That's good, Sandra," Bob says quickly, so maybe he

can hear what's going on. He hears Corky saying that she's sorry, that it wasn't his fault she got upset and that boy is saying no, that he's sorry. Bob thinks that that boy is sorry, too, sorry as anybody can be, and he can't help but wish that Corky had said all of that to him, told him that she was sorry for all those awful things that she said. It might be that he should just give up on Corky Revels and concentrate on another woman. He could snap his fingers and have Sandra Rhodes just like that. He can hear his Mama and what she always says, "Always want what you ain't got. You get big wonders, eat rotten cucumbers."

Sam Swett watches that cop disappear around the corner. "He's sort of strange, isn't he?"

"Well, that's an understatement!" Corky laughs. "I bet you think he's like everybody else, don't you?" She is suddenly lightening up, laughing, like her whole mood has changed. "And I'm just like anybody and everybody. I'm just like Loni Anderson. I'm just like Dolly Parton." She holds back her shoulders and thrusts out her chest, her small breasts held there.

"Not quite." He shakes his head. "You're not like anybody I've ever met."

"Same for you." She reaches for his hand and holds it, even though Sandra is watching. "Let's go somewhere else. I've been here all morning."

"You've got a birthday party." He pulls his wet money back out of his pocket and unfolds it, five twenties. That boy's got a hundred dollars and didn't even know that he had it.

"Not for an hour." She stands up and stretches, takes

one of the twenties up to the cash register. "Here you go, Sandra."

"This money's wet." Sandra shakes it out and opens the drawer. "Did you see what Bob gave me?" Sandra points over to the lamp.

"Isn't that something?" Corky holds out her hand for the change and counts behind Sandra. It wouldn't be the first time that Sandra had overcharged somebody.

"I just can't get over Bob doing that for me. How did he know that I'm an old Elvis fan?" Sandra is over by that lamp now, running her finger up and down Elvis' nose.

"He must have been checking up on you." Corky crooks her finger and Sam gets up and follows her. "He must be getting up his nerve to ask you out."

"You reckon?" Now Sandra is all smiles, even smiles at Sam Swett. "You children have fun now," she calls and Corky hardly gets out the door before she starts laughing, her eyes crinkling, the pink flowing back into her face. She loops her arm through Sam's and pulls him off down Main Street.

"Do you ever feel mean?" she asks and laughs again. "I mean do you ever just feel so good deep down inside that it makes you a little mean acting?"

"I don't know if I have or not." Now Sam can't help but laugh, even though he's not certain what he's laughing about.

"Well, it's a good feeling sometimes. It feels good right here." She stops and takes his hand, puts it over her heart and he can feel the outline of her small breast underneath her uniform. "Right in my heart is where it feels good sometimes when I feel mean." She takes his hand away and he is sorry; he was just about to put his other hand up there. God, what is he thinking? He is here in the middle of this town and he's losing all sense of privacy, losing all sense.

"Do you want to go to my room?" he asks and points to the Hotel down on the corner.

"I don't think that would look so nice, now, do you?" She puts her arm back through his. "I'll show you where I live, though, if you want to see?"

"Yeah, that's fine."

"I mean, for all I know you may have a bus to catch?"

"No, not right now. I'm in no hurry." And that's true, a concrete statement. He has nothing to do and nowhere to go, at least for the time being. "I'd love to see where you live." He quickens his walk to match hers, those little feet almost skipping down Main Street.

Thomas McNair knows that his Mama is coming before he even sees her or hears her voice. He recognizes that shuffling walk, those scuffed up terry cloth slippers that she wears year round everywhere she goes. A policeman is leading her down the hall and she's going on and on with that white man about the weather. She doesn't even know when somebody's talking down to her, using that slow pronunciation that people use with children and idiots.

"Here he is," the policeman says and leads her into the room. Thomas doesn't even look up at her and she can tell by the way he's clenching his fists, tightening that jaw, that everything he said on the phone was an act, prayers in the dark. He's the same old Thomas.

"What took you so long?" he asks when she has shuffled her way over to him. She seems to have aged in just the past few weeks, gray hairs creeping from that scarf that she has rolled and tied up around her hairline like some kind of Aunt Jemima.

"I had to wait for a taxi. I work way out in the country, you know." She sits down across from him and shakes her head like he's to blame for something. "I never thought I'd have to see this."

"What? See what? Your son falsely accused of something? Accused only because I'm black?" Thomas cannot help but raise his voice; he'd like to scream, and he doesn't care who would hear him. "I don't even know what's going on!"

"The truth will come out," she says. "If you're innocent, then you've got nothing to fear."

"If! You say that like you're not sure you believe me! What if little M.L. was sitting here? What would you say if precious little M.L. was all of a sudden the token nigger accused of something?"

"I do believe you. I do." She reaches over and touches his arm but he jerks away. "I'm here, ain't I? I came as soon as you called."

"You got to help me get this mess straight." Thomas stands up and starts pacing back and forth. "Don't you see what could happen if that witness comes in here and says I'm the man? It happens, you know. Innocent people get convicted."

"You got to have faith, Thomas, cause the good Lord ain't gonna let any such wrong happen."

"Faith! That's all that ever comes out of your mouth. Tell me, Mama, where was Jesus Lord God Almighty when the black man was out in the fields? Where was he when we were sold and beat?" She won't look at him and he'd like to grab her face and make her look, make her hear what he's saying. "I know before you even say it, The Great Lord works in mysterious ways." Thomas lifts his hands to the ceiling and waits for her to respond.

"It's the truth, Thomas, and you see that I ain't been sold or beat a day in my life!" She grabs him by the arm and he lets her, because she's about to cry and because if he grabbed her arm right now he's afraid that he'd twist it until it snapped like a twig. "You listen to me, Thomas Alva McNair. You listen."

"You sell yourself every single day and that's worse! You were beat the first day that you ever went and cleaned up after that white man!" Thomas gets right in her face.

"Anybody that holds down a decent job, I don't care who they are, is selling themselves. A body's got to do what they got to do." Now she is starting to shake a little, her hands trembling, the tears coming to her eyes, making him feel guilty as hell; his whole life she's made him feel guilty. "You call me away from my work to come and be with you, and then this is what I get."

"Yeah, I reckon you'll lose about two dollars and fifty cents, huh? And let's see, what would that buy?" He rubs his chin like he's thinking, giving her time to hear every word. "That would just about buy a watermelon for you and little M.L. so you could sit out on that dirty front porch and spit seeds.

"You shut up, Thomas McNair. This don't concern M.L., and besides, I make a good salary and earn every cent of it." She picks up her purse and her paper bag and puts them on her lap. She acts like she's got such a good job out there and they don't even feed her, she probably has some old piece of side meat slapped between bread in that bag.

"Oh no, this doesn't concern little M.L., little Martin Luther McNair who's going to grow up and be some-body, probably be a doctor or a lawyer. Little M.L. who's gonna rise above it all because he's got faith and the Lord on his side and an old grandmother who thinks he's going to take care of her."

"Prayers in the dark. I should've known." She stands up and faces him. "Only time you need me is when you're aching to air out that ugly mouth of yours because you ain't got the guts to speak out to who you'd like to tell it all to." She backs up to the door. "I'm ashamed of you, and I'm not going to stand here and take it."

"Wait, wait." He goes and takes her hands in his. "Don't leave. I'll stop, I'll stop if you'll help me. For once, just help me. I'm your real son, remember."

"I don't know what you think I can do."

"I got an idea, please." He pulls her back over to the chair and though he hates to do it, he lowers his voice, he begs her. "You could call up those people that you work for, that man, Mr. Foster, he's got a lot of pull in this town, doesn't he? He can get me a lawyer, tell you somebody to get that can come down here and say it's a mistake. I don't want to spend the night here, and besides, what if this witness thinks I'm the man?"

"Lord, I can't believe my ears right this second."

"C'mon, please, it's my one chance." Thomas grips her hands tighter. "You said once that they said you were like part of the family."

"Everybody that's got themselves a housekeeper says that at one time or another." Fannie loosens her hands from his. "I'm part of that family as much as you're white. I'm part of that family as long as I'm doing what I'm supposed to be doing as an employee."

"But you could ask. Just ask them!"

"Listen to yourself, Thomas McNair, just listen to yourself. You ain't got a bit of pride, not a thread to cling to. You make fun of what I do in my life, and then turn around and you want me to go and beg to these people that you say have wronged me so. Well, I got too much pride for that, I'm proud to say."

"But it's not begging. You'd just be getting something back for all that you've given." Thomas grips her hands again.

"I get what they owe me every Friday and I don't owe them a thing and never will. That's selling yourself, Thomas."

"You don't give a damn, do you?" He shakes her and then shoves her aside. "You've never given a damn about me!"

"Tommy? I got here as soon as I could. They're not going to keep you here, are they?" Janie is waiting outside that barred door now and he is sorry that his Mama is here to see it, give her one more thing to throw up to him.

"That's my woman," he says and stares his Mama down. "Her name's Janie."

"I'm Thomas' Mama, Fannie McNair." She turns and stares back at him like he might be nothing.

"Oh, pleased to meet you. Thomas has told me so much about you!"

"Knock it off, Janie," he says and she goes back to her sniffling. "If she had been at home and in bed where she was supposed to be," he stops, giving his Mama time to react, but she's sitting there acting like she hasn't heard a word, acting like she's some kind of saint and never had a man other than his Daddy. "If she'd been there this never would've happened. She could have told them that I was at home when that man was killed."

"But, baby, how was I to know? I did it for us. I wanted to earn enough money so that you could concentrate on your studies and not the bills. And I'm getting a promotion real soon!"

"I reckon she ain't selling herself," his Mama says. "Only black folks work like dogs and sell themselves."

"What can I do, honey?" Janie asks, but he puts his head down and doesn't answer.

"I reckon the same as me," his Mama says. "We just got to wait and know that they'll sort this mess out."

"That's easy for you to say." He looks up. "It's not your goddamned black ass sitting in here."

"I'll check on you later," she says, and then calls out to

that policeman that's waiting in the hall. "I reckon your girl wants some time with you." She turns and looks back while the policeman is opening the door. "You're my child and I do love you, Thomas, whether you think so or not." She turns and walks out and does not look back a single time. He watches her shuffle down that hall, her purse swinging slowly by her side, and for a second he almost calls out to her to come back, not to leave him, but he doesn't. Right this second he hates her. He hates her for everything she's ever done, hates her for raising him with no Daddy in that old cheap room, hates her for playing along with people, playing Mama or Mammy to all those white children through the years, hates her for hovering over M.L. when she never did that for him.

Janie rushes in and squats down right in front of Thomas' chair, puts her head on his knees like some child or dog that wants its head patted.

"What the hell were you doing last night?" He asks suddenly when his mother is out of sight. Janie lifts her head and stares up at him.

"I told you, honey. I was at work."

"Why didn't you lie? Why didn't you say you got home at one?"

"Thomas, you know I can't lie to the law." She rises up on her knees and wraps her arms around his waist. "That man would've talked to Mr. Stubbs, and then you would have looked guilty."

"What do you think I look now?" He pushes her away and she lands on the floor, her legs sprawled out in front of her. For the first time all morning all those drunks in the other cells laugh and point. He hasn't even got the guts to tell them to shut up.

"Knock it off!" Janie yells and gets back on her knees. "I know, Honey, I know how horrible and hard this is."

"You don't know shit." He wants to push her again, to grab her neck and beat her curly head against that floor.

"Well I never!" she says and looks at Thomas, but he is staring out the window, his jaw clenched tightly; he isn't going to say a thing.

Janie waits a minute and finally he turns and looks at her.

"We'll talk about it all later," he says, and then glances around at all those men, especially that cop. None of them say another word. "There's a lot we need to talk about, but first I gotta get out of here."

"You're right, honey, I'm sorry. Here we are fussing and you in here with your life on the line." She hugs him around the middle and kisses his forearm. He'd like to slap her out cold but he just nods and she kisses him again, up and down his arm. She is disgusting to him right now.

"C'mon, miss, time's up," the policeman says and opens the door. "Can't let you get all worked up like that in front of all these other men, might be asking for trouble."

She looks up at Thomas and he nods. Damn right, she asks for trouble. "You go on," he says and pulls her arms from around him.

"Maybe my boss, Mr. Stubbs, can help us out?"

"He'd help you out, sure." Thomas stretches his legs

out, crosses his feet. "He's not likely to help me out. Bet he doesn't even know about me, does he?" Janie stares back at him with that stupid blank stare of hers. "Does he?"

"I told him I've got a boyfriend." She holds up one finger to the policeman so that he'll give her another second. She smiles at him even, so that he'll give her that extra second.

"Did you tell him that you've got a black boyfriend? Huh? Did you tell him that?"

"Why should I?" She steps back closer to Thomas but the cop grabs her arm and holds her there.

"Yeah," Thomas laughs, throws back his head and laughs until the tears come to his eyes. "You go tell him and see what happens."

"Tommy, I don't want to leave you like this," she screams while the cop pulls her out of the room. "I'll be back, honey. We're going to get you out of here!"

Now, Thomas watches her all the way down the hall, turning and screaming, waving and blowing kisses. At least his mother didn't make a scene. At least she just walked right out without causing any sort of ruckus. She's the one person with sense enough to get him out of this mess, and goddamn her, she isn't going to do it. He knows that it's true; he knows that there ain't any use to fight a losing battle when his own Mama ain't even going to help him; there ain't any reason to stop saying "ain't" or to try to groom himself in any way, cause it ain't gonna work, nothing's gonna change.

4

Granner is so happy to see Harold's pickup truck pull up and stop, even if he is a full hour early. Usually, she'd think what she always thinks about Harold, that he's rude and coming over early to get first dibs on the food, but today she's too glad to see him even to fuss. That damned Mr. Abdul has just about driven her crazy all morning long and that on top of that article in the paper that Ernie Stubbs set up.

"Come in, son!" Granner screams and smiles great big at Harold. The only times that Harold has ever seen her looking this happy were the few times that she has accidentally gotten lit. "I'm so happy to see you, Harold, and I've got so much to tell you."

"I got some things to tell myself." Harold goes over to the stove and takes two big brownies out of the pan, and Granner doesn't even fuss. "You been drinking a little bit, birthday girl?"

"Harold Weeks, you know better! Can't a woman be nice to the one child who ain't done her wrong on this day without being accused of something?" She sits down right beside him. He might've known that she's being all sweet to him cause she's mad at everybody else. "I want you to see what Ernie Stubbs did to me."

"Okay, but first I got to tell you." Harold swallows and wipes the brownie crumbs away from his face. The crumbs land on the floor and Granner stares down at every speck, but she still doesn't say anything. "Charles Husky was murdered down at the Quik Pik last night and I was the one that found him."

"Do tell," she says and licks her finger, bends down and dots up those crumbs. "Well, that's something, Harold; now you go over and look at what I put up on my refrigerator with magnets so that Ernie Stubbs will see that I know what he did, that is if he shows today. He might have to hit the field, play a little golf, you know."

"Mother, did you hear what I said?"

"I heard you, Harold, but I'm telling you that I've got some worries of my own, that on the refrigerator and Petie Rose, getting hit by that car, and that Mr. Abdul calling every other breath."

"Petie Rose? What happened to Petie Rose?"

"Her cat got hit by a fast little car, knocked the life right out of him, deadest thing you ever saw."

Harold takes a deep breath. His Mama scares the hell out of him, the way that she tells stories without all the words that belong in it. "Charles Husky was the deadest thing I ever saw."

"I'm sure, Harold, now go look on my refrigerator before Mr. Abdul calls me back. I want you to answer if he does, so that he'll know that I'm not some old lady all by herself, which I am most of the time."

Harold sighs and gets up and goes over to the refrigerator. "All it says is that you turn eighty-three today, what's wrong with that?"

"Look at that ad underneath it, that's what!" She creeps over and stands right behind Harold. He puts his finger up at the ad and moves it along while he reads aloud, "We take old, worn out, used up things that get in your way." He shakes his head and laughs. His mama can tickle him slam damn to death sometimes.

"It ain't funny, Harold Weeks. Kate and Ernie have got it set in their heads that I need to be in that old folks home and I ain't aiming to go!"

"Now, what does Ernie have to do with The Salvage Bin? I know he wants you to move, but he can't go making up ads for some company that's not his."

"He's got power, I tell you." Granner's eyes bead up and she points her finger right in Harold's face. "Money enough to buy out that place or to pay 'em to put that ad in under my birthday announcement."

"Ernie's crazy, but he ain't that crazy." Harold goes back to the table to finish his brownie.

"Foot if he ain't, watch those crumbs, Harold, I've slaved for a week to clean and scrub and you're already messing. Foot if he ain't crazy and rotten, it's the Injun Street coming out in him." She shakes her head from side to side, stares up at the ceiling like she's looking God square in the face, and then walks all around Harold's chair.

"What you looking for, Mama?" Harold asks, as if he doesn't know.

"Nothing, I'm probably looking for more crumbs, the way you eat like a pig."

"Your present's in the truck."

"I wasn't looking for no present." She sits down at the table and rearranges the plastic fruit in the bowl. "A truck is no place for one, though. God knows who could walk up and steal it."

"Them."

"Them? You mean I got more than one, Harold?" She breathes on that red plastic apple and wipes it on her dress.

"One from me and one from the kids." Harold tries to smile at her but he thinks of Maggie again; he thinks of Charles, and it makes him squeeze his eyes tightly and shake his head.

"Why didn't Harold, Jr., and Patricia bring it themselves?"

"I don't know if they're coming or not." Harold watches his Mama's eyes blare up and she taps her feet on the floor.

"You mean that you and Juanita ain't patched things up yet?" She shakes her finger again. "I swear Harold Weeks, you are the stubbornest man alive!"

"Stubborn? After what she did to me?" Harold gets up and gets himself a big glass of milk, drinks it halfway down. "You know what happened. You think I'm gonna just walk up and forgive her just like that?" He snaps his finger and downs the other half of the milk.

"That's what I done, Lord year back." Granner leans back in her chair, and Harold knows a story is coming. The damned trouble is that these days nobody knows what's the truth and what ain't.

"What are you talking about, Mama?" Harold sits back down.

"Talking about that time Buck got hisself mixed up with this woman that worked down at the five and dime."

"I've never heard this!" Harold can't help but feel a little impatient with her when she starts these stories.

"You were just a little baby at the time and I never wanted you to be hurt by it, just like I never want Petie Rose or this baby on the way to be hurt by the fact that their Mama and Daddy had to get married, and that Pete might not even be Petie's Daddy. Lord knows, though, you ain't protected Harold, Jr., and Patricia one pea turkey bit."

"Get on with it." Harold rolls his hand around to motion her to speed things up. He's sick of that story about Pete and Rose, whether it's true or not.

"This woman came from the bottoms, not real pretty, real plain looking." Granner makes this simple looking face and slumps her shoulders to show him what this woman looked like. "Her husband went around giving people an address for a quarter. Nobody had addresses up on their houses like we do nowadays, and this man would take a little piece of charcoal and draw you a number for a quarter, not that it meant anything of course because everybody had a post office box in them days, and if anybody was wanting to visit you they knew where you lived anyway." Granner stops and closes her eyes, holds her hands up to her head. "I remember! He wrote 509 on our house and I sort of tossed that quarter to him cause his hands were so black with charcoal. Washed away first big storm that blew, but I always said it was 509 Main Street even though really it's 1208 like what's out front now."

"Goddamn." Harold leans over and beats his forehead against the table.

"Stubborn and impatient. I won't tell you then."

"Go on, Mama," Harold says, knowing that his day will be more miserable than it already is if he doesn't go along with her.

"Anyway, this woman took to Buck and why wouldn't she, considering what she was married to herself. She come around to see me one day and said that she loved my husband and meant to have him." Granner purses her lips now and tilts her nose in the air. "I didn't say a word, didn't know if that hussy was telling a lie or what. I didn't lower myself, no sirree, I acted like a lady and I walked up to her and looked her square in the face, had to look up a little, though, because she was a big woman, much bigger than you'd have thought if you had seen a picture of just that plain simple face or had just seen her sitting behind that candy counter at the five and dime, looked like this." Granner makes the face again, rolling her eyes back in her head, her mouth dropped open in a stupid way. Harold can't help but laugh. "I said dogs will follows bitches, and she gave me that simple look like I just showed you and I never ran into her again, and neither did Buck that I know of, and when her husband come around after that big rain that washed my 509 away, I told him that he ought to be lookin after that wife of his better, and that, no, I didn't want another number to have it wash away and leave a black smudge on the side of my house."

"Well, had Daddy been messing around with her?"

"I don't know for sure to this day. All I know is that I let him know that this woman had come by and I let him know that never in my life would I put up with such tomfoolery, again or ever, just in case it had or hadn't happened."

"But I know that Juanita was with Ralph Britt, cause I saw them."

"Ralph Britt might've forced her!" Granner polishes a banana now. She wants it to look so good for Kate to see, because Kate has been ashamed of that fruit bowl her whole life. Why on earth would a child get so upset over plastic fruit, Granner'll never know, but Kate always has. Kate hates the birdbath as well; even when Granner points out to everybody a pretty little cardinal which is the bird of this state or points out a big mean blue jay, Kate still turns her nose up.

"Shit, Mama, I could put Ralph Britt in my pocket. He couldn't have forced nothing on Juanita that she didn't want forced. Juanita may be crazy as hell but she's strong."

"That's what Nautilus has done for her."

"I reckon." Harold rubs his hands through his hair. "I

wonder if she'll show her face here today. She better not, is all I've got to say."

"Selfish. Add selfish to stubborn, impatient, and rude! This is my birthday, and how do you start it but to come in here with all that depressing talk, and now wishing off three of the people on my guest list." The phone rings and Granner freezes with her eyes wide open and that banana held up to her chest. "You get it, Harold. I know it's him again."

"For God's sake, Mama." Harold pushes his chair away from the table and walks over to the phone.

"Tell him that you're living here, now. You know you could live here really, instead of that trailer." Granner creeps over to where Harold is standing, creeps closer when he picks up the receiver.

"Hello?" Granner squeezes closer and gets her head right beside Harold's. There is a pause at the other end of the line. It is just as Granner though; Mr. Abdul ain't going to talk his trash to anybody else. "Who is this?"

"Harold?" He recognizes Juanita before she even finishes his name, and he hands the phone to Granner and goes back to his chair. His Mama is standing there holding the receiver away from her. "It's Juanita," he says, and Granner tosses the banana onto the table and puts the receiver to her ear.

"You give me a scare, Juanita. I thought it was Mr. Abdul again." Granner breathes a sigh of relief and shakes her head. "How bout from now on you let it ring once and then call right back and then I'll know to answer."

Granner is listening now, nodding her head. Juanita is probably the one woman that can talk as much about crazy things as Granner. Harold opens the newspaper, what part Granner hasn't shredded all up, and pretends not to be listening. Granner says, "that was Harold, your husband, that answered," then she just nods and whispers, keeps looking over at Harold. "All right, Juanita, all right," Granner says and hangs up.

"That was Juanita." Granner points to the phone. "She had been to the Burger King. Got back and the air-conditioning unit was on the blink, doing the shimmy shake, Juanita said, making noises like a transfer truck."

"She's probably burned the damn thing slam damn up, doesn't know her ass from a hole in the ground."

"She's got a man coming over to fix it." Granner goes and peeks out the window where she can see Harold's truck. "Sure hope my present ain't something that can spoil."

"I bet that's not all that man's coming for." Harold clenches his fists and bangs them on the table. "I could fix that air myself and here she is calling in a repairman, got to spend some money." Harold? He hears her saying his name over and over. It sounded for that second like she was glad to hear him. "What else did she say? Everything in that house is probably tore up."

"Said she'd be here after a while." Granner turns from the window. "Sure hope my present ain't plastic. It'll melt out in that truck."

"Well, I ain't going to be here when she comes, I'll tell you right now." Harold puts on his cap and stands up.

"I better go get your presents." He pulls his shirt where it is sticking to his back and under his arms, where there are already large circles. "Damn, it's hot in here; I'm surprised you don't smother.

"I was thinking I might slip on my sweater." Granner follows him out on the front porch. "You might have a fever, Harold."

"I got a fever like you got three titties." He lets the screen door slam shut.

"Don't you start that talk on my birthday. I mean it. Here comes Kate and Ernie, so don't you start that ugliness." Granner is still talking when Harold climbs in the cab of the truck and sits for a minute. He's tempted to just crank it up and leave. He looks in the rearview mirror and watches Kate and Ernie get out of that car of theirs. Harold would love to get under the hood of that car, but he ain't about to ask. Somebody ought to tell Kate that she looks like shit in those rainbow shorts, and that Ernie Stubbs looks like a white-bellied gone-ass queer in those pink britches. God, talk about going from bad to worse, this day is shot to hell. Harold opens the glove compartment and pulls out a pint of gin. If he's got to be here, he might as well drink. He gets Granner's presents out of the passenger seat and goes back in. His Mama is as two-faced as that trick penny that Harold always carries around. She's going on and on about how good they both look, after all that fuss about the article in the paper, just because they've brought in this great big box all wrapped in fancy paper. Harold puts his two Woolco bags down beside it.

"Well, Harold, didn't even see you." Ernie holds out his hand.

"I saw ya'll." Harold eyes Ernie's pants and Kate's shorts. "Ya'll like those bright colors, don't you?"

"We're colorful people," Kate says, and fans herself with one of Granner's copies of *National Geographic*. "It's a little hot in here, isn't it?"

"Pleasant." Granner lifts one end of that box and lets it fall back, doesn't make a sound. "I bet I know what is in this box."

"It's something that you've been needing." Kate goes over and turns on that one window unit that Granner has.

"Yep, I sure do know what's in this big box." Granner has to bite her tongue not to say something to Ernie about what he put in the paper. He wants to bribe her is all, give her that whirlpool foot relaxer that she wants so bad. She's not going to say a word to spoil it, either. He'll know that she knows what he's up to as soon as he sees that paper up on the refrigerator, and he'll be going in there all right, because he's brought that little suitcase bar that he always totes along. "What pretty slacks you're wearing, Ernie," she says, though deep down she doesn't mean it. A woman's got to do what she has to do sometimes.

"Bet you don't know what's in those bags, Mama."

"I can't imagine, Harold."

"Sorry I didn't wrap 'em." Harold goes and sits down on the far side of the room. He's going to go mix himself a drink in about two shakes.

"Heard about the murder," Ernie says and glances at

Kate. "What were you doing down at that Quik Pik so late at night?"

"Visiting." Two shakes is up. Harold gets up and goes into the kitchen, only thing to mix with is milk or iced tea. Harold gets out the iced tea and mixes himself a strong one.

"Visiting? At that hour?" Kate picks right back up on the conversation when Harold comes back in. "Ernie was still at work."

"I work in the daytime." Harold takes a big swallow and it feels like pine needles sliding down his throat.

"So do I, just had some big business to take care of." Ernie crosses that pink leg and stares at Harold. "Heard you saw that man that did it."

"Yeah." Harold clinks the ice round and round in his glass. "Saw Charles Husky, too. You remember Charles. He was in school with ya'll, lived right up from your old house, Ernie."

"I can't place him." Kate snaps. "He must not have run around with us."

"Yessir, I know just what's in this big box." Granner pats the box and then pulls up her foot stool and sits right there in front of the present. "This is probably what Buck would have give me if he was here. Buck would be sitting right there where Harold is, probably drinking a little Postum, and he'd say, 'I swear Irene, you're just like a child at Christmastime.' That's what he'd say, all right."

"They picked up the killer," Kate says, and Ernie gives her a quick look. She's not about to let Harold know that

Ernie's secretary lives with that man. "Did you go down and identify him?"

"Nope." Harold wishes to hell they'd stop this talk.

"Nobody's sung to me, yet," Granner says. "I reckon we'll wait for the others. Ernie why don't you go get yourself something from the refrigerator? I see you brought your stuff."

"In a minute." Ernie walks over to Granner's china cabinet. "See, Kate, I knew your mother had some depression glass. It's going for a lot of money these days."

"Oh, I know. Helena Foster had gotten some exquisite pieces at an estate auction." Kate opens the door and pulls out a cobalt blue vase.

They're dying to get their hands on everything Granner's got, she knows it. "I bought that at the five and dime way back." Granner waves her hand. "Cost near bout nothing."

"It's probably worth something now," Ernie says, and holds the vase up to the light like maybe he can see it better. Granner wouldn't let him have that vase for nothing in this world, just because he wants it.

"Maybe I'll sell it, then, and redo my bathroom."

"Why on earth would you redo the bathroom, Mother?" Kate whirls around like she might have said something crazy.

"I'm thinking of a bright canary yellow. Corky suggested that, bright yellow, something cheerful."

"Oh, Granner, I wouldn't go to all of that trouble." Ernie talks to her like she might be a baby. He wants the place to run down and fall apart, just like his Mama's house did before he stripped it away and sold that land for a liquor store. Granner is fixing to say that, in spite of that present, when Pete Tyner comes running in all out of breath, dragging Petie Rose behind him. "It's time!" Pete yells, that white face a little flushed around the edges.

"Oh my, where's Rose?" Kate and Ernie run out on the porch and down to where Pete is parked on the street. "Call us first thing!" Kate screams to Rose, who nods and grips her stomach. "Won't we have something to tell tonight!" She puts her arm around Ernie and they stand out there watching, while Pete jumps back in the car and drives off. Petie Rose is standing out on the front porch pulling every gardenia that she can reach on Granner's bush, and throwing it to the floor of the porch.

"Hi Petie." Kate bends down and kisses her and Petie pulls away. "You're going to have a little brother or sister real soon."

"I want a cat," Petie says, and jumps down behind the bushes there in front of the porch.

"You stay right there now, Petie," Ernie says and unbuttons another button on his shirt. "Might be time for that drink." Kate nods and he suddenly grabs her by the arm and stops her. "Not a word about Janie Morris, you hear?"

"Goodness, Ernie, I'm not a fool." Kate pats her hair. Already the heat is getting to that natural look and her hair is going flat around her full face. "Besides, the way Harold's already drinking, he's not going to notice anything."

Granner is pacing all around the table when Harold goes in to mix himself another drink. Here it is, her birthday, and all this commotion. Lord knows, Rose waited this long for that baby, and here it is coming on her birthday. If she wasn't going to have it yesterday, she should have held on to it for one more day, or at least until later on in the afternoon when the party was almost over. They didn't even leave her a present, didn't even bring those deviled eggs and baked beans that Rose promised.

"What's your problem?" Harold asks, and takes a big swallow. "Seems to me you ain't too upset about that article in the paper."

"Ssh!" Granner hisses. "Don't you talk to me that way. You tend to your ownself, and I think you got plenty to tend to, especially with that wife of yours loose as a goose coming over here."

"The leopard has changed its damn spots!" Harold sits down at the table and opens a bag of potato chips.

"Those are for the party!"

"Well, it looks to me like the party has started."

"The party starts when I say it starts. This is my party and my birthday, and I'm the oldest one here and what I say goes!"

"Ain't going to argue that."

"Well, you best not. I'm going to go sit on that porch and wait for the other guests and don't you eat all of that food." Granner pushes past Ernie, and Harold hears her talking to Kate and then the screen door slams shut. Ernie opens his little travel bar, takes out a highball glass. "Can I fix you one of these, Harold?"

"Nah, I don't go for that strong stuff like you and Kate." Harold rolls his head back and laughs. He wishes that Ernie Stubbs would go the hell on, because he ain't interested in a thing he can say.

Sam Swett has taken in everything about Corky's room, from the corn-husk dolls, the single iron bed pushed up near the window, a faded quilt folded over the bed, the table set for two to the little glass bottles that she has in her kitchen area, each bottle with something different, macaroni, tea bags, dried beans, rice. He sits down on the bed and leans up against the window frame. He can see the hotel from here, cars passing on Main Street, the glare of the heat, but it feels cool here, the ivy around the window, the shade of the big tree out front. The shower stops running and he looks toward the door of the small bathroom, which she will open any minute now. It's comfortable here, smells old for some reason, cool and old and comfortable.

"I feel much better!" Corky steps out, her hair wrapped up in a towel, her body in a thin cotton robe. "You want to take another shower?" She looks over at him and he shakes his head. He watches her undo the towel and drop it to the floor, then she leans her head back and starts combing through her hair.

"This is a nice place," he says, and watches her take the end of her comb and form a perfect part. She doesn't even use a mirror.

"I like it, you know, it's not much but I like it."

"You have a nice view." He turns back around and

looks out the window. "You could even climb out on the roof and sit."

"I've done that before." Now she is sitting beside him and he can smell the shampoo, her hair squeaking when she combs it. "You know sometimes at night when there's a breeze, I sit out there. It's sort of peaceful." She leans right beside him and looks out the window. "Some nights I can see people in the hotel, you know, just the shadows of people behind the shades." She shrugs and turns to look at him. "It's sort of scary to do that."

"Why? I like it. I used to sit out on my fire escape in New York and do the same thing." Corky tries to get a picture of this but it is difficult to imagine. "It's sort of like what I was saying earlier about observing people, just sitting back like a fly on the wall and observing."

"Yeah, I see what you mean." She sits back now and leans against the window so that she is facing him. "But still, it makes me think that somebody might be watching me. I feel like that sometimes, like somebody's watching me, somebody big and powerful, and it's not like thinking about God, you know, it's something different from that."

"Like aliens?" He leans close to her, wanting to kiss her, but she turns her head away, props her chin in her elbow. At that angle, with her arm propped on the window sill, her robe hangs loosely on one shoulder, tiny freckles on that shoulder.

"No, not aliens, but maybe something like that, maybe this great big feeling, you know?"

"Yeah, yeah, I think I do." He nods and backs up, studies her profile again with a feeling of for some reason wanting to always remember it, the freckled nose, the full lips. "I think it's fear."

"What?" She suddenly turns like he had just awakened her or snapped her away from some thought.

"Fear. I think that when I get that feeling, it must be fear."

"What are you afraid of?" She laughs now and reaches her arms straight up, makes a weeeooooooo spaceship noise. "Aliens?"

"I think I'm more afraid of things right here." He rubs his hands over his head, wishing so much that he had his hair, that he looked his best.

"Like death?" she asks, those large gray eyes widening, not blinking. "Like feeling like you might die at any given second?" She stares at him now, leans closer.

"Yeah, something like that."

"Scared of other people, maybe. People who might make you hear things you don't want to hear?" Again she stares away. "Scared of losing someone or something that means everything to you?" Her voice trails off lingering into the soft hum of the fan that she has over on the table. He feels that sudden sense of fear now, as though she had taken every thought from his head. "Scared of, of losing," she turns around, her voice almost a whisper, "of losing your hair?" She quickly rubs her hands over his head and laughs, stops with her hands locked behind his neck.

"I'm not scared right now," he says and slowly reaches his arms around her waist. "Are you?"

She leans forward and kisses him on the nose, presses her cheek against his forehead and he is staring right into that throat, can almost see the pulse there. "I'm afraid of what Granner will say if I'm late." She sits back, her pulse hidden. "I'm sorry, but I've really got to go."

"Yeah, I understand." He slumps back and she watches him, those hound dog eyes. He looks at this minute as lonely as she often feels.

"You know it could be just plain lonesome," she says, and gets up. She opens the small chest of drawers and pulls out some cut-off jeans and a light blue tee shirt. Then she opens the top drawer and quickly pulls out underwear and a bra and tucks them between the shirt and the shorts.

"What's that?"

"The clothes?" She holds them up and walks off toward the bathroom.

"No, what could be lonesome?" He gets up from the bed and follows her.

"That feeling, the feeling that we both get." He follows closer and then she shuts the door. "Hey, Sam."

"Yeah?" He presses his ear up against the door.

"Do you want to go with me?"

"Would it be okay?" He feels a sudden rush, like it's his first date, his birthday, Christmas. "I mean, I don't want to intrude."

"You won't be." She opens the door and walks out, pulls a pair of old tennis shoes from under a chair and puts them on. "It's sort of a family thing."

"I thought you didn't have a family."

"Well, sort of my adopted family. We are related, though. Granner is my great-aunt, but I never knew her before I moved here." She laces her shoes, pulling the strings tightly, the ends of her hair drying in light wisps around her shoulders. "You met Harold and he'll be there."

"I'd love to if it's really okay." He reaches out his hand and pulls her up. He would like to pull her closer, to press his face against her neck. His legs feel like rubber, as if she has removed all fear, as if he is losing control.

"Sure, it's fine!" She steps away, pulling him by the hand. "You're not scared, are you?" She laughs again, that mood of a little earlier returning, like she might start skipping at any second.

"I just wish I had some different clothes, you know? Some hair."

"You look fine." She pushes him back and stares him up and down, the dirty tennis shoes, that old green shirt, the wornout jeans. "We can say you just had brain surgery or something, and they gave you that shirt as a souvenir." She pulls him into the hall and locks the door. "That didn't happen, did it?"

"No." He follows her down the dark stairwell. "I just wanted to be different, that's all. You know, I was afraid of being like everybody else."

"Oh yeah, well, you look different all right." They go out on the front porch and it is so bright that it makes Corky squint, that flicker of heat above the hot tar pavement. They walk down the sidewalk, both of them stepping over the cracks in the warped old cement. It is cooler once they get past the far end of Main Street and have the big shade trees to line the sidewalk. "How long you guess you'll stay?" she finally asks.

"I don't know." He squeezes her hand. "I just don't know."

"You want to eat dinner with me?" She doesn't even look at him or give him time to answer. "I promised that I'd watch M.L. McNair a little while tonight but he's six and you know he'll watch T.V. or something. We could eat late. I like to eat late because it's not so hot then."

"Okay."

"Huh?" She goes to the edge of the street and walks on the curbing, her hair down around her face while she watches her feet.

"I'd like that," he says, now simply trying to remember just that little bit ago when he was sitting so close to her, the profile when she was leaning against the window. He would like that very much.

Harold spots that yellow Toyota from a block away and gets up to go fix himself another drink before the others see her coming. Kate and Ernie may as well have stayed at home, the way that they talk among themselves about this person or that hotsy totsy. It makes Harold sick and it makes him even sicker when he peeks out the kitchen window and sees Juanita standing there in those tight terry cloth shorts and that bushy hair flying every which way. What the hell if she stays or if she doesn't? Juanita opens the trunk of the car and pulls out this great big box all wrapped up in bright paper, probably last week's Sunday comic section. That's what Juanita always does, even at Christmas, she wraps things up in newspaper and puts big red bows on top. She says it's for the paper shortage, but he knows she does it cause she thinks it's cute. Juanita Suggs always has thought that she was cute, and the damn shame of it is that she is, everything about her is cute. Juanita Suggs can even thump her chest and burp great big like a man after she's had some Coca Cola or beer, and even that's cute. Harold takes another big swallow and decides he'll just stroll on out there. After all, he ain't got a thing to be ashamed of.

"Hi Harold," Juanita says as soon as he gets out that screen door, and all of them, even Kate and Ernie, shut up and wait to see what he's going to do. Hell if he's gonna let them get any satisfaction out of this.

"Getting that way," he says, and rubs his hand over Harold, Jr.'s, head, acts like he's gonna sock Patricia in the stomach, and sits down.

"Huh?" Juanita looks at the others and rolls that curly head from side to side. "Oh hi, like high. I get it."

"Oh Mother," Patricia says and goes and sits near about on top of Harold. Juanita would think that she'd say "Oh Daddy," with him sitting there getting crocked. But no, it's all her fault, and she's paying too high a price for that little accidental happening with Ralph Britt.

"Happy Birthday, Granner!" Juanita yells and puts that present down in front of Granner. "This is from me and the kids."

"I got a present for her from the kids already!"

"All right, then this ain't from the kids. It's from me."

Juanita sits down right there on the porch, one leg tucked up under the other. She does just what she damn well pleases when she damn well pleases.

"What you got in there, big slab of meat? The W-D brand?"

"Harold, you hush up and look at this fine big present that Juanita has brought, wrapped, too." Granner thumps that box and then sits back in her rocking chair. "That's cute, the way that Juanita always wraps with the funny papers, isn't it?" Granner looks over at Kate and Ernie, and Kate gets that strained, exasperated look that Granner hates so in her but loves to see her do.

"Yes, cute," Kate says.

"Probably got a big batch of pork chops in that box." Harold swirls his glass, tips his cap and then pulls it forward on his head. "Probably got them special cut in that back room."

"Please now, Harold!" Juanita glances at the children and then stares at Harold. Harold, Jr., is getting down in those bushes with Petie Rose to look for roly-polies or some kind of bug, but Patricia is taking in every word.

"Probably got Ralph Waldo Emerson Britt to cut them for you." Harold laughs and stomps his foot. "Or maybe you just thought you got some pork chops, maybe you just thought all of that and there ain't nothing inside of that box." Harold is on a roll now. "I reckon Ralph Waldo Emerson Britt has to slip into Harold, Jr.'s, pajamas when he comes over cause he's such a teeny little thing."

"I don't have to stand for this!" Juanita looks at Granner

as if she might say something, but Granner's too busy fiddling with that present.

"Then just keep your seat." Harold waves his hand at her. "I believe Juanita likes teeny little things."

"I have never in my life!" Kate twists around in that swing. "Of all the disgusting things."

"It was disgusting!" Harold takes off his cap and puts it on Patricia's head. "It was so disgusting when I found Juanita back in that meat room."

"Harold!" Juanita's face is fiery red now, just the way he likes to see it.

"You both make me sick!" Patricia throws Harold's cap to the floor and runs inside.

"Now you see what you've done," Juanita hisses. "I never should have come over here but, no, I thought maybe you could act decent. I wanted the kids to come and I wanted them to see that I wouldn't miss Granner's birthday, either."

"Thank you, Juanita." Granner leans forward. "Will you get the phone the next time that it rings and tell Mr. Abdul that I'm not home? Kate answered a little bit ago and she didn't tell him what I asked her to." Granner glances over at Kate and Ernie. "I do like this comic strip paper; by the way, did you see today's paper with my birthday greeting?"

"No, I didn't, must've missed it." Ernie says, and Granner just looks over at him and laughs, winks and laughs, to show that she ain't a fool.

"Mother, I told you that those were children playing

on the phone. That's probably what's been going on the whole time to confuse her," Kate says, mostly to everyone but Granner.

"Mr. Abdul pulled one over on you, Kate." Granner nods her head and pushes off the floor to get a good rock going. "He's a sly one, foreigners are, you know."

"I'll answer it next time," Juanita says and moves over to where she's sitting on the top step. "What are you two finding down there?"

"Petie found a granddaddy longleg," Harold, Jr., yells. He looks so happy down there in the dirt, and Juanita is so glad to see him having a little fun. All it took to make him happy was to have his drunk Daddy rub his head. God, she wishes she could get down there in the dirt with the bugs and spiders, and it would make her feel that good.

"That's good, honey." Juanita is thinking that she ought to go inside and see if Patricia will talk to her, but she thinks she should let her calm down a little bit. The phone rings and it gives Juanita a good reason to get up and leave, except for the fact that Granner is right on her heels with Kate right behind her. "Hello?" Juanita holds the phone close and she can hear some children laughing in the background. "Is your refrigerator running?" that little voice says, and Juanita just laughs. "Mr. Abdul, we're tired of this and we've got this number tapped. Right this minute the policemen are coming to get you, and believe me, they'll catch you a hell of a lot easier than I'd catch a refrigerator." Juanita stands there twisting that cord around and around, even though those children have hung up. "I'm telling you, Mr. Abdul, Granner don't want to date a foreigner."

"Oh be serious!" Kate says and goes into the kitchen.

"Okay, you do the same, Mr. Abdul, as long as it's elsewhere and you're not calling here every breath. I'm telling you that we'll have you arrested." Juanita hangs up the phone. "Now, Granner, I bet he won't call back another time."

"Thank you, ma'am," Granner says, and hugs Juanita. "At least somebody believes me," she yells, so that Kate can hear her. Granner goes and gets her other presents and carries them onto the porch so that she'll be right ready for the opening as soon as Corky gets here. Juanita goes into the kitchen to get herself some iced tea.

"Thanks a lot," Kate says. "Here I am trying to keep my mother on course, and you, what do you do but play along with her?"

"I just did what I thought might help." Juanita opens the refrigerator and gets the jug of iced tea. There's only a little bit left, which means that Harold has just about had the rest of it. Juanita's got enough on her mind without having to deal with Kate. "I like those shorts. Did you get them at J.C. Penney's?"

"No, these are designer's. I drove all the way to South Cross to buy these and several other things."

"I wish I'd known, because they've got some here in town that look just like them, same cloth and everything." Juanita sits down and massages the back of her thigh, tight as a drum that muscle is. "I started to buy me some, but plaid makes me look big around the hips."

"I rarely go to Penney's. It's always so crowded and you can't get anybody to wait on you." Kate leans back in her chair. "I enjoy getting out of town once in a while, too."

"I buy most of my things at Penney's. Some people just don't have the time or money to go shopping all over creation." Juanita leans forward and props her elbows on the table. "Sometimes I find cute things at Woolco. They have cute shorts and tops, and I love to walk around and help myself."

"Unless you're at the grocery store."

"That's not fair, Kate." Juanita sits back, and now she feels her face getting warm. She knew Kate must have heard all about it, but she never thought that she would bring it up.

"Well, it's not fair for you to sit there and make fun of me, make me feel like it's some kind of sin that I can afford to shop somewhere besides Penney's."

"I never said that," Juanita says, and is about to ask Kate just what all she's heard, what all those women out in Cape Fear Trace are saying about her, but Patricia walks in.

"Could I talk to you, Aunt Kate?" Patricia stands there slump shouldered and does not look at Juanita once. "Alone?" Juanita starts to say something again, but decides to leave well enough alone. She stops at the door and is about to tell Patricia that she's sorry, about to tell Kate that's she's sorry, but Patricia is waiting for her to leave. She goes back out on the porch right when Corky Revels is walking up. Corky is a cute little thing, but that boy that she's with is a sight. Juanita smiles and speaks, though, because she's friendly to most everyone.

"Hey, Buddy," Harold says, and lifts his hand to that boy. "Thought you would have caught yourself a bus by now." The boy just shakes his head and looks at Corky, shifts around from one foot to the other.

"Everybody, this is Sam Swett," Corky says and pulls him up on the porch. She takes an envelope that's all folded up in her back pocket and hands it to Granner.

"My, what you reckon this is?" Granner asks and drops it on top of that big box that Kate and Ernie brought. It's the biggest and the prettiest in Granner's opinion, even though Juanita's paper is cute. Harold Weeks either didn't care enough or didn't have sense enough to even wrap his.

"His Daddy's a Shriner over in South Cross. You know that area, don't you, Ernie?" Harold pulls some Red Man out of his pocket and puts a little in his jaw. It's a fine art to be able to chew and drink at the same time, learned it when he used to be in the softball league. It makes Juanita sick to her stomach to see him do it, which is why he is doing it. She looks over at him and he makes sure she sees a little of his chew before he takes a big swallow.

"Nice area." Ernie nods his head and stretches his arms out over the back of the swing. "Kate and I have thought of retiring there."

"Thought you just now retired out in Piney Swamp or whatever it is." Granner says, but she can't bear to take her eyes off of those gifts. She just can't wait any more.

Ernie chuckles and shakes his head back and forth,

looks at Sam Swett. "It's called Cape Fear Trace, fairly new neighborhood, outside of the city limits."

"Except it's really called Piney Swamp, Snot Face Trace." Harold spits a straight line over the bannister, and Petie Rose and Harold, Jr., both come scrambling from behind those bushes with their hands held over their heads. It makes Harold laugh till he could split wide open.

"Have you ever thought of using a can or something?" Juanita asks. "Instead of spitting out in the yard, spitting on the children?"

"Does a deer wear a brassiere?" Harold stands up and holds onto the bannister, leans over so he can see Harold, Jr., down on all fours near the dogwood tree. "How bout if I spit off to this other side?"

"Good!" Harold, Jr., says and lifts his leg like he's a dog pissing on that tree. It tickles Harold so, got him to do that when he was just a tiny boy and he still remembers. Harold sits back down and looks at Ernie and starts laughing again. "Cape Fear Trace. Shit by another name smells like shit."

"Watch it, Harold," Granner says, but now she is focusing on that boy with Corky; he looks like he might be foreign, with that head shaved. "Where did you say that you're from?"

"He's from South Cross, Mama, where've you been? Been daydreaming of Mr. Abdul?"

"I asked him, Harold, not you." She looks him up and down. He's a sight, and Corky such a cute girl. His head makes her right sick to her stomach, reminds her of a rotten coconut, probably won't be able to eat a bite of that coconut cake she worked so hard on.

"South Cross."

"Ever been out of this country?"

"I went to Europe when I was in high school." He is twisting one foot around and around. It makes him nervous for everybody to look at him this way.

"Did you hear that, Ernie? A Mason that's been to Europe, you never been to Europe, now have you?"

"Not yet." Ernie stretches his arms. "We're planning to go real soon."

"Do you use the telephone right regular?" Granner asks, and he can't bear to look at that old woman. She looks wild-eyed, looks like she could fall over dead any minute. He shakes his head.

"So do you golf?" Ernie asks before Granner can ask her next question. "I may have met your old man before. I know a lot of people over in South Cross." That boy just shakes his head, and that aggravates Ernie so when he's trying to make connections. "What does your Daddy do?"

"He's in textiles."

"How do you like them apples, Ernie, a mill worker who's a Shriner? Sounds to me like I ought to retire in South Cross, sounds to me like I'd fit in better." Harold spits off the side of the porch.

Sam Swett grabs hold of Corky's arm and clings to it, his hand lightly cupped around her elbow. It has always bothered him for people to ask him questions, even when he was in college and went around to some fraternity houses they asked that same kind of question about what does your Daddy do, where did you go to high school, as if that mattered, as if those things would make him a different person. What bothers him most is that there were times when he did want to fit in, even though he didn't really have anything in common, even though it would have been a lie. "My Dad's a neurosurgeon," he had said at one of those places, and he didn't belong there; it seems that he doesn't belong here. His Daddy was a mill worker, a mill worker that worked himself like a dog and got way on up, making good money so that Sam could have everything that his parents never did, Europe, college, a car, graduate school if he decided to go back, but not the kind of money the man in the pink pants is talking about. Sam Swett is not blue collar or white collar; he is the product of hard-working people who want him to have the best of everything, to do everything that they've never done. Why did they do that? Why have they settled for such a life that revolves so around him, worked all those years so that he would have all these decisions to make that are so difficult to make? "Where are you going to apply for school?" they had asked. "If you could have a car," his father had said, looked across the table at his mother. "I said 'if' now, we're talking wishes. What color would you want?" Why did they do that to him, even now, "What are you doing, Sam?" Why is it important to them what he decides to do? What if he never decides what to do, what then? What if he can't decide?

"That boy can drink some, too." Harold points at Sam and it makes him jump, clutch Corky's arm tighter. "Drinks like a fish, can't hold it worth a damn, but you sure do try, don't you, boy?"

Sam starts to tell him that he doesn't do that all the time, but he just nods. He feels like he's been pinned up on the wall for everyone to pick at and question, the outsider, and this is what he's been saying that he wants, but not this way. He wants to be the one that sums everyone else up, to be the observer, not the one that's being observed. And the strange part is that it's because they do belong and do fit in that they can do this to him, make him feel so self-conscious and unsure of himself. They're not giving him a fucking chance.

"So maybe you've met your match." Juanita stands up and stretches, those little shorts riding way up on her thigh. She acts like she doesn't know they're riding but she does, and Harold sees Ernie Stubbs looking. It always has burned Harold slam damn up the way that Ernie Stubbs looks at Juanita when he gets the chance. "It's time to get this party rolling. I'm going to go get Patricia and Kate."

"Please do," Granner says, because she is sick and tired of all this chitchat, chitchat that don't involve her, and on her birthday.

"Juanita, you look great," Corky says. "You have really gotten yourself into shape."

"It's Nautilus." Juanita takes her thumbs and pulls down the back of her shorts. "That and swimming at the YMCA."

"Probably getting some other kind of exercise, too," Harold says, and stares at her.

"Corky, if you like I'll take you in as my guest one day and see if you like it."

"I'd like it if my guests would come on out and have my party," Granner says, but it's no use. Now, they're starting up again. It makes her sick, sick as a dog, too, when she sees that boy's head and him clinging hold of little Corky like he might be blind.

"The only problem," Juanita continues, "is that sometimes it gets crowded and there're some people in there like Al Taylor, do you know him?" Corky shakes her head and Juanita has to speed up, because she knows that she is getting Harold's goat with the very mention of Al Taylor. "Al Taylor smells something awful when he's done. I don't know if it's his feet or what, and I can't stand to be by him when he does this cross chest exercise." Juanita puts her hand up to her chest and laughs, leans closer to Corky to whisper. "He poots every time that he pulls those weights down." Juanita holds her hand straight up. "I swear he does, and I'll bet that's why he lets himself his feet or whatever get so stinky, so maybe he can hide the fact of what he does during his workout." Sam Swett cannot help but laugh at this, and so Corky laughs, too. She was afraid to laugh at first, afraid that he might think she's a nasty person, but he's laughing all right, those big dark eyes watering up a little and this little wheezing laugh coming through his shut lips like that Precious Pup on the cartoons.

"That's a lie, Juanita." Harold pushes his cap back on his head, takes a big swallow, the drops of water on the outside of his glass dripping all over the front of his shirt. "Men don't poot anyway. Men fart and all you women like to say 'poot' cause it sounds cute and ladylike, but I'll tell you, Juanita Suggs, that women fart, too!"

"Thank you for that testimony!" Juanita leans up against the doorway and her face is red as can be, but she can't help laughing. Lord, she tries to catch her breath, but everytime she looks at Corky and that Sam boy doubled over on that top step, she can't hold it back, and there's Harold leaned back in his chair like he hadn't said one word that was funny.

"That is disgusting." Ernie switches his leg crossing, and that makes Harold laugh. It looked like four legs crossing, like an octopus in pink tight tights.

"We all know you're a pooter, Ernie," Harold says. "You look like that's what you are, but we all know better. People out in Piney Swamp like to act like they never have cut one, but everybody knows that somebody from Injun Street grew up doing it as entertainment." Juanita cannot control herself now, though she should, because she knows that Harold is working his way around to her and that won't be funny. "Your Mama probably cut holes in your pockets so you'd have something to play with."

"I've heard that before," Sam Swett yells and laughs again. He is losing control, trying to fit in for some reason.

"You heard it from down this way," Harold says. "Ernie's Mama invented it."

"I know one." Sam Swett cannot believe he is doing this, cannot believe that he is suddenly having fun. "My Uncle Larry told somebody that they were so ugly that their Mama had to tie pork chops around their neck to get the dogs to play with them." He laughs again, but no one else does; Corky giggles a little and nods, but Harold just spits over the railing.

"I've heard that, too," Corky says and laughs. "It is funny." She is embarrassed for him, though he doesn't seem to notice, doesn't seem to be embarrassed.

"That's so old that when Columbus told it to the Indians they shot him," Harold says, again without laughing. "But it is funny." He looks over at Sam and nods. "Ernie's Mama did that, too, and that's why I'm not laughing now. I was there when it happened."

"I'm sick and tired of all this." Granner stands up and puts her hands on her hips. "Why don't you all just go on, go on and have a ball. Don't let me and my party keep you from having a ball."

"Juanita will probably do just that later on." Harold gets up and dumps the remaining ice from his glass, and doesn't even look at Juanita. She has got herself collected now, and is ready to go inside before Harold jumps on her.

"I'm sorry, Granner." Juanita pats that old woman on the back and can feel every bone of her spine sticking up like a railroad track. "We just got carried away. I'll go on in and get them."

"Don't take much to get you carried away, now does it?" Harold laughs great big and so does Sam Swett until Corky nudges him. He didn't know what he was laughing at, anyway.

Juanita gets to the kitchen door and just stops off to one side. Patricia has her head down on that table and she is crying her heart out. "I know you don't like us," she blubbers. "But I can't help it, Aunt Kate. I can't help it."

"I know that." Kate rubs her hand over Patricia's hair and down her back. "I felt the same way when I was growing up."

"You did?" Now Patricia has sat straight up, and Juanita backs up a speck more.

"Sure." Kate nods and looks a way that Juanita has never seen before, looks like she might cry.

"I knew that I wanted more! I knew that I was going to be somebody with nothing to shame." Kate has her fists clenched now like she might be getting ready to give a speech. Now she looks more like herself. "I didn't want to spend my life in some small rundown house or trailer park. I didn't want to buy all of my clothes at Penney's. I didn't want other people acting like they were better than me!"

"That's how I feel," Patricia sniffs. "My mother buys all of my things at Penney's and she tells people! She told a friend of mine one day about the cute summer tops at Woolco! Woolco! and I could've died. Nobody goes to Woolco and my mother doesn't understand, she says there is nothing wrong with buying clothes at Woolco."

Patricia puts her head back down. "I can see why ya'll don't like us. I can see but I can't help it. I can't help all that talk going around about my mother and father. They hate me or they wouldn't do this to me!"

"I know how you feel."

"And then she wonders why I don't want to have a pajama party!" Patricia wails. "I'm lucky that I even get invited to one, and then what about when I have a steady boyfriend, I think I've almost got a steady, but what do I do when he wants to come over and he sees those loud colors in our living room, a red couch!"

"Well I never knew that ya'll had a red couch." Kate shakes her head. "Of course, I haven't been by your house in years."

"Yes! We have a red couch and bright blue walls and then these two chairs that don't match anything, a big olive green lazy boy with a split down the side and this blue and white flowered chair!"

"Oh my, my." Kate shakes her head and gets this pained look on her face. "What kind of lamps do you have?"

"Just plain wooden ones." Patricia shakes her head. "I'm sorry, Aunt Kate, I didn't mean to tell all of this but I, I just wanted you to know that I'm not that way."

"Oh I believe you." Kate rubs her hand up and down Patricia's back. "You can always talk to me, honey, really. I'll do what I can to help you."

"You will?" Patricia asks, and Kate tries to figure out what to say next.

Juanita is leaning flush against the wall now, her eyes clenched tightly to keep the tears back. Here she's been thinking that Patricia was upset about that rumor and with good reason, but it's not that at all. Patricia is ashamed of her, ashamed of her own mother, ashamed of their home. Juanita thought that girls wanted to be like their mothers, but hers is just the opposite. Patricia hates her and Juanita feels like she has been slapped square in the face. She holds her finger up to her lips when she sees Harold coming in with his empty glass but he just keeps walking. "What you doing, Juanita? Spying?"

"No, I was just coming in to get Kate and Patricia." She wipes her eyes and steps into the kitchen. "Are you all ready? Granner is about to bust to open those gifts!" Juanita makes herself laugh but can't bear to look at Patricia or Kate.

"Well hell, you come in hours ago. Mama sent me in to see what had happened." Harold looks around at all three of them, and damned if those aren't three kinds of strange faces.

"Well, I did have to be excused," Juanita says and smiles again. She watches Harold mix himself another drink and she hopes that he won't say anything about anything at this point. "Let's go." She turns and hurries out where Granner is waiting, the Woolco bags and Corky's envelope on her lap. She goes and sits on the bannister by the chair where Harold has been sitting, and stares out where Petie Rose and Harold, Jr., have drawn all kinds of pictures on the driveway. Now Harold, Jr., is sitting up in that dogwood tree and Petie Rose is under the tree barking. "Look at me, Mama!" he yells and she smiles back at him. In probably no time at all he'll start up being ashamed of her, and she can't bear to think about it. She has never felt so let down in her whole life.

"Time to sing!" Corky yells when Harold steps out followed by Kate and Patricia. Harold, Jr., comes sliding down out of that tree and he and Petie come up and sit on the floor right in front of Granner. Juanita thinks that she can't bear it if Patricia goes and sits in that swing with Kate and Ernie, but she doesn't. She goes behind the swing and to the far end of the porch and hops up on the bannister, hidden from Juanita by the long line of posts. "Happy birthday dear Granner." Harold eyes Juanita before sitting back in his chair, and it looks to him like she wants to smile at him; it looks to him like Juanita might bust out crying at any minute; it looks to him like he couldn't get a fight out of that woman right now with anything, her face a little sickly looking and those blue eyes as cloudy and sad as Maggie Husky's had been. "Happy birthday to you!"

"Wait a minute!" Corky holds up her hands. "Where are Rose and Pete?"

"Gone to get Petie a little brother or sister." Kate leans over the swing and nods at Petie. "Right, honey?" Petie Rose just looks at her grandmother and goes right back to picking the scab on her knee. "Oh, I hope it's another little girl just like my Petie."

"That's great," Juanita says, and looks at Kate. "I'll never in my life forget the day that Patricia was born. It was the happiest day of my life." She looks at Patricia and Patricia glares back.

"What about me?" Harold, Jr., looks up.

"I was happy both those days just to see that neither of you was deformed or retarded."

Harold looks at Juanita and grins. "Your Mama was happy, cause being so full and round didn't set well with her free and easy lifestyle."

"Honey, I was happy the day that you were born as well," Juanita says. "Those were the two happiest days of my life to have such fine babies."

"Sure hope this baby ain't retarded." Granner holds up the envelope from Corky. "Let's see what this is."

"Mother, that's a horrible thing to say!" Kate glances down at Petie and then back to her mother. Her mother has no couth whatsoever; senile or not, it's no excuse.

"Corky knows I didn't mean that in a ugly way; we all know she can't afford much, right, Corky?" Corky nods, and then turns her head away from Sam Swett. She wishes she could grab that envelope and rip it up right now before everybody hears.

"I was talking about what you said about the b-a-b-y," Kate says, and looks at Ernie and nods.

"My whole life you have corrected me, Kate Weeks Stubbs, or rather your whole life. All I said is that I hope that child ain't bad off, and I don't think there's a thing wrong with that. You can't go around with your head in high cotton acting like things don't happen, cause they do." Granner points her finger past Sam Swett and on down the street. "Myra Henshaw who used to live over there had herself a mongoloid child. I'm telling you it happens."

"It was the way you, oh, forget it, just forget it." Kate

shakes her head and twists around in that swing. If she keeps that up, with it making all that noise, it's gonna break, Granner's sure.

"Mrs. Henshaw lives in the new highrise." Ernie puts his arm around Kate and pats her shoulder. She has a harder time putting up with her family than he does.

"That's what having children like that will do." Granner opens the envelope. "It's a wonder I've held onto my sense, the way that my children treat me sometimes, but I have." Now Granner is talking to Sam Swett and he is taking in every word. "This here is from Corky, now listen." Granner opens up the piece of paper and reads, "I Corky Revels am at your service for fifty hours of chores and errands."

"What a nice present!" Juanita squeals and winks at Corky. "I sure wish I'd get a present like that."

"Thank you, Corky. That's a fine present and I'm gonna take you up on it when I redo my bathroom." Granner eyes Kate and Ernie and smiles great big. "Have you ever heard of anything so nice?" She looks around and waits for everybody to nod, even that boy with the rotten coconut head. If he's a friend of Corky's, she reckons she can stand him. And there, that's enough fuss over that gift, and she can move on to the next without hurting Corky's feelings.

"I do windows, too," Corky says and everybody kind of laughs. Granner laughs, too, and she wishes she could spend a speck more time raving over Corky's gift, cause that girl is starved for attention, but she knows that if she doesn't get on with it, she will never get all these gifts opened without another interruption.

"Those are from me and the kids," Harold says when she picks up the Woolco bags. God, Juanita hates to see those bags, cause she knows that Patricia is probably about to crawl under the porch. Never in her life is Juanita going to say Woolco if she can help it, at least not in front of Patricia. Granner shuts her eyes and sticks her hand down in the first bag.

"Foaming milk bath," she says. "And a gallon of it. Well sir, I'm fixed up." She takes off the lid and smells. It's strong smelling and she bets will keep her tub clean, it smells so strong. "That's nice Harold, Harold, Jr., and Patricia. Here," she hands the bottle to Harold, Jr. "Take that over and let Kate and Ernie smell it. I want them to smell it."

"That isn't necessary, mother," Kate says, but Harold, Jr., is already standing there holding that huge jug out in front of her face.

"Bring it back, Harold, Jr. Seal it up and put it right here by my chair." Granner sticks her hand down in the other bag. "There's more than one thing in here!" she says and pulls out some fuzzy socks, a pack of three pairs that are striped in cotton candy colors. "My feet sure won't get cold in these, bet Patricia picked these out, didn't you?" Everyone looks at Patricia and she just smiles this sort of sick smile and turns red. It makes Juanita ache inside to see that face. Granner reaches back into the bag and pulls out a mini-flashlight. She looks at it, turns it off and on. "Well, this is cute." She puts it beside the milk bath and socks and reaches again.

"That's in case you got to get up late at night and can't see," Harold says. "You know if you got to tee tee, ain't that what women do? tee tee?" He stares at Juanita and laughs great big, dumps the leftover ice again. He's gonna go in for a refill as soon as the opening is over. He's feeling much better than he did earlier, that's for damn sure.

"This is the last one." Granner pulls out some cologne. "This is called Tigress." She opens it and smells. It's more powerful smelling than that milk bath, could kill every weed in her garden. "Take this over and have Kate smell it." Granner hands the bottle to Harold, Jr., and he walks over to the swing with it. Kate bends forward but holds her breath; God, she hasn't heard of Tigress in years. She didn't even know they still made that stuff. It's simply awful. She leans back in the swing and nods to Granner. "You smell it, Ernie. Put a little on your wrist to get the effect."

"Oh, I wouldn't want to waste your cologne." Ernie sniffs the bottle and sits back. Come to think of it, that does smell familiar, that may be what Janie Morris was wearing that he recognized last night, and where would he have recognized it before that? Certainly not at a cocktail party. Harold, Jr., carries the bottle back over and sits back down.

"Awful, isn't it?" Kate whispers and he nods. "I remember that time you bought me some, remember?" She giggles and clutches his arm. That's what it was. He had liked the way that it smelled, and then Kate had told him that that was not good stuff at all. Kate had given it to the maid because she had said that the maid would probably like it. He had learned since which were good colognes and which were not, but why did he think that one that was not smelled enticing? Maybe that's what had made him want to nuzzle into Janie Morris, Tigress. He can't tell one good cologne from one cheap one unless he has the price tag there in front of him. He learned a long time ago that if you buy the most expensive thing, then you're getting the best.

"Open ours, mother," Kate says, and Granner pulls it over in front of her. She had planned to open theirs last, so that nobody else would feel put out to have to come after the best one. Still, she may as well go ahead with it now. Granner carefully tears away the paper, trying not to tear it cause there's enough pretty paper there to wrap at least a dozen small presents. Still, she can hardly wait. She folds that paper and puts it under her chair and starts pulling open the box. "I got to say that I know what this is and it's just what I've been wanting." Granner pulls the box open and slowly starts pulling away the tissue paper on top. Never has she been so put out in her whole life. She pulls out a pink robe and holds it up for everyone to see. "Ain't this something?"

"That's not all, mother." Kate gets out of the swing and takes the robe from her mother, holds it up against her own chest. "This is a Gucci. Did you see it, Ernie?" She turns like she's a model in a fashion show.

"Looks like a robe to me." Harold laughs great big, just the sight of Kate twirling around makes him laugh. "You put that on and dab a little of that cologne on your neck and Mr. Abdul won't know what to do!"

"We took care of Mr. Abdul," Juanita says.

"God, yes." Kate goes back and leans over her mother, starts pulling out tissue paper like maybe Granner can't do it by herself. There, Kate uncovers another pair of those fluffy shoes just like those dust mops she already has. "I thought your others were probably worn out, mother, so I got you some new pink ones."

"Well." Granner holds up those shoes for everybody to see. "Won't these look pretty with my new socks?" Granner knows what they're doing, giving her that new robe and shoes, getting her ready to move into a home, don't care what an old woman looks like in her own home, but Lord, put her in a home where people might see and she's got to have a fancy robe. It's just like Ernie buying his Mama that silk dress for her burial when she had spent her whole life looking like a withered-up raggamuffin.

"And there's more!" Kate takes the shoes and starts pulling back paper again. Before Granner can even see for herself, Kate announces what's in there. "A new bath-set, mother, the towels match your robe, and there's a pretty soap dish and a new toothbrush, bath oil, some Halston cologne with the bath powder."

"Well, looks like I'm gonna be spending a lot of time in the bathroom" Granner plows through all those things, and there's still another box down at the bottom. She pulls it out and opens it. "And a transistor radio, well."

"You can keep that right by your bed," Ernie says. "Then you won't have to get up so often." Granner just looks at Ernie because she knows what he's got in mind, have her in some home bed listening to a radio like some old worthless thing.

"And," Kate reaches to the very bottom of the box. "The matching gown!" Kate holds it up again for everyone to see and does another turn.

"That's beautiful, Aunt Kate," Patricia says and walks over. She walks hunch-shouldered especially when she passes by Corky and Sam. She is so self-conscious, and Juanita is sorry that she had not noticed that so much before this day. "May I smell the Halston?" she asks, and Kate reaches down and hands her the bottle. "Oh, that's nice. Is that what you have on, Aunt Kate?" Kate nods, and Patricia just smiles at her and creeps back over to her seat on the bannister.

"Maybe you'd like some of that, Patricia," Juanita says and Patricia shrugs. "If you want some, that is." Juanita gets up to smell it, too. "My, that is nice. Where did you buy that, Kate?"

"Well, I got it when we were in Raleigh. I don't know if anyone carries it around here." Kate takes the bottle from Juanita and puts the lid back on. "You know no one around here sells nice cosmetics and it's a shame. I was talking to some ladies about that the other day. We were thinking that we should ask the manager of The Fashion Place to see if she could get a good line."

"Oh," Juanita says and sits back down. She vowed one

time that she would never go back in that place after that plastic-haired looking woman was so rude to her. Juanita was just standing there and was looking at this real pretty sweater, though Lord knows it was sky high, and that woman came up and said, "Are you going to buy that?" It made Juanita so mad that she said, "I was until just now," and she walked right out of that store. Still, if Patricia wants that stuff and they get it, well, she might just have to go back in that place. "We'll try to find you some, Patricia. I might like some myself, you know if you really want some."

"It's no big deal," Patricia says.

"Hell, I've never heard such a fuss over smelling. I'll just go to Woolco and get you some of that that I bought for Mama." Harold gets up and stretches, and Juanita would like to slap him square in the face for saying that, or worse, she'd like to hug him close and tell him that their very own child is ashamed of them. "I'm going for a drink, can I get somebody else one?"

"Not me," Ernie says. "We're going to a cocktail party tonight."

"That's right," Kate adds. "We've got to be at our best."

"Then you probably need a drink to bring out the best, don't know that I've ever seen the best." Harold pats his Mama on the shoulder. "Hold your horses, Miss Smell So Right, and I'll be right back, gonna get me and the Mason over there a drink." He looks at Sam. "Gin and Coca Cola suit you?" It makes Sam Swett feel a little sick to think of it, but he nods, goes along with him.

"I'm not waiting for Harold." Granner pulls Juanita's present closer and starts opening.

"I hope you like it," Juanita says. "You've gotten so many fine presents today already." Patricia has her head turned away. If she had wanted some say-so in the present, why didn't she tell Juanita?

"Lord, I got it! I didn't think I would, and here it is!" Granner rips open the box and pulls out the blue plastic tub. "My whirlpool foot relaxer! How on earth did you know?"

"I've heard you mention it once or twice," Juanita says, though it's more like one or two hundred times. Granner puts it down in front of her and puts her feet on top of the plastic bag that covers it. "Ain't this gonna be the life of Riley, come in from weeding that garden and rest old Pat and Charlie good now." Granner leans back in her seat and grins. "This is the finest present an old woman could ever hope to get. This, and of course little Corky's present." Granner cannot bear to leave Corky out of this, knowing the way that she is. "I can use this for years, use it until I'm old, worn out, and used up." She eyes Ernie with that, and he smirks at her, and Kate just stares down at those loud shorts. "I appreciate my stuff from ya'll, too."

"What you got there?" Harold comes back and hands Sam Swett a drink. It makes Sam's whole face feel like it's been turned inside out when he takes a sip. He nods to Harold as a thank-you because he can't get the words out. "Better take it easy on it, boy, that's a strong one."

"Juanita got me just what I've been wanting, a whirl-pool foot relaxer."

"That's just what you need." Harold sits back down, looks over at Ernie. "I ran out of liquor so I mixed a little of that scotch of yours with the gin. Says that scotch is old. Hope it ain't bad." Harold laughs and kicks one foot up on the bannister, right there behind Juanita's ass, and so easily he could kick her right off that rail and into the bushes.

"Scotch and gin?" Sam Swett looks up, those eyes great big like he's scared. That boy is greener than Harold thought, green as grass. Harold can tell he ain't been hanging out at the Mason lodge too often.

"You what?" Ernie rubs one hand over his face, switches those pink legs again.

"You should have asked first, Harold." Juanita stares at him, hoping that Patricia is seeing her doing this.

"You should have asked first, Harold," he mimics. "I reckon you should have asked somebody in the Winn Dixie if you were awake or asleep before you got all twisted up in the meat room."

"Just shut up, Harold." Juanita can feel the tears coming now, and more out of fury than anything else.

"Why you getting so huffy, everybody knows." Harold takes a long drink and watches her look away, that bushy hair hiding her face. "I reckon you know that everybody knows. We all got skeletons in the closet, now don't we?" Harold looks around and he enjoys the way that everybody on the porch looks away from him except his Mama, but that doesn't bother him. "Who here don't know what happened to Juanita down at the Winn Dixie?" Harold grins great big when Sam Swett's hand goes up.

"I don't," Harold, Jr., says and looks up. Patricia is inching her way inside the house. God, what is he doing?

"Well, sorry folks, that story ain't worth the time it'd take to tell." Harold winks at Sam. "Corky can tell you that one later on." Sam nods and Corky looks away. She hates when Harold gets this way. "Hey Patricia, how about sitting over here with your Daddy?"

"I'm going to get something to eat," she says without looking up. "Hey, you two want something?" She nudges Harold, Jr., with her toe and he and Petie Rose both jump up and follow her inside.

"Don't eat it all. The rest of us are coming to get some, too." Granner gets out of her chair and stacks all of her presents neatly inside her whirlpool and carries them inside. Lord knows, anything can happen to a present if it's left outside. "Come on everybody, get some food." Granner motions, but Harold stands and motions that everybody sit back down.

"Let me have a few minutes of your time. Let's have a few minutes of silence in memory of Charlie Husky." Harold's voice rings loud and clear and he straightens his collar and bows his head like he might be a preacher.

"That's not funny, Harold," Kate says. "You are so sick."

"Charles Husky?" Juanita looks around and nobody else looks surprised. "What happened?"

"It all started when I had to leave home," Harold says. "It all started because I go to the Quik Pik late at night."

"Harold, you're not making any sense."

"Mr. Husky was killed last night and Harold is the one that found him, Harold and Sam here." Corky rubs her hand up and down the hair on Sam's arm, and it gives him chills, gives him chills to think of that man again.

"Oh my." Juanita looks at Harold and she starts to reach out and touch him, but quickly draws her hand away before he sees. "I had no idea. And Harold, and you," she looks at Sam. "You two found him?"

"Dead." Harold presses his palms together. "Dead as can be, suffocated, murdered." He sits back down and laughs. "The damnedest thing is that I went by to speak to Maggie Husky and she was waiting for him to come home, had breakfast cooked and was there waiting on that dead man to come home and eat!"

"What did you do?" Corky looks up, her eyes watering with just the thought of Mrs. Husky.

"I told her he wasn't coming home, told her he was dead."

"Oh Harold, I hope you were tactful with her," Juanita says, those blue eyes as sad as can be.

"Goddamn, what do you think? What would you say? Your husband has passed away up to the angels, Saran Wrap around his face and enough napkins for a boy scout picnic stuffed down his throat?"

"Oh God." Juanita puts her hand up to her mouth. "Do they know who did it?"

"Harold saw the man," Ernie says, and realizes that Kate is about to explode. "Hey, I wonder how Rosie is doing? We ought to be hearing pretty soon."

"It took her hours with that first one," Harold says. "I reckon you might hear before you go out to a party."

"Petie Rose was a C-section and I doubt seriously if we'd go to the party without knowing," Kate says.

"You might would. Old Juanita there went in and those babies slid right out of her." Harold claps his hands and slides one forward. "Everybody knows why that was, why those babies were able to just fall right out."

"I don't," Sam says, and takes another swallow. This drink goes down real smooth now and he doesn't even have a trace of a headache. Corky nudges him and he doesn't know why, doesn't know why those babies would have slid right out, oh yeah, yeah, he does. "Oh I get it!" he says and looks around. Harold just laughs and Juanita looks mad, and that couple in the loud clothes look like they just smelled something rotten. Corky nudges him again, those gray eyes dull and begging.

"You saw the man, Harold?" Juanita asks, keeping her voice soft and even, hoping that he'll leave her alone.

"Yep." Harold squints one eye so that he can get Juanita in focus and stares her down.

"Come get some food," Granner yells out the door and Kate and Ernie get up.

"I better go get a little something, because we've got to leave in a second." Kate takes Ernie by the arm. She's mostly talking to him instead of everyone else, anyway. Harold isn't about to let it all end here, not when Charles Husky is dead, not when Charles Husky is stretched out on some table with some man seeping the blood out of him and Maggie having to make all kinds of arrangements, not when the person that did it is out running loose, somebody that could be white black or purple. It makes Harold cringe. "Come on everybody. Ernie and Kate will have it all eaten up if we don't go on in." Juanita follows him, with Sam and Corky right behind her. Sam is having a ball, just like that old woman said, and this is only the beginning. He can't wait to get back to Corky's room, to see her in that bathrobe again, to sit and look out the window, watch the world going by.

Patricia, Harold, Jr., and Petie Rose are sitting in the living room in front of the T.V. set and that Petie Rose is sitting there kicking her feet as hard as she can up against Granner's sofa. It seems to Juanita that if Kate was so willing to help somebody, that she'd spend a little time with that grandbaby. "Did you all already eat?" Juanita asks, and Harold, Jr., nods. "Granner says we have to wait for some cake," he says.

"My cat is dead," Petie rose says and kicks her foot again. "This woman killed Tom."

"Well, I'm sorry to hear that." Juanita squats down beside Petie. "What happened?"

"A car. A big fat woman in a car." Petie puts her head down on the sofa, but keeps right on kicking until Juanita takes hold of her feet.

"I bet you can get a new kitten, Petie, and just think. You're gonna have a new little brother or sister soon."

"I want Tom, that's all." Petie twists her feet away from Juanita and kicks at her. "I want my Mama." Juanita wants to jerk a knot in that child, but it isn't her place.

"Did you get enough to eat, Patricia?" Juanita smiles, but Patricia whirls around and stares her square in the eye.

"Everyone at school calls me Patricia, the way it's supposed to be said!"

"Honey, I named you saying it that way. That's your name."

"Well, I don't like it. I'm going to tell all of my friends to call me Tricia or Patty!" Her face is fire red now and she's got her arms crossed over her chest.

"Juanita, you better hurry. The food's going fast." Juanita turns around to see Corky standing there with a plate of food, that boy right behind her. Juanita nods and turns back to Patricia.

"Honey, there are loads of Tricias and Pattys. I gave you a name that I thought would be different."

"I don't want to be different!" Patricia slumps back in her chair. "I want to be just like everybody else! I want that more than anything and as long as I'm wearing shorts from Woolco and going around with some stupid name, I can't be!"

"You want to be like everybody else?" Sam Swett steps closer but Corky puts out her arm and stops him. He cannot help but stare at this young girl. To him she already looks like everybody else, every nondescript long-legged, thin, light brown haired, self-conscious teenager, and that's what she wants; she wants to be like everybody else.

"Yes! Yes, I do." She glares at that boy and it surprises

Juanita to see Patricia speaking up to a stranger. "I don't want everybody staring at me cause I'm different. I don't want people laughing at me and talking behind my back!"

"Honey, people don't do that. You have lots of friends." Juanita puts her hand on Patricia's arm, and she jerks away.

"You don't know! You don't know anything and it's your father, too." Now Patricia is crying. "Just leave me alone, all of you!" She gets up and runs down the hall, slams the bathroom door.

"Patricia's mad," Harold, Jr., says and gets that very old look on his face. "So's Petie." He frowns and looks back at the T.V. Lord knows, a child his age shouldn't be so worrisome.

"Adolescence," Juanita says to Sam and Corky, and tries to laugh it off. "You all must remember how it was." Corky nods but Sam doesn't. This is the first time in his life that he's thought that maybe everybody feels a little different at some time or another. He is wondering right now if people have ever laughed behind his back, if they're in that kitchen right now talking about him. He watches Juanita go into the kitchen and Corky takes his arm and pulls him back on the porch.

"Do you think I'm different?" he asks when they sit back on the steps. He takes a sip of the drink that Harold just mixed for him and it makes his throat go dry, makes him cough.

"We've already talked about all that," she says, and he cannot help but notice those slight circles below her eyes, the fragile blue blood vessels on her eyelids. "Lord," she shakes her head and laughs, the dark smudges disappearing into laugh lines. "Everybody's the same but everybody's different, and everybody's different but they're the same." She takes a small bite of a potato chip, a nibble off the edge. "You're different, but it's a nice different, and you're also like everybody else. You eat and sleep and get scared and feel lonesome and you drink. You probably drink too much." She takes another nibble and he watches her jaw muscle clench, release; she chews without making a sound. "You know some people just can't drink very good. It makes some people say sort of stupid kinds of things." She looks at him so seriously now, the darkness returning below those tissue paper lids, the wide gray eyes. "I can't drink much because it makes me say stupid things."

"Like what?" He cannot imagine anything stupid rolling from those full soft lips.

"Oh, I don't know, makes me say things like that I'm no good, that nothing's ever going to go right for me, makes me cry like a baby." She shakes her head, the wisps of hair around her eyes. "It got to my Daddy that same way." She takes a small bite of her ham biscuit and stares at him the whole time she chews, and he watches that small chin going round and round, the swallow that he can almost trace down her throat. "Listen to me, telling you what you ought and ought not to do. It may not affect you that way at all. You might be different from me."

"No, I think we're alike." He wants to kiss her right

now, to squeeze her as hard as he can. The door slams shut and both of them jump.

"Hope we ain't interrupting you lovebirds." Harold goes back to his chair, and in a second everyone else except the children files out, with Granner coming out last, carrying what's left of the cake.

"Whew! I thought I was going to roast inside that house." Kate fans herself with her hand and goes back to the swing. "I never thought that it could feel so nice outdoors in July, but that house is a sweat box!" Ernie goes and sits down beside her, both of them looking at their watches and nodding to one another. Granner puts the cake down on the small table by her chair. "You all help yourselves," she says, and stares out into the yard while she's getting herself adjusted, twisting her back a little and moving her head from side to side so the arthritis won't settle in. She loves this time of day when the sun is so bright yet the shadows of the big trees start to darken the porch. She gets the morning sun on the porch, so this time of day sitting on the porch is almost like being inside and looking out a big picture window. She always sits out here this time of day just to remind herself of all those times that she and Buck would sit out here and swing and talk while he chewed tobacco. They'd sit till dusk and then they'd start counting the bats that would fly out from under the eaves of the old Sampson house that used to be across the street. Those bats would file out one at a time, like they were in the army or in a parade, and then soar way off, probably ready to dive on something white at any given second. At least that's what

Buck used to say. Buck said that colored folks as long as they wore dark clothing would never have to fear a bat nosediving on them.

"Going to the movies, Mama?" Harold asks, and grins. Lord knows, sometimes he can look just like Buck Weeks, though Buck Weeks never acted as rough as Harold.

"I've never in my life been to the movies. You know that."

"Oh, I though you were cause I saw you picking your seat." Harold takes his hand and pulls on the back of his work pants.

"I was not!" She sits back down in her chair and stares off again. She doesn't care what a one of them says or does right now, because as far as she's concerned the party is over. As far as she is concerned she'd rather sit and think about Buck, talk to him a little bit in her head. Sometimes when she talks to him in her head, she feels like he's right beside her, sometimes he even talks back to her. He was the only person who would listen to her telling about Mr. Abdul until Juanita took an interest.

"You know, Charlie weren't the first dead man I ever saw," Harold says right out of the blue. "I saw so many dead men when I was in Korea. Used to count 'em. Got to be where seeing a dead man was like seeing a tree or a bush, all looked alike." Harold pushes his cap back and laughs. "Thought to myself one time that was gonna be some kind of fertile soil once they all rotted."

"Please," Ernie says. "Don't start with your old war stories. We all know them. We've all seen your scar."

"You don't know shit, Stubbs. You were sitting in some office doing some shit right here in America."

"He's flat-footed," Kate says. "And I was glad they wouldn't have him."

"He's a pussy."

"Harold, I'm not gonna have it." Granner gives him a sharp look, but she knows from experience that that look probably won't do a bit of good. Ernie starts to say something, but Harold cuts him off.

"But it was like a different thing altogether when I saw Charlie stretched out on that floor."

"Because you weren't in war." Sam says, takes another sip of his drink and sets it aside. "You were accustomed to it in war, you accepted it then. You forgot that those people had lives of their own, that they belonged somewhere, that there were people who cared about them." He squeezes Corky's hand and waits for her to look up at him, the slight nod, the tears in her eyes. She smiles and returns his squeeze and it makes him feel funny all over. He has surprised himself, those words coming from his mouth, and now he no longer feels self-conscious around these people who have asked him all the questions, because he does fit in with her. She has somehow made him fit.

"No, I don't think I did and I don't think you would." Harold puts both feet up on the bannister. He could wrap his legs around Juanita right now and squeeze the life out of her. "How old are you anyway?"

"Twenty-one."

"Twenty-one, prime age, but you're a baby, don't

know a thing about it all." Harold stares at Sam now. "You ever seen a dead man before last night? Not all fixed up at a funeral but just dead, still warm, still got the blood left in him?" Sam shakes his head. "See, you don't know what I'm talking about, either, or maybe you do now that you've seen one. Makes you feel sick as hell, don't it?" Harold points at Corky. "She knows what I'm talking about. Yessir, Corky knows about as good as anybody what I'm talking about."

"Leave her alone," Juanita whispers.

"Juanita don't want to hear nothing because she's never had nothing horrible to see, had to make herself up something in her head so she'd have something horrible in her mind like everybody else." Harold glances back at Corky. "You know what I'm talking about, now don't you?"

"Yes." Corky looks away from him and stares out in the yard. "It sure has been a pretty day, hasn't it?"

"Oh yes," Juanita says.

"Pete ought to be calling any minute," Ernie says. "I'm afraid to leave because I want to be among the first to hear."

"Well, if we leave now, we can hurry home. They'll try our house first, I'm certain." Kate sits up straight but Ernie doesn't budge. For some reason, for the first time ever, he'd rather stay here than go home. As hard as Harold is to take, he doesn't want to be alone with Kate right now, not the way he's feeling, not the way his chest feels so tight, a feeling that he hasn't had since his Mama died, since he waited on pins and needles to find out if they had been accepted into the club. He's afraid of himself, afraid of everything he's done or hasn't done in his entire life.

"We will in a minute, honey." He takes hold of Kate's arm and squeezes. He can still wrap his fingers all the way around her arm, though her arm has gotten plump, but it's the same arm, the exact same arm that he has held for all these years. "It's not even four yet."

"Yeah, little Corky must know," Harold says now, as if Corky isn't even present. "Go in that room and see her Daddy with his head blown off. She knows what can happen. She knows what it can do to a person."

"Harold, this ain't the time nor the place for this," Granner says. She's ready for them to all go home so she can be right by herself with Buck in her head, try out that milk bath that Harold gave her, put her feet in that whirlpool and watch something good on T.V.

"Look what it did to her brother." Harold looks around, and everyone except Sam is ignoring him. Ernie would like to speak out, to tell Harold to leave Corky alone, but he knows that Harold would start in on him. "Course look at you, young green boy, don't know a thing about war, playing with building blocks or playing with yourself during Viet Nam, right?"

"Harold." Juanita grabs hold of one of his brogans and he starts to move his foot, to give her a good swift kick, but no, he'll let her hold it, he'd like to see her lick that shoe.

"I know it was wrong," Sam says. "I know I wouldn't have gone."

"You know it's wrong cause that's what you've heard

by now." Harold leans forward, his legs inching forward, that one foot in Juanita's lap and she doesn't even move, just holds that shoe, damn her.

"What do you think you would have done? Been a pussy?" Harold looks over at Ernie and laughs great big. Kate is about to open that fat mouth of hers, so Harold keeps talking. "Maybe run off to Canada?"

"Maybe." Sam feels uncomfortable now; he feels as helpless as that young girl had looked a while ago. He wants Corky to rub his head again, to hold him close.

"Don't blame you," Ernie says, and nods at that boy. For some reason he is feeling sorry for everybody today, even Harold, but mostly for himself.

"Damned if you do and damned if you don't." Harold twists his foot around, and now he's got the heel of his shoe right near Juanita's crotch. He could grind her right out of business if he took the notion. "You either could've been a pussy or you could've been like Corky's brother. He couldn't take it, could he?"

"What do you know?" Corky looks up now, those large eyes filmy. She looks at Granner because Granner and Fannie McNair are the only two people that she's ever told all about her brother, but Granner is staring away, far away, and Corky realizes that Granner has shut them all out and is right by herself now.

"Ain't nothing to be ashamed of, Corky. We all got skeletons. You can't help it if your brother couldn't take it."

"Well, he tried."

"Sure he did and that's what I'm saying. Either that

boy sitting there with you could've done nothing and run away and spent the rest of his life being a good for nothing pussy, or he could have gone and maybe not been able to take it and wound up in a hospital making doll babies out of corn for the rest of his life." Harold takes a big swallow of his drink and pulls out his Red Man. "That's what I was saying, damned if you do and damned if you don't. I tell you when I saw Charlie with his mouth crammed full of napkins and that plastic on his face, I knew what happens to people like your brother, people who let themselves care a little bit, people who lose their fucking shit."

"Harold, you are so crude," Kate says, and he ignores her. It may be the first time in his life that he has ignored her.

"I'm sorry," Sam says and touches her arm, the slight goose flesh that runs up her shoulder. "I really am."

"Yeah." She looks at Harold once, quickly, then looks away.

"Corky knows what the hell I'm saying, and God knows Ernie should, after what happened to his Mama."

"Stop right now, Harold," Kate says, but Ernie doesn't say a word. He knows that Harold's going to say it sooner or later. He knows he may as well get it over with, let Harold pull up all of the old bones that he can.

"Course the mailman would know even better. Old Donnie Capps been delivering over on Injun Street for years, putting mail in Mrs. Stubbs' box." Harold looks at Ernie now and Ernie stares right back, doesn't even blink. "What was it, third day? Was it the third day when

Donnie saw that your Mama hadn't come out to get her sale catalogue from two days before?" Ernie is still staring. "Yep, third day so old Donnie knocked real loud on the door and he waited and waited, got a little worried so he called the police, tried to call Ernie but he was out of town for the day, golfing or shopping I forget which."

"I mean it, Harold." Kate stands up but Ernie doesn't budge. "Are you going to let him sit there and humiliate you?" Ernie just looks at her, opens his mouth but then closes it and shakes his head. His chest is so tight right now that he can't even speak, doesn't want to speak. Kate goes inside and slams the door.

"Anyway, they busted in that door and when they did, they got a whiff of an awful odor, and there she was, Donnie Capps saw her first, on the kitchen floor, a frying pan with grease dried in it down beside her wheel chair and grease everywhere, with Mrs. Stubbs stretched out in front of that chair with her head cut open." Ernie doesn't want to hear it all again, but there is something in him, some part that does want to hear it, to get a picture of what he never saw. "Juanita went down there and mopped that floor after they had got Mrs. Stubbs to the funeral home. Mrs. Stubbs had on a frock that looked like it was a hundred years old, ratty old underwear, too, that's why Mamas always tell their children to wear clean underwear in case something was to happen where people would see them." Sam Swett looks up and nods, yes, he knew that, his Mama had always told him that, though nothing had ever happened to him, though later on, Corky might see, it's very possible that Corky might see that big footprint on his underwear. That story made him feel sick all over again; he feels a little sick. "For three days, though, she was like that." Harold inches his other foot up near Juanita's thigh, that firm hairless thigh. "Three days and it took the mailman to go in there and find her. I thank God that I found Charlie when I did. It could've been seven hours before anybody else went in that store."

"I called once," Ernie says. "I thought she was probably in bed and couldn't get to the phone." He shakes his head, tries to shake away that picture of his mother that Harold has brought so vividly to his mind.

"She was sleeping, all right." Harold taps his foot against Juanita's thigh and she looks at him, those blue eyes so clear and begging, not a trace of anger in them. "Oh well, I reckon that covers skeletons in the closet, unless of course Ernie's got himself a new story to tell."

"Why do you say that?" Ernie leans up in the swing, his hands clasped so tightly together that his knuckles are white.

"Oh, I don't know. Seems like that lifestyle of yours might cause a bone or two here and there. You know a bone to pick?" Harold spits over the side of the porch, a straight shot that ends with a splat on the dry dirt. "You act a little fidgety, them pink legs crossing and uncrossing.

"I've got a grandbaby being born." Ernie sits back and wipes the sweat away from his temples. "I've got a reason to be edgy."

"Yes, you do," Juanita says, and nods. She looks down

at her hand on Harold's shoe like she's surprised to see it there, surprised that he hasn't moved away from her. She takes one finger and rubs it around and around the lace eye. She will sit here all night long if Harold does, because she's not going to be the first to go. It has been so long since she's been close to any part of him and she ain't about to budge.

Bob Bobbin has had some kind of day. Now, he's sitting in this little air-conditioned room down at the station trying to cool off, drinking a Coca Cola and flipping through some mug shots to see if he can find the suspect. For all Bob knows, this man could have done all sorts of bad things; he very well could have been the one that went into the First Baptist Church and did all those nasty things, wrote those nasty words on the wall. That case was never solved though rumor had it all over town that some kids from nice homes had done it. Bob doesn't believe that for one second, no child raised in a fine home in a nice neighborhood would do such a horrible thing, had to be trash that did it.

"Bobbin, what in the hell are you doing?" Chief Williams sticks that red Santa Claus face of his into the room. "You ain't getting paid to loaf, son, gonna wind up right back downtown writing traffic tickets if you don't watch it."

"Working on the case, sir." Bob stands up straight as an arrow. "Thought this man may have been in here before for something."

"This ain't New York City, don't you think we'd remember?"

"Oh, yeah, yeah." Bob shifts from one foot to the other. "Thought I'd wait for the lab reports."

"What lab reports? That bottle that you brought in don't tell us a thing. It was all wet with sweat. Somebody got it out of the cooler and then it sat out for who knows how long."

"Couldn't have been too long, cause Harold Weeks saw that guy leaving." Bob rubs his chin. "We could get prints from that cooler," Bob says, but the Chief just shakes his head.

"What the hell, if you've got a witness, then go get him!" The chief backs up and Bob takes himself a long swallow of Coke. It's so hot that his uniform is sticking to him all over. "Now!"

"Yes sir." Bob drains the last bit of his Coke and goes and puts it down in the crate by the machine. He sure doesn't want that downtown duty again, walking round and round that parking lot behind the old dime store and Belk's, walking up and down Main Street measuring cars from the curb, checking meters. The only nice part about that beat was that he had been right there near the Coffee Shop and near Corky. He picks up his car keys and walks down the hall and outside. It's so hot that he can hardly breathe when he steps outside, can't hardly see, either, so he puts on his mirrored sunglasses. Harold is probably still at his Mama's party and Bob hates to go to that house. That old woman is crazy, and what's more, Corky will probably be there and he hasn't gotten himself ready for another apology. Damn that woman for the way she keeps him dangling. He opens the door of his car and stands there a minute to let some of that heat out.

"Have you heard anything?" He turns around to see that little curly-headed woman standing there, crept up on him without a sound. "I've been here all day long. Tommy told me to leave and that big man inside told me to leave, and I just don't know what to do!"

"I think you ought to leave." Bob whips off his glasses so that he can look her square in the eye. "Get yourself a new start, you know?" He looks her up and down, puts his glasses back on so that she can't tell how closely he is looking her up and down. "You know I might want another one of those lamps." He nods while he talks. That was so stupid of him to give that lamp to old Sandra. Corky didn't even notice, or if she did, she pretended not to. "Might get two as a matter of fact, one for me and one for a present."

"You'll have to wait until Tommy is out. Those are his lamps."

"Well, might have to forget it, then. My witness that I'm bringing in might identify him as the man."

"I'm telling you that Tommy didn't do it." She grabs his arm. "He's innocent." She starts to cry and Bob can't hardly stand to see that. "I'm so hot and miserable," she wails. "You've got to help me."

"Seems to me that we're on two sides of the fence." Bob shakes his head.

"Let me go with you to get the witness." She clutches his arm again, those pretty shiny nails glistening there on his uniform.

"Police work," he says. "I can't go carting around the mistress of the suspect."

"Please, I'll just sit right in the car and not open my mouth." She runs around and opens the other door. "Let's turn on the air-conditioner." She slams her door and Bob gets in and slams his. He has never been able to say no to a begging woman. Besides, it would serve Corky Revels right to see him with a cute young woman, even if she is a little on the cheap side. Yessir, this will get Corky's attention.

"You just sit right there," he says and cranks the car, turns on the A.C. "We'll ride around a few minutes and get cooled off. Got to look my best on the job."

"Oh, I know what you mean. That's exactly why I bought these shoes." She picks up one of her legs and sticks that shoe practically in front of his face.

"I'll ride by my place, show you how the other half lives, might ride by your boss's house, show you what you could have someday if you get yourself straight."

"You're wrong about Tommy," she says and puts her foot back down. "But I would love to see where Mr. Stubbs lives. You know that he said that I'm his protégée, that's French."

"I know French, all right." He speeds up, leans back in his seat. That steering wheel is burning the hell out of his hands but he ain't going to let on, just like that Chinaman on Kung Fu when he used to pick up that boiling hot pot, if you got the mind for it then you can handle any kind of pain. Bob Bobbin has that kind of mind. "Everybody knows French."

"I didn't," she says and lifts her skirt up in front of that A.C. vent. She's a hot number, all right. "But a protégée is somebody that learns everything from the boss, you know, advances fast."

"I know what that means." Bob flexes his fingers, damn they're scorched. "You ain't talking to your colored boyfriend, you know."

"Tommy took French. He knows some German, too."

"Um um, like he might have call to ever use it." Bob shakes his head and laughs. He will never in his life understand how some people can get such big notions in their heads. "I got to tell you, Miss, that Mr. Stubbs weren't too pleased about where you live and with who."

"You told him?" Now that little face is as white as can be.

"Had to, had to check our your story. His wife weren't pleased more than him." Bob pats her on the knee. "Don't you worry. You can start fresh and new."

"But I like my job. I've worked hard to get that protégée position!" Lord, now she's got to shed another tear or two. This girl can turn it on and off like a faucet. He can't stand it. "I know what'll cheer you up but we ain't got much time."

"What?"

"You'll see." He's gonna ride her by his place; one look at where he lives and she's bound to make some changes in her life, bound to set her sights a little higher, and after all, that's as much a policeman's job as arresting criminals, reforming those who ain't on the right track, making them fit for society so that this world can be a better place, saving people. That's why Bob had been so torn in his younger years as to whether to be a policeman or a preacher. The way he saw it, they had about the same kind of job, only a policeman had more excitement and a policeman did not have to live such a reserved life, and a preacher wasn't allowed to carry a gun. All those things swayed him into his profession, though every now and then he has a little doubt or two, especially like last Sunday when his church voted to collect enough money to send the preacher, his wife and their four children on a mission to the Virgin Islands. Bob Bobbin would like himself a vacation in the Virgin Islands, that's for sure, but there wouldn't be any virgins left in the place if he went, which when you weigh it all out is why he's a cop instead, and a damn good cop, got his sights set on chief of police and he'll get there one day, he'll get it sure as that preacher is going to get his wish of a mission over to Paris, France, after he has saved some souls in the Islands.

"Here we are," Bob says and drives through the parking lot.

"Where?" She asks and looks so funny. Bob realizes now that though this girl's got right much going for her in the looks department, that aside from being cheap, she's a little dumb.

5

Rose Stubbs Tyner has never been in so much pain in her entire life. She wishes that that doctor down there, framed by her legs in those stirrups, would give her some drugs to knock her out or just give her drugs and cut her stomach wide open like they did for Petie Rose. God, not a word that anybody has ever told her is true, and to think that Lady Di got herself in this position and huffed and puffed and sweated like a pig. She clutches Pete's arm and digs her nails into him. He tries to get his hand away and she's not about to let him, stupid son of a bitch; it's his fault anyway.

"Relax, now, pause," that doctor says and Rose just grits her teeth. What the hell does he know anyway? He's never had to squeeze a watermelon out of himself, probably never has had a hemorrhoid and here he's saying that he's just going to clip hers after the baby is out, God, if that baby ever comes out. Relax? How the hell can she relax with her legs pulled up off the table.

"Okay push, now," the doctor says, just as calm as can be.

"You push!" Rose screams and digs into Pete's arm again. "You damn push!" Oh, Lordy, it's killing her.

"Jesus! God! Jesus!" she screams and Pete off to that side panting like some dog, telling her what to do. If he knows so damn well what to do, then he ought to get up on this table and have the baby and have the hemorrhoids and have had the enema and the shaving and the episiotomy.

"It's okay, honey." Pete rubs her face. "Come on, breathe with me." He pants again and if she wasn't in so much pain, she'd spit right in his panting mouth.

"Fuck off!" she screams and it feels so good that she says it again. "Fuck off! Fuck off!"

"Rose, honey." Pete has pulled his hand away now and is staring at her. "How can you say that when our baby is being born?"

"Fuck off!"

"Okay, I've got the head," that doctor says and Rose rises up as far as she can and screams. "Push, don't strain."

"Jesus God!" Rose lies back down. "Don't fucking strain," she gasps.

"Rose," Pete says like he might be talking to Petie Rose, calling her down for saying "poot."

"It's okay," that doctor says. "She won't even remember this probably."

"The hell I won't!"

"She never talks this way!" Now Pete has gone down there to watch, like there might be a movie between her legs, the doctor, the nurse, and Pete all staring into her crotch and her hurting so damn much!

"A lot of women do this." That damn doctor has the

nerve to smile about it all. "They should have warned you in your Lamaze."

"Fuck Lamaze!"

"Okay, here we go," the doctor says, and Rose can barely hear him cause her ears feel all stopped up from pushing so damn hard.

"Is it a boy or a girl?" Pete's a damn fool, standing there in the front row of the show and asking what's happening.

"Shut the fuck up!" She screams and rises up from that table again. Now there is a nurse there with a cool cloth on her head.

"Almost there," that nurse says, and it makes Rose burst out laughing and crying. Everybody in that room is about to burst out laughing or crying because of her baby. It's like a current running through the room, like everything is flashing and buzzing and it's about time. Jesus, it's time.

Granner is starting to feel like she just might give up on having birthday celebrations, the way that everybody acts, not a one of them pays her a bit of attention, won't even wear those Uncle Sam hats that are such a tradition. If Buck Weeks was alive they'd wear them, cause Buck Weeks had a way of making people do things; he could make people feel so guilty down in their guts. Granner thinks right now that she might be ready to die, to drop dead with that Uncle Sam hat on her head and then they'd be sorry, then they'd have to live the rest of their lives out thinking about her stretched out on the porch dead as a doornail at her own party. Corky had her hat on for a second and then took it right off, probably cause she thought that boy might not like her looks in it, and Juanita just up and said that she didn't want her hair going flat. Kate didn't even offer an excuse. Kate said that it was bad enough to all sit out on the front porch like a bunch of hicks.

"This will probably be the last party," Granner says and takes off her own hat, puts it down beside the chair.

"You say that every year." Harold pulls his foot away from Juanita and plants it firmly on the floor cause he's starting to feel the spins a little. It must be the heat, because Harold very rarely gets the spins.

"I mean it this year." Granner rocks back and forth, crosses her arms because now that the whole porch is shady and a slight breeze has picked up, she's a little chilly. "I doubt if I'll be around."

"Oh mother," Kate says, and Juanita cannot help but think how much she sounds like Patricia, who is now back on the far end of the porch. Petie and Harold, Jr., stayed inside to watch T.V., and Juanita wishes that Patricia had too in case Harold starts shooting off his mouth again. "Please don't start with that old story today." Kate runs her hand through her hair and it slicks straight back, with those dark roots showing. Juanita would like to know right now what Patricia or Tricia or Patty Patsy thinks of that hairdo, since she thinks that Kate Stubbs is so great. "You know that we do everything that we can to make you comfortable and here you start trying to make somebody feel guilty." Kate turns and faces Ernie now.

"If they don't call soon, we're going to have to go on home. Look at me." She lifts a strand of that hair and lets it fall back. "I look like I've been working in the yard and I've got to have plenty of time to shower and fix my hair before the party."

"You're right," Ernie says and nods. She does look like she's been working in the yard.

"I know that you think I'd be comfortable in a home." Granner crosses her feet and flexes them so that the arthritis won't set.

"Please, don't start that." Ernie looks at her, and she thinks he looks right pitiful now. He knows how to do that, probably did it to his own Mama for years and years.

"No, I know what's so." Granner nods her head while she rocks and stares out into the yard. "Nobody wants to spend any time with an old person, just leave 'em alone, find 'em after they've been dead awhile."

"Harold has already covered that, Mother," Kate says. "Besides, we check on you constantly."

"Oh bout once a week. Mr. Abdul checks more often than that."

"Mama, I come over here near about every single day," Harold says and props his foot back up. The spins are gone now and he places his foot further away from Juanita than it was before. He wants to see if she'll inch her way back over close to him.

"Yeah, to eat," Kate says and shakes her head. "Oh, let's talk about something else."

"Let's talk about how much you eat," Harold says, and looks at Kate. "I'd say you eat a plenty."

"I'd say that you're drunk. God, I hope nobody that I know rides by here." Kate crosses her legs and swings her foot back and forth like she's fit to be tied, that barefoot sandal looking like it might slip and clatter to the floor at any second. It makes Juanita so mad, the way that Kate can make a person feel small. If it weren't for her services, Kate couldn't wear barefoot sandals.

"I'm not drunk," Harold says, looks right at Kate, thumps his chest and burps great big. Juanita sees that boy with Corky trying so hard not to laugh, and it's difficult to keep herself from laughing. All she has to do to keep from laughing, though, is to look over there at Patricia and see that sad look on her face. Patricia looks like she might cry at any second.

"I like those barefoot sandals, Kate," Juanita says real loud, so that she can cut Harold off. "You have attractive toes."

"What do you mean by that!" Kate glares at her. There ain't any way that you can be nice to Kate Stubbs cause she ain't going to let you.

"I mean the shape of your toes, those nice square nails that are nice for painting." Juanita stretches her leg out and stares down at her own foot. "See, my nails are sort of fan shaped and the cuticle grows way up on them. Never have been able to paint my toenails. Now, Patricia, I mean Tricia, has nice nails as well and not a single hair on her toes." Juanita smiles at Patricia but she looks away, and so does Kate when she mentions hair on the toes.

"I can see straight up your crotch with that leg lifted,"

Harold says and shakes his head. "I reckon you think I'm interested in what you've got to show."

"Well, you don't have to look." Juanita puts her leg back down and cannot control her mouth, even though Patricia is over there soaking in every word like a sponge. "I reckon you wanted to see."

"Looks about the same, got a little more mileage, I reckon."

"Even the preacher has stopped coming to see me," Granner says to nobody in particular. A bomb could probably drop and Corky and that dirty-looking boyfriend of hers probably wouldn't even hear it, they're so busy staring at one another and touching hands.

"He's a busy man, mother," Kate says. "Besides, he's out of town right now."

"Yeah, I heard he went to the Virgin Islands," Juanita says, and almost starts laughing when that old picture of that preacher singing Jailhouse Rock comes to her mind.

"Oh, mother!" Patricia leans her head up against that post, her hair falling all around her face.

"That's what they're called, The Virgin Islands," Juanita says. "That's some fine vacation."

"Bet it cost a bundle." Harold inches his foot just a speck. There, now he's made the first move.

"The church raised the money," Ernie says. "I think it's wonderful, good man, and he deserves it. We're lucky to have a man like him."

"I reckon that church is as rich as it ever was," Harold says. "Just as snotty as it ever was."

"That's not true, Harold," Kate says. If there's one of

many things that makes her mad, it's for someone to talk about the church. "We accept members of all kinds. Why, there's one man in our church who works at a gas station and another that works at a grocery store."

"Lord, that's enough to get Juanita up and going every Sunday morning." Harold laughs, but Juanita looks away.

"I go to church from time to time," Juanita says. "But I go to the church where I was raised."

"That church out in the county?" Kate asks and Juanita nods. "I had no idea that that little church was still there."

"I'm going to join the First Baptist," Patricia says. "All of my friends go there. Do you know Billy Foster, Aunt Kate?" Patricia creeps up a little closer.

"Sure, he lives next door to us. Is he a friend of yours?"

"Sort of." Patricia looks away and gets all giggly and slump shouldered. "I've spoken to him a couple of times."

"Oh where have you been Billy Boy, Billy Boy." Harold waves his cap at Patricia and she goes back to her seat.

"Don't tease her. It's time that she starts having boy-friends," Juanita says.

"Oh mother, nobody says boyfriend anymore!"

"That's cause of the sexes getting mixed up," Granner says out of the blue, and everyone stops and looks at her. "I've read all about it, all about the boys liking boys and girls liking girls and some go back and forth trying to decide and getting that sickness."

"That's not why nobody says boyfriend anymore," Patricia screams.

"Really, mother, don't get on that again." Kate crosses her legs the other way.

"All I know is that I'd rather know a person who had the first disease than one who's got this second disease," Granner says and stops rocking suddenly, glares at Harold. "That church hasn't always been uppity." She sits forward in her chair. "It was the pillar of the community when Buck and I first come to town. We tithed. We went to Wednesday night prayer meeting, too."

"It's not uppity, now," Kate says. "People just say that about our church because we do have a lot of money and a lot of influential people."

"Gotten too big to serve," Granner says. "Used to the preacher went and visited old shut-ins."

"But, you're not a shut-in," Ernie says. "If you wanted to go to church, we could pick you up some time."

"What would a body who ain't a shut-in be doing in a rest home?" Ah ha! Granner has caught him now. Besides, they don't go to church near as much as they like to pretend. "How often do you all go anyway? Seems to me you're out of town lots of Sundays."

"Well, that's understandable with Ernie's business, but we do tithe, and sometimes we give well over ten percent when it's for a good cause." Kate says and looks around for some support. Ernie nods, Patricia smiles, but what in the hell does that ignorant little blasé child know? The rest of them are sitting there bathing in stupidity, Corky and that boy look like they're about to bathe each other the way they're getting closer and closer together.

"A good cause? What do you call a good cause, that purple shag carpeting and purple walls?" Harold notices that Juanita's thigh is just a speck closer to his foot and he is trying to figure out if she moved closer or if he accidentally moved closer to her.

"It's not purple and it wasn't shag," Kate says, her face so red now that she looks like a lobster. Harold loves to see her get that way as much as Granner loves to see it. "The walls are a lovely pale lavender and the rug is thick wool lavender, slightly darker than the walls. It's beautiful."

"Finest carpet you can get," Ernie says. "It looks royal."

"Sounds a little bad to me," Granner says. "Back when I was an active member, we had pretty wooden floors with light gold carpet down the aisle."

"But think about it," Kate says, and she wonders for a second why she's even trying to explain anything to these people. "So many of the brides like to use pastel colors and the lavender will be perfect."

"Unless a bride should choose red for her color," Juanita says.

"What?" Kate whirls around.

"I said unless a bride should pick red or some shade of orange."

"Well, I can't imagine anybody choosing those colors in the first place."

"I can't imagine anybody choosing purple for a church," Granner says and shakes her head. "I reckon Jesus wouldn't like it."

"I was on the committee that chose the colors!" Kate says. "And how would you know what Jesus would or would not like?"

"Maybe they shouldn't have chose you to be on the

committee to choose that choice," Harold says. "Maybe Jesus should have had his say."

"Don't be sacrilegious, Harold Weeks," Granner says. "You don't even go to church, so that gives you double bad trouble for making up Jesus jokes."

"No it don't, cause if Jesus knows everything then Jesus knows that I ain't meaning any harm by laughing at him, and he also knows that it's out of love all these years that I stayed at home on Sunday mornings." He stares at Juanita and she stares straight back at him. It looks like she's about to smile at him, and the thought of their Sunday mornings way back must have got her excited cause she's got goose flesh up on her thighs. "And if Jesus knows everything, then he knows that purple ain't no color for a church and the Virgin Islands ain't no place for a preacher."

"That's your opinion, Harold," Kate says.

"And Jesus' opinion. He just now told it to me."

"I mean it, Harold. I want you to get off of my porch with that kind of talk. Go right out there in the yard to get struck, but don't ask for it right here on my porch." Granner's arms are waving now, lifted straight up, and she's whispering something.

"Is she serious?" Sam Swett whispers to Corky, or he thinks he is whispering. He can't tell now that he's almost done with that third drink that Harold mixed.

"What do you mean?" Granner asks. "You should be serious. You may be one of those people that don't believe in anything. Are you?"

"It's called an atheist, mother," Kate says, and Granner

cannot help but think that she wishes Kate had been a schoolteacher so that she could have gotten paid for making so many corrections. "And I'm sure he's not one. I'm certain . . ." Kate stops abruptly when the phone rings and she jumps up and runs inside with Ernie right on her heels.

"They painted the walls to match Ernie's pants," Harold hoots. Juanita's thigh is almost within kicking distance.

"I bet it's the baby!" Patricia gets up and dashes right behind Kate and Ernie. She wants so much to be accepted that it makes Juanita ache inside her heart. It aggravates the shit out of her as well.

"It ain't the baby on the phone, that's for sure," Harold screams.

"Are you one of those?" Granner leans forward toward Sam Swett and clenches her teeth together. She gives Sam the creeps. He shakes his head. "Then what are you?"

"Granner, it doesn't matter," Corky says, but Granner cuts her off immediately.

"Tell me," she says.

"I'm not sure." He shakes his head, squeezes Corky's hand, that warm little hand that he would like to fit inside his mouth right this minute. "I grew up going to a Presbyterian church."

"Believing that everything was lined out for you, huh?" Granner starts rocking again. "Mm Mm, that's bad business, thinking that everything is planned out for you by God, cause then people take to doing whatever they durn well please and think that God will reach down here and set them straight when they need it. Just like the way that Catholics go around and can do all the bad stuff that they want to do as long as they go and sit there in front of that box where the preacher stays and tell him about it. They tell that preacher now, not the Lord. Don't you know that that preacher could ruin every soul he knows if he should up and lose his mind and tell all he's heard?" It makes Granner rock that much faster, the madder she gets. Religion is something that can get Granner all riled up, especially when it's the wrong religions that she's discussing. She's a Baptist through and through, and these days even they make her mad, that preacher acting about as uppity as Kate and Ernie, and probably not a one of them interested in a thing other than padding their pockets. Granner ain't about to set foot in a place that's so filled to the brim with hypocrites, and it hurts her so to think of little Corky going to that very church hoping to be a part of it all, when they ain't about to let her considering she's not got the cash flow. "Is that what you think? You think you can walk around and do as you please and then God'll fix things his own way, that maybe you've been as low as a snake and God up and puts you in the White House, or maybe you've been so good and fine and God up and makes you kill a person. Is that what you think?"

"No, no." He shakes his head, but that old woman still won't back off, even though there's all kinds of laughing and screaming inside, she won't back off.

"That's what happened to Corky's Mama, tell him Corky."

"Maybe some other time, Granner." Corky stands up when she sees Kate running to the door. "Here comes Kate."

"You can't wait too late, son," Granner says. "I'll tell you about Corky's Mama."

"It's a boy!" Kate squeals, and Ernie rushes out right behind her and wraps his arms around her waist. It's times like this when he knows why he married Kate.

"Congratulations!" Juanita screams. "How's Rose?"

"Fine!" Ernie comes over and hugs Juanita tightly and then looks at her, those clear blue eyes of hers watering a little with the excitement. Some day he's going to thank her for mopping his Mama's floor, apologize for twisting her nipple that time. "Thanks for asking, Juanita."

"Hey, don't choke her," Harold says, and puts a hand on Ernie's shoulder, pulls him away. Juanita is staring at him, so he has to do something so she won't see that he didn't want Ernie Stubbs touching her flesh. He sticks out his hand. "Congratulations, there." Harold nods his head toward Juanita. "Couldn't let you choke her, gonna do that myself." He laughs but so does Juanita. It sounded like something he would have said when they were still together. "I'm going to do it right after the divorce," he adds, and Juanita stops dead in her tracks right in the middle of a laugh. Harold goes over and drapes one arm around Kate. She starts to move away from him but then gives him a quick hug. He smells awful, but after all, he is her brother, no matter how different they may be.

"Baby ain't deformed or anything, is it?" Granner asks, and Kate gets that exasperated look all over again.

Granner has a way with words; she can make everybody get quiet as a mouse in the midst of a commotion.

"He's healthy, perfectly healthy," Ernie says, and shakes Granner's hand. Ernie is out of his skull at this point. He picks up Petie Rose and cuddles her like she might be a baby. "Just like Petie!"

"What's his name?" Corky asks.

"Buck Robert Lee," Granner says, but Kate shakes her head.

"They haven't named him yet," Ernie says. "Right, Petie?"

"His name is Tom! I want a new Tom!" Petie squirms out of her grandfather's arms and runs back inside to watch some more cartoons.

"We've got to run now," Kate says. "Thank God, that's over. Mother, do you mind if Petie stays with you until Pete gets home?"

"You reckon somebody as old and helpless, worn out, used up and crazy as me can look after a young one?"

"She won't be a bit of trouble." Kate gives Granner a brisk kiss on the cheek. "Happy birthday."

"Thank you." Granner looks at Kate real hard. She never can tell if Kate is really being nice or putting on. "And thank you for my gifts. That cologne smells real nice, that Tigress."

"Harold gave you that," Kate snaps, and then softens a little. "You remember."

"Yes, I remember." Granner looks at Sam Swett. "I remember that I was fixing to tell you about Corky's Mama."

"Not now, Granner," Corky says, and watches that police car coming down the street. She knows even from that distance that it's Bob Bobbin's car. God knows he rides by her building often enough. "Oh no, look who's coming."

"Who?" Kate asks and they all look down the street where Bob is slowing at the corner. He doesn't even stop at the stop sign, runs right through it and then stops in front of Granner's house.

"Bob Bobbin," Corky says and grabs Sam's hand.

"Well, I know we're leaving now," Kate says and takes Ernie's arm, but he is frozen now, watching Janie Morris hop out of that car.

"Hi, Mr. Stubbs!" Janie waves and walks up slowly. "I sure do like where you live. Bob rode me by."

"Ernie, who on earth is that?" Kate clutches his arm tighter.

"You must be Mrs. Stubbs." Janie Morris sticks her hand out in front of Kate, those silvery nails flashing. "I'm your husband's protégée."

"You're what?" Kate stares at Ernie, her mouth dropped slightly. "Do you mean to tell me that this is that secretary you hired?" Kate looks her up and down. Imagine, spectator pumps with a short culotte skirt and a tee shirt. Ernie had told her that he had hired an attractive, bright girl, one that would be an asset to the business. She has on enough eye shadow for everyone in Marshboro.

"Mr. Stubbs, please, I know that you know about who I stay with sometimes, but please don't fire me because of it. I'm a hard worker, you know that I am." Janie Morris grabs hold of the sleeve of Ernie's shirt. "I've shown you what I can do." She tilts her head to one side and stares at him. This is blackmail.

"I told her you weren't too pleased about her nigra boyfriend," Bob says and shakes his head.

"I tell you, Tommy didn't do it!" Here come those tears again. It makes Bob want to sing that song. It makes Bob want to take his billy stick and hit that crazy boy with Corky square in the head. "You've got to help me, Mr. Stubbs." Janie rushes up and wraps her arms around Ernie's waist, presses her face against his chest.

"How dare you!" Kate gasps and steps back. Ernie is just standing there like a fool, his arms held out to the sides, his chin lifted like he doesn't want to touch her.

"I've got to go," Ernie says.

"I'd like to know what's going on." Granner gets up from her chair and walks up to Bob. "I thought I told you that I'd call if I needed a police."

"I've come to get Harold," Bob says and looks over at Harold. "You've got to go down and see the suspect."

"What?" Harold blinks several times to get Bob into focus and he feels Juanita's hand back on his brogan now, just where he wanted it. "What man?"

"The murderer," Kate screams, still staring at Ernie who has not moved an inch away from that slutty looking woman. "The murderer that this woman lives with."

"Let me get this straight." Granner turns away from Bob and looks at Janie Morris. "You live with a nigra and this nigra is the one that Harold saw kill that man."

Granner shakes her head. "Ain't that something, and what did you say that you are of Ernie's? Something other than secretary."

"She's his protégée," Bob says. "That's French." He looks at Corky but she rolls her eyes and looks away.

"I don't know what that is," Granner says. "Ain't gonna try to say it either, or Kate there will correct me. Kate used to be a secretary but she was never one of those that I know of."

"You were a secretary?" Janie Morris finally lets go of Ernie and steps back, stares at Kate Stubbs. "Why, that's hard to believe."

"Well, I wasn't one for long!"

"Mr. Stubbs took you away from all of that, huh?" she asks, and Kate puffs up her chest and cheeks. It makes Harold laugh, makes him think that she might cut loose and blow away like a balloon set loose.

"I took them both away from it all, and now what do you think but that they want to put me away." Granner rocks faster.

"Oh my," Janie Morris gasps. "Can I have some of that cake? I'm starving."

"May I!" Kate says through gritted teeth.

"Help your damn self," Harold says. He'd like another drink right now, but he hates to move his foot away from Juanita. How does Bobbin know he's got the man? It gives Harold a rush all of a sudden. The man that killed Charles could be a woman, could be Chinese, could be anywhere. "Hey Sam, how bout going and getting me and you another drink?" Sam looks back at him, his eyes glazed all over again. That boy just can't drink worth a damn.

"I'll do it." Corky stands up and Sam Swett suddenly realizes that she is going to go inside, that she is going to leave him out here with all of these people. He can't let that happen. He jumps up, weaves a little, grabs hold of Bob Bobbin who pushes him away.

"You're drunk, Harold," Bob says, and watches Corky prance right inside and let the door slam after that boy has squeezed in past her. "You can't go down to the station that way."

"I can't go down to the station." Harold shakes his head and then slumps forward, his face cupped in his hands. He had almost forgotten it all, had almost forgotten Maggie's face.

"What is it?" Juanita creeps forward, puts her hand on Harold's back and he doesn't even jerk away.

"Come on, Kate," Ernie says.

"Not until I find out what's going on!" Kate sits back down in the swing and pulls Ernie with her. "What did she mean, protégée? All you needed was someone to type a little!"

"Harold?" Juanita shakes his shoulder, but he just rolls his head back and forth in his hands. Corky comes out carrying a drink and stands beside Harold's chair. Sam Swett stands behind her, his hands on her shoulders, his face pressed into the nape of her neck. It is cool there.

"Really, Harold, it's the only way that we can convict the man." Bob cannot take his eyes off of Corky letting that boy nuzzle up to her like a pony.

"I can't tell you anything." Harold looks up, his eyes red, runs his hand through his hair. He knocks his cap off and doesn't even pick it up. Juanita bends over to get it and then holds it. "I didn't see anybody coming out of the store. I don't know who killed Charles."

"You lied!" Ernie Stubbs stands up.

"I had to say something. I sure as hell didn't think they'd go and pick up somebody."

"Where were you?" Kate asks, and everyone is staring at Harold now. Patricia is staring straight through him, it seems, and he can't hardly stand it.

"I was passed out in the backroom." Harold looks around, looks everyone of them in the eye with that. He is completely sober. He has never felt so sober in his whole life.

"But you said," Sam Swett lifts his head off of Corky's back and stares at Harold. He sees two Harolds.

"Well, then what about him?" Bob points to Sam Swett, then walks over and pulls him away from Corky, pins him up against the porch post.

"He came in after I had already found Charles."

"Where were you before you went in that store?" Bob shakes him and he feels sick all over again. He had been feeling so good, too.

"He was outside throwing up," Harold says. "Kid was drunk as a skunk. We both were and that's why I made that up."

"Let him go, Bob." Corky squeezes in between Bob and Sam. Bob has never been this close to her before, and he'd like to press in closer and closer, except that everybody and their brother is watching. "Now!" she says and he lets go. Sam slumps down along the bannister and sits on the floor. Corky squats right down beside him and rubs his head. It makes Bob sick.

"I knew Tommy wouldn't do such a thing!" Janie Morris hugs Ernie and then hugs Kate. Kate has smelled enough Tigress for one day and she pushes her away.

"He could still have done it," Bob says. "Somebody drank that T.J. Swann—unless he did." Bob points at Sam.

"He didn't. I smelled his breath." Harold looks up at Juanita, suddenly feels angry about it all. "I reckon you're enjoying this, all of you, old drunk Harold telling a lie to the cops because old drunk Harold was scared." He stares over at Ernie and Kate. "That's something else for you to be ashamed of, all of you, scared to death that somebody will hear that Harold Weeks gets drunk and goes to the Quik Pik in the wee hours." He looks over at Patricia, who is now sitting on the railing facing the street as though none of this is happening. "Give Patricia over there one more reason for hating her Daddy, give Juanita here one more reason to screw around."

"Shut up!" Patricia screams. "I am ashamed of you! I do hate you!" Before Patricia can scream another time, Juanita is over there and has slapped her in the face. Juanita draws back her hand and watches Patricia, whose eyes are flashing like she hates Juanita more than anything on this earth. Patricia looks at Kate as if Kate might offer some help, but Kate doesn't even look at her. Juanita wants to hug her now, to say that she's sorry, but Patricia has run into the house and slammed the door.

"Well, now I've had enough," Kate says. "I have never seen such a fiasco in my life." Ernie follows her down the steps. "We don't even have time to get by the hospital and get to the party on time." Kate just keeps walking toward the car, doesn't even turn to wave. "I'm sure Rose will understand, though, that we simply couldn't make it."

"Wait, Mr. Stubbs!" Janie Morris goes running down the steps, those pumps clicking down the sidewalk. "Am I still your protégée?"

"Certainly not," Kate says, without even glancing back at the girl.

"Mr. Stubbs? What about all of that overtime that I did for you? What about last night?"

"We'll see. My wife is upset right now. You come in on Monday and we'll discuss it."

"There's nothing to discuss, Ernie," Kate says. "Fire her!"

"I can't just fire her," Ernie whispers. "Her boyfriend didn't do it. She is a hard worker."

"Remember how you said that you needed me?" Janie Morris grabs his sleeve again and slips her thumb up under the cloth, rubs over the hair on his arm. Kate doesn't see; Kate is in the car. "You said you were going to teach me so many things," she whispers. Again Ernie is getting that tight feeling in the pit of his stomach, even if she does have a boyfriend, even if she does wear Tigress and sparkly shadow. Just once Ernie wishes that Kate would look like this. Just once he wishes that Kate would let go of this act that she puts on and act a little loose.

"Ernie!" Kate screams, and he opens his door.

"Come by Monday," he says, and watches Janie Morris smile and wave, watches her almost turn her ankle on the edge of the sidewalk.

"Why did you tell her that?"

"Honey, I pay her peanuts. There is no place that I could get such a cheap worker."

"She's cheap." Kate nods. "Protégée! Ha. Like she could learn something. She needs to learn how to put on makeup." Ernie nods in agreement. But, God, she could teach Kate a few things.

"Let's go get Tommy!" Janie Morris runs up the steps and wraps her arms around Bobbin. Corky isn't paying attention to anything but that drunk boy. "Oh, poor Tommy, in that jail all day."

"Are you positive that you didn't see the nigger in the foreign shirt?"

"I swear it." Harold lifts his hand. "I'm sorry, Bobbin. I'm sorry that I don't know anything, cause I'd love to see whoever done it strung up by his balls."

"Harold!" Granner yells. She is glad that Kate and Ernie have left, glad that this commotion is near bout over. "Well, I'll tell you about Corky's Mama."

"You know lying is serious business, Harold! I could run you in," Bob says and looks away; those guys at the station will have a fine laugh over this.

"He didn't mean to lie," Juanita says. "He had too much to drink; he was scared and upset." Juanita has both of her hands on his back now and she is kneeling beside his chair. She ought to be on her knees. "Please, just let it go at that."

"Yeah, okay. But take it as a warning, Harold. Don't you never lie like that again!" Bob shakes his finger right in Harold's face and Harold never in his life thought that he would back down to Bob Bobbin, but he is doing it now. He nods and Bob steps back, throws back his shoulders. He points to Sam. "He ain't above suspicion. And if I didn't know you as good as I do, Harold Weeks, you might be under question yourself."

"He's the one that called the police!" Juanita screams.

"That's a trick used lots of times." Bob rubs his chin. He'd like to stall as long as possible. He'd like to get in his car and drive as far away from Marshboro as he can. It's going to be worse than when he saved that man's life. Here, all day long, he's told everybody that he caught a prime suspect and now all of this. God, the least Harold could have done was to go in and say, yep, that's the man. Hell, he lied once, he should've carried it through and lied again. Though, if the nigger didn't do it, that was that. But why couldn't he have just kept his big fat mouth shut in the first place? That's what Bob Bobbin would like to know.

"Tommy will be so happy!" Janie Morris pulls on Bobbin's sleeve and heads down the steps. "I've enjoyed being here. The cake was delicious!"

"It's homemade. Made it myself." Granner waves and watches them get in the car. "She's a right cute girl, ain't she?" Nobody answers Granner, so she keeps right on talking. If what these people want to do is touch one another, then they should go on home and do just that. Nobody should touch and carry on on the porch. It's so hicky, hicky, something awful. "That police ain't too cute though. If I was that girl I'd probably date a nigra over him, too." Corky looks up and laughs at this, and that is enough to get Granner to keep right on going. "Corky's Mama was a sort of odd girl to begin with. She was real pretty when she was young, like Corky there, but when she took to the bottle, she got to where she looked haggy."

"Leave her alone," Harold says.

"Well, if the pot ain't calling the kettle black. I'm telling of Corky's Mama." Granner looks right at Sam Swett, and he has to keep one eye closed to keep her in focus. He decides to open that other eye and forget being in focus. "I knew that woman was odd when I first heard of what she did with her coffee pot."

"Granner, that never has made a bit of sense." Juanita realizes now that Harold has his arm around her waist, and he has slowly pulled her closer and closer to where she is near about on his lap. He looks so pitiful, so sad.

"Yessir, it does. She was so afraid of running out of coffee or not being able to make it, so it got to where before she went to bed at night, she'd set up the percolator so all she'd have to do in the morning was plug it in. You see?"

"I don't get it," Corky says.

"I never have gotten it." Juanita rubs her hand up and down Harold's back, and all of a sudden he turns on her.

"You know if all that hadn't happened, I never would have been at the Quik Pik so late at night, never would have seen Charles dead!" He pushes her away and she lands flat on the floor. "I must be slam damn crazy to have sat here thinking that maybe you really cared. I must have been drunk."

"Must have been drunk," Sam says.

"Get that goddamned mynah bird out of here!" Harold screams.

"He didn't do anything." Juanita gets up from the floor and brushes off the back of her shorts. "And I do care, Harold Weeks. I care more than you know!" Juanita is crying now, brushing the tears so that they don't make her mascara run. "You won't even try to understand what happened!"

"What happened?" Sam asks, but Corky just shakes her head. Things had been going along so well, it had seemed, and here all of a sudden the bottom has fallen out.

"I understand that Charles Husky is dead, and I really can't stand to think of nothing else right now." Harold grabs Juanita's arm and twists the skin, squeezes until her flesh goes white underneath his hand. "Your goings-ons ain't worth nothing, just like you." He knows that he's hurting her, hurting her feelings as well as her arm, but she's too damn stubborn to say so, too damn stubborn to admit that she's the one that doesn't understand anything.

"You don't get that about the coffee pot, Corky?" Granner asks. "It was your Mama."

"I don't want to talk about my Mama any more, okay?" Corky raises her voice at Granner, something that she has rarely done, but she can't help it. It seems like everybody has been after her today, bringing up old bad sad things. She wishes she was right by herself now.

She wishes that she had never gotten out of her bed this morning, never met Sam Swett, never heard about Mr. Husky.

"Well, pardon me for breathing." Granner gets up and goes to the door. "I'd rather talk to Mr. Abdul right now than any of you others! This is the worst party that I've ever had!"

"Granner, I'm sorry. Really, I didn't mean to snap at you." Corky runs over and hugs Granner. Lordy, now Juanita's got Corky crying. They are all out to make an old woman's last birthday pure T miserable. "I just don't like to think about my family sometimes."

"I know just how you feel," Harold says.

"Me too," Sam Swett murmurs, and leans his head against the post. The shadows in the yard are getting longer now, almost cool-looking, and the sky is gray and hazy, as gray and hazy as Corky's eyes. Sometimes he wishes that he was all by himself without any family at all, and then he wouldn't have to think about them, then he wouldn't feel so torn up so much of the time.

"Well, very well," Granner says and pats Corky's head. "You all leave when you're ready. I'm gonna rest a little."

"I'll take Petie Rose home with me if you want," Juanita says.

"Yes, please do. If I hear 'Tom' once more I might slap her. It has been some kind of day." Granner comes back out and gets her Uncle Sam hat, puts it on her head and goes back inside where she can hear the T.V. going full blast. It's just gotten to be too much for her all of a sudden, all of that talk and fussing and fighting. If Buck

Weeks was alive all that wouldn't go on. If Buck Weeks was alive she probably wouldn't care if it did go on. "You left me with the short end of the stick," she says right out loud, mostly to herself but partly to Buck just in case he can listen in on her. Sometimes she even gets a picture of Buck, sitting right up there with Jesus, happy as a Jew lark and feeling pity for her that she's got to live with all this craziness on earth. Course, Buck got to be right crazy himself in his old age, when he'd slip into the bathroom and read what Harold Weeks calls beaver books. Granner thought for the longest time that Buck had took up drinking, but when she checked the back of that commode there was a baggie hanging there with naked pictures. It liked to have given Granner a stroke, and it's a wonder that she outlived that man. Granner goes and gets on her bed and pulls her afghan up around her neck, closes her eyes, and in her head says the pledge of allegiance. Usually that puts her right to sleep and if that doesn't work, she goes to reciting scripture and that does the trick, especially if she tries to remember who begot who.

Well, I guess I'll be going." Juanita moves closer to the door. "I'll just get the kids and go on."

"Yeah, we need to leave, too," Corky says and stands up. She nudges Sam's knee with her foot. "Come on. I knew you shouldn't have had all those drinks. You need to take a nap."

"You taking him home with you?" Harold asks.

"Damn, Corky, I didn't know you were that way, too." He nods toward Juanita.

"I've invited Sam to eat dinner with me and we're going to babysit M.L. McNair."

"Just ignore him," Juanita says.

"Well, that sure is what you did, wasn't it?" Harold stands now, scratches his chest, and Juanita catches a glimpse of the chain that she gave him on their last anniversary, solid gold filled, and she thought it looked so good hanging there in all those hairs. Harold didn't give her a thing for that anniversary, but he did take her over to Newton to the Long John Silver restaurant. At least he's still wearing it. "What if I said that I'm going home and that you can go to the trailer park?"

"I'm not about to go to any trailer park." Juanita steps back out on the porch. "Patricia would have a fit and we're not going to do it!"

"Well, see ya'll later." Corky pulls Sam Swett up from the porch and down the steps. "It was good to see you."

"Take care now, Corky," Juanita yells, and smiles as if nothing else in the world is going on. It has always amazed Harold the way that Juanita can put on that friendly cheerful show right in the middle of a fight. "You'll have to go to Nautilus some time, you hear? You two have fun. Nice meeting you." She waves and that boy just nods his head, says some funny sounding word and does his hand this odd way.

"Don't do that, you damn fool!" Harold screams. "Nobody is supposed to know those secrets!"

"What secrets?" he asks and stops, thinks. "Oh yeah. I won't do that."

"Put him on a bus, Corky," Harold calls. "He's crazy and he's drunk."

"Thanks to you," Corky says, and pulls Sam Swett on down the sidewalk. It surprises Harold so to have Corky speak right up to him that he doesn't even say anything back to her.

"Oh, leave them alone. They're having fun." Juanita puts her hands on her hips and steps closer. "I can't live in that trailer. But, you know, you can come home if you want. I never said you couldn't come home."

"Damn right you never said that, cause a hell of a lot of good it would do!"

"So do you want to come home?"

"I might! I might just!" He slaps his hand against the post. "I wouldn't want to mess up your love life, of course."

"I don't have any love life. I haven't had a love life since you left home!"

"Had two and then none. That's how it works. Didn't you ever hear of a bird in the hand?"

"Does a wild bear shit?" she asks, thinking she can get him to smile. It doesn't work. "I didn't really have you in my hand, now did I, Harold?"

"I never went after another woman!"

"But you never went after me, either." Juanita steps closer. "You know it was so nice a little while ago when you let me touch you."

"It was all right." Harold sits back down in his chair.

"I swear it's just too much to think about. I mean I don't know if I can ever forget what happened, and so it might be hard for me to forgive it all."

"It'll take time." Now Juanita is perched right back up on the bannister in front of him, those hairless shapely thighs right in his line of vision, that key chain that he gave her that says Massey Ferguson dangling from her fingers. "But we got that, Harold. Think of all we've got in the past. Think of those nights over in Pedro's country; think of the children."

"That's who I am thinking about. I don't want to get them all confused, cause it might not work right. What if something happens again?"

"I swear it won't!" Juanita lifts her hand. "I've been to a doctor, Harold. I tried to tell you that I have and I'm fine now, I tell you, I'm fine."

"What was it, sexitus?" Harold starts to laugh great big, but then catches himself when he sees that serious look on Juanita's face. She is serious; she wants him to come home.

"I told that doctor that I have never loved anybody but you," she says, and those blue eyes start to fill up with tears. "I don't know what made me go out and do what I did, Harold. If I did know, then I reckon I never would have done it, you know? I never would have done something to make my husband and my children, the only people that I care for, to hate me!"

"You told that to a doctor?" Harold takes his cap off now and runs his fingers through his hair. "What did he say?"

"Well, he said I ought to tell you so." Juanita sits there playing with that key ring, staring down at it like a baby with a rattle. "He said I might have been frustrated for a long time and the more I tried not to think that I was, the more crazylike my thoughts got."

"So it was my fault," Harold says. "Well, here we go again."

"No! It was nobody's fault, really, or mine. It was my fault, okay?" She tries to smile, but it looks like she's gonna bust out crying any second. "So, can we try again?"

"Maybe we'll try it. That trailer park is so loud and dark, dark as pitch, just about wrecked the pickup coming in the other night. But," he points his finger at Juanita, "we can't rush it cause deep down I'm still mad as hell, Juanita. Deep down, I feel like I could break your neck when I think of Ralph Britt. I mean the whole town knows! Ralph Britt's wife knows, everybody knows."

"Well, I can't change that." She wipes her eyes again and straightens up. "I thought about moving away."

"I can't get in that bed next to you right yet." Harold puts his cap back on but keeps messing with the bill, flipping it up and down. "I mean, maybe a lot of men would make fun of me but that bed was like a church, you know, just like what I used to tell you on Sunday morning." He flips his bill down now so that it hides his eyes. "It's special that way, Juanita. It's just like what I do at the Mason Lodge. If it means something to you, then you got to treat it right and it's your private business."

"I know, Harold."

"No, it is. It was like all them years me and you had

had our own club with our own rules and our own secret words and such, you know like me calling you cooter clam. That was our private joke, a bedroom secret, and then when you done what you did, it was like you had broken every rule of our club."

"Harold, I'm sorry. I've never told anybody about cooter clam or anything else. I've never told a living soul about how you like to have me pinch the arches of your feet when we're in bed!"

"Well, it's going to take a while. Take me a while to be able to trust you."

"But you'll come home?" Juanita is begging now, and this is just what he's been hoping to see, ever since that day he moved out. He nods and she smiles back at him. He feels like he could take a little nap himself right now. "Are you going to come now?"

"I'll be there directly. Might wait for Mama to get up."

"What would you like for dinner?" Juanita is talking a mile a minute now. She goes to the screened door. "Come on, kids! We'll go get Slurpees if you like." She walks back over and he starts to tell her about that Slurpee machine, about how Charles looked, but he doesn't. If those children want themselves a Slurpee and if Juanita wants one, he sure doesn't want to ruin it for them. "How about ribs? I can run to the store, the A&P, and get us some pork ribs and we can do them on the grill."

"Don't go to any big trouble."

"Or steak, I can buy us some pretty steaks and maybe a bottle of wine."

"Whatever you say."

"You don't act happy about this, Harold." She stands right by his chair, pulls his head up against her stomach but he pulls away.

"I said it's going to take time."

"I know! I know!" She squeezes his arm. "What time are you coming?"

"I don't know, not too late. Got to go out to the trailer first and make sure I got my valuables."

"Hey, can Petie go, too?" Harold, Jr., yells and runs out on the porch. "Petie doesn't want to stay here with Granner, cause Granner will make Petie Rose go to bed."

"Petie's going with us," Juanita says and smiles at Petie, who doesn't smile back. That Petie is a sourpuss for such a young thing. "We'll all get big Slurpees!"

"Hey, I'm gonna get cola!" Harold, Jr., screams and Petie Rose mimics him exactly. It is a shame that Patricia is not as kind to him as he is to Petie Rose.

"Thrills," Patricia says.

"Honey, I'm going to the shopping center, too, to the A&P, you reckon that the new drugstore out there would have that cologne that you want so bad?"

"God, I said I like it. It's not like I just smelled it for the first time." Patricia glances at Harold and then traipses on down the steps, with Harold, Jr., and Petie Rose racing behind her.

"We'll see you in a little bit then?" She waits now, holding her breath, afraid that Harold might burst out laughing and say that he was teasing her, or worse answer with that old, does a deer wear a brassiere? or does your Mama have three titties?

"Does a fat baby burp?" he asks, and Juanita is so nervous and so in the dark as to what to expect that she has to think for a second. Yes, yes a fat baby does burp. She nods and runs down the steps herself. Harold watches her and she looks almost like a child herself with those curls in her head so loose and sparkly. She toots the horn and then waves her arm out the window to him. She keeps waving and just about backs right out in front of a car.

"Mother!" he hears Patricia scream, but Juanita just laughs and waves again. Without a doubt she is the prettiest thing in town, but he can't let her get off the hook that easily, can't let her tell some little doctor story, flash those thighs, let a few tears well up and everything be okay. Harold Weeks has got to be slam damn sure of what's going on before he crawls back on top of that velvet spread with that woman.

6

The walk back makes Sam Swett feel much better; as long as he's moving, he's just fine. He never should have had all of those drinks, doesn't know why he let a man like that big hairy crude one have such an effect on him. But he does know; he knows that he wanted to fit in, to be liked and accepted, and it bugs the hell out of him because it goes against everything that he has been telling himself, that he needs no one, that he is different. He watches Corky walking on the edge of the curb, her arms held out gracefully to balance her, her hair falling down around her face as she watches her feet. He can't imagine what it would feel like to be Corky, to really have no family to speak of, to have seen all of the things that she has. And maybe that's been his biggest fear all of this time anyway, the fear of something bad happening, something that he cannot control; he can't even control himself. He feels so weak and helpless and how can that be? He doesn't know what the dead man's wife is feeling right now, what he felt when he was gasping that last breath, what Corky felt when she found her Daddy, what she feels when she visits her brother; what that old woman feels when she talks about her husband; what the man in pink pants felt when the mailman found his Mama. What would it feel like to suddenly have a child? a grandchild? a great-grandchild? What would it feel like to be the girl sitting there, with her parents talking about what made them split up? What would it feel like to be either of those parents? Sam Swett never even had a pet; he doesn't even know what that little girl is feeling with the loss of her cat. He doesn't know anything; he can only imagine how it all must feel, and he can't help but wonder how he can possibly write it all down as he has planned to do without really knowing and understanding; he can't help but wonder how people manage, how they keep going instead of doing what Corky's Daddy did. What do they have that keeps them alive when their lives appear to be so empty, so routine, like his parents? What do those people have that made him want to be a part of it all? They are settled; in spite of everything they are settled. "When are you going to settle down, Sam?" his father has asked. "You've got so much going for you and I wonder why you won't settle down." Settle. Settle down; his father said it as if it were a positive thing to do; so many people say that they want to settle down, to have a family, but what does that mean, settle? Settling, sinking to the bottom like silt and sand, orange juice pulp in the bottom of a glass, or settling like cream, rising to the top, finding a place, sticking together. They have settled; they've accepted; just that easily they have accepted the good and the bad, the indifferent; they even accepted him in an odd way just by letting him be there. Settling, accepting; that's what makes it different.

"What are you thinking about so hard?" Corky grabs his hand and swings it back and forth. "Feeling better?"

"Yeah, fine." He rubs his thumb up and down the back of her hand. "Sorry I drank too much, should've known better."

"Well, Harold has a way of getting people to drink too much." She laughs. "He and Juanita are some kind of pair. I hope they'll get back together."

"Why? Seemed to me like they couldn't agree on anything."

"That's how they've always been. You know people love in lots of different ways."

"They do?"

"Well, yeah." She faces him, gives him an odd look like he might not know anything. "Like my big brother, Chip," she says and shrugs. "You know, the one Harold was talking about." Sam Swett nods. "When we were little or at least when I was little, Chip would get me on the sofa and pin me down and he'd get this real serious look on his face and he'd say, 'I am never going to let you go.'" She laughs and looks away from Sam. "He would say that over and over and of course, I'd scream and cry and tattle and my Daddy would get after Chip." She stops and reaches down and picks up a piece of pine straw, braids the three pieces of straw like a plait of hair. She holds it up. "I used to braid straw all the time." She hands it to him and he bends it up and puts it in his back pocket. "Oh, but you know, that was Chip's way of loving me. That was his way of being close to me and holding me. He used to beat up anybody that picked on me."

"I can't imagine anybody picking on you."

"Shoot, everybody gets picked on some time or another." She pulls his arm and speeds up. "There's M.L. sitting on the porch," she says when they round the corner, and Sam looks over to see a small black boy sitting on the steps. "Hi M.L.!" Corky yells and he stands up and waves, then runs to the door and yells that Corky's home.

"Whatcha doin, M.L.?" Corky rubs her hand over his head.

"Playing." He stares up at Sam Swett, his eyes zeroing in on Sam's shaved head. M.L. has a G.I. Joe that he is playing with. "Who's that?" he asks without taking his eyes off of Sam.

"His name's Sam," Corky says. "He's gonna be with us tonight, cause he's a friend of mine." Corky sits on the step beside M.L. and motions for Sam to have a seat. He really probably ought to keep walking but he sits. At this point he would probably do anything that she said. "You don't mind, do you?"

"Naw." M.L. bends his G.I. Joe's legs and makes him sit down. It is a white G.I. Joe and that bothers Sam Swett. Does the child pretend that he is black? It is something that has always made Sam stop and wonder. It is only in the past few years that they have even started making black dolls, and Sam cannot help but wonder what it must have felt like to be a black child with a white baby doll, to be a black child and for Roy Rogers and all the good heroes to be white. Which M&Ms did black children choose for themselves, the dark browns or the light browns? "I did a dive off the side of the pool," M.L. says to Corky.

"That's great!" she screams and claps and hugs him close. Corky needs to love people. Obviously, she loves this black child. Sam Swett has never had much to do with children; he's not even certain that he knows how to talk to a child.

"I might try it off the board pretty soon." He stands up and bends his knees up and down, holds his hands over his head, one hand cupped over the other. "Do like this. I jumped off the board today, done like this." He goes to the edge of the porch, winds up his arms and then jumps off. He lands in a squat position with his knees bent, but can't hold it there; he tumbles over.

"Good jump," Sam says, and the kid just grins at him and nods. "What does M.L. stand for?"

"Martin Luther." He holds his arms out and spins around and around with his head thrown back. "Martin Luther McNair."

"Nice name. Martin Luther King was a fine man." Sam Swett shakes his head and looks little M.L. square in the eye once he has stopped turning and is standing on that sidewalk swaying back and forth. Sam Swett has to sway with him to keep eye contact. "You should be proud to have such a fine name."

"My Mama named me," he says and flops down on a grassy spot by the walk. "Fannie said that name was too big for somebody so small so she named me M.L. for shortness." He lies back in the grass now, his legs crossed, one shoe untied. It looks so comfortable that Sam Swett would like to do it himself.

"Where are your parents going tonight?" Sam asks and Corky gives him a quick look that he doesn't understand.

"My Mama's in New York," he says. "I don't know where they go at night."

"M.L. lives with his grandmother, Fannie McNair," Corky says. "They're my best neighbors, right, M.L.?"

"Yep." He sits up and looks at Sam. "Who you stay with?"

"Myself." He leans back on his forearms, stretches his legs.

"You talk with Corky?" M.L. creeps up closer, now that he has gotten used to this funny looking man.

"Well, sure, we've been talking all day," he says, and Corky starts laughing.

"No, do you talk to her, you know."

"He means are we going together," Corky says and then looks at M.L. "He's a lot older, you know, hasn't heard the new things to say."

"Oh," M.L. steps closer and grins again. "I talk to a girl named Lareesie Polk. She's seven."

"Older woman, huh?" Corky asks, and M.L. spins around again and laughs.

"So, you two talk?" he asks again, and Sam Swett doesn't know what to say; he doesn't know how Corky can laugh so hard. She may think it's just that funny to imagine herself going with him.

"We haven't known each other long," she says. "We're just friends."

"Oh." He stops spinning again and walks crooked all around the yard. "This is what a drunk man does," he says and falls flat down. Sam is getting a little self-conscious now. Is this child making fun of him. Can everybody tell that he's been drinking?

"How was the party?" Fannie McNair steps out on the porch, and M.L. comes running up when he sees her. She stops and stares at Sam Swett first thing. "I'm sorry, didn't know you had company."

"Fannie, this is Sam Swett." Corky stands up. "He's a friend, just visiting the area." Sam gets up too, and his knees feel a little rubbery. He sticks out his hand. "Pleased to meet you," he says and smiles. Her hand is rough and warm, her knuckles as gnarled as the roots of a tree.

"Any friend of Corky's is a friend of mine," Fannie says, and Corky cannot help but notice the sad distant look in Fannie's eyes. It makes Corky feel a little scared, because she has never seen Fannie look this way.

"They don't talk, though," M.L. says and picks up his G.I. Joe, fixes Joe's arms like he's about to dive.

"Are you okay?" Corky touches Fannie's arm and she nods her head slowly.

"Baby, how about you running upstairs and eating your supper," Fannie says, and wraps her hand around the back of M.L.'s neck. "I got it on the table for you. I want you to go ahead and eat and take your bath cause I'm leaving pretty soon."

"Right now?" He reaches up and hugs her around the waist.

"Don't you put on that act now, M.L." She gently pushes him away and laughs, though the laugh seems strained. "You run on and put on your pajamas, too. Then you'll be all set to watch T.V."

"All right," he says, and turns when he gets to the door. "You ain't gonna leave right now, are you?"

"No, I'll be up there before I leave. You go on and you put on those bedroom slippers before you come back down here." Fannie watches him go inside and then listens while he goes up the stairs. She pulls that old kitchen chair up near the steps and sits down, wipes her forehead where beads of sweat have formed. "I appreciate you keeping him, Corky. I wouldn't have asked if I knew you had company."

"We don't mind, do we?" She looks at Sam and he shakes his head. "Are you okay, Fannie?"

"Lord only knows," she says and it looks to Corky like Fannie might cry. "I tell you it has been some kind of day."

"What happened?" Corky asks, and slides over to where she is sitting right at Fannie's feet. She looks like a little girl in that position, and Sam Swett suddenly has the urge to know what she looked like as a child, what she looked like when her brother held her down on the sofa, what she would look like when she got old.

"My boy, Thomas was picked up cause he looks like a murderer." She stares out in the yard, focuses on an old poptop at the edge of the street that is glaring in the late sun like a bright star. "They got him in jail, too. I know Thomas ain't a real good person, but I don't think he'd kill nobody."

"Fannie!" Corky grabs her arms. "Does your son have a white girl friend?"

"I didn't know it till today but yeah, I spose so." Fannie shakes her head. "See, that's how Thomas is. He'll do anything to be different from what he is. I mean no offense, but he knows I wouldn't like the notion of him being with a white girl."

"Then he's okay," Corky says. "They don't have any evidence to keep him." Corky is up on her knees now and talking so fast that Sam can barely understand her; she's telling about the big hairy Harold and the lie he told and the girl with the cop and so on. It amazes Sam the way that both of them sit there and say "white" and "black" and draw out all of these differences between the two. He has always treated black people like he didn't notice that they were black, like they were all the same. He had always thought that that was the way it should be, that that was what civil rights was all about, and yet these two are sitting here talking about all of the differences, talking as if there is a need for differences to be made.

"Well, that is music to my ears," Fannie says when Corky has finished the story. "I knew that Thomas couldn't have killed that man. That was a nice man and it's a shame. I didn't know him that well, but everytime me and M.L. went in that store, he'd give M.L. a piece of gum or candy."

"He was a fine man," Corky says and then squeezes Fannie's arm and laughs. "You feel lots better now, don't you?"

"Yes, Lord, I sure do." Fannie smiles and Corky can see the relief in her eyes. It makes her feel relieved herself to see that Fannie isn't upset any more. "I sure hope they catch that man that done it, though."

"I do, too," Corky says. "You know Sam here went in the store after it all happened, and he saw Mr. Husky."

"Oh, how bad that must've been." Fannie clucks her tongue and looks at Sam. "I am sorry for you."

"Yeah," he says and nods, but he remembers seeing the man before he was dead as well, or did he dream that?

"All done, Fannie." M.L. comes running out in his blue striped pajamas and bedroom slippers. He has swapped his G.I. Joe for an old stuffed monkey.

"Um um, I bet that was some bath, give what you got a lick and a promise and that was it, huh?"

"No, I scrubbed, scrubbed so hard it near about hurt!" He swings one leg up on Fannie's lap. "How late you gonna be gone?"

"I'll be home about eight or so."

"Can I sit up till you get home?" He slides up and sits on her lap.

"I reckon you can." She wraps her arms around him and it makes Corky feel so good to see them that way. It makes her want to squeeze Sam Swett, but she can't do that in public, so she just reaches over and takes his hand. His hand is cool and clammy and his face looks a little pale. He probably needs to get some food in him to soak up those drinks. "I tell you what, M.L. I might bring you home some goodies from the party, too," Fannie says.

"Please!" He pulls that monkey right up under his chin and swings his little feet back and forth, one of his corduroy slippers about to fall off.

"There's my ride," Fannie says when a big black New Yorker pulls up. "Hop up, baby, I gotta go get my purse and that dress for Mrs. Foster."

"I'll get them for you." Corky hops up and goes to the door.

"They're on the bed, honey, thank you." Fannie turns and holds up one finger to Billy Foster, who has already blown the horn two times even though he sees her standing there.

"Hey, do this," M.L. says to Sam, and starts spinning round and round up on the porch. It makes Sam dizzy to watch him; it makes everything feel like it's spinning; it makes the saliva in his mouth double its production; makes his stomach churn. He has to look away from M.L. and stare at something stable, concrete, that big black car, that boy with the punk-cut yellow hair, that big black car. Sam puts his head between his knees and stares down at a spot of grass beside the steps. He remembers squatting outside of the store; he remembers everything spinning so fast and he felt so sick and he heard a car; he heard the bells on the door ring. It seems they rang several times. He looks up and now that boy has gotten out of the car and is walking around, opens the passenger side. "What's the hold up?" he asks.

"I'm on my way," Fannie yells.

It was a hold-up. He remembers stretching out in the grass beside that building, remembers staring at that light in front of the store where moths were gathering, remembers the bells ringing, remembers he was thinking of M&M's, remembers seeing all that bread land on the sidewalk, slice after slice of bread that reminded him of the ants in the gutter, going after the bread, but he had been too tired to think about it; he had closed his eyes; he had taken a nap.

"Here you are." Corky hands Fannie her purse and a green dress wrapped in plastic.

"You do what Corky says, baby." Fannie kisses M.L. on the cheek and then heads down the steps. That boy is already back in on his side and has the car cranked and the radio blasting. Fannie gets in the car and Sam Swett suddenly bounds up and runs down to close the door for her. He waits while she gets her skirt in and folds that dress in the plastic just right. He has seen that boy before; he had seen him dump out a whole loaf of bread.

"Thank you, Sam," Fannie says and makes him jump. He closes the door and watches them drive away, rubs his head.

"What's wrong with you?" Corky asks, and he shakes his head. If he could just remember for sure. If he could just take a little nap, maybe he could remember better, or maybe he'd forget all over again. He has done this before, remembered something that happened when he was drunk when he was drunk again but forgetting it while he was sober.

"Who was that in the car?" He weaves a little and sits down on the sidewalk, takes her hand and pulls her down beside him, almost pulls her on top of him.

"Don't do that with M.L. right here," she whispers and sits up straight, glances up on the porch where M.L. is running back and forth, tossing that monkey up in the air and catching it.

"I didn't mean to," he says and grabs her arm tighter. "Who was that?"

"His last name's Foster. He's the son of the people that Fannie works for." She takes his hand off of her arm because he's hurting her. "Why?"

"I've seen him before." He gets right up in her face and whispers. His breath just about knocks her out, might have to lend her toothbrush to him if he plans on kissing her later on.

"So?"

"Do you know him?"

"Nope." Her eyes look so blank right now, so dull and blank. "Fannie can't stand him cause she says he's spoiled rotten." She shrugs and pulls up a piece of grass, makes a tiny slit and tries to whistle through it. "I never did learn to do this, did you?" He shakes his head. "Chip could do it real good. He could whistle with his fingers, too."

"Why doesn't Fannie like that boy?"

"I told you, he's spoiled and too, he's a troublemaker." She glances back on the porch to make sure that M.L. is still up there playing and not getting dirty. "Well, nobody knows for certain but when the church was all messed up, rumor was that that boy and two others did it. Nobody ever found out for sure, but Fannie said she could believe him doing such a thing."

"What did they do." Now he is in her face again, those brown eyes wide open, darting back and forth like he might be crazy.

"I can't even say it was so bad." She leans back so that he won't be breathing right in her face.

"Please, tell me." He leans toward her again and she thinks he'd crawl right up on top of her and hold her there like Chip used to do if she gave him half a chance.

"Okay, but sit up," she says, and he does. He sticks his little finger in his ear and jiggles it around to make sure he can hear good. "They wrote all this bad stuff on the walls, bad words, you know. They did it with spray paint and so the church had to be repainted, then they," she looks away. "They did something filthy there on the altar."

"What?"

"Well, I'll tell you this much, they got it from messing with themselves, you know?"

"God, that's sick." He squints his eyes, jiggles his ear again. "And that boy did that?"

"Well, it wasn't proven. Everybody figured that those boys' daddys paid somebody off, might have paid to redo the church, you know?"

"God, my father would've probably killed me and turned me in." He remembers suddenly the time that he took a tape from K-Mart's, one lousy Eagles tape and he didn't even get caught. But he couldn't hack the pressure, he told his father what he had done. His father had slapped him in the face, driven him to K-Mart's, made him go up to the register and confess there in front of everyone. He was in high school, for God's sake, and his father was standing right there behind him, forcing him to confess, forcing him to pay for the tape. He had begged for forgiveness on his own. The woman smacking gum behind the counter had not accepted the apology; she had just rung up the tape and smacked her gum.

"You never know," Corky says and he looks back at her quickly. "Your Daddy might have thought you deserved another chance, you know?" She leans her head to one side, a small sprig of hair blowing right near her eye. "Still, though, everybody else was hoping that they'd catch who did it."

"I saw that boy last night," he says and grabs her hand, this time not as tightly so that she will let him hold it; he needs to hold it. "I saw him at the Quik Pik. I was outside of the store; I was sick and now I remember that car, the same car, pulling up and I remember seeing that bread fall out of the wrapper."

"What are you talking about?"

"He did it." Sam gets on his knees now and moves from side to side. "I tell you I think he did it!" He can't keep himself still now. He feels like he needs to start moving again. "You got anything to drink?"

"Are you sure? Are you positive that you saw him?" She sits up straight again, those gray eyes opened wide, her mouth dropped open, those full lips. "I mean you're sure?" He nods faster and faster; he jiggles his ear. He has never felt this way before.

Juanita has got her Tammy Wynette album turned up about as high as it will go so that she can hear it while she's taking her bubble bath. Stand by your man. She lathers her legs up real good so that she can get a close shave. She has done electrolysis on part of her legs, and probably in about five years will finish them up. She will probably be the only woman on the face of the earth who always has smooth silky legs, who never has her nylons catch on a stubble. She just does it a little at the time because it is a skill-requiring, lengthy process.

"Mother! Can I turn that record off?" Patricia is outside of the bathroom door.

"Sure, honey," Juanita yells, even though she would really like to go right on listening to Tammy instead of those Talking Heads. She knows that's what Patricia's going to play, too. Imagine, calling yourselves the Talking Heads. Still, Juanita wants to do everything in her power to make up to Patricia, to see if she can make it to where Patricia won't be ashamed of her. Juanita finishes shaving her legs and lets the water start draining out of the tub. She likes to sit there until all the bubbles gather around the drain, and then she turns on the shower and just stays there like she might be stretched out in the rain. It is invigorating and exhilarating. That's what she always told Harold when he told her that was a stupid thing to do and she likes those two words so much, invigorating and exhilarating, that's how she feels right this second, especially now that her skin is all tingly and red where she has rubbed good and hard with her loofah sponge. She gets out and puts on her robe without even drying off just like they always do in the movies, and it does feel good to air dry sometimes.

Patricia is sitting in that lounge chair with her legs thrown over one arm. She is reading *Seventeen*, listening to the Talking Heads and eating a Milky Way all at the same time. That chocolate ain't good for her face and Juanita has to near about bite her own tongue to keep from saying it. Harold, Jr., is on the floor playing himself a game of checkers. Juanita loves to watch him do that, the way that he'll move around that board from side to side. He writes down on a piece of paper "me" and "I" and then he keeps track of how many games he wins.

"Where's Petie?" Juanita asks and fluffs her hair.

"Her Daddy came and got her." Harold, Jr., jumps himself two in a row.

"Well, why didn't you tell me?" she asks. "I would have liked to have congratulated him. Besides, we could have run Petie home."

"Well, he got her." Patricia looks up from her magazine as if she is the Queen of Sheba and has just been interrupted.

"What's for dinner, Mom?" Harold, Jr., asks and makes a mark on his little score pad.

"Ribs!" She goes into the kitchen, stopping in the doorway. "Your Daddy's favorite." She stands there grinning and waiting for them to say something.

"Dad's coming?" Harold, Jr., asks and runs into the kitchen.

"Yes sir. He's coming home." Juanita presses her robe up against her leg where there is some water dripping down. Maybe she should have dried off a little.

"Oh great." Patricia throws down her magazine. "So ya'll can finish your fighting?"

"No ma'am." Juanita goes back into the living room. "So we can work things out between us."

"You mean he's going to come back after what you did?"

Juanita is so tempted to go over there and slap Patricia's face again, but she stops herself. Why on earth is that child doing this to her?

"We both made some mistakes," Juanita says and steps closer.

"But I didn't" Patricia balls up that Milky Way wrapper and tosses it toward the trashcan. It misses and she doesn't even get up to get it. "I haven't done anything at all, but I have to put up with it."

"I'm sorry, too." Juanita goes over and stands right beside Patricia's chair. "I never wanted to hurt anybody." She touches Patricia who jerks away. "I love you; I love all of you."

"Then why did you do it?" Patricia stands up. "Why did you . . ." She glances over at Harold, Jr., and stops short. At least she cares enough about him not to tell everything that she knows.

"I don't know why. If I knew that then I wouldn't have

done it." Juanita feels like she might cry right now and Patricia looks away from her. "I had some problems, honey. I just wasn't myself." Juanita steps closer. Patricia goes and picks up her magazine and then puts that wrapper in the trash. Juanita watches her slouch off down the hall.

"He's here!" Harold, Jr., screams and runs out the front door. She hears Harold, Jr., squeal and she knows without even looking that Harold has picked him up and swung him around.

"Come on in," she yells as if Harold had never even been here before. "I'll be dressed in a minute!" She rushes off to the bedroom and puts on her stretch jeans and a full loose blouse, one that Harold picked out for her all by himself one time. She leans her head over and brushes all her hair forward, so that when she slings it back it will be full and bushy, the way that Harold likes it. She looks at herself in the full length mirror and she does look good. Harold cannot help but notice how good she really does look. She sprays a little Aviance on herself and for a second catches herself wishing that she had some of that fancy cologne for herself right now. Harold likes Aviance, though; he always liked that commercial where the woman says, "I can bring home the bacon, fry it up in a pan." Juanita moves her hips in front of the mirror just the way that that woman always did. Her heart is going a mile a minute, like this might be her first date or something. She knocks on Patricia's door when she passes by. "Your Daddy's here, honey," she says, and Patricia doesn't even answer.

"Hi, Harold," she says. "I hope ribs sound good to you."

"That's fine," he says and goes to the refrigerator and gets himself a beer.

"I might have one of those, Harold," she says and he pops open another one and hands it to her. "Do you want a glass for yours?"

"Now, when have I ever used a glass?"

"I didn't know, thought I'd ask is all." She smiles great big but Harold doesn't. He goes over to his lounge chair and rears it all the way back. "Cut on the sports station," he says to Harold, Jr. "And cut off that stereo." Harold, Jr., goes right over and does both of those things. It is just like old times.

"Here's some chips and dip," Juanita says. "You sit here and rest and I'll do the grilling."

"Why don't you cut it out, Juanita?" he asks, right when Patricia comes into the room.

"What?" Juanita smiles great big and tosses her hair from side to side.

"This act you're putting on. I'm here to eat, here in my own house, and you're acting like I'm a guest."

"I thought you were here to stay."

"Maybe, haven't decided." He takes a big swallow of his beer. He is going to give her a hard row to hoe. He leans his head back in the chair and closes his eyes. He's just going to take a little nap and let her sweat it out for awhile. She got herself all fixed up and he knows she's dying for a compliment, fishing for one. Juanita always has fished for compliments if you didn't give them to her.

"Tricia, will you help me?"

"Why are you calling me that all of a sudden?"

"You said that's what you wanted to be called," Juanita says, and looks over at Harold. He has one eye open.

"Why in the hell would she want to be called that?" he asks.

"She doesn't like her name as it is."

"I didn't say that," Patricia wails and grunts.

"I'm sorry, I thought that you did." Juanita goes over and gets herself a chip and dip. Harold is not even touching them. "Will you help me?"

"I said that I might want to change my name," she says. "What do I have to do?"

"Well, you don't have to do anything, honey. I thought you might help me with the salad." Harold sits up and stares at Juanita. She is acting crazy all the way around. "I thought we might use the good china this evening."

"Why in the hell would you put ribs on good china?" Now Harold has pushed his recliner back down and Juanita doesn't even answer him. She comes over and runs her finger over the tear in that chair. "I declare we've got to patch this old thing up, maybe get a new one."

"This one is fine. Who the hell are you expecting, the Reagans?"

"I've been thinking that I might want to redo this room" Juanita puts her hands on her hips and looks around the room. "Maybe paint the walls white or off-white, you know, something sophisticated. I might get new drapes and a whole new set of furniture."

"Is that what this is all about?" Harold looks at her but she is going around the room now, stepping back and looking at everything from ceiling to floor. "You want me to come back so you can get some money?"

"No, Harold. I've just been thinking lately that we haven't done a thing to the house in years and you know, Tricia will be having dates before too long."

"So what?" Harold gets up and follows her around the room.

"Well, we want our home to look nice when her friends stop by, now don't we?" She stops and looks at Harold. "I mean things like that are important when you're young and entertaining."

"I hadn't noticed anybody knocking the door down," he says, and then looks over at Patricia. She is staring down at her feet. "Of course, I'm sure they will be" he adds. God, now Juanita's got him acting crazy.

Juanita loops her arms through Harold's and he lets it stay there. "I mean sometimes you just have to have something new to make you feel better. I mean just the other day I came this close to buying me and you and Harold, Jr., some of those shirts that everybody wears with the alligator."

"Those fox shirts that I wear are just as good," Harold says, but Juanita shakes her head slightly at him and keeps right on going.

"You know with Patricia going to the high school, she'll need some new things, especially if she makes flag girl." Now, Patricia's mouth is wide open.

"Why are you saying it like that? like Patricia instead of Pa-tree-sia. You said when she was born that that was the prettiest name you could come up with."

"I did say that, Harold, but you know that name is hard for people to pronounce, and what's more, when it's spelled out it looks just like Patricia." She looks over at Patricia. "Right, honey?" she asks and Patricia nods. "Don't you remember P.R. Riley, Harold and how his Daddy meant to name him Pierre but always said P.R.?" Harold nods and starts to say something but she doesn't give him the damn chance. "You know, P.R. was embarrassed by his name and it made him ashamed of his Daddy cause he thought people would make fun. Now we don't want our Patricia being ashamed of us now do we, heaven knows we've already caused her enough heartache." Juanita shakes her head back and forth, the tears springing to her eyes all of a sudden. Harold would like to know what in the hell this is all about and where Juanita thinks all this money she's talking about spending is going to come from, when one look at Harold, Jr., and them rabbit teeth of his would tell you that that boy is going to be in bad need of braces one of these days soon.

"Hey Mama, want me to sing it now?" Harold, Jr., asks and Juanita shakes her head back and forth.

"Sing what, son?" Harold asks.

"Nothing, Harold. He was thinking he might sing a song he learned just recently."

"I learned it off of Mama's Wayne Newton record," Harold, Jr., says and smiles great big. He is so proud of himself.

"What did you learn?" Harold asks, and can't help but laugh to see him standing there, those dirty hands on his hips like he might be all grown up.

"Goes like this," he says and throws back his shoulders, opens his mouth.

"Not now, honey," Juanita says. "Not while we're talking about the redecorations."

"Let him sing," Harold says. "God knows, it's nice to see somebody that feels like singing for a change. Go ahead, son."

"Daddy don't you walk so fast, daddy don't you walk so fast!" Harold, Jr., holds his hands behind his back and sings as loud as he can. Patricia has to cover her ears up cause he's off key something awful. "Daddy, slow down some cause you're making me run. Daddy, don't you walk so fast." Harold, Jr., bows and Patricia claps her hands together and laughs; she actually laughs.

"Who told you to learn that song?" Harold asks and Juanita gives Harold, Jr., a quick glance.

"I learned it off the record," he says. "You want to hear it again?"

"I bet I know who put you up to that." Harold looks at Juanita. "You trying to make me feel like I done wrong by walking out of here?"

"No, Harold. You know me better than that."

"Yeah, I know you too well," he says and goes back to his chair. Juanita can't tell if he's mad at her or not. She certainly never intended that Harold, Jr., would sing that song with her standing there. Thank God, Harold, Jr., was too busy playing with Petie Rose at the party to sing it there. Kate and Ernie would have gotten just what they wanted from that.

"Now, let's finish talking about this room," Juanita says and Harold interrupts her, tells Harold, Jr., to go get him a beer. "Patricia, I'll let you decide. You might want to ask Aunt Kate what she thinks."

"What?" Harold shakes his head from side to side and then points his finger at his head like Archie Bunker used to always do, and acts like he shoots himself in the head.

"Daddy, don't you drink so fast." Harold, Jr., hands him the beer and is so tickled that he sprawls out on the floor. Patricia is laughing, too, laughing up a storm until her eyes get all watery and she sits over there crying.

"What's wrong?" Juanita asks. "I mean that you can decide, and what's more, we'll go to that decorator furniture place over in Newton, too. I mean we can't do the whole house but we can do this room and maybe your room, Patricia."

Patricia shakes her head back and forth and then she jumps up and wraps her thin arms around Juanita and puts her head up against Juanita's neck. "I'm not ashamed of my name, Mama. I'm not." Patricia looks up and shakes her head back and forth.

"It doesn't hurt my feelings if you are. You got a right to say what you want to be called."

"No, no, I'm sorry that I ever said that. I didn't mean it. I know we can't afford to do all of those things."

"We can, too," Harold says. "Not all at once by any means, but we can do those things."

Patricia wipes her eyes and runs over to hug Harold; Juanita stands there crying, too, wiping her nose on her apron. Harold doesn't know what in the hell to do. If he had known it was going to be so damned crazy over here, he probably would have stayed over at his crazy Mama's house. He presses his large hand against Patricia's back and hugs her.

"Okay, okay," he says. "That's enough, now. You're gonna get snot all over my shirt."

"Harold!" Juanita says. "You could at least say mucous."

"Mother, that sounds worse than snot." Patricia stands up and laughs. "I'm going to go fix that salad now, okay?"

"If you don't mind," Juanita says, and watches her walk to the kitchen. Already it looks like those shoulders have straightened up. "Harold, Jr., why don't you run outside and see if the paper's been delivered. He nods and goes outside. The screen door slams behind him and he starts singing again.

"You thought that song would get my gut, huh?" He rolls his head to one side in that chair and watches her standing there, that hair so curly and sparkly. "Might as well admit it Juanita Sucks Weeds, I know you like a book."

"I thought it might make you want to come home, yes." She goes over and sits on the footstool in front of the window. "I know we can't do all of that decorating at once, but you just don't understand why I . . ."

"I reckon I see what you're doing." He shakes his head

and takes a big swallow. "We been going round and round and not thinking a thought of those two. We been stupid, Juanita."

"I know." She moves over to his chair and kneels right there by his feet. "I want to make it up to them." She rubs her hands up and down his calves. "I want to make it up to you."

"Well, that's gonna take a while." He shifts his legs around, crosses them and she sits back. "But I reckon it's best for the kids that I stay here. Else, no telling what you'll have Harold, Jr., doing, probably have him wearing girl clothes or such."

"Thank you, Harold," she says. "It hurts me so bad to think that our children could ever be ashamed of us."

"Well, they're not. I mean all children get mad at their parents, but it don't mean they'd really be ashamed. Ernie Stubbs was ashamed of his Mama. Now, I can't picture either of ours ever acting that way."

Juanita is on the verge of telling Harold what she heard today, but she simply can't bring herself to do it. "Let's make sure that never happens," she says and wipes her nose again. "Now, what would you like with the ribs?" She stands up and shakes her hair from side to side.

"I'd like a beer, Nita. I'm gonna sit here and think a little." That's the first time that he's called her Nita in ages and she'd like to run over there right now and kiss that filthy mouth of his as hard as she can. But, no, she can't push it; he's gonna make her pay, and she might as well go along with him. It's a hell of a lot better than having to move out of town.

"I'll bring you another," she says, and she doesn't even tell him not to drink too much, though she hopes with all of her heart that he won't, considering she's made a little breakthrough with Patricia. This room does look a little bad, though Juanita had never seen it as being as bad as the picture that Patricia painted for Kate Stubbs. Deep down that's what bothers Juanita the most, the fact that Patricia never let on to how she felt to her own mother, but instead went to somebody like Kate who already turned her nose up at them. "Oh, that salad looks so good," she says, and Patricia halfway smiles at her, her eyes still red and a little puffy. "I'm sorry that I slapped your face, Patricia," she says. "But you know your Daddy isn't a bad man; he's a fine man deep inside where it counts." Patricia swallows hard and her eyes well up all over again. She nods. Juanita goes and gets a beer from the refrigerator, pops it open. "My mother made me the ugliest dress that you've ever seen in your life one time. I got up on Easter Sunday and there it was right next to my brother's basket full of eggs." Juanita tilts her head to one side and snickers. "It was this purple ruffly dotted swiss dress with a big bow at the neck. I'd much rather had those Easter eggs."

"What did you do?" Patricia asks and scrapes all the tomatoes she has chopped into the big salad bowl.

"My mother was standing right there when I first saw it and she was so proud of it, said that she had worked for days on that dress while I was in school." Juanita gets to the door with the beer and stops. "I said that I loved that dress even though I hated it, and I wore it to church that day even though I was scared to death that somebody was gonna say something about it."

"Did anyone?"

"No, I don't think it was really as ugly as I saw it, or rather not sticking out like a sore thumb like I imagined." Juanita laughs again. "The worst part, though, was that it made me feel ashamed of that dress and ashamed of my Mama for choosing such ugly cloth and an ugly pattern, and then I felt so guilty for thinking all of that because I knew that my mother hadn't meant to hurt me at all. She had wanted to make me happy." Patricia stares back at her and doesn't say a word. "I know now that I just should have looked at my Mama and told her that I didn't like it, but something inside of me kept me from doing it."

Patricia puts down her knife and steps closer, those shoulders slumping again. Juanita straightens up herself and Patricia gets the hint and stands straight. "You heard what I said today, didn't you?" Juanita starts to look confused, starts to shake her head but there is no way to lie her way out of this. She nods her head and Patricia lets out a little sob, pulls up her tee shirt and wipes her nose. "I'm sorry, Mama, I didn't really mean it."

"Look at that snot on your shirt, would you?" Juanita puts her hands on Patricia's shoulders and pushes her back, looks her up and down. "You are gonna be the prettiest flag girl in all of Marshboro! Yes, you are, and what's more before you start wearing those little suits, I'm gonna thin out that thigh hair for you."

"Mother!"

"I mean it. You'll be so glad when you're out there lifting your legs and such!"

"Juanita, did you forget my beer?" Lord, she'd like to tell that stinking man to come get it himself, but no, gotta make her slave it for awhile.

"I'm coming, honey."

"Mama, I am sorry that I said all of those things."

"I know you are," she says. "I was sorry as hell myself that that dress my Mama made was so ugly. But you know what? That didn't make it any less ugly, and so sometimes people need to be told the truth."

"Hey, Juanita!"

"I'm coming!" she yells. "Patricia, why don't you cut up a few radishes while you're cutting?" Patricia doesn't even bitch about that, either. Now all Juanita has to do is get Harold back to where he can trust her, back to where he'll say that about the shit and the pony, back to where he'll call her cooter clam late at night when just the streetlight shines in their bedroom window.

Granner is fixing to take herself a bubble bath and then put on that new gown and robe that Kate bought for her, though she wouldn't want Kate to know it, when Pete Tyner and Petie Rose ring her doorbell. Petie is standing out on that porch with the biggest stuffed cat that Granner has ever seen and Pete's got a grin on his face that goes from ear to ear. Better than that, he's got a great big pretty present under his arm.

"Look!" Petie Rose screams as soon as Granner opens the door.

"I bet I know what that cat's name is, too," Granner says and goes to turn on a lamp. Very rarely does she even need to turn on a lamp in the summertime, because as soon as it gets dark she goes to bed.

"His name is Harold Pete," Petie Rose says, and goes and crawls up on the couch with that big cat right along with her.

"Well, that's some name for a cat," she says.

"Isn't that a good name?" Pete asks and winks at Granner. "I completely forgot to bring in your present this morning. I'm really sorry about that."

"No need." Granner takes the box from him before he even offers it to her. After all, it's getting late. "Go on and get yourself some cake, Pete."

"Maybe tomorrow," he says. "Petie and I just went to Burger King."

"Me and Harold Pete got a pita," Petie Rose says.

"A what?"

"It's like a salad, something new." Pete goes and sits down. "Open your gift."

"I can't keep up with all those new things." Granner goes and sits in her chair and starts taking the ribbon off slowly. After all, this is the last present that she will open until Christmas. It could be the last one that she ever opens.

"It's a stove!" Petie screams, and that makes Granner so God blessed mad for somebody to do that to her. Petie is as bad as Kate.

"Not a stove, honey." Pete comes over now to get in the act. He's got to take it out of the box for her. "It's a toaster oven. You see? This way you don't have to heat up your stove all the time. We've got one and it saves on electricity and your kitchen doesn't get so hot."

"Well, that's nice," Granner says. "That's a nice gift." She nods at Pete and motions for Petie Rose to come over so that she can give her a big hug and a kiss. "I'm proud of that boy, Pete. Have you named him?"

"Yes, just now. His name is Brantley Rhett Tyner." Pete shakes his head and grins that great big grin again. That grin is bigger than Pete's head near about. "I just left Rose and she's fine, just fine."

"She waved to me from the window!" Petie Rose says. "She held up our baby and I held up Harold Pete."

"Well, that's fine. What are you going to call him? B.R.?"

"No, I think we'll call him Brant," Pete says and Granner has never in her life heard of such. Whatever happened to all those good names like Charlie and Sam or Joe, Gus or Buck? Who in their life ever heard of a baby called Brantley Rhett? Lord, Buck and Jesus are probably mopping up the floor laughing about now. She can just hear Buck's great big laugh, though she can't imagine how Jesus' laugh might sound. She'll know one of these days soon, though.

"Well, we better go on. It's about Petie's bedtime and I know you must be tired, too." Pete leans down and kisses Granner's cheek. "We've all had a big day, haven't we?"

"Yessirree." Granner stands up and walks to the door. "It's been about the biggest that I can remember. Did Kate and Ernie get to the hospital?"

Pete shakes his head and calls out for Petie to wait for him. "They didn't get the chance, said they'd be there tomorrow. They sent Rose two dozen red roses, though."

"Roses for Rosie," Granner says and laughs, lifts her hand to Pete and then stands there watching them walk across her yard to next door. "You're the last rose of summer," Buck used to tell her, which was a nice way to tell her that she was old as a dirt dauber. She shuts the door and locks it tight, turns on her outside floodlights and goes to the bathroom. She is just about to turn on the water and pour in some of that foaming milk bath when the phone rings. If it ain't somebody at the door, it's somebody on the phone, and it all comes in one day. Now, she'll probably go days with hearing from nobody but Harold Weeks. She picks up the receiver and waits. She hears some breathing at first and then she hears him, clear as a bell with that foreign tongue.

"I thought Juanita told you to stop calling me!" she screams, but Mr. Abdul said that he never heard anything of the kind. He says that he wants to know what she is wearing and since Granner didn't get much of a chance to talk at the party today, she tells him, right down to her new bright fuzzy striped socks and her old terry cloth scuffs. She doesn't even give Mr. Abdul the chance to ask any more questions because she has got too much to say, and she's gonna say it even if he is an Iranian. "I got me a new great-grandbaby, today," she says. "It's my birthday as well. I'm eighty-three years old, born in nineteen hundred so I'm always the same as the new year, makes it easy to remember, too. This baby's name is Brantley

Rhett Tyner which I don't like so good; they want to call him Brant and I know if my Buck has heard that that him and Jesus is either laughing or mad about it all. Brant! I never heard such. It's a Thursday child and that means that he's got far to go. My daughter Kate Weeks Stubbs was a Wednesday child and you know that's full of woe and it always has suited her so well. You know that's why they call them homeless children that they show on the news sometimes, Wednesday's children, cause they're woeful. If I was a younger woman and Buck was alive, I've thought that I might get me a Wednesday's child. My son Harold is Saturday, which means he works hard for a living and that fits him as well. What day are you, Mr. Abdul, or do ya'll have days over there in Iran? Mr. Abdul?" Granner sits there holding the phone next to her ear and she cannot believe that Mr. Abdul would hang up on her. Well, sir, she ain't going to be friendly to him one more time. She didn't even get to tell him that she is a Saturday's child, which means that she works hard for a living and that's the gospel, though she always has thought she should have been a Monday's child because she was so fair of face. There was a time when Irene Turner was the prettiest girl in Flatbridge County, not a soul around could hold a candle to her, and Buck Weeks was smart enough with common sense that he knew a good thing when he saw it. He told her that; though, Lord, if he's seeing her right now he probably doesn't think so, with her so old and feeble and withered up. Jesus is probably saying that he sure doesn't know what Buck Weeks ever saw in her, and Buck is probably telling him that he should have looked down and paid more attention to Irene Turner about sixty years ago, though Lord knows the Lord has watched over her and blessed her. Buck Weeks says, "She was the most beautiful woman in the whole state, the country even. She was the smartest and the prettiest and the very best in the Christian ways and I never could have found myself a better wife." Buck says, "Happy birthday, old gal. Goodnight Irene, Goodnight."

"Night, Buck," she whispers and goes to run her bath water. "You take care of yourself, you hear?" She brings that pretty new gown set into the bathroom and sits on the commode seat and watches those bubbles sudsing up in a pretty blue color. "Buck? Don't ya'll watch me take my clothes off. You wouldn't want to see me now, yourself. My body has lost its fairness as much as my face." She steps into that hot water and it feels so good. It's just what an old woman needs to get her circulation going full blast; that's all that she needs.

7

Fannie McNair takes herself a swig of that brandy before she pours it all over that flin, flun, flan, whatever that dessert is. Lord knows, she deserves a little taste of something to keep her going and to get her through this night. People are just starting to arrive and already she has rewashed dishes, fixed Parker and Billy something to eat, finished that knick knack tray, and filled up what seems like a hundred tiki torches to go around that pool. Now she smells like a kerosene stove, and if it weren't for M.L. she'd probably have the mind to go stand on that diving board, take a match to herself and flame up just like that dessert is going to do. She'd like to see the faces of all those dressed-up people when they saw her out on that board burning slam up.

"Oh, Fannie, everything is going smoothly." Mrs. Foster glances at the clock and then looks at herself in the window and fluffs her hair a little. "Everyone is enjoying the cocktail hour so much that we may extend it just a speck, okay?"

"All right by me." Fannie sticks that dessert in the refrigerator and slams the door harder than she means to.

"Are you okay, Fannie?" Mrs. Foster stirs her drink

around with that olive on a pick that Fannie had fixed for her; she must have stuck a hundred of those, too, and Mrs. Foster wanted so many done in each color pick, like people notice that kind of thing. Well, maybe they do, but Lord knows, they ain't got a thing in their mind if they do. "Oh what about your son? I completely forgot to ask you."

"What are you doing in here?" Mr. Foster comes into that kitchen sour as ever. "People are going to wonder what you're doing."

"I only came in to check on things," Mrs. Foster says and smiles at Fannie. "I don't know what we'd do without her."

"I know," Mr. Foster says hurriedly, without even giving Fannie a glance. "Where's Billy? Ted Miller wants to speak to him, says he might hire Billy to look after his boat since Billy is so interested in sailing."

"That would be marvelous. I think Billy should think about working, the way that he spends money. Fannie, have you seen him?"

"Out by the pool," Fannie says, and refills another tray with some of those little rolled up sandwiches. Everything's got to be complicated; can't just make square sandwiches and cut off the crust, gotta layer them and roll them up, stick 'em together with some more colored picks. All them colored picks, and where do they wind up but on the floor and strewn on every table, in the ashtrays, in the candy bowls. Mr. Foster calls to Billy from the door and he comes slouching in.

"I don't want to go in there," Billy whines and plops down in a kitchen chair.

"Get up. Don't act this way." Mr. Foster pulls on that boy's arm and he glares back at his Daddy like he could spit on him. "Come on, Billy. Ted Miller is trying to do something nice for you and you're not going to act this way."

"Oh no, I can't disappoint one of your friends, now, can I?" Billy goes over to the refrigerator and gets a beer, opens it and stands there drinking it in front of his parents. Fannie would like to slap him down herself, but it is sort of pitiful the way that that boy just don't seem to fit in with his own folks. "Oh hell, no! Not one of the friends."

"I think you've had enough beer, Billy," Mrs. Foster says and he starts to put the can down until his Daddy says the same thing. Then he takes another great big swallow. Well, Fannie knows one thing for sure and that's that she'll get herself a taxicab home, cause she ain't about to ride with that drunken boy.

"Please, Billy, go speak to Mr. Miller," Mrs. Foster puts her hand on Mr. Foster's arm, but he doesn't even look at her. "Your father only wants to help you."

"Yeah, maybe if you work you can keep your nose clean," Mr. Foster says.

"Hey Dave, I like the way you mix a drink!" That fat old Mrs. Stubbs' husband sticks his head in the kitchen door. Lord have mercy, he's got on the reddest pants that Fannie has ever seen, looks like he just jumped from a frying pan or hell, one. Mr. Foster grins great big and waves and then cuts it off like a light switch.

"What do you mean, keep my nose clean?" Billy Foster backs up when his Daddy steps toward him, and now he looks like a pitiful scrawny chick instead of the bantam rooster with that hair sticking straight up in front.

"You know good and damn well what I mean." Mr. Foster is speaking like Fannie might not even be there, like she might be a fly on the wall. She'd just like to know where they expect her to go while this fussing is taking place. She ought to go on out in that living room and stir herself up something with a colored pick. It's a funny thing how people who can act so proper will up and show their tails.

"Please, Dave, let's not get into that right now." Helena Foster looks like she might cry any second, and Fannie sure would like to bring a stop to all of this, call attention to the fact that she is standing here and hearing every single word, just in case somebody might care. "Mrs. Foster, my son didn't kill that man," Fannie says loud enough for all three of them to hear. "I knew my boy wouldn't kill a person."

"I'm so glad, Fannie." Mrs. Foster looks like she just let out a ton of air, and Fannie is certain that that air wasn't let out for Thomas McNair but for her own self; she wanted that fussing to stop, too. "Fannie and I had quite a scare today when we heard her son was in jail."

"I'm sure I wouldn't know how it felt." Mr. Foster glares at Billy again, and if Fannie didn't know any better, she'd think they'd break out into a fist fight any second.

"What's that supposed to mean?" Billy is moving around that kitchen now like he might have ants in his pants. "I've never been to jail."

"And don't I know why." Mr. Foster pulls out a wad of money from his pocket like Fannie has never in her life seen. God knows, if they weren't fighting, she might ask for a raise. "You suppose you'll ever have any of this, Billy? Any of your own?"

"Oh Hell-eena! Everything is wonderful! Absolutely marvelous!" Mrs. Stubbs steps into the kitchen and it is a funny thing to see the way that Mrs. Foster smiles and sticks out her hand to that woman. Lord God, Fannie thought those shorts were something, but tonight she's got on this bright-colored dress with little old straps cutting into those round shoulders. It makes Fannie hurt to look at that tight dress. "I didn't get the chance to tell you that I have a grandson!" Mrs. Stubbs claps her hands together and smiles.

"Oh, how splendid." Mr. Foster goes over and hugs and kisses Mrs. Stubbs. "You look marvelous, Kate, simply terrific!"

"Why thank you, Dave. Ernie was just now saying what a great drink you mix and after having two, I'm inclined to agree!" Mrs. Stubbs just laughs and laughs and then kisses Mrs. Foster on the cheek. Fannie never has been able to stand the way these people hug and kiss one another all night long at these parties; the men stand around with their arms wrapped around one another, kissing every woman they see and the women go around kissing both women and men. Fannie has imagined that this is what one of those orgies would look like, except that people probably wouldn't have nothing on. "Did I interrupt something?" Mrs. Stubbs asks, and Fannie is tempted to say, "Yes, ma'am!" but Mrs. Foster knows just how to handle it.

"Billy needed to speak to us in private for a few minutes." Mrs. Foster pushes Mrs. Stubbs toward the hallway and whispers. "You know how these teens are. When they want to talk, they want to talk right then." Mrs. Foster keeps smiling until Mrs. Stubbs pushes her bright-colored self back into that smoky crowded room. Fannie can't help but feel a little sorry for Billy right now, the way he's all hunched up in that chair, looks like he'd blow sky high if you touched him.

"They didn't find the real person that killed that man, though," Fannie says. Mr. Foster is clicking his fingers on that table; he's about to blow himself. "It was a nice old man that was killed, too. Man that runs that little Quik Pik store right near where I stay."

"Oh my, Fannie, I didn't know it happened in your neighborhood!" Mrs. Foster puts her hand on her chest. "How frightening for you!"

"It doesn't surprise me," Mr. Foster says. "No offense, Fannie, but that's a mighty rough section once you get to the end of Main where you live." He eats his olive and drops that colored pick right there in a clean ashtray.

"How was he killed?" Billy Foster crumples up that beer can with his hand and sits there working it back and forth, trying to break that can in two.

"He was snuffed out. His head was wrapped up in plastic so he couldn't breathe." Fannie goes and gets that pick out of the ashtray. "I declare, I can't believe they'd have thought that Thomas would do something so mean."

"Maybe it was an accident." Billy Foster puts that bent-up can in the trash and goes and stands at the sliding glass doors. "Maybe they didn't mean to kill him."

"Well, dead is dead," Fannie says. "And whether they meant to or not don't count in the Lord's eyes. That person will suffer one day whether they find out or not."

Mr. Foster drains the last bit of drink from his glass. He raises those eyebrows at Fannie and stares at her like she might be a cockroach. "Come on, Helena. We don't want people thinking that we're rude. Billy? I'll expect you out here soon."

"Oh my, no, we don't." Mrs. Foster looks at Fannie. "I'm going to float around a little and see if everyone is about ready to eat."

"Wait!" Billy turns from that window and steps toward them. His face is white as a sheet. "I did it," he whispers and stares down at the floor.

"Did what, Billy?" Mr. Foster shakes his head and makes a humming noise. "You would do anything to mess up our party, wouldn't you? What did you do? I know you took that twenty off of my dresser, but what else?"

"Oh no, honey, I took the twenty." Mrs. Foster laughs. "I didn't have a cent in my purse when Betty Booth came by with raffle tickets."

"I killed that man at the Quik Pik." Billy stares at them, the shocked look on his mother's face. He feels down in the back pocket of his jeans where he still has the rolling papers. And just last night he had laughed about it all; just last night. God if he could do it over, if he had asked some girl to the movies, if he had stayed home and watched T.V. "I didn't mean to do it." Billy is talking fast now, moving around the room, crying, his fist in his pocket, clutching those rolling papers.

"Billy, do you expect us to believe that?" Mr. Foster laughs great big, and then his face goes as solemn as Billy's. "This is for attention, right? The doctor told us that you'd do anything for attention, to hurt us."

"Fuck that doctor!" Billy screams, and Mr. Foster slaps his face and pushes him against the refrigerator right there in front of Fannie, but Billy doesn't stop. "The doctor is your friend, not mine! I did it, I tell you, but I didn't mean to!"

"Oh God." Mrs. Foster feels her way around and into a chair like she might be blind. Fannie steps backwards slowly. She's going to get her stuff and she's going to walk out that back door, going to walk to the nearest phone and get herself home.

"I'm sorry, Mama. I didn't mean to do it. I was just going to scare him, you know?" Billy slumps over and Mr. Foster lets him slide right on down to the floor. Fannie gets her purse and loops it over her arm.

"Fannie, you stay right there," Mr. Foster says, and Billy stretches out on the floor with his hands over his face. "I'm going to go in there and I'm going to tell everyone that dinner has been delayed, that there has been an emergency involving Helena's parents and that we're waiting for a call, and please to drink all they want and that dinner will be coming soon." He nods his head up and down while he talks; he is cool as a cucumber and Fannie doesn't know how he can be so cool. Every bone in her body is shaking. "By the way," he turns at the doorway. "Where is Parker?"

"At a friend's," Mrs. Foster whispers. Now she is crying, and Fannie feels completely helpless. Nobody says a word while Mr. Foster is out of the room. The voices in the living room die down to soft whispers when he starts talking and then the voices build right back up to a loud murmuring buzz.

"Okay, let's hear it." Mr. Foster comes back and goes to stand over Billy. "Get up off of the floor." He raises his voice but Billy doesn't move. Mr. Foster reaches down and pulls him up by the arms.

"I think I better go on now," Fannie says, her voice quivering with every word.

"You may as well hear it all, Fannie. You're family and anything that you ever hear in this house goes no further, do you hear?" He turns on her now and she doesn't know what on earth to do. "I said, do you hear me?"

"Dave, please leave Fannie out of it," Mrs. Foster whispers. Her face is pale white.

"Leave her out of it? How can we leave her out of it

when she's heard as much as we have?" He faces Billy now, a vein in his forehead bulging and buckling like it could pop right out of his head. "If this is a joke, if this is your way . . ."

"No, it's true. It's true!" Billy opens his mouth to cry but nothing comes out.

"Well, I don't know what we're going to do." Mr. Foster pushes him up against the refrigerator again. "I mean, what in the hell do you expect me to do this time?"

"Nothing, just don't do anything!" Billy starts to slump back down but Mr. Foster snatches him back up.

"Do you know who just paid to have that church re-carpeted and repainted? Do you know how much that cost?" Mr. Foster is right in Billy's face now, and Billy's eyes are blinking like he is expecting a punch any second. "I did, and why? Why did I do that? To save your lousy ass!"

"You did it to save your own," Billy murmurs.

"What?" Mr. Foster has Billy by the collar and is shaking him, hitting his head up against the refrigerator. Fannie can't hardly bear it. She picks up the phone and is about to dial 911 when Mrs. Foster jumps up and stops him. Fannie is standing there holding the phone, listening to that buzz. This is like a nightmare; everything is getting blinking and twisted like a bad dream.

"I said you did that for yourself." Billy steps back from his father and it looks like his whole body is trembling. "You did that so that you wouldn't be embarrassed by me."

"Oh yeah, just like Ron told me you believe. It's all our fault." Mr. Foster is talking a funny way now, laughing, and patting his chest, but that vein is still bulging. "It's all my fault, right, Billy Boy? Every time that you've gotten in trouble it's been our fault." Mr. Foster steps toward Billy with Mrs. Foster right behind him, clutching his sleeve. "I mean hell, why wouldn't it be my fault? You're my son. All that I've ever done is taken care of you, patched up your mistakes to give you another chance, thinking that some day you'd amount to something, not that I have real high hopes for you, especially not now, but I always thought that maybe you'd pull through. You know, I thought you deserved to get away with a childish prank here and there."

"Okay, Dave." Mrs. Foster steps in between her husband and Billy. "Just stop for a minute, hold it." She holds her hand up to her husband and then puts her other hand on Billy's shoulder. "Why, baby? Why?" she cries and Billy latches onto her and stands there crying in her arms like a baby.

"Put the phone down, Fannie." Mr. Foster comes and takes the receiver out of her hand. "Everything is going to be fine. Now, you go right ahead and do what you have to do for dinner."

"It's done." This time Fannie stares right back at him and she feels like she has every right. Family member, foot; he wants her to keep her mouth shut, pretend like she's heard none of this. What Corky Revels had heard about the Baptist Church was true after all, and it didn't sound like no childish prank. Corky hadn't even been able to tell Fannie what was done up on that altar, said it would make Fannie sick on her stomach. Fannie has thought all along that they probably collected some dog mess or dead animals or such. Um um, it makes her ache inside to think of what Helena Foster must be feeling right now. Fannie feels it bad enough but Lord, if it had been her Thomas or worse, if it had been M.L., she doubts that she could live with herself, cause she'd have to tell the truth; she'd have to send her baby to his death, she reckons, and that would be sending her to her own.

"Fannie, why don't you begin serving the salads?" Mr. Foster doesn't even look at her. He lights a cigarette and stares out the window. "Tell our guests that I will join them in a second." Fannie gets up and starts taking the chilled salads out of the refrigerator. It's a blessing that she went ahead and made them up individually, cause there's no way that she could've managed dishing them out, with these hands of hers like putty.

"Well, Fannie, I see you made it after all," Mrs. Stubbs says. "I do hope that Helena's parents are okay. Has she heard?" Fannie shakes her head. "Oh what a shame, and here this party going on." Mrs. Stubbs follows Fannie all the way around the tables. "Please tell Hell-eena that I'll do anything. I'll be glad to go and sit with her or I can mingle out here and act as hostess."

"I'll tell her." Fannie places the last salad and turns to Mrs. Stubbs, who is squinting one eye and looking around the room. Fannie reckons she is looking for her husband, and that woman must be blind if she can't spot them red britches in the far corner talking to Mrs. Ted Miller. "Mrs. Stubbs, would you please tell all these people their salad is ready and that Mr. Foster will be here directly."

"Well, I doubt if I say 'DI rectly' but I will tell them, yes." She laughs great big and then clinks a spoon against one of the iced waters. ";May I have your attention, please?" She calls in a sing song way. "Before we begin this scrumptious salad, I want to announce for those of you who haven't heard that Ernie and I are the proud grandparents of a simply perfect little boy. He is more adorable than Prince William and no doubt has a better background!" She bends over and laughs, that blonde hair not moving a speck. Fannie doesn't know which is the worst sight to be seeing and hearing, this spectacle or the one in the kitchen. Mrs. Stubbs is so drunk from having been waiting all this time and drinking. "By the way, where are our honored guests? There you are little bridesy, come on up here. None of us are familiar with you and yours, so do step forward and introduce yourselves." Mrs. Stubbs motions with her hand. "Where's that handsome groom, now? Come out, come out, wherever you are!" This tall dark right handsome boy steps up, nods his head, laughs a little. Fannie ought to walk right out that front door is what she ought to do, and if it weren't for Mrs. Foster she'd do just that. "Oh give me a kiss, you." Mrs. Stubbs hugs the groom and then faces the bride. "We all love Justin so much. I just hope that you and yours can love him half as much! You are getting a real prize!"

"So am I," the groom says.

"That's right," this man says, and Mrs. Stubbs immediately turns to him.

"You must be her father," she says and he nods. "I knew that the bride's parents would be the two people that I didn't know! Makes it easy to spot you, you know?" Now Mrs. Stubbs goes and gets her husband and leads him to the head seat. "Please, find your places," she calls. "Ernie is going to serve as host until Dave comes back, right, love?" Mr. Stubbs nods, raises his hands and says a long prayer that near about puts Fannie to sleep; he's thankful for friends and sunshine and grandbabies and brides and grooms and parties and land and salads and just about everything but the kitchen sink. People snicker all the way through that prayer, but Fannie waits for them to be seated and to make certain that everything is going smooth. Now she can give them at least fifteen minutes before the meal.

When she gets back in the kitchen, Mr. Foster is hanging up the phone and Billy and Mrs. Foster are sitting at the table. Mr. Foster claps his hands once and then squeezes his lips together in a thin straight line. "Okay," he says. "I'm going to get Ronnie's father up from that table and have him come in here. He's got to know, too." Mr. Foster starts to go to the door and then stops. "Better than that, Fannie, you go and tell Dr. Booth that I need to see him. They'll just think that I want some medical advice about Helena's father."

"What?" Mrs. Foster asks.

"Your father has just had a stroke, okay?" Mr. Foster

waves his hand to shoo Fannie like she might be a fly. She goes out there and excuses herself, gets Dr. Booth and tells him that Mr. Foster needs to speak to him. While she's out there, Fannie goes over to tidy up the bar, and already people are moving around, getting up for another drink or a cigarette. Fannie goes and starts picking up those picks that have been dropped all over the top of that bar, some of them with the olive still on the end. That Mrs. Miller is standing there talking to a woman that Fannie has never met.

"Can you believe her?" Mrs. Miller asks and giggles. She leans her head closer to the other woman. "Nobody but Helena is even nice to her, because no one can stand to be around her."

"What a shame, because I really like Ernie," the other woman says. "He got us such a good deal on our house."

"Oh, he's a doll! Getting a little pudgy but he's really a sweetie!" Mrs. Miller says and giggles again. High as a kite, Fannie figures, and gossiping up a storm. She sure would hate to be the poor soul whose ears are burning up.

"What's her problem?" the other woman asks and leans closer to get the answer. Fannie just keeps right on picking up picks and wiping off the bar. They don't even know that she's there.

"Who knows? She's just one of those people that is desperate for everyone to like her. You know, if you do something in your house, she'll turn right around and do the exact same thing to her own, except that she has to make hers a speck better. For instance," the woman leans closer. "When Dave and Helena put in their pool, they immediately got one and they went all out for one bigger and better. I mean, if you're going to get right down to it, Ted and I had about the first pool in town."

"Do you think Helena copied you?" The woman asks. She's got enough gold on those wrists to start her own jewelry store.

"Oh no, Helena's not that way." Mrs. Miller waves to someone across the room. "Oh, God, here she comes now. I hate to be cornered by her."

"Hi, girls!" Mrs. Stubbs walks up. "Why Nancy, I've been meaning to compliment your hair all night long. Who cuts it for you?"

"I had it cut in New York," Mrs. Miller says and then turns right back to that other woman. "Now as I was saying, I go over to the antique shops in Newton quite often, if you'd like to ride some time."

"Oh Nancy, that would be super!"

"I've never been to any antique shops in Newton," Mrs. Stubbs says. "Do they have some pretty things?"

"They have marvelous things, all kinds of small accessory pieces as well that can just make a room." Mrs. Miller and the other woman are talking among themselves again, with Mrs. Stubbs standing there on the outside of the circle, like children in a schoolyard. It's almost as pitiful as Helena Foster is right now, and Fannie wants to get back in the kitchen, to help Mrs. Foster if she can, but now she's afraid to move from behind the bar. She hates to own up to it, but she doesn't want to talk to Mrs. Stubbs any more, either.

"Well, I'll just have to go sometime," Mrs. Stubbs says, and smiles. She isn't acting near as silly as she was a while ago. "You know there are some nice shops in South Cross and I go rather often. If either of you would ever . . ."

"I used to go over there all the time, and then it seemed to me that they simply did not have as much to offer, at least not to my taste." Mrs. Miller drops her pick right where Fannie has just wiped.

"Oh, there's Betty Booth," Mrs. Stubbs says. "You girls will have to excuse me. I haven't talked to Betty all evening and I've simply got to swap some grandparent stories with her. I can't wait for you girls to have grandchildren. It's so fantastic, just super!" Mrs. Stubbs squeezes both of those women's hands and then hurries off across the room. "I'm getting a little hungry," Mrs. Miller whispers.

"I'm getting a little drunk," the other one says. "I certainly hope we eat soon, I mean, emergency or not, they should either have the party or call it off." Mrs. Miller nods to that woman and Fannie hurries back to the kitchen. She is so tempted to tell everybody that the party is over and that they should just go on home or to McDonald's or wherever they please.

When she gets in the kitchen, Dr. Booth's boy Ronnie is sitting at the table as well, and Mr. Foster is back on the phone. "Will do, buddy, I appreciate it," Mr. Foster says. "We'll have him there tomorrow."

"I don't want to go to Montana!" Billy cries and puts his head down on the table.

"It's better than the reformatory in Raleigh, isn't it?" Dr. Booth asks, and then looks at Fannie. He stops abruptly.

"She already knows," Mr. Foster says. "Billy gave his full confession with an audience." Mr. Foster leans against the counter. "She won't say anything, we've covered that." He eyes Fannie but she looks away; she goes over to the oven to check the mariner casseroles. She's had them on warm forever now; those crab legs are probably tough as leather, and the shrimps curled up to nothing.

"We had thought about sending Ronnie off to that school in Denver, anyway. He may as well start a little early," Dr. Booth says.

"Won't it look funny for them both to leave at the same time?" Mrs. Foster asks, her smooth fair brow all wrinkled up.

"Nah, they're going two different ways. Billy's going for some summer vacation on a dude ranch, and Ronnie's going away to school," Mr. Foster says and lifts his hands, shrugs. "Last night they were both right here in this house, popping popcorn and discussing their upcoming trips with us."

"Did you call everyone?" Dr. Booth asks, and Mr. Foster nods. Fannie has heard all that she wants to hear. She starts putting the small casseroles on trays. It's a blessing that these were done individually as well. It's almost as if Fannie foresaw it all.

"I think you boys better get packing. Ronnie, go on home. We'll talk some more when I get there. This is going to kill your mother." He looks that big boy up and down, and who would think from looking at that large boy, that round face with teen acne and those large brown eyes, that he would have been a part of it all? "Dave, can I tell everyone that Helena's father is fine and that we'll all eat together?"

"Yes, that's fine." He takes Mrs. Foster by the arm. "Are you going to be all right, honey?" he asks and she nods, wipes her eyes again.

"What about me? You guess I'm going to be okay?" Billy asks after Ronnie has gone outside.

"You sure as hell better be, after I've stuck my neck on the line for you!"

"So why'd you do it? Why didn't you turn me in? Why don't you get them to gas me? to fry me?"

"Because I love you, Billy." Mr. Foster leaves the room and Billy breaks down all over again. He just slumps right there on the floor, curls up like a baby and cries. He cries and cries, sniffs and beats his hands against the floor the whole time that Fannie counts and arranges the casseroles. Those people out there are so drunk by this time, she could feed them cat-food tuna and they wouldn't even know the difference.

Corky is squatted outside on the window ledge where the roof slopes out over the porch. It is nice this time of day when the lights in the downtown businesses begin to go out and those in the hotel and the homes further down Main Street begin to come on. The breeze has picked up and the leaves of the large oak tree out front are rustling;

that damp fresh smell that promises rain mingling with the scent of wisteria. She leans inside the window and watches Sam Swett sleeping on her bed, one foot dangling off the edge, one arm crossed over his eyes. "Hey, wake up." She shakes his leg and he rolls toward her, rubs his face up and down on her pillow. "Sam, dinner's almost done."

"Huh?" He opens one eye and sees her there, that pale hair blown back from her face, her hand on his leg. "Did I doze off?" He rubs his hand over his eyes and props up on one arm. The last thing that he remembers, she was here beside him, no, she was under him, her arms wrapped around his neck, her legs wrapped around his.

"I'll say." She laughs. "Hey, if you still feel bad, there's some aspirin in the bathroom." She props her elbows on the sill and cups her face in her hands. "Hamburgers are almost done."

"What are you doing out there?" He sits up now, stretches.

"Cooking the hamburgers. How about getting that plate off the table and handing it to me?"

"Yeah, okay."

He gets off the bed and feels his way to the table.

"There's a light right over you if you'll pull that string," she says and laughs again. He pulls the string and it takes a few seconds for his eyes to adjust. That big doll that had been in the window is now over on the counter. It is hard to believe that there is someone that sits and makes those dolls all day long. He gets the plate and goes back over to the bed.

"Hey, come on out," she says and moves away from the window. "The fresh air will wake you up." He hands the plate to her and then crawls through. The tar shingles are still warm from the afternoon. He slides over closer to where Corky is standing.

"Where are the hamburgers?" he asks, and she crooks her finger and walks up the slope to the top eave of the roof. Sam Swett doesn't stand up; he keeps sliding, inching himself with his hands and feet until he is at the top and can swing his other leg over and straddle the roofline. It feels safer that way.

"See, here's the barbecue." She points to a small flat area where the eave hangs over enough to break the wind. There is a sterno stove there, two hamburgers cooking and dripping into a can of sterno. "I hope you like yours done. I can't stand bloody meat, you know? Some people think it's not good unless you can see some blood, but I don't."

"I like mine done," he says and watches her carefully flip the burgers on that tiny stove. "Did I miss something?" he asks, his head cocked to one side. "I mean, you know, when we were in bed?"

"Like what?" She smiles at him, bats those long lashes.

"Well, did we?" He looks away, the streetlights getting smaller and smaller as he looks down Main Street.

"You mean that you don't remember?" She sits down in front of the stove and pulls her knees up to her chest. It makes him nervous for her to do that, just the thought of her suddenly tumbling over backwards. "I can't believe that you don't!"

"I'm sorry, really." He slides closer and puts his arm out behind her, lets it drop behind her back. "I must be crazy, God, I must be."

She nods her head slowly and then faces him, leans closer. "I would be so mad if we had've and you didn't even remember!"

"You mean we didn't?" He feels a sudden relief. Maybe he's not so crazy after all.

"Nah" she shakes her head and stares down at her feet, those small dirty tennis shoes with the bright red strings. "We were lying there kissing and the next thing that I knew, you were snoring into my neck."

"Not snoring."

"Honest to God you were." She holds up one hand. "You sounded like a chain saw."

"I'm sorry, really." He moves his hand up her back, slowly, as if she won't notice. "Forgive me?"

"I reckon I do. I've been out here cooking you a hamburger, haven't I?" She hugs her knees closer and leans into him. "Feels nice out here, doesn't it?"

"Do you think that maybe we can try again?"

"Maybe." She picks up a small pebble from the roof and tosses it out to where it disappears in the dusk. "Look at those trees over there," she says and points in the direction of the highway. "I love those trees in the wintertime. I love the way those bare limbs curl and wrap around one another like a piece of black lace this time of day. They don't even look real when they're that way." She picks up another pebble and tosses it. "Tell me about your family."

"There isn't much to tell, just me and my parents."

"So, what are they like? Must have money to have sent you to Europe and New York and all those places." She leans away and pulls the can of sterno out from under the burgers. "Let's sit here another minute, okay?" She squeezes his hand and he nods. "Now, tell me."

"They're real nice people." He shrugs. Suddenly, he feels a little twinge of guilt, of homesickness. They would be worried sick if they had tried to call his number in New York. She is waiting for him to tell more. "They both work, always have; they've done all right for themselves."

"You sure don't tell much," she says. "I bet your Mama is about seven feet tall and four hundred pounds and eats raw snakes, and your Daddy is . . ." He puts his hand over her mouth and pulls her closer, kisses her.

"No, my Mom is about your height but she's got more meat right here." He moves his hand to her hips. "She's a secretary and she's got the prettiest clear blue eyes. Her name is Shirley."

"So why did you run away from home?"

"I didn't run away. I just wanted to find out what I want to do, you know?"

"I know, finding yourself. That's what people always say on the soaps, and that's what my brother Chip used to say back when his hair was so long." She laughs. "My Daddy said, 'Chipper, if you'll take your hands and grab a hold of what's in between 'em, you might just find yourself.'" She laughs louder now, louder than he has heard her laugh before. "I thought it was funny, even if Daddy was a little out of his mind when he said it. I mean, it is sort of dumb to have to go off somewhere to find yourself when you've got to go with yourself to get there, you know?"

"I guess I just wanted to be alone," he says and she stops laughing and looks away from him.

"Maybe you felt like you were different, maybe you felt like you were a little better."

"No, no that's not true, really. It's just that there's no reason why I shouldn't know what I want. After all of that, I should know." He reaches over and grabs her hand but she doesn't squeeze back.

"You're still doing it," she says and pulls away, "still acting like you're the only person who's ever felt that way." She laughs what sounds like a forced laugh, shakes her head. "Maybe you've been looking in the wrong places. Maybe you need to take your hands and feel what's in between." She glances down at his hands resting on his thighs, what's in between them, and smiles. "I didn't mean it like that," she says and laughs again, but he doesn't.

"Don't you see? Everything that my parents have done, they've done for me, for Sam Swett." He puts his hand up to his chest. "And they've never had all the doubts and questions like I do."

"Did they get married because of you? Did they hold hands for the first time because of you?"

"No, but you know what I mean. You can see it, can't you?" He puts his hands up over his face now, and Corky can't tell if he's crying or what.

"They must have done what they wanted to do, got

brains, don't they?" She reaches over and pulls his hands away, and he stares back with this blank watery stare. "I mean they cared enough to use their brains to decide what to do instead of blowing them all over a bedroom, didn't they?" She picks up the plate and scoops the burgers onto it. "These damn things are cold as ice."

"I'm sorry," he says. "I wasn't even thinking, I mean."

"It isn't your fault!" She shakes her head. "It's nobody's fault but his own. It's just that me and you think a whole lot different from one another. You see I'd give anything if I could say that somebody cared so much for me that every thought in their head near about went in my direction, or if I could say that I had a home and family where I could go when I pleased and never be alone. You say that you want to be alone and all I know is that you must not have ever really been that way." She inches away from him. "I reckon we better go in."

"No wait." He grabs her hand. "You see they did all of this so that I would have things better than what they've had. I don't think I could stand it if I ever did do better than them, though."

"So you're gonna do nothing and then they'll feel like they've done nothing."

"You know, you're right." He lets go of her hand and swings his leg over and inches down beside her. "How'd you get so smart?" He slides down behind her and wraps his legs around her waist, presses his face into her hair.

"Don't you make me drop this meat!" she screams, and then stops suddenly, slowly leans her head back against his. "I got brains. Nobody believes it but I do. Nobody thinks that some waitress in a coffee shop can use her brain. You said it yourself, said I'd get like Sandra."

"I didn't know what I was saying," he whispers and kisses her forehead. "Hey, where's the kid?"

"I was wondering how long it would take you to think of him!" She inches away from him, the burger plate held in one of her hands off to the side. "Fannie's son stopped by, the one that was suspected," she whispers. "He said that he'd stay with M.L., cause he needed to talk to Fannie."

"But what about . . . ?" He waits for her to crawl through the window and then he crawls through. "What about what I remembered, that boy, that boy in the black car?"

"Well, you were sleeping right there on the bed when I called the police," she says and goes into the small kitchen.

"I was?" He squints his eyes against the light as he walks over to the table.

"Lord yes. I'm surprised you remember who you are!" She puts a bag of potato chips on the table and two paper plates. "Hope you don't mind if it's not fancy." He shakes his head. "I spoke to Bob Bobbin, Good Lord, if you say you can't remember that jerk, I'll know you're mentally out of whack."

"No, I remember him."

"He's not on that case any more but said that he'd pass the word, said that they might need to speak to you and then he said on the other hand, he doubted if anybody would believe a thing you said." She sticks the hamburgers into the oven to heat them back up. "It's not your fault. Bob just had to say that for my benefit, you know? He acts like I belong to him or something." She gets two glasses and fills them up with ice. "I doubt if they ever prove or say who killed Mr. Husky." She pours tea in the glasses and brings them to the table. "Talk about people who get everything bought for 'em, ha!"

"But I saw him!"

"Would you swear to it? As drunk as you were, would you swear to it?" She pulls out a chair and sits down, crosses one leg over the other and pulls on her shoe-string. "No, you're not absolutely certain yourself."

"I'm almost certain I'm certain," he says and sits down in the other chair. He takes some matches off the table and lights the red candle, reaches up and pulls the light string. "You know, I'm glad I met you."

"Yeah, me too," she says and turns her chair into the table. "Hey, after we eat maybe we can take a walk. I do that a lot. There's this house not too far from here, a yellow house. It's for sale and the grass is all grown up high, but I just love to look at it." Her skin looks warmer in the candlelight, not as fragile. "It's no great house. You probably wouldn't even see why I like it, but I do."

"It must be nice if you like it so much."

"It's more than that." She sits up straight, perkier than before. "Do you want to?"

"Yeah, okay, and maybe we can go sit on the bed and talk some more?"

"Why, so you can snore on my hair?"

"The floor, then? We could sit on the floor and talk."

"Talk! Why don't you just ask for it? Why don't you place your order?" She reaches and pulls on the light and goes to get the hamburgers out of the oven.

"I didn't mean it that way," he says. "I'm sorry."

"Oh, so you just said it for something to say." She drops a bun and a hamburger on his plate. The sudden bitterness in her voice surprises him and he sits staring down at his open bun, the catsup and mustard spreading and mixing, a paler shade of red.

"No," he says. "I mean I know that I just met you but I've never known anybody like you."

"We forgot to say grace," she says and puts her burger back on the plate.

"Grace, grace, grace," he says and takes another bite and when she doesn't laugh, he closes his eyes and stops chewing. She says "God is great, God is good," just like practically every child has grown up saying. "Do you do Now I Lay Me Down to Sleep, too?"

"Maybe I do," she says and takes a sip of her tea. "And maybe we can. Maybe we can sit on the roof to talk, huh?" He looks up at her and shakes his head, back and forth, back and forth, like some kind of windup doll. There's something about him that makes her want to hold him as tight as she can, something that makes her wish that he wants to hold her in the same way.

Fannie McNair stretches her legs out in that taxi cab and it feels so good to just sit; it feels so good to be out of that house, and she doesn't know if she ever wants to set foot there again. Lord have mercy, she has never in her life had such a bad day, not even those last days with Jake were this bad. She can't get it all out of her mind, Billy Foster sprawled out on that kitchen floor; Helena Foster with her eyes all red and swollen, a plain sad face underneath that makeup; Mr. Foster going on with that party like nothing had ever happened. Mr. Foster had put those large hands on her shoulders and looked her in the eye with a look such as she has never seen. "Billy has an alibi. You've got a little boy to support, what's his name? M.L. is it?" After all those mornings that he's picked her up, and suddenly he had to ask M.L.'s name. It sent a chill down her spine. "I'm sure you could use some extra money, couldn't you?" He had pulled out that same wad that he had shown to Billy earlier.

"No sir, I'm doing fine. I'm not about to take that kind of money."

"What kind? It's money, that's all," he had said, and Mrs. Foster had come into the kitchen and asked him to stop. Mrs. Foster had asked Fannie if she would stay on.

"I'm not sure what I'll do," she had said.

"Take tomorrow off, Fannie," Mrs. Foster had said. "We'll be driving to the Raleigh airport anyway." Mrs. Foster had grabbed Fannie's arm and held onto it like a frightened child, and her eyes had looked that same way, so small and frightened. "Please, Fannie."

"I'll see." That's all she had said, and now she can't see her way clear of any of it. If only she hadn't heard it come out of Billy's mouth. If only she had never heard the truth.

She pays the driver and walks up the sidewalk. Corky's

light is on and so is her own. She gets to the top of the stairs and starts to knock on Corky's door when she hears Thomas' voice coming out of her own room. She turns the knob and there he is sitting in her chair, and M.L. is stretched out on that rug in the same way that Corky was just last night. That seems like ages ago now.

"What are you doing here?" she asks, and hangs her purse on a nail in the closet.

"Well, that's a fine way to greet your son. I suppose you would have been happy if I had never gotten out of that jail."

"You know better, Thomas," she says and sits down at the kitchen table. "M.L. should have been in bed by now."

"Well, I'm real sorry." Thomas stands up and walks over to her. "I mean we can't have little M.L. getting tired, now can we, not when he's got a full day of playing ahead of him." Thomas squats down in front of her. "You look like you've had it," he says. "You'd think that you had been in jail, you'd think that you had been taken in on some stupid nigger lie by some stupid white pig."

"I just don't feel like talking about it all now, Thomas," she says and he stands up, walks around the table.

"Oh, well, what should we discuss, mother? Should we discuss M.L.? Should we talk about his fine future? The one that you're saving every penny that you can pinch for when your own son is out making tacky lamps and pots so that he can go to school?" He sits down at the table, puts his hands over his face.

"All right, Thomas, get out." Fannie pulls his hands

away from his face. "I just can't take any more of this tonight. God knows that I can't."

M.L. squeezes his eyes together tighter and doesn't move a muscle. He barely breathes while he waits for Thomas to leave. He hears Fannie's slippers scuffing across the floor. She opens the door and lets it fall back against the wall.

"Well, you think about what I said," he says. "You think about when you're gonna be all by yourself, Mama. I'm too big for those fairy tales that you save up for M.L. You're getting old, Mama, and I'm sorry for you." He turns and goes down the stairs and Fannie presses her face against the door and cries, softly, almost silently so that she doesn't wake M.L. She waits until she hears the door downstairs slam shut and then she closes her own door, latches it, and then goes over to M.L.

"C'mon, Baby," she whispers. "It's late and you gotta get in your bed."

"Fannie?" he calls, and stretches out on the rug. She is bending over him now, pulling his arms, lifting him. He grabs hold of her arms, and when she hugs him close he feels so sad, though he really isn't certain why. He's never going to ask about his parents again, not ever, cause they might come and take him far away from home. He has always thought that one day they'd come there to live. He has always thought that Fannie would be there with him forever. He climbs over to his side of the bed and pulls F.M. up from the floor in the corner where he keeps him. Fannie goes now and turns off all the lights and then puts on her gown there in the dark by the bed. She eases herself onto the mattress and then rolls over and puts her cheek just above M.L.'s mouth to feel his breath.

"I'm awake, Fannie," he whispers.

"I'm sorry I woke you, baby," she says. "I thought you'd get right up and walk in your sleep, like you used to do when I'd get you up to use the bathroom."

"I was a baby, then."

"Yeah, and you ain't a baby no more." She turns away, her back facing him. "Scrooch up to old Fannie." She waits for him to say that he's too old for that as he usually does, but instead she feels his arm reach around her stomach; she feels that old stuffed sock monkey pressing against her back, and M.L.'s breath rising and falling as he buries his face against her back and holds on to her as tight as he can.

"I'll never leave you, Fannie," he whispers and she answers with an "I know," though she doesn't know.

Kate Stubbs sits down in front of her dressing table and brushes her hair back over and over to get all the hair spray out while Ernie gets into the bed.

"Nice party, wasn't it?" he asks and props his pillow behind him. "They really know how to give one."

"Oh yes." Kate puts down her brush and comes over to the bed. "I hope that Helena's father is okay, though. You know, I don't know how she got through the evening the way that she did." Kate gets in and pulls the sheet up, props her pillow up as well. "I know how upset I was when Daddy had his first stroke."

"Well, I'm sure that she was more upset than she was letting on. I mean, when have you ever heard Helena go on and on about her children and what they are doing?"

"Never." Kate shakes her head. "People never want to hear about someone else's children and Helena knows that." Kate moves toward the center of the king size bed. Sometimes they go through the entire night without so much as even brushing feet or legs. Sometimes Kate likes to be able to stretch out her foot and feel Ernie there. "I probably talked too much about the grandbaby. Did I, Ernie? Do you think that I talked too much about the grandbaby?" She faces him now.

"No, no, everyone knew that you were excited."

"Well, sometimes I feel that maybe I talk too much." She rubs her hand over her hair. "I don't know why I get that feeling sometime, like that I talk too much or get on people's nerves, but I do."

"Nonsense. You were a hit when you offered the toasts." Ernie turns off the lamp on his side and slips down beneath the covers.

"I was afraid that people thought that maybe I had had too much to drink or something and I hadn't." She rolls closer to the center. "I was only excited, felt festive, you know?"

"Sure, sure. No problem." Ernie pats her hand and rolls over, faces the window. "We've had some kind of day all the way around."

"You know, Nancy Miller is not real friendly," Kate whispers, as if that makes a difference in Ernie's trying to get to sleep.

"Oh, I think so," he mumbles. "You must have caught her at a bad time. I think she's really charming."

"Yeah, I must have caught her at a bad time. She was probably a little miffed with Ted, I mean after all, there is that rumor going around."

"Oh, I don't think there's anything to it."

"Well, I'm glad that I've never had anything like that to worry about." Kate turns off her lamp and reaches her foot over to Ernie's. It makes him jump.

"Look at us, Kate." Ernie rolls over and he can barely see the shape of her head in the darkness. "We came up differently from a lot of other people. I think it's natural that maybe we've never gotten over the feeling that someone is putting us down."

"Yeah, I know you're right. I try so hard to forget but you're right, sometimes I feel it, especially when I see some poor child like Patricia. I remember so well how she feels. I mean when you get right down to it, Juanita is probably more like Mother than anyone else. They're both so stubborn and outspoken. They both have no sense of common decency. They say whatever pops into their minds."

"You're right there."

"I'm proud of what we've done with ourselves, Ernie. I really am."

"I know." Ernie is just about asleep now, just about, her hands moving slowly up and down his back. He is too tired to even worry about anything that has happened. Kate could find out about Janie Morris, everyone could know that he came from Injun Street, he could have herpes and at this point he wouldn't even care, though that feeling won't last. It will ease away from him in the morning, just like the picture of his mother that sometimes is so clear in his mind, only to return at another time, returning when something sparks some bit of his past, some moment when he does not feel so close to Kate as he does now, the furrowed brow, the flat yellow hair. It will return and there is no guarantee ever that it will dissolve in the morning, only the guarantee that it will come to him with the same degree of pain as being pushed aside, a sharp gash in the temple, an arm covered in searing oil.

"I bet they named him after you," Kate whispers. "I bet that baby will carry on your name." She snuggles up to his back now, closes her eyes and almost instantly drifts off to sleep.

Bob Bobbin has his car parked on the corner of Main and First Street. His shift is up but it seems there's nothing else to do but sit in the car and listen to the radio. He should have known that he wasn't going to solve some big case, should have known that those guys were going to give him all kinds of hell. "Did you kiss this one on those big black lips?" Bob punched him in the face, broke the guy's glasses, made all the others laugh that much more. For all he knows what Corky called up to tell him might be true, maybe that filthy guy that she's with right this minute did see the Foster kid there. But, who would believe it? No, he isn't going to say a word more about it; he isn't going to make a fool of himself again, not for anybody.

There are some headlights coming down Main Street and he decides he's going to pull somebody just for the hell of it, check their license, maybe catch a drunk, maybe just to make himself feel a little better. He waits, his foot above the accelerator, the car in drive while this little sports car starts creeping up. Why is it going so slow? Damn, if he had himself a car like that he'd drive the hell out of it, like Magnum P.I. does in that car of his. He pulls out at ten miles an hour and turns on his light and siren. That fool keeps right on going for a while and then finally pulls over and stops. He gets out and walks up to the window.

"What did I do?" This pretty girl yells through her window. She has herself locked in that car tight as a drum.

"I need to see your driver's license," he yells and raps his knuckles against her window. She fumbles through her purse and then cracks the window just a speck and slips it out to him. He shines his flashlight on it. She's damn pretty. Most people look bad on their license but she doesn't, looks a little like Olivia Newton John. Let's see, blue eyes, blonde hair, 110 pounds. If he didn't know better, he'd swear that he was talking about Corky Revels. Of course, Corky doesn't have herself an address like Primrose Boulevard.

"Live out in Cape Fear Trace, huh?" He squats down and motions for her to roll down the window and she does, about a quarter of an inch. "Has anyone ever told you that you look like Olivia Newton John?"

She breaks down crying, gets a tissue from her purse and wipes her eyes.

"Hey, I'm sorry, didn't mean to upset you. You were going so slow, I wanted to make sure that you were okay."

"You were?" she asks. "You were making sure that I was okay?"

"Yes, this is a bad neighborhood, parts of it, Frances, isn't it? Frances Miller? Is that Dr. Miller?"

"Yes, yes it is," she says and rolls down her window. "I'm sorry, officer, but my father always told me to lock my doors through this part of town. Do you know my father?" She eyes the policeman up and down. He seems nice enough; he's even a little cute with that hat cocked to one side.

"Know of him." Bob takes his hand from his gun now and hands back her license. "I live near that area myself but I've never seen you around."

"My parents came here after I was starting college, so I'm not here often."

"College coed, huh?" Bob pulls a handkerchief from his back pocket and hands it to her.

"I'm through now. I just finished in June." She wipes her nose and hands back his handkerchief. "I'm in K-3."

"In teaching school?" he asks and she nods. "That's a fine profession there." He holds onto the handkerchief because it looks like she may need it again. "What's got you all upset?"

"Oh, I drove all the way to Myrtle Beach to see my

boyfriend." She leans back in her seat. "Well, did he ever turn out to be a jerk!"

"I'm sorry to hear that," Bob says.

"Well, I'm glad I found out." She lets out a loud sob and he hands the handkerchief back to her. "He said that he never wanted to have a house! He said that he wanted to move all over the country and live here and there but never one place for too long. I mean how can you make friends or be a club member if you move all the time?" She looks up at Bob and he shakes his head back and forth.

"Clubs are important, too," he says. "It's important that a person belongs to a group."

"Exactly!" She opens her car door and steps out. "I was so hot sitting there. I hope it's okay for me to get out." She is wearing this short little white thing, looks like a bathrobe. "Oh, I forgot that I'm still wearing my bathing suit."

"No problem," Bob says. "This is some kind of car you've got!" He pulls out his flashlight. "Mind if I look at it?"

"Oh, not at all." She sniffs a few times and then lets out with another big sob. Bob shines the flashlight first at her and then inside the front seat. This car is something, almost as pretty as that girl. He checks out all of the instruments on the dash, fine leather seats, enough room probably for a suitcase back there. Good God! "Hey, uh, do you know that there's a dead cat in your car?" Boy, if this girl turns out to be crazy, too, Bob will be convinced that all women that look good are insane.

"Oh, I forgot!" She presses her hands against her cheeks and cries that much harder. "Will you get him out?"

"Sure thing." Bob reaches into the car, gets that stiff cat and hurls it into the vacant lot. "What was it doing there?"

"I killed it," she says. "Right on this very street, I killed it this morning."

"God, and you've carted it around all day?"

"I couldn't help it, officer, honest, I couldn't!"

"It's okay, it's okay. You can call me Bob, name's Bob Bobbin."

"Oh, Bob, I'm so glad that you stopped me," she says and she does not even make one crack about the red, red robin like most people on first meeting. "Oh, I hate to tell my parents that the wedding is off. They were so pleased!" She shakes her head. "I know they'll be upset!"

"I bet they wouldn't want you to marry someone that you didn't want to marry." Bob looks her in the face now. This girl may be prettier than Corky Revels.

"I guess you're right," she says and dries her eyes, blows her nose in his handkerchief and hands it back to him. He puts it in his back pocket this time.

"Hey, why don't we go have ourselves a drink so that you can unwind before you go home."

"Aren't you working?" she asks.

"Not right now I'm not." He smiles at her and he is cute. She thinks he's getting cuter all the time. "How about it? You can follow me and then you'll be closer to home."

"I didn't know there was any place in this town to get a drink!"

"I have some champagne at my place." He leans against the car. "If you like champagne, that is."

"Oh I do but I really don't know," she stops and stares at him again, those large innocent looking eyes, that moustache. "Well, sure Bob. I'd love to."

"Great!" Bob runs back to the police car. He can't believe that this is happening to him. "You follow me, okay?" She nods and gets in her car. "Don't get lost," he yells and cranks up his car. He watches her pull out behind him and he goes fifteen miles an hour so that he won't lose her. He passes by the diner and there's Sandra sitting in the window, reading a magazine, that Elvis Presley lamp right in front of her. She lifts her hand and smiles great big but Bob just nods. He keeps looking behind him all the way, forgetting the way his heart had raced when he heard Corky's voice on the phone, when he thought she was calling to say that she was sorry, forgetting what happened down at the station and how he's got to face them all again in the morning. He is planning just how he'll pour the champagne, planning just how he'll dim the lights and turn on some slow easy-listening music, how he'll tell her about the way that he saved that man's life. Frances Miller does not even stop to think and ask herself what she is doing. She will do that later, time and time again, in years to come when she thinks of past lovers, this one-night stand.

Juanita Weeks is just about asleep when she sees a shadow in the doorway, hears the floor creak, and then feels the bed slope off to the other side. She doesn't move a muscle, just lies there, and then she feels those big hairy arms reach around her middle, feels Harold's manhood pressing against her thigh.

"Is that you, Harold?" she whispers.

"Now, who the hell were you expecting?" His arms get tighter around her waist and he presses closer.

"I just couldn't believe it was you."

"Does a wild bear shit in the woods?" he asks, and now his face is nuzzled into her neck under all that curly hair.

"Oh, Harold." She rolls over and presses herself against him. "I love you, Harold. It was all my fault, every bit of it and I'm so sorry. I know you can't forgive and forget right off but I'm willing to do anything, honey, anything that I can to make up for it."

"I reckon there's probably a pony close by," he whispers and twists her nipple. "You reckon so, cooter clam?"

"Yes, yes, I know it." Juanita can't help but get a little tearful when he hugs her so close and rolls her over on her back.

"I rinsed, Nita," he whispers.

Sam Swett wakes to the darkened room and at first he thinks that he is in the small studio apartment in New York. Then he sees Corky in the slight glow from the corner streetlight, her head on his chest, the small hand resting on his stomach. Now, he remembers. He remembers everything. He lifts a strand of her hair and rubs it between his thumb and forefinger, lets it slip back down on his chest. He watches her sleeping, her chest and stomach moving up and down slightly with her breath, the slight jerks and twitches of her hands and feet. It is as if everything is clearing up now and he has not felt so good and safe, so sure of himself in ages. Slowly he lifts her head and slips out from under her, kneels by the side of the bed and gently places her head back on the pillow.

He can barely find his clothes in that dim light but he does, at the end of the bed, and he dresses there in the darkness while he watches her sleep. There is a part of him that wants to crawl back in beside her, a part of him that would like to be there when the sun comes up. He goes over now and strokes her hair, kisses those full lips lightly, a slight brush, but enough to cause her eyes to open.

"What are you doing?" she whispers in a voice so childlike that he would like to wrap her up in that quilt and rock her back and forth in his arms.

"I've got to go." He kisses her again and she sits up.

"To the hotel?"

"Yeah, gotta get my stuff." He shifts from one foot to the other. He had wanted to slip away, or so he thought, but he never could have done that, never could have left her without a word. "I need to be getting home," he says. "My folks are going to start worrying probably. You know they may have tried to call me."

"Yeah," she whispers and reaches for her robe, throws it around her shoulders. His eyes have adjusted now and he can see the blank open expression on her face. Then she laughs softly. "Bet they'll really like your hairdo."

"Yeah." He laughs again and steps away from the bed. "I sure have enjoyed being with you."

"Same here." She gets up and walks toward him, her hands holding the robe around her. "You know if you're ever around, of course, who in the hell is ever around Marshboro?" She laughs again, though he can hear the crack in her voice. "But I mean if you ever do come back and you'd like to call . . ."

"I'll be back," he says and kisses her forehead.

"I'll walk with you."

"No, go back to bed. No telling what time a bus pulls out." He grips her hands and then lets them go limp in his own. "If the bus is too late, I may just get on the highway. That's how I came, you know?"

"Be careful," she whispers and the tone in her voice is such a frightening and foreboding one.

"I may just call my Dad." He goes over to the door and she follows him. "I meant what I said," he says. "You are one of the nicest people that I've ever known, ever."

"You too," she whispers and watches him walk away, down the stairwell. She runs back over to her bed and sits, staring out the window. He is walking down the sidewalk and he turns around once but she ducks down behind the doll that she had placed back on the window sill. He walks around the corner and then disappears and she gets back under the sheet, her arms wrapped around her waist just as his had been. She closes her eyes and tries to sleep but there is that impulse to jump up and run out into the street, to run to the hotel, the bus station, the highway, just to tell him good-bye again, but she talks herself out of it, turns her thoughts to the possibility that he may come back some time soon, the faceless stranger of her dream replaced by Sam Swett, shaved head, dirty green shirt and blue jeans: Sam Swett.

He doesn't even check the bus schedule. He gets his things and walks straight to the highway. He walks to Howard Johnson's and sits in the lounge area while he waits for his father to arrive. His parents sounded so frightened at first, his mother's hello after that long distant ring, and then there was relief. He doesn't talk to the night clerk who is sitting there watching some old movie on the small black and white T.V., though it is obvious that the clerk would like to talk. Sam supposes that man would be talking to himself if he weren't sitting here. He is tempted to go over to the phone, to call Corky, to hear that sleepy child's voice answer, but he's not sure what he would say. He feels like he has time now, time to let his hair grow, to get cleaned up, to decide what he wants to do. He thinks of her standing under the streetlight in front of that house that she likes to go see, the distant look, the lull of her voice when she described why she likes that house, that big front window and front porch, and he asked her if she ever thought of settling down, and yes, she nodded, but then looked away. He had had to ask why. "I reckon it's something to look forward to," she had said. Now, he can't help thinking about that, remembering everything about her, that blue cotton robe, freckled shoulder, wide gray eyes, her room decorated in corn husks, while she pours coffee, while she wishes herself into that yellow house. He feels now that he will always have her to turn to when something spurs his memory, an Uncle Sam hat, a miserably hot July afternoon, the smell of pancakes, and if he ever finds himself seated in front of his typewriter with world-solving words somewhere in the back of his mind, it will be her image that comes to him, an unchanged face. But, what if he wants for someone to really be there, a real person with a life of their own? It has all come to him so slowly, so simply; he can go anywhere and see the Howard Johnsons and familiar service stations and restaurants that line the highway at every stop, and it will all seem the same at first glance, though when given the chance will prove to be so different. It's knowing that makes it count, settling and accepting that makes it different; it's something to look forward to.